Juno Rushdan is the award-winning author of steamy, action-packed romantic thrillers that keep you on the edge of your seat. She writes about kick-ass heroes and strong heroines fighting for their lives as well as their happily-ever-afters. As a veteran air force intelligence officer, she uses her background supporting Special Forces to craft realistic stories that make you sweat and swoon. Juno currently lives in the DC area with her patient husband, two rambunctious kids and a spoiled rescue dog. To receive a FREE book from Juno, sign up for her newsletter at junorushdan.com/mailing-list. Also be sure to follow Juno on BookBub for the latest on sales at bit.ly/BookBubJuno

Addison Fox is a lifelong romance reader, addicted to happy-ever-afters. After discovering she found as much joy writing about romance as she did reading it, she's never looked back. Addison lives in New York with an apartment full of books, a laptop that's rarely out of sight and a wily beagle who keeps her running. You can find her at her home on the web at www.addisonfox.com or on Facebook (www.Facebook.com/addisonfoxauthor) and Twitter (@addisonfox).

UNSUSPECTING TARGET

JUNO RUSHDAN

COLTON'S COVERT WITNESS

ADDISON FOX

MILLS & BOON

First Published in Great Britain 2021
by Mills & Boon, an imprint of HarperCollins*Publishers* Ltd
1 London Bridge Street, London, SE1 9GF

www.harpercollins.co.uk

HarperCollins*Publishers*
1st Floor, Watermarque Building,
Ringsend Road, Dublin 4, Ireland

Unsuspecting Target © 2021 Juno Rushdan
Colton's Covert Witness © 2021 Harlequin Books S.A.

Special thanks and acknowledgement are given to Addison Fox for her contribution to *The Coltons of Grave Gulch* series.

ISBN: 978-0-263-28339-6

0521

UNSUSPECTING TARGET

JUNO RUSHDAN

To J, my hero and the love of my life.

Chapter One

Laughing at her escort's flirtatious comment, Wendy Haas glanced across the crowded reception hall of the gala and froze as she spotted trouble incarnate.

The bubble of amusement in her chest burst and she struggled to breathe. Staring back at her was *Jagger Carr*. The one man who could derail her life, for a second time.

His dirty blond hair was shorter, the cut cleaner. Half his face was cloaked in shadows, but he looked older, more rugged and chiseled by hard times. He was broader and taller than Wendy remembered, his muscled body filling out his tux to perfection.

No doubt about it, that was Jagger.

How? He was supposed to be locked up—a fifteen-year sentence for murder.

A murder that never would've happened if they hadn't been together. A prison term that was her fault.

He hated her as much as she hated him, but how could he have the gall to be in the same room as her, make eye contact and not bother to say a single word? Even one of contempt.

"Hey, babe, are you okay?" asked Tripp Langston, her on-and-off lover. "You look like you've seen a ghost."

If only. A phantom couldn't do any harm.

But Jagger free and in the flesh could wreak all kinds of havoc.

Wendy made a pleasant humming sound, masking the lead weight in her gut. "I'm fine," she said as if she didn't have a care in the world and turned back to Tripp.

The photographer dressed in a simple black suit with a dark shirt circled closer. He'd been prowling about them shortly after she and Tripp had arrived. She believed he was one from *Page Six*. Since she hadn't been up to dealing with a sensational tabloid tonight, she hadn't gotten close enough to see his badge clearly.

"He's just going to keep stalking us until we give the paparazzo what he wants," Tripp said.

It was the least of her concerns, though inevitably true. The bloodhound wasn't going to stop.

Wendy owned an up-and-coming PR firm that worked miracles in the image consulting department. She was the go-to person if you needed to reinvent yourself, as she had done after Jagger sent her world in a tailspin.

At twenty-eight, her career was on a trajectory into the stratosphere, and her name opened doors that made socialites envious.

As for Tripp, he was on the current cover of *New York Magazine*, named number one on a list of the top thirty under thirty in the city. All thanks to her company rebranding him from a barracuda in a toilet bowl to the Orca of Wall Street.

A photograph of them together would have the readers of the gossip site and tabloid talking. Still, the last thing she needed to worry about was ducking a shutterbug. Not when Jagger Carr was lurking somewhere in the room.

"Let's just get it over with." Wendy tucked her handbag under her arm and swept a hand over her hair, checking her chignon was in place.

Then she looped her arm through Tripp's, pasted on a saccharine smile, raised her champagne flute and posed for the camera.

The photographer adjusted his telephoto lens, snapped the picture and blew a kiss of thanks.

"He didn't bother to use a flash," she said, irritated at how the photo would turn out in the low lighting. *What a waste.*

"Let me get another for Instagram, babe." Tripp held his camera phone up, shifting it to get the best angle for both his six-foot frame and her standing at five feet six inches in heels. Wendy turned her face, giving her profile for the shot, and drained her glass of champagne as Tripp captured the moment with a bright flash. "That's a good one. I'll send it to you, so you can post it, too. This time write something that makes me sound fun and hip. Okay."

Handsome, wicked smart and wealthy, Tripp was a catch by many standards. He was also the walking definition of an egomaniac, always trying to tell her how to do her job. That was precisely why they were currently in off mode. They'd decided to go together to the Youth Literacy Gala—one of the most anticipated nights on New York City's cultural calendar, second only to the Met Ball—but there were no amorous strings attached.

Disentangling herself from Tripp, Wendy glanced over her shoulder.

Watching her back was second nature and came with the job. Once you identified a threat it was best to deal with the problem head-on, before it became a headline that had tongues wagging.

Wendy scanned the crowd, but it was as if Jagger had never been there. *Poof.* He'd vanished into thin air.

For a long moment, she doubted he'd been real. Only a figment of her imagination, perhaps her eyes playing tricks in the dreamy rose-tinted lighting that reflected off the marble surfaces. But the way her pulse had kicked and her nerves had danced when she'd locked eyes with him had been bona fide and irrefutable.

No other person had ever given her an inkling of butterflies, whereas being with Jagger had been like riding the ultimate roller coaster, the wind rushing over her, arms raised recklessly in the air, her heart doing somersaults, her body tingling. Not a single thought in her head of what was at stake. Of her mother's desperate pleas. Of her brother's warnings.

Until it had ended.

Her throat closed at the memory of all the tears she had shed over him ten years ago.

Wendy grabbed a glass of champagne from a passing tray, swapping it for her empty flute, and sucked the fizzy alcohol down. The chilled bubbly eased the terrible tightness in her throat, if not the sudden ache in her chest.

"What's up?" Tripp asked, typing away on his phone and staring at his screen. "You've barely had anything to drink all night, and in the past two minutes you've inhaled two glasses."

"Who are you? A ruthless cutthroat or my father?" Her dad had died when she was sixteen, a year before she met Jagger. She had still been grieving. Her brother, Dutch, had tried to step up, fill their dad's shoes, but she hadn't needed a replacement.

"You can call me daddy later if you want." Tripp chuckled at his own crass joke, and Wendy rolled her eyes as she dug her tense fingers into her satin clutch. "Let's skip dinner and cut out of this snooze fest. What do you say, babe? Your place or mine? I believe it's time to pay the piper since you signed Rothersbury."

Thanks to an introduction from Tripp, Wendy had seized an opportunity to pitch Chase Rothersbury, a bad-boy billionaire in jeopardy of losing his trust fund if he didn't clean up his image fast. After she'd given a knockout presentation last week, she had landed her biggest client and a lucrative contract that had everyone at the gala buzzing about her.

"You're on the cover of *New York* because of me," she said, sugar dripping from her voice. "I scratch your back and you scratch mine, remember. *Babe*." How could he have possibly forgotten?

"Yeah, of course. The cover was fab." Tripp didn't even look at her as he spoke, keying away with his thumbs on Facebook or Twitter. A chirp sounded. Texting someone.

"But in terms of equity, come on, there's no comparison. You owe me, right?"

All too familiar with this sport, Wendy suppressed a sigh. For Tripp, everything was a transaction, a deal he had to win. He'd tell his own mother that she owed him.

"I'm not a pink sheet stock. This feels more like arbitrage than equity." She wasn't sure if she'd gotten the terminology right and doubted herself as his eyes took on a narrowed glint.

Then she caught his shrug, a gesture of acquiescence that she attributed to his preoccupation with his phone, and she decided it didn't matter.

Off the proverbial hook, she was back on the hunt. For Jagger.

The last she'd heard he'd gotten involved with Los Chacales cartel in prison.

Which would do wonders for her reputation if old photos of her and Jagger, intimate snapshots that would make her mother screech in horror, found their way into the voracious hands of the press. At least her mom was traveling outside the country with her new husband for the next few weeks, but this was going to be resolved tonight.

What were the odds of Jagger being *there*? A million to one?

When did he get out of jail?

A better question, the one churning in her mind and making her stomach roil: What in the hell was he doing at a black-tie event for Manhattan's literati and culturati?

Unless he was there deliberately playing a sick game, taunting her with his presence. Had he come to blackmail her, extort her for hush money to keep quiet about their scandalous past?

Wendy's ears were hot, burning, as if they were on fire. As though someone was talking about her, and not in a good way. An old wives' tale, she knew, but still...

Pivoting on her heels, she turned slowly around Astor Hall. She glossed over the elaborate floral arrangements, the designer gowns, inconsequential hobnobbing and every atmospheric inch of the famed institution. Then she tuned out the jazz music and chatter in the air.

There!

Moving stealthy as a thief up the stone steps to the closed second floor was Jagger.

Jaw squared. All that muscular power striding up the stairs, looking like he'd stepped out of the pages of *GQ* instead of a cell block. God, he looked so damned good.

Hotter than a hostile ex had a right to be.

She flicked a glance at security near the entrance off Fifth Avenue. The guards were focused on an incensed late arrival who refused a pat down after setting off the metal detector.

Wendy shoved her champagne glass at Tripp. "I'll be back in a minute."

Disregarding his questions, she made her way to the broad staircase on the left.

The musical bell chimed, marking the end of the cocktail hour. The drone of voices in the room grew louder in anticipation of the early dinner. In ten minutes, the next chime would sound, and the well-dressed crowd would head for the grand hall to find their seats at the lavishly decorated banquet tables.

Perfect timing.

Appetizers should keep Tripp occupied long enough for her to have the conversation with Jagger that was a decade overdue. Tell him how much she loathed him. Then she'd send him scurrying back to whatever hole he had crawled out of, before he had a chance to do any serious damage.

No matter what it took.

She'd worked too hard putting the pieces of her heart back together, transforming herself into someone new—*better*—

sacrificing everything to build her company and create a life worth living…without him.

No one, least of all Jagger, was going to bring the whole house of cards crashing down.

She darted under the velvet rope cordoning off the stairs while four guards were distracted with Mr. Upper East Side, who was now causing a scene. She lifted her rented black Cavalli gown to keep from tripping on the hem and tiptoed up the stairs, not wanting the clack of her heels to draw the unwanted gaze of the guards.

At the top of the landing, she caught the subtle sound of a door closing.

Up ahead was a sign for the lavatory. She hurried down the corridor, entered the restroom vestibule and hesitated in front of the men's door.

All the other guests were downstairs, and she'd already seen and touched everything Jagger had to offer. Clenching her jaw, she shoved inside and found an empty two-stall bathroom. No one at the urinals or sinks.

"Jagger?" she muttered under her breath.

Disappointment leaked through her, but outrage was quick to chase it away. She was as acutely attuned to his presence as she had been all those years ago.

He was up here somewhere. It was possible he'd seen her coming and was waiting for her in the ladies'.

She pulled open the door and went back into the vestibule.

Footfalls sounded in the corridor headed in her direction. She peeked out and glimpsed the photographer from *Page Six*.

The paparazzi never quit. Now he was going to harass her for a quote about the status of her relationship with Tripp.

She ducked into the ladies' room, only to find the small two-stall bathroom just as quiet and vacant as the other. Unease niggled at her, as if she was missing pieces to a puzzle.

Maybe she *was* losing her mind. The relentless hustle of

working sixteen-hour days, the constant stress and never making time for a vacation was obviously taking a toll on her sanity. Instead of being downstairs relishing a once-a-year event, she was running around New York City's flagship public library, looking for a man who wasn't eligible for parole for two more years, seven months and three days.

Not that she was counting.

Trudging to the sink, she wished she'd stayed home, curled on her sofa watching a show on DVR, and hadn't come tonight. But getting tickets from the mayor for helping his daughter avoid a scandal had been an honor that she couldn't refuse.

Wendy checked her makeup and reapplied her lipstick.

The door swung open, and the photographer strode inside.

"Listen, I admire chutzpah," she said, zipping her purse. "I wouldn't be such a success without it, but this is crossing a line. Don't you think?" She swiveled, facing him, and her whole body tensed.

His dark eyes hardened as he kept walking toward her. She had the sudden unnerving sensation that the walls were closing in. Each confident step he took ate up the distance between them, dampening her bravado and ratcheting her pulse to an alarmed high.

She rocked back on her heels, uncertain what was happening.

Then she realized he hadn't asked for a quote, hadn't uttered a word. And he was blocking her path to freedom.

She glanced down at his press pass and read the name *Krish Kapoor*.

Ice water ran through her veins.

The Krish she knew was bald, stocky and in his fifties. The complete opposite of the twentysomething, wiry guy with a full head of hair stalking toward her, emanating menace.

Don't panic. Stay calm.

Her mind raced as she strategized options.

Simple and direct was best. She had to get back to a public space where a guard or guest could see her, where anyone could hear her if she needed to scream.

Swallowing hard, she straightened. Her mouth tasted sour with fear, and she did her darnedest not to let a flicker of it show on her face. "Excuse me, I'm sure my date is looking for me." She marched forward, brushing past him.

He caught her by the arm, yanking her to a vicious stop that left her teetering on her heels.

"How dare you." On reflex, she pivoted, twisting her arm up and around, breaking his hold. Her next instinct was to shove him out of her way, yell, run—all at once.

But he slapped her with so much force she went spinning and fell. Her head smacked against the edge of the countertop on the way down and she hit the floor. Hard.

Pain blasted through her skull, radiating to her limbs.

The world tilted. She gasped for air.

Shocked and hurting, she dragged herself along the cold tile floor, trying get away. Even though there was nowhere to go, nowhere to hide. Fingernails scraped against grout as she hauled herself farther. Shaking, she feared she'd splinter into pieces from the pain.

"Sorry," he said. "I was told to rough you up first. Make it look like you suffered."

First. Suffered. The words swam in her mushy brain. She couldn't make sense of it.

What was going to happen once he was done making it *look* like she'd suffered?

Red droplets hit the white tile, streaking as she slithered toward the wall. She was bleeding. From her nose? Her lip? She couldn't tell.

Her attacker closed in with a few short steps. She had to do something, anything. Using all her strength, she kicked his leg. Her sharp heel connected with bone.

The guy swore bitterly. "Now, I'm really going to hurt you."

Inhaling deep, Wendy clawed up the wall, pulling herself upright as much as possible. She turned, shifting her butt onto the floor, and blinked through the agony ricocheting in her head. Her vision started to clear.

She put her back against the solid wall and faced her attacker.

The guy unscrewed the long lens on the camera and dumped a gun suppressor into his palm. He dropped the lens and slammed the body of the camera on the counter. The inside was hollow except for a gun. The pistol was so small it looked like a toy, but Wendy knew it was all too real.

She shook her head in confusion. "Why are you doing this?" she asked, wiping the moisture from her nose with the back of her hand. Blood smeared her skin.

"Orders."

"Whose orders?" She choked on a sob.

Wendy wasn't in the business of making enemies. Her success depended on smoothing things over, making trouble disappear, keeping people happy. She certainly didn't drive people to murder.

"Don Emilio Vargas."

The name sounded vaguely familiar, from the news. He was the nation's current biggest headline, the leader of Los Chacales cartel, arrested in San Diego. Why would he want her dead? How did he even know who she was?

The man screwed the sound suppressor onto the barrel of the gun.

Paralyzing terror swamped her. *No, no, no! I don't want to die.*

So much for work hard now and enjoy the rewards later. She should've taken that vacation to a warm, sunny tropical island, even if she had been alone. The same way she woke up and went to sleep. *Alone.*

She pushed back the fear and chaos raging in her mind. Forced herself to think.

"I have money. I—I can pay you a lot. Whatever you want." That was far from true, but this circumstance warranted any lie that would work.

"Once the Brethren have been ordered, money can't save you."

Wendy screamed as loud as she could, screamed until her throat burned and her lungs ached. Fearing that no one would hear her over the music and chatter downstairs, she kicked out again, this time striking his knee.

He grunted in pain, but he managed to raise his weapon and aimed.

Her heart clutched.

The door to the bathroom swung open and the guy spun, refocusing the barrel in the opposite direction.

Her attacker blocked her view, but he didn't shoot whoever walked in and let the door close. "Hey, man." The gun lowered. "What are you doing here?"

Oh, God. Her attacker knew this other man. The cavalry hadn't arrived. Tripp hadn't come looking for her. No one had heard her scream.

Wendy pressed up against the wall, wanting to disappear through it. A desperate whimper left her.

"I was sent as backup." The husky, masculine voice was a shock to her senses, a lightning strike straight to her heart.

A voice that was deeper, coarser than she remembered, but nonetheless familiar. Even in the haze of panic and pain, she'd recognize it.

"You, too? How many of us did the Brethren send to off one chick?"

"By my count, a lot."

Wendy's stomach dropped. Tears leaked from her eyes as the terrible reality struck her, and the pain was too intense to bear.

Jagger wasn't incarcerated.

He *was* here…and he'd come to kill her.

Chapter Two

This was hell.

Not damnation with fire and brimstone.

Wendy wanted to wake up and find herself safe in her bed, in her Chelsea apartment, far from any danger.

"You barely messed her up, Zampino," Jagger said, stepping closer.

Zampino's position blocked her from getting an up-close look at Jagger, seeing his face, his eyes, but she stilled as horror and agony bled through her. Hell was knowing that he musttruly hate her to the bone to betray her this way. To seek brutal revenge.

"Yeah, I'm getting to it," Zampino said. "But she's a hellion."

"The two of us together will be faster and easier. You'll still get the credit for the kill, but I'll help."

I'll help.

Agony.

The words were a dagger twisting in her heart and cleaving it in two. Her brain flashed to past moments with Jagger. Kissing him. Being held by him. Making love to him. Soaking up his tender attention and devoted affection. Sharing everything. Getting so caught up in *him* that a life without him had been torture.

Wendy swallowed around the cold lump in her throat, not believing her ears.

"Please, p-please," she muttered in between uncontrollable sobs, the misery growing and spreading. "Don't do this."

Jagger had thousands of reasons to despise her—one for every day he'd spent locked up in a cage, denied his freedom and the possibilities she got to enjoy. But never—not in her darkest dreams, not in her worst nightmares—did she imagine him capable of physically hurting her, much less killing her.

Not Jagger.

Not the man she'd once given herself to completely, in every way.

Not the man who'd sworn on his life that she'd always be safe with him. That he'd protect her no matter what.

Not even after she was the cause of ruining his life.

It was clear that their history meant nothing to him. She meant nothing.

"Sounds good." Zampino tucked the gun in his waistband against his lower back as he turned to face her.

Wendy clenched her hands into fists and braced herself. Not for the pain that was to come. She prepared to punch, kick and fight with her last breath. With any luck, she'd get in a good scratch or two and have their DNA under her fingernails.

"We'll make it quick," Zampino said to her, as if he was about to do her a favor. He lowered in front of her and balanced on the balls of his feet. Unfortunately, he was smart enough to stay out of the kicking range of her foot. "Then we'll put you out of your misery." He smiled. It was a cruel expression, devoid of any kindness.

Wendy looked up, needing to see Jagger, and it was like time slowed. He was still everything that had first attracted her. Rugged and beautiful, he didn't have the build of a hulking bruiser, but he had a formidable physique and a big presence that dominated any room. And those green eyes she'd loved so much had lost their warmth. They were severe and piercing, burning with resolve.

All those years she'd wasted, hating herself for losing him, craving him, trying to convince herself that she hated him, too. Maybe even more for pushing her away.

And after everything, her love for him had never died.

What a fool she'd been.

Zampino snatched her ankle and yanked her away from the wall. Wendy screamed, scratching at the floor. He dragged her closer, and when he started to rise, he lifted his foot as if getting ready to smash his heel into her face.

In a blur of movement, Jagger exploded into furious action. He drew something from his pocket and swept up behind Zampino. Jagger slipped a thin cord around Zampino's throat, tightened it across his windpipe and hauled him back.

The hand around her ankle slipped away and Wendy scrambled up onto her feet.

Eyes blazing with alarm, Zampino kicked at the air and clawed at the cord. His expression was frantic.

Wendy scampered backward and pressed against the wall, wanting to keep her distance from both men.

Zampino dragged his feet, swung his arms, grabbed for a hold onto a bathroom stall. His rubber boot heels caught on the tile flooring and he threw his skull back. Jagger defended against the move by keeping his head out of the way.

Clutching two plastic handles on either end of the wire, Jagger jerked Zampino down at a lower angle where he was unable to gain any purchase. Face flushed, Zampino continued to struggle, thrashing in vain, his strained breathing turning into a gruesome wheeze.

Zampino pushed with his legs, scratching at his throat, his fingers slipping in the wetness of blood. His mouth opened as if to scream, to shout for help as she had done, but his airway was closed. He kicked the sink cabinetry, the edge of the stall frame.

It was futile. The hold was too tight, too absolute.

Jagger swung him to the right and to the left, thwarting Zampino's attempts to get free by shifting the man into unstable positions. Jagger's honed body was tense, every muscle flexed.

He dug in harder with the crude weapon, applying more pressure. His jaw clenched, his fists shaking from the strain.

He dropped to the floor, getting better leverage while keeping Zampino on top of him. Rolling from hip to hip, Jagger avoided the elbows thrown at his sides.

Seconds slowed to a crawl. Heart pounding so hard that her chest hurt, Wendy stood frozen from the shock of watching Jagger kill a man. Again.

The first time hadn't been like this, deliberate, with merciless focus.

But, once more, he was taking a life because of her.

She wanted to close her eyes until it was done, but she couldn't look away, like there was some law in the universe that obligated her to bear witness.

Zampino's flailing arms weakened and finally fell to his sides. The last breath punched from his lips. His head flopped to the side and his panic-stricken eyes went vacant.

Jagger stayed on the floor with the cord around Zampino's neck for a drawn-out minute that felt like an eternity. Rocking to the side, he slid the dead body off him. The impulse to help him up came over her when he climbed to his knees, panting, but she was paralyzed.

Although Zampino was no longer a threat, a shiver of fear ran through her staring at him.

Jagger struggled to his feet. Then he lugged the dead body into one of the stalls and laid it on the floor by the toilet. Backing out of the stall, he stuffed the bloody weapon into his pocket.

The pulsing tension eased from her limbs, but she was rooted in place.

Jagger's voice drifted to her. He turned, his green eyes finding hers. "Are you badly hurt?" He sounded winded. "Are you okay?"

The answer was the same to both questions. "No." Her throat was coarse, like she'd swallowed sand.

His gaze roamed over her as he went to the sink and

washed his hands. He dampened paper towels, shut off the water and hurried to her.

At six-two, his size was imposing for someone of her build, but this was the first time she had been intimidated by it rather than comforted. He towered over her when he reached for her face.

Wendy shrank back, a reflex after the threats and violence. Also, a small part of her wondered if she could trust him. Once you were part of Los Chacales, you were always a member, and for some inexplicable reason the top dog of the cartel wanted her dead.

Did that make Jagger part of the problem or the solution?

He hesitated. "You can't walk out like this. I need to clean your face," he said matter-of-factly, but he didn't move toward her.

She glanced at her reflection in the mirror and drew in a sharp breath.

Blood was smeared under her nose and across her cheek. Tears had streaked her makeup.

Wendy nodded to Jagger, giving him the go-ahead. With her whole body trembling, she needed the assistance. Since he'd been arrested, she wasn't used to being protected and cared for. She'd had to learn to fend for herself.

The damp paper towel pressed to her face and the coolness of it brought immediate relief, jump-starting her brain. "We have to get security. Call the police."

"No. No police." His tone was sharp, no-nonsense, but he wiped her face with careful, gentle strokes. "No security."

"Why not?"

"Because they can't help you." He picked up her purse and stuffed the bloody paper towels inside. After tossing the handbag to her, he started wiping down the handles on the sink and the surface of the counter. "Some of the cops in the city are on Los Chacales payroll. It's safe to assume they were told to keep their ears posted for any calls involving you." Even as he cleaned up what he could of her blood from the floor, she suspected he was more concerned about leaving behind the DNA of a convicted felon. "Once I received the order about you, it took me less than ten minutes to figure out you'd be here tonight." He took her arm, his grip firm yet not hurting her, and started walking. "We can't linger."

They stepped into the vestibule after he wiped down the door.

"How did you find me?"

"Instagram. Your social calendar is splashed all over it in perfectly posed pictures with cute little captions."

Oh, God. Social media was a necessary evil for her job. She hated posting about her life, sharing her workouts, hangouts, whereabouts—a necessary part of the biz. As the number of her followers grew, so did the status of her clients.

"You even posted about the dress you were going to wear tonight."

They'd used information that she'd made public to find her. Anyone could, at almost any time, with her social media track record. She grew light-headed, weak-kneed and swayed.

He caught her by the waist and brought her up against him. His arms were hard and possessive around her, steadying her on her feet as well as something inside her. The world stopped spinning. The raging terror and confusion settled. Her racing heart slowed. Calm stole over her.

"Take a couple of deep breaths."

She did and leaned into him, grateful for the physical support, glad of his body heat and protective instincts.

He looked her over. His intense gaze was so palpable it caressed her skin. A surprising awareness flowed between them, and she went weak in the knees again. She'd never been attracted to someone like she was to him—and had been from the moment she'd set eyes on him.

"Excellent choice on the dress by the way," he said. His features lightened.

For a heartbeat, she blocked out the gruesome images from the bathroom and let herself see the man she'd once known. He was still beyond handsome with the most gorgeous green eyes. Hair that couldn't decide if it wanted to be blond or brown. No one wore rough and tumble as enticingly as he did that tux. He always had a dark sense of danger, an edge that drew her even though reason cautioned her to pull away. There'd been a hundred reasons he'd been wrong for her and still so right.

But he was different now, too. There was a new hardness to him that made him seem out of reach even though he was touching her.

"You were an unsuspecting target, and with your social media posts you made yourself easy pickings," he said, his voice softening, hints of his Southern drawl peeking through.

Any lingering doubts about him didn't evaporate, but she was cognizant of a terrible certainty. If it hadn't been for him, she'd be dead. She had no idea what she was up against or even why. For now, she needed him.

He released her from the embrace. "We need to move," he said, and she nodded in agreement.

They left the vestibule and entered the hall. He guided her toward the side stairwell that led to a different part of the library, away from Astor Hall, where the security guards were.

"I get your concern about the cops," she said low, "not knowing who to trust, but why can't we get help from security?" The odds of them being involved had to be nil.

"The more people you come in contact with, the more you'll endanger. Security is only armed with Tasers and batons. They're collateral damage waiting to happen. We need to get out of here now before we run into the others."

Earlier he'd said that there were *a lot*.

"How many?" she asked, praying for a low, single-digit number.

"So far, I've dealt with two and half of them."

How do you deal with half a person? "What does that mean?"

"I didn't finish the one that was up here. Only knocked him out," he said as they rounded the corner headed for the stairwell. "I heard you scream and—"

A man wearing a dark gray suit swept in front of them from the intersecting corridor. He held up a gun with an attached silencer.

Jagger shoved her backward behind him while he simultaneously threw a kick. His foot connected with the other man's arm, knocking the gun from his hand.

The pistol clattered to the floor out of her reach.

Both men took up a defensive fighting stance, squaring off against the other with fists poised.

"What are you doing?" the man asked.

"You wouldn't understand, Corey."

"Try me. You took a vow. If the Brethren find out that you interfered—"

Jagger launched an elbow at Corey's head, knocking him off balance. Corey staggered a few steps, then recovered, countering with a fast jab. Jagger deflected the blow. His face became a mask of intensity and determination as the two men exchanged punches and kicks, went at each other blow for blow. Their movements were powerful, brutal and shockingly quick.

Wendy had seen Jagger work out years ago, going through martial arts katas that he'd learned before they met, but never anything this fast with another person.

Corey grunted from the latest strike and tried to spin away. But Jagger pivoted into a high roundhouse kick that struck Corey's face, sending him falling to the floor in a motionless heap.

Breathing hard and sweating, Jagger stood over the man. His brows shot together in a worried expression.

"What is it?" Wendy asked, glancing around, on the lookout for any incoming danger.

"I knocked him out earlier, came up behind him. He never saw me. I should kill him. Otherwise they'll know that it was me who saved you."

"Then why don't you do it?" she asked in a harsh whisper, never believing she'd ever utter such a thing.

It was unlike her. Rewind an hour—heck, ten minutes—and she would've screamed, *No, you can't kill him*, the thought of him doing so horrifying. The cruel words had come from a dark place of desperation. She was fighting to survive and that man on the floor was a threat. When he woke up, he might very well try to kill her again.

"I can't." Jagger shook his head, staring at the helpless man. "He's my friend."

A chill shot through her. The realization that he not only knew the people coming after her but also was friends with some of them made the situation even more terrifying.

But she clasped Jagger's shoulder, relieved the young man she'd fallen in love with was still in there. Jagger Carr would never take another person's life in cold blood. In self-defense, yes, but only if he had to. He would do anything to avoid hurting a friend and wouldn't kill an unconscious person.

"Jagger." Her voice was shaky and uncertain as she pressed a palm to his cheek.

Calling his name brought him out of his tormented trance. Lowering to one knee, he pulled out zip ties from his pocket. He restrained Corey's ankles and his wrists behind his back. Jagger patted Corey down. He found his cell phone, removed the SIM card and tossed both.

Jagger found Corey's gun on the floor and stuffed it in his waistband.

His gaze snapped up to hers as he stood. "Let's go." He held out his hand to her—a lifeline, a choice she had to make.

She took his hand. His palm was warm, comforting and so big it engulfed hers. His callused fingers were rough against her skin, his grip steely.

They hurried down the stairs side by side.

It was like déjà vu, and she was that teenage girl, following him blindly. Attached to Jagger and going wherever he led. Confident he'd keep her safe.

She also remembered the dire consequences that had ripped their world apart.

"Wait," she said when they reached the ground floor near the Forty-second Street exit. "I need answers about what's happening. Why does the head of Los Chacales cartel want me dead? Where are we going? How are we supposed to survive without help from the police? What's going to happen to you when they find out that you saved me?" The shrill questions tumbled over one another in a dizzying rush.

Jagger pursed his lips, and she could tell there were things he didn't want to say. "I'll answer all your questions. Later. I promise."

Based on experience, he'd always kept his word, but fleeing the scene of a murder was a critical moment that could not be undone. There might not be any traces of his DNA in that bathroom, but there was plenty of hers. Hair. Blood. Not to mention the problem of the Brethren.

Jagger resumed moving, his stride speeding up while he tugged her along.

"This might be a mistake." She stopped, jerking him to a halt. "Take me to the police. Sure, there are a few dirty cops out there, but I'll be safe inside a police station." She had to be, surrounded by police, right? "There's one three blocks away on Broadway. Maybe I should take my chances with the authorities."

"Not on my watch." His tone brooked no argument.

But she had to try. For his sake as much as for her own. "Drop me off at the station and walk away. You can tell your friends where I am to make things right on your end. I won't breathe a word about you to the police. I'll say someone I didn't recognize killed Zampino." She didn't want to cause trouble for him. He'd done far too much already.

As tallies went, it was looking as if she'd be eternally indebted.

"The second I interceded and chose to help you, I forfeited my life." His voice was raw and unfiltered. "I didn't step aside and call the police, because it only takes *one* dirty cop to give the wrong person the right opportunity and you're as good as dead."

Wendy's heart stuttered. She pressed a hand to her chest. Jagger's words had knocked the air out of her.

This was her worst fear. Not the part about being hunted and the kill order on her. She'd already messed up Jagger's life once. The last thing she wanted was do it a second time, but apparently that was already too late.

"You took my hand." He squeezed his fingers tighter around hers. "Let me keep you safe."

He didn't say the words: *Don't let me forfeit my life for nothing.* Yet, it was there, hanging in the air, connecting them in a hundred different ways.

"Once I'm sure you're not in any more danger," he said, "I'll get out of your life and you'll never have to see me again."

Right. He wasn't back for good, only to help her.

A new kind of agony assailed her, along with shame. To think that she'd believed he might've hurt her. He'd shown up in the bathroom to rescue her, though, considering what had transpired the last time they'd seen each other, she didn't know why.

In her heart, she wanted him to be her hero, although she'd learned the hard way she needed to be her own heroine.

She held back, studying him. Green eyes glinted with wicked street smarts.

The only person she could completely depend on was herself, but there was an inescapable caveat. Jagger understood the code of the cartel, how they operated, who they paid off, what they controlled.

He was also the only person who could give her answers that might save her life.

What choice did she have other than to trust him? "Okay. I'll do it your way."

"We need to hurry. Run while we can. Once Corey wakes up and gets loose, he'll call the others. Then it'll be that much harder to get out of the city."

Chapter Three

Adrenaline pumped in Jagger's veins like he was in a war zone.

He'd killed another man, but Zampino had been Brethren, and Jagger didn't have authorization. That in itself was a death sentence. Even worse, more would come to hunt him and Wendy down.

But all he could think about was the sound of Wendy's voice as she'd called his name, the feel of her palm gliding across his cheek.

His chest constricted with emotion.

Years ago, while sitting in a cell, he'd given up the far-fetched fantasy of *ever* touching her again. Now here she was right beside him, close enough to kiss.

His throat tightened, and he shoved the thought of it aside.

Crouched on the balls of his feet in front of the door that led to Forty-second Street, Jagger slipped the lock-picking tools out of his pocket and he attacked the pin tumbler. First, he worked the L-shaped part into the cylinder to keep pressure on the pins. Next, he slid the straight piece into place and searched for the right angle to access the locking mechanism. He had tackled this kind of lock before and estimated it would take him thirty seconds tops.

What worried him was not knowing if the library had set the alarm on the exterior doors that weren't supposed to be in use, but he couldn't fret about that.

He glanced at Wendy. Her honey-blond hair was up in a fancy twist that showed off her gorgeous face, and her light blue eyes, set against smooth, tanned skin, burned through him. In the low moonlight, her gaze shifted from aquamarine to the color of the sky at dawn.

"You should take down that updo," he said, "let your hair frame your face. So it's not so easy to recognize you."

"All right."

One tumbler clicked into place, then a second and third. Jagger worked feverishly on the next two.

The straight tool slipped from his sweaty palm and clattered to the floor.

Exhaling in frustration, he felt around for the instrument with only dim moonlight to guide him. Trying to calm his nerves, he brought himself down from totally wired to on guard.

Wendy knelt next to him as her hair tumbled loose around her shoulders in curly waves. The smell of her perfume slid over his senses, drawing him closer. The scent was soft and sensual, sophisticated like she'd become. She grabbed the thin tool and handed it to him.

Their faces were a breath apart in the low light, her proximity adding oxygen to the fire already burning inside him. Even strung tight and prepared to do whatever was necessary to keep her safe, he was tormented with a need for this woman that had never gone away. Never eased a day they'd been separated.

As a free man there were things he wanted to say to her, things he had lost the right to say, but first they had to get out of the city and survive the night.

He took the tool and got back to work.

Any second Corey would wake up. Getting free of the zip ties wouldn't take his industrious friend too long. Once that happened, Corey would contact the Brethren and holy hell was going to rain down on Jagger and Wendy. Unless they could get somewhere safe.

Got it. The last pin gave way and the tumbler fell into place.

Standing up, he braced for the possibility of an alarm

sounding. If anyone else from the Brethren was waiting outside, the noise would draw dangerous attention, giving away their position.

There was no way to avoid it. They had to take the risk in order to get out of the building.

He grabbed Wendy's hand and hit the push bar. The door swung open. No alarm blared.

Releasing a breath, he peeked outside. No one loitered in the immediate vicinity. Nothing appeared amiss, although there were plenty of places for a sniper to hide in the surrounding skyscrapers.

The one thing in their favor was that if there were more hit men lying in wait, they were most likely covering the main entrance.

They stepped into the cool night, hurrying down the steps.

"Where are we headed?" Wendy asked.

"Parking lot." Jagger led her down the block in the direction of Sixth Avenue, wanting to bolt with her like two bats out of hell, but instead he forced himself to walk. She'd never be able to run in those sexy heels, and it would only cause people to notice them when they needed to blend in. "I've got a car there."

He caught the surprised glance from her. Keeping a car in the city wasn't practical or economical.

Deciding to spare her the trouble of asking, he said, "I sort of borrowed it. I co-own a car repair shop. We do a lot of custom work." He left out the fact that the other owner was his former cell mate and that the majority of their business came from the cartel.

The service of providing souped-up vehicles that were outfitted with turbocharged engines, bulletproof windows, reinforced doors and fortified chassis to handle the extra weight proved to be quite lucrative. Though there was a small pool of clientele looking for that sort of thing and hardly any of them had legitimate reasons for wanting it.

They stopped at the corner and waited for the light to change.

Shivering, she rubbed her arms. "When did you get out of prison?"

"Are you cold?" It was April, and the fickle spring air had dropped ten degrees over the past two hours. The night wasn't frigid, but decidedly chilly.

"I'll be okay."

He pulled his shirt from his pants, covering the gun with attached silencer that was tucked against his back in his waistband. Despite her protests, he took off his jacket and draped it around her shoulders. His adrenaline would keep him warm.

"Thank you," she said reluctantly, and slid her arms into the sleeves. "How did you manage to get released early?" Her tone was sharp, almost harsh. "You're not supposed to be eligible for parole yet."

"Sorry to disappoint you." He fired back.

"Jagger." It was a plea as well as a warning. "When did you get out?"

He gritted his teeth as he checked their surroundings. Many of her questions he couldn't answer because he simply didn't know. Only the top lieutenants in the cartel had any clue why Don Emilio wanted her dead. The Brethren didn't care. They'd been tasked by the leader of Los Chacales himself. The order was sacrosanct.

Jagger was the only one who'd dare violate it.

As far as how to get out of this mess, he was winging it. The order had been short notice, not leaving time for him to fully strategize, much less contemplate the consequences that would come down the pike. His business, the life he'd rebuilt after prison were at stake, but he'd given little thought to any of it when he'd seen Wendy's name attached to the termination command. He was taking things one step at a time, weighing the pros and cons of every choice. Not to be a hero. His sole concern was keeping Wendy alive, and the one thing he knew for certain was that going to the police would be a mistake they wouldn't live to regret.

"How long ago were you released?" she asked again, her voice growing more strained.

This was one question he was capable of answering, even though it was the last he wanted to discuss. "Three years."

Gravity pulled his gaze from the steady stream of vehicles and heavy foot-traffic around them back to hers.

Without fully registering her shocked expression in the bright lighting from the streetlamp, he took in how beautiful she'd gotten. Wendy had always been a looker. Heart-shaped face. Creamy skin. Cat-shaped eyes. Flawless figure that was somehow both slender and voluptuous. But everything about her had matured and been refined. She'd gone from gorgeous to exquisite.

Still took his breath away, but now the sight of her also made his heart ache.

A second or two ticked by as the little color that was in her face drained. She stared at him, her eyes huge and features pinched with pain that was unrelated to Zampino hitting her.

"Three years," she said in stark disbelief that twisted his gut in a knot.

The impulse to hold her was overwhelming. He wanted to comfort her, kiss her, taste her lips one more time, but if he did, he wasn't sure he'd be able to walk away.

The traffic light changed, saving him from himself.

"Come on." He reached for her hand, but she folded her arms across her chest, stepped off the curb and strode into the crosswalk.

Ignoring the sting of her rebuff, he was at her side in an instant.

They rushed across the street and hurried in the direction of the parking lot in silence. Their arms brushed once or twice, and each time she put a couple of inches between them as they navigated through the evening flow of pedestrians.

"Wendy." He caught her arm, but she jerked free of his hand.

Not that he blamed her for not wanting him to touch her. Their history was messy and complicated. Too ugly to dive into if he knew what was good for him.

"Why didn't you tell me that you were out? Didn't you think I'd want to know?" Her words were barely a whisper, yet the hurt attached hit him with startling gravity.

She cared. After so many years, he still mattered to her. She hadn't buried the memory of him.

Despite the fact he'd hoped she would've forgotten him—awful as it was—a selfish part of him was relieved she hadn't.

He took extreme care selecting his next words. What sprang to mind didn't seem to fit the awkward moment or the grave situation.

Nothing was right. Everything was wrong. What was he supposed to say?

That he was sorry for not contacting her after he was released?

Well, he wasn't. Any more than he regretted the harsh things he'd said to her on her last visit to see him inside Sing Sing prison.

"You didn't have a *need* to know. It was my personal business." Staying dispassionate and pragmatic was the only viable option if he was going to figure out a way for them to get through this and survive. "I didn't think it'd make a difference to you. We're nothing to each other anymore."

"Nothing?" She choked on the word and then straightened. "The last time we saw each other, you told me that you hated me. So if we're *nothing* and that hate is still festering inside of you, why are you here?" There was no missing the anger tightening her voice.

As if he'd ever let someone kill her—regardless of their history. Hell, because of it.

It would've been a blessing if he could safeguard her without speaking at all. But that wasn't possible. Wendy would push and prod and question until he answered.

"I made your brother a vow." To always protect her. That was what Jagger had sworn to get her brother and mom to back off and give their relationship a chance. "I'm a man of my word. I'll uphold it and do the right thing whatever the risk."

He never bothered with a cost-benefit analysis when it came to Wendy. Risk versus the odds of success be damned. His intervention was a necessity. He had to find a way to keep her alive.

"You're really not here for me," she said low, as if speaking to herself.

He *was* there for her, but he preferred to downplay that part. It was bad enough he was feeling emotions he shouldn't. "This is a mercy mission." How simple, how clear-cut things would've been if that was the whole truth. If he was no longer a devil-may-care fool in love with Wendy Haas, but his actions were proof to the contrary.

Only a fool would go up against the deadliest, most powerful drug cartel on the continent, and he sure as hell wasn't doing it because she didn't mean anything.

Mercy mission. More and more it was starting to feel like a suicide mission.

"We should pick up the pace a bit if you're able." His voice was cool steel. Giving way to sentiment did no one any good.

Wendy lifted the hem of her dress and quickened her step. Her heels stabbed the pavement with a strident clickety-clack. "Why does the head of Los Chacales want me dead? And please don't give me the brush-off."

"The order came down short notice. Immediate execution." Figuratively and literally. "There weren't many details, but I think it might have to do with Dutch."

Wendy's gaze snapped to Jagger and a befuddled look fell across her face. "My brother? That doesn't make any sense. He works in fugitive recovery. I saw on the news that Vargas was only just arrested. Dutch goes after fugitives on the run, so how on earth could he have angered the head of the cartel so much that he wants *me* dead?"

Jagger shrugged, wishing he had the answers. Without insight into the particulars, he'd only be able to buy Wendy time, not save her. "The order was issued as a blood debt."

"What does that mean?"

"That this is really bad. Somebody who is very close to you must have killed or harmed an important person Don Emilio cares about. I don't know specifics. I'm not privy to that sort of information."

"These days I'm only close to my mom and… Dutch."

"I figured your brother is more likely to be connected to this than your mother. What I know for certain is that this is a life-for-a-life kind of thing. The Brethren are invested beyond money. It's a matter of honor." Under normal circumstances, Jagger could pick and choose his assignments, but no one—absolutely no one in the Brethren—could refuse a blood debt kill order.

"Honor in the cartel?" Wendy scoffed. "Give me a break. Los Chacales, those Jackals, have no regard for human decency. They're all vicious drug dealers, thieves and murderers."

His heart froze, and he blocked out the surge of pain in his chest.

Jagger hadn't spoken to Wendy in almost a decade, and the first time she saw him again, he'd wrapped a homemade garrote around someone's neck and strangled the man. He was appalled at his actions, regardless that they'd been necessary.

Another reminder of what had driven them apart years earlier. "Yep, drug dealers, thieves and murderers. That's us."

"Oh, Jagger," she said, flicking a cautious glance at him. A glimmer of regret caught in her gaze. "I didn't mean you. I wasn't talking about you. Just them."

But he *was* them. In every way that counted. Not that it was the entire story.

"Don't worry about it," he said. "I am Los Chacales." A long, dark road paved with self-preservation had led him there. "I'm Brethren, too." They were a well-trained, highly organized lethal extension of the cartel. Not gangbangers and foot soldiers. They were *sicarios*—hit men with specialized skills, loyal to the cartel. "We are a pack of murderers. You're right, except for one thing. There is a code in the cartel, and those who don't respect it suffer the consequences." As he would soon find out, but he'd cross that bridge when he got to it. Or burn it down. He was undecided.

A visible shiver ran through her. "Well, then, how do we fix this?"

He didn't have a clue.

Fix wasn't a part of his current plan. Only keeping them both above ground and breathing. "I'm working on it."

"Your tone doesn't inspire confidence."

"Who stopped Zampino and Corey and has gotten you this far?"

"You're right. I'm sorry. I'm scared."

One block to go and they'd have wheels. On foot out in the open on the streets left them too hideously vulnerable. Exposed. He felt like they had bull's-eyes on their backs. There was no telling how many from the Brethren were looking for them or what resources they might use. "You should ditch your phone."

"Get rid of my phone?" She stared at him like he was crazy. "Are you serious?"

"Let me rephrase. The sooner you dump your phone the better."

"It has all my contacts. My calendar. My appointments. My whole life is on my phone."

How convenient to be able to reduce the essence of your life down to what was accessible on your smartphone. "Sounds valuable," he said, keeping his voice curt, not a hint in his frosty tone of the man who'd once had all his hopes and dreams and desires tangled up in this woman.

"It is extremely valuable. I don't know what I'd do without it."

Perhaps take a break from posting on Instagram and live to see another day.

"I should point out," he said, "that if the Brethren track you through your phone, you won't have much of a life left. Correction, *we* won't. And forget about keeping any of your appointments."

Looking up at him, she let her dress slip from her hand and tripped on the hem. Instinct had him reach out and grab hold of her to keep her from falling—a hand at her waist and the other cupping her palm.

The one little gesture sent sparks of heat and electricity tingling through him, and he could have sworn he'd seen the same in her eyes, in the way her jaw unhinged and in the breath that left her perfect lips.

Once she was steady, she yanked her arm free of his grasp and tore her gaze from him in response. "No one has had physical access to my phone to download malware, and without a court order not even the FBI can get information from my mobile provider."

That was the naive thinking of a law-abiding citizen with no idea of what the underworld was capable of.

Jagger gave a bitter laugh. "We're talking about Los Chacales. The most formidable cartel in North America. How do you think they got so powerful? It wasn't by using court orders to get what they want. They circumvent the law. They have people everywhere. You name a mobile phone provider and I guarantee that they have an inside person who is looking for you in their system as we speak. When your name pops up, they'll ping your phone and will have your location within a one-hundred-fifty-meter radius. Brethren will be dispatched, and that radius will shrink until we're surrounded and dead."

She lowered her head and crossed her arms, tucking her purse along with the phone stashed inside of it in a protective position. "What about *your* phone?"

"I left it back at my place." Fingers curling in his palms, Jagger checked their rear. Still no signs of any shadowy members of the Brethren tailing them, but they needed to get to the car quickly. He had the feeling their luck was going to run out sooner rather than later. "So, are you going to scrap yours?" Or was he going to be forced to do it for her? This was his world and she was in way over her head. She needed to trust him. To follow directions. If he said run, then she had better run. If he said ditch your phone… "Decide now before we get in the car."

He stopped at the corner and gestured to the hourly paid parking lot across the street.

Huffing a defeated sigh, Wendy unzipped her glitzy purse and handed him her cell phone.

Jagger removed the battery, tossed the SIM card on the ground and raised his foot, getting ready to crush it under his boot heel.

Wendy winced. "Wait. Are you sure that's absolutely necessary?"

It wasn't. Removing the battery was sufficient to prevent the phone from being tracked, but the extra precautionary measures were the only way to be certain no one made a desperate phone call while on the run. "Do you swear to leave the battery out and not use it under any circumstances?"

Her baby blues brightened. "Yes, yes. I promise."

"Okay." He scooped up the SIM card and handed everything back to her.

Exhaling as though he'd saved her life again, she dumped the components in her purse with a shaky hand.

At the corner, they waited for a break in the traffic to get across.

A vague sense of alarm had him swiveling around, doing a 360-degree check of their surroundings. At the intersection, one block over to the east on Fifth Avenue, he spied a large black truck stopping at the traffic light. A prickle of warning slid down his spine at the familiar outline of the vehicle.

Jagger grabbed Wendy by the shoulders and whisked her back from the curb and behind a building.

"What is it?" she asked.

"I'm not sure." He peeked around the edge of the brick building and trained his sights on the truck. From that distance, he couldn't see the driver.

The traffic light changed, and the truck rolled through the intersection down the parallel avenue, heading in the direction they'd come from.

The hairs on the back of his neck raised at seeing the shiny black vehicle, an M2 Freightliner. Twenty-two-foot-long custom tactical body with metal reinforcement and a pull-down rear ramp. Interior features comprised an armory cage with enough storage for a small arsenal and custom flip-up bench seating that, when in the upright position, provided space for two motorcycles to fit on board.

Jagger knew this because he was the one who had done the custom work on the vehicle, including the installation of the bulletproof windows, and tires filled with silicone so they wouldn't go flat or get shot out.

That beast on wheels was the property of Los Chacales cartel. More specifically, it belonged to the Brethren.

Chapter Four

The tendons in Jagger's neck tightened as he cursed their rotten luck. A handful of hit men pursuing them individually was one thing. A united mobile unit following one person's direct instructions was a game changer and not in their favor.

He raked a hand through his hair. "Corey must be awake. The Brethren dispatched a mobile unit."

"How do you know it was Corey?" Wendy asked. "You trashed his phone, the same way you were about to with mine."

"But not Zampino's." In the bathroom, Jagger had been focused on a hundred different things—chiefly the blood on Wendy's face, the stark terror in her glassy eyes—and had forgotten one that was critical. Corey must have found the phone after he had gotten loose and then called in reinforcements.

Jagger double-checked that the street was clear of any immediate threats and gestured for her to follow him.

They hustled across the road, darting through a break in traffic, to the parking lot.

Digging in his wallet, Jagger fished out two twenties and paid the attendant.

They climbed into the navy Mustang, and he turned the key in the ignition. The engine roared to life. This car was his personal pet project, loaded with all the bells and whistles and a few extras he'd never added to any previous vehicles. Another customer, a high-ranking lieutenant in Los Chacales, had spotted him finishing up the muscle car and offered to buy it. The guy had been so adamant, offering to pay more than the vehicle was worth with the upgrades, that Jagger had agreed to sell it. The new owner was supposed to pick her up tomorrow, but a customer's disappointment was not on his list of priorities.

Throwing the car in Drive, Jagger did another quick search of their surroundings before pulling out of the lot.

"Where are we going to go?" Wendy asked.

"Out of the city. Somewhere safe. Then we'll regroup and come up with a plan."

Taking the FDR Drive north was one option to reach the Upstate New York destination he had in mind, but the 495 might be faster at this time of night. Not only to get to where they were ultimately going, but also it was the quickest route out of the city.

To say that Wendy wasn't going to like it was an understatement. The 495 meant taking the Lincoln Tunnel—a tube that was a mile and a half long, less than twenty-two feet wide, ninety-seven feet below the Hudson River. For someone claustrophobic like Wendy, the short drive through would probably feel like several hours, but every minute they were in Manhattan counted and he wasn't going to waste any.

"Put your purse in the bag in the back."

Wendy reached between the seats, grabbed the black duffel and hefted it onto her lap. "This weighs a ton. What's inside?"

"Supplies."

She unzipped the duffel and peered down at the contents. "What in the hell? You had all this stuff on hand?" she asked in disbelief as if he wasn't a hit man for the cartel. Rifling through the weapons, she gasped. She held up a canister that had a pin. "Please tell me this isn't a grenade?"

"Okay, then I won't."

She shrank back in horror.

"Relax. It's only smoke, nonexplosive." Though it had a variety of uses and one never knew when it might come in handy.

Lifting what looked like, to an untrained eye, a piece of

molding clay the size of a deck of cards, she said, "Are you going to tell me this causes smoke, too?"

Truth be told, C-4 did create a lot of smoke, after the explosion. "I told you to put your purse inside, not to take inventory or to ask questions if you don't really want to hear the answers."

He took a left onto Seventh Avenue, heading south. To reach the 495 they had to backtrack, and this route would take them within two blocks of the library. Dangerously close. As much as he hated that, there was no choice with the city's network of one-way streets. Since traffic wasn't gridlock, they should be able to move smoothly, and the car's windows were tinted, offering a small degree of concealment.

"What do you plan to do with all this? And yes, I want the answer."

"I don't have a plan. I just wanted to be prepared."

"Still a Boy Scout, I see. Only you're playing for the bad guys these days." Wendy stowed the plastic explosives and her purse inside the bag. After zipping it closed, she heaved it into the back.

"It's complicated."

"Which means you don't want to talk about it."

No, he didn't. Jagger tightened his grip on the steering wheel. He had no desire to dredge up the hard, ugly choices he'd had to make that led to his current predicament. Maybe a part of him was afraid she wouldn't understand. When they had been together, she'd never judged him or made him feel he had to prove himself. Things had changed. She had every right to question the decisions that had put him on the cartel's payroll as an assassin.

"I noticed a flip phone in your bag." Wendy leaned back in her seat, and her shoulders relaxed. "I thought you didn't bring one."

"It's a burner phone. For emergencies only. No one has

the number. I'm not tied to a plan that can be traced, and that model doesn't have a GPS chip, so it can't be tracked."

Wendy ran her hand along the dashboard and the seats. For a long, silent moment she looked over the interior. "You restored this beauty, didn't you?"

She had always had an affinity for the things he loved—cars, the outdoors, hunting, football. Things she'd learned to appreciate from her father before he died, and her brother. But during their time together, anything that was important to him became important to her and she showed genuine interest. It was one of the things he loved about her.

"Guilty," he said, biting back a small smile. His heart warmed at knowing that she hadn't lost her eye for spotting his work. Just as quickly, he realized it might be wishful thinking on his part. She could've easily made an assumption based on the fact that he'd picked this car to drive.

"You leave a little piece of yourself in your work. Always did. I can see it in the details."

This time he let the smile ghost across his lips. That she still knew him so well gave him hope. Of what exactly, he wasn't quite sure, but even as vague as it was, he'd grab hold of it with both hands.

A right turn took them onto Thirty-seventh Street through the Garment District. Traffic slowed, growing heavier. They'd put some distance between them and the library, where he hoped the mobile Brethren unit was parked and not out searching the area.

In a few more blocks, they'd start to merge onto the 495.

"You said you own or, rather, co-own a car repair shop."

"Yeah."

His partner and good buddy, Sixty, who had earned the nickname because he could boost almost any car in sixty seconds, had an arrangement with the cartel for tricking out their rides before he had been incarcerated for grand theft auto. Jagger was a mechanic, loved tinkering with anything on wheels. At night in their cell, he came up with ways to take the upgrades to the next level. Sixty thought they'd work well together, and as it turned out did. A match made in heaven. Or hell, considering they worked for the cartel. Jagger had increased the shop's profits three hundred percent in the first six months.

Sixty was the closest thing Jagger had to a best friend after getting released.

"Here in the city?" she asked. "In Manhattan?"

He dipped his head in response, his gut churning in anticipation of the next question, the much heavier one that he didn't want to answer.

"Where exactly?" she asked.

He took a deep breath. Best to spit it out and let the cards fall where they might. "Hell's Kitchen."

Her jaw set hard and her eyes lifted to his.

"Your shop is in *Hell's Kitchen*." A pregnant pause swelled in the car, sucking up the oxygen. "I would've guessed Brooklyn or the Bronx. Hell's Kitchen is about what, twenty minutes from the heart of Chelsea? That's where I live, by the way."

An eight-minute car drive to get to her place from his, depending on traffic. With a bus ride on the M11, fourteen. If he took the C train and transferred to the E, it would be closer to sixteen. He was aware of which posh building, the floor and unit she lived in, and had before he'd even stepped foot out of Sing Sing.

Not seeing her didn't stop him from keeping tabs on her, ensuring that she was all right.

"Twenty-five minutes, give or take," he said, and it was true, if he was walking.

He lived above the car shop and sometimes, when he had trouble sleeping, he'd stroll the streets. Always found himself out front of her building, with gut-wrenching memories battering him while he contemplated ringing her bell.

Deep down, he realized that would do more harm than good. Regardless of how he had ended up behind bars, he was the one who had pushed her away. She didn't deserve him mucking up her situation. It was impossible for him to turn back the clock and be the man she used to know and love. That guy was gone, but if she was ever in danger, then he'd be there for her. Protect her the way he swore on his own life to Dutch that he would.

A kill order definitely constituted danger with a capital *D*.

"Twenty-five minutes, huh. From Chelsea, or my apartment specifically?" When he didn't respond, she asked, "Did you already know where I lived?"

"I'm pretty sure every member of the Brethren who received the kill order on you knows where you live. It's a good thing you weren't at your apartment earlier when I swung by there first."

"I got ready at my fashion stylist's loft." She shifted in her seat, facing him. "But that's not what I meant. Did you know where I lived before tonight?"

He didn't want to lie, but would admitting the truth make him seem like a stalker?

Good God, was he a stalker? Not the creepy kind, but one nonetheless?

His intention was to watch over her from a distance, keep her safe without intruding in her life.

"How long have you known where I live?" She put her hand on his thigh and shook him, demanding an answer.

Heat sparked from her touch, radiating up his leg. Parts of his body loosened while the rest stiffened, kicking into gear. He'd craved the feel of her touch, imagined her caress against his skin, and this simple brush of her hand left him aching for so much more.

Jagger glanced at her. Gleaming blue eyes drilled into him, penetrating past the barrier he'd erected after he'd slammed the book closed on their relationship ten years ago.

The connection between them flared, tugging at him, alive and animate. It stole his breath, but the one awful thing that had gone wrong for them was there, too. The one thing that had separated them for nearly a decade was front and center, and the pain he'd caused her was just as palpable.

"I do have a confession," he said. "And you're not going to like it." He pursed his lips, trying to ignore her enticing fingers sliding across his thigh.

"Try me."

Tempted as he was to give in to the distraction of the physical contact and get lost in her eyes, this wasn't the time or place. It was too easy to be lured into a false sense of security in the confines of the car, and in the next three seconds she was going to be furious with him. There was no telling how she'd react.

"We have to go through the Lincoln Tunnel," he blurted out. No way to sugarcoat it and there was little point trying.

Wendy reeled back, her eyes flaring wide with hollow misery. Her hand on his leg retreated and she clutched her chest. "No! Go a different way."

"Too late." He hiked his chin forward, redirecting her attention. "We're already here."

The Lincoln Tunnel lay in front of them. Long gone was any opportunity to turn around. They'd passed the last exit and were now on the ramp to the westbound portal. He merged into one of the lines funneling toward the tube about two hundred feet up ahead.

Twenty-foot-high concrete walls bracketed either side of the two lanes of vehicles. Metal lane dividers kept cars from veering off course, channeling the traffic in one direction—forward. Headed straight for the dark gaping mouth of the tunnel.

"I can't do it," she said, her voice rising. "Not the tunnel."

"You can. I'll be right beside you the entire time."

"No! I'm not going inside that death trap. I'd rather surrender to Los Chacales and let them put me out of my misery quickly."

"It'll be fine. Close your eyes and breathe through it."

"Did you read the article in the *New Yorker* that said the tunnels are the biggest targets for terrorists? The soil above the tunnel has shifted and there are cracks. What if something happens inside and—"

"Not today. The tunnel will hold." He grasped her hand and interlaced their fingers. "Take a deep breath," he said, and she did. "Another, slower."

He understood how serious her claustrophobia was. She had difficulty in elevators, which was hell in Manhattan, and avoided the subway, a more expensive kind of hell in the city. Flying was okay for her, and he suspected it had something to do with being able to see outside through the window. The tunnel, however, was intolerable.

Wendy flicked a terrified glance at the current source of her fear. He put their clasped hands on his chest, and her gaze returned to his.

"I don't know." She shook her head and squeezed her eyes closed. "I don't think I can make it."

He tightened his grip on her soft hand, needing to find a way to stem her anxiety. "Hey." The single word drew her focus back to him. "We'll make it through, together. I promise. Besides, there's no way the cartel is lucky enough for some freak accident to take us out."

She gave a small, sad chuckle. "That's a good point," she said. "What would be the chances? It would take insane odds. Right?"

"Exactly."

Wendy gulped and nodded slowly. "I'll try."

"Try? You're Wendy Haas. The most determined person I know when you set your mind to something. Strong and beautiful and smart. A fighter with guts, who never gives in." And it was for all those reasons that he'd been cruel to her on her last visit with him in prison.

She heaved a deep breath. "Well, that's a lot to live up to."

"Not for a tough cookie like you."

Something changed in the air as she turned her mesmerizing blue gaze on him. A hundred memories floated into his mind. Kissing her in the rain. Long chats snuggled together in front of the fire. Making love to her, consumed with a breathless need, only for her. Never wanting to let her go.

"Don't look at me like that," she said.

"Why not?"

"Because—"

The lights on the monitor below the dashboard and the instrument panel flickered. The radio turned on and pop music filled the car—Imagine Dragons' latest song from whatever movie was dominating the box office. They exchanged a surprised glance.

He released her hand and hit the button to switch off the radio.

Nothing happened. Music continued to blare, lyrics wrapping around them.

It was the strangest thing.

He stabbed the button for the radio again—the music kept playing.

"What's happening?" Wendy asked, pressing back against her seat.

"I don't know."

The radio bounced from FM to AM. Static boomed across the airwaves.

Wendy turned the dial for the volume with no effect. "What the hell?" she asked over the noise.

Suddenly the radio cut out.

Silence descended and a chill shot up his spine, but he kept a bead on their progress toward the tunnel. They were almost there. One hundred yards from the entrance.

Racking his brain for an explanation as to why his car was possessed, a terrible suspicion slithered into his head. There were two possibilities. Best case, a short in the electrical system somewhere, somehow. Worst case, they were being hacked.

These days a car was a big computer on wheels.

The Brethren employed individuals from a variety of backgrounds and skill sets, but none of them would be able to infiltrate his vehicle's system. They'd need the VIN number, engine model, to know what electrical system he was using.

Jagger looked up at the sluggish traffic.

They had to make it to the tunnel. Once they were inside, he'd know one way or the other. The structure of the tunnel provided natural shielding. If they were being hacked, the disruptions would stop until they exited on the other side, and if they weren't, the issues would persist.

Either way, he could ditch the car in New Jersey, but they had to cross through first.

Eighty yards to go. The line of cars crept forward.

Inside the tunnel, the speed limit was thirty-five miles per hour. Their approach to the entrance with the bumper-to-bumper traffic was closer to a painful ten miles per hour crawl.

The monitor on the dashboard flipped through screens and flashed from Radio to Settings to Bluetooth. The wireless connection activated.

Sixty yards.

Trimble, the telematics system, popped up. It was a more robust version of OnStar or Teletrac Navman, which could transmit information from the vehicle to the outside world and allow an occupant to call for help.

Fifty yards.

"Jagger." The shaky male voice over the speakers gave the identity away.

Recognition sliced through him. "Sixty, is that you?"

"I'm sorry, man," Sixty sniveled, his voice tight with pain. "They're making me do it."

Jagger's heart punched into his throat. "Do what? Who's in charge?"

Static crackled through the 4G network connection. Voice mode deactivated.

"Sixty?" His stomach turned inside out. If the Brethren had control of the vehicle's telematics, they were hosed. "Sixty?" Jagger hit the Call for Help button on the screen. When nothing happened, he jabbed an impatient finger at the disconnect icon, trying to sever the connection.

The steering wheel lurched, and the brakes engaged, slamming the car to a jerky stop twenty yards from the entrance of the Lincoln Tunnel. They were close, so close.

Jagger pressed the accelerator, but nada. The engine didn't even rev in response, and the steering wheel had locked.

His heart galloping, he stomped on the gas pedal, smashing down on the accelerator in the hopes of getting the slightest movement. The car didn't budge. The gears were stuck in Park.

"Nothing is working," he said, jamming his foot on the gas as hard as he could.

Horns blared from the cars stuck in line behind them as the rest of the vehicles in front proceeded into the tunnel. Onlookers from the adjacent stream of traffic in the next lane gawked as they passed by.

"What do we do?" Wendy asked.

The monitor on the dashboard blipped from Trimble to Navigation with mind-blowing speed. A map came up on the screen.

Trimble combined a GPS system with onboard diagnostics that could cross-reference the data from the sensors in the vehicle. Within seconds, the Brethren would know the exact location of the car.

Jagger had installed the system in case of an emergency

or to track the vehicle if it was ever stolen. Now his resourcefulness was being used against him, to trap him and Wendy, and someone was torturing Sixty to do it.

No good deed goes unpunished. I should've killed Corey. If he had, they wouldn't be in this bind. He shoved the thought to the back of his head.

Their coordinates were highlighted on the monitor. Latitude and longitude, degrees, minutes, down to the seconds.

Slapping the steering wheel, Jagger let loose a string of foul words. "We've got to move. We need to get out of the car."

They both tried the handles, but the doors wouldn't open. He pressed his thumb frantically on the tiny button on the key fob even as he knew it wouldn't work.

Pushing the keyless ignition button to shut down the engine was equally as futile.

Jagger would've fired a couple of bullets at the windows, but the glass was bulletproof.

He'd been shut out of his own vehicle's system. The brakes and locks were under Sixty's control, or rather the Brethren's.

No doubt the mobile unit he'd spotted earlier was already on the move, coming straight for them. They were sitting ducks in a tin can with no way to escape.

Thanks to the bulletproof windows, the Brethren wouldn't be able to take them out with gunfire from a distance, but the alternative wasn't better. To kill them inside the car, the Brethren would have to blow it up.

Wendy scrabbled at the door handle again with no success. Jagger threw his shoulder against his door as he tried the handle, gripping it so hard his fingers hurt, and failed to get it open.

Dread constricted his chest.

Think. There had to be a solution. He couldn't let fear cloud his reasoning.

"The lock won't give!" Wendy said. "They're coming, aren't they."

Their eyes met. The terror in her gaze tore at him, but it was knowing that the longer they stayed the likelihood of the Brethren killing her increased that spurred him into action.

He released his seat belt and climbed into the back, ignoring the steady stream of agitated beeping coming from the cars jammed up behind them.

"What are you doing?" she asked.

"The trunk. That might be our only way out." Unlike the convertible Mustang model, his fastback came with flip-down rear seats. He found the first tab on the right upper corner and pulled the rear seat into a horizontal position. Once he got his hand on the second tab, he got the other seat down out of the way. "Come on."

She scrambled into the back beside him.

Jagger scooted into the trunk, feet first, hauling the bag of supplies along with him "The emergency release isn't connected to the electrical system, so it can't be controlled or disabled by anyone on the outside. I'm going to need you pull on it while I give the trunk door a good kick, since the lock is electronic." He pointed out the glow-in-the-dark T-handle latch.

To reach it, she'd have to enter the trunk headfirst. Wendy crawled in next to him, slid into position and grasped the handle.

"On my count," Jagger said, and she gave a quick nod. "One. Two. Three."

Wendy yanked the latch and Jagger kicked with both feet, giving it everything he had.

The trunk door popped up. Fresh air whooshed in over them.

He hopped outside and then helped Wendy. Slinging the bag of gear onto his shoulder, he glanced at the long line of cars clogged to a standstill.

Over the horns blaring, he picked up another sound. Motorcycle engines. Fast. High-powered.

Two sleek black motorcycles roared around the corner. The drivers wore tinted black full-face helmets, gloves and matching sinister outfits, and their bikes turned them into an even more terrifying threat.

Jagger had personally upgraded the motorcycles to make them the fastest things on the street. He'd also equipped them with a specialized magnetic panel where they could rest a weapon without fear of losing it. The feature enabled the drivers to confidently discharge a gun, knowing they could they secure it within two seconds and reclaim a two-handed grip on the handlebars.

This eliminated the need to have an extra person on the bike—one to drive and one to shoot—allowing faster performance and improved agility on the road. He'd done fine work on those motorcycles. Now that they'd been unleashed against him, he realized he'd probably done too good a job, but they weren't indestructible. He'd left a couple of easily overlooked vulnerabilities that he'd exploit.

"Are they the Brethren's mobile unit?" Wendy asked.

"Unfortunately, yes, but only part of the unit." The others were in the tactical vehicle making a beeline to provide backup.

Both motorcycle drivers hesitated, almost certainly catching sight of them and reporting back. Their engines revved and they started weaving around cars, circumventing the stalled traffic.

Jagger grabbed Wendy's hand and took off running around the Mustang.

"We'll never make it on foot through the tunnel," Wendy said.

She was right.

"And we can't stay here either," he added.

They bolted for the entrance. The sound of the motorcycle engines grew louder.

Jagger glanced over his shoulder.

The drivers were easing their way past the stuck cars. The lanes were wide enough, and their motorcycles were so streamlined that they were able to squeak through, even with the metal dividers.

Bullets pinged behind them, ricocheting off the raised trunk door.

Wendy screamed. She let go of his hand and covered her head as they ran.

Jagger drew his weapon and returned fire. "Keep going without me." He dropped the bag on the ground, knelt and unzipped it.

"What?" Wendy stopped dead in her tracks. "Go without you?"

"Don't think. Trust me. Run! Now!"

She looked as if she wanted to argue, but she turned and ran for the tunnel.

The click-clack of her shoes receded in the distance as Jagger grabbed the M18, pulled the pin from the smoke grenade and tossed it toward the Mustang.

He snatched another from the bag and did it again.

Thick layers of white phosphorous bloomed. That might slow the riders down, provide enough concealment for Jagger to pull a Hail Mary and get Wendy out of this alive.

Jumping up, he hoisted the bag on his shoulder.

She was almost inside the tunnel. With the gap in traffic, the lane was wide open. Once the Brethren made it by the traffic clogging the road behind them, they'd be able to run him and Wendy down.

Jagger fought to keep his fear for Wendy under tight rein, but his hand was shaking. He shoved emotion away. If he was going to save her, he had to stay focused. He bolted toward the tunnel, his pulse thrumming in his temple.

A motorcycle drew nearer, the rumble of the engine growing louder. Jagger couldn't see it, yet, because of the smoke, but he sensed it, felt the power of the thrumming motor, though that could have been his adrenaline pumping.

He kept running. Risked another glance behind him.

One of the bikers roared through the smoke, down the lane after them and lifted his gun with an attached suppressor, taking aim.

Heart racing, Jagger raised his weapon and trained his sights at the same time. He fired once, dropping the rider in his tracks, and sent him tumbling across the pavement. But not before a second shot whispered through the air and a searing hot bullet ripped into Jagger's body.

Chapter Five

Wendy's breath punched from her lips. She sprinted as fast as her three-inch Louboutins and long dress allowed. She dodged and changed direction in an attempt to avoid flying bullets that hadn't been fired yet.

I can do this. I have to.

Don't think.

Run!

But her thoughts pounded in her head like her heels against the asphalt. An underground tube that ran almost a hundred feet below the Hudson River was not her idea of safety. Rushing toward it challenged her sense of self-preservation. The closer she got, the stronger the urge to turn back, to avoid the dimly lit confines. Her fear nearly undid her, but Jagger was counting on her not to fall to pieces.

Wendy ducked inside the tunnel and stopped.

She turned around to check on Jagger, make sure he was all right and catch her breath.

One motorcycle rider was down on the ground, but she could hear the engine of the second.

Jagger raced toward her with one hand gripping the strap of the heavy bag on his shoulder and the other, holding the gun, was pressed to his side.

Was he hurt?

If he was injured, there was no indication of it on his face or in his hard-charging pace as he rushed flat out into the tunnel.

Before she could say anything to him, he leaped in front of a sedan in the adjacent lane of slow-moving traffic with his gun raised and stopped the car. "Unlock the doors!"

The driver, an older man in his late sixties, raised a hand in compliance and unlocked the doors.

"Wendy! Get inside." He motioned to her with a hand.

She hurried to the driver's side and hopped into the back seat, leaving the door open for Jagger.

He shifted around the car, keeping the gun pointed at the driver, and slipped inside. "Go! Drive!"

A red stain on Jagger's white shirt spread, blooming wide over his right side. He was bleeding.

She went cold with fear. *Oh, God.* He'd been shot.

"I don't think you want to do this, son," the driver said in a soft, steady voice, but the stony expression on his face gave the words bite.

"You're right. I don't," Jagger said, "but we don't have a choice. Drive."

"A person always has a choice. As both a former United States Marine and a retired cop, I'm telling you that you're making the wrong one. Someone is calling the cops as we speak. They'll have officers waiting on the New Jersey side."

"And I'm telling you that if you don't start driving, cops on the other side will be the least of worries and you're going to have two corpses in your back seat. There's a high probability that you'll be killed, too." Jagger turned and flicked a glance through the rear windshield.

"If you're in some kind of danger, then you need to drop your weapon and call 911," the driver said. "I'll wait with you until the police arrive."

The older man with salt-and-pepper hair was tough as nails, but there was also something tender and kind about him. "Please, sir. Help us. This is a matter of life and death," she pleaded, but he looked skeptical and unmoved.

There was a growing gap between the stationary car they were in and the vehicles transiting the tunnel farther ahead. That alone would draw attention to the Buick if they ever got moving.

"I could put this gun to your head and force you, but I'm asking." Jagger's full attention snapped forward. He undid the shirt button along his wrist, yanked the sleeve up and flashed the driver the tattoo on his forearm—a shield with a lightning bolt across the center. "As one former Ranger to a Devil Dog, I assure you we don't have time for this. Los Chacales cartel is about to storm the tunnel to kill this innocent woman who has done nothing to warrant it. They'll be here any second. Do you really think dialing 911 is going to make a difference?"

The driver raised his scruffy eyebrows at that. "Los Chacales," he echoed, concern entering his voice. "Why didn't you say that from the get-go?" He hit the gas and the silver Buick jolted forward.

A motorcycle zipped out of the smoke. The driver rolled by the cars in line behind them, peering into the window, searching for them. They both scooted down in the back seat.

The older man exceeded the speed limit, trying to catch up to the traffic in their lane, but if he went much faster, it would draw attention.

The inside of the car was dim from the lack of moonlight and the dull fluorescent lighting of the passageway. The grungy walls of the tunnel closed in and the ceiling seemed to press down, as the length of the underground tube elongated.

Tension spiraled in her chest and ballooned, filling her lungs and squeezing out the air.

She closed her eyes, tried to stop her mind from spinning before she had a full-blown panic attack.

Jagger grunted in pain. The distinct sound tore her away from her private misery, had her head coming up and her eyes flying open.

She put a hand on his shoulder. "How bad is it?" Taking a deep breath and forcing herself to focus, she lifted his shirt and looked at the wound.

He glanced down at his side where he was bleeding. "I got lucky."

It sure didn't look lucky, but rather than a gaping hole, the wound was more of an ugly gash.

"The bullet only grazed me, passed clean through." Blood trickled liberally down his side and her heart clenched. "Only a superficial flesh wound. Better than catching one between the L2 and L3 vertebrae."

The cocky smile that tugged at his lips was quickly supplanted by a grimace.

He was putting on a brave face for her, which meant that he didn't want her to worry, but she was worried. Not only because he was the one thing standing between her and certain death, but… She wasn't ready to face any of the other reasons yet.

"We need to stop the bleeding," she said. "Disinfect it. Get it bandaged." Would he need stitches? It wasn't as if they could waltz into a local ER. The doctors would be able to tell the wound was from a gunshot. That would trigger an automatic call to the police.

He knew better than she did about the severity, but in this, she couldn't trust his answers. His injury would be glossed over, his pain left unacknowledged, and he'd muster on like a good solider.

Though he hadn't been on active duty for years, had been fresh out of the army when he met her, once a formidable Special Forces operator, always one. It was the way he was wired. As much as she admired his doggedness, at such times it made her want to shake him in frustration. All she wanted was to help him, keep him from bleeding out in the back seat of a stranger's car in the middle of the damn Lincoln Tunnel.

He gave a curt nod and pulled his shirt down, covering the wound. "Later. It's fine. There's no time. They're coming."

"We should at least apply pressure to it," she said, recalling what she'd learned from watching episodes of *Grey's*

Anatomy. She looked around, but they didn't have anything clean to use.

A motorcycle raced up the adjacent lane. The sound of the thunderous engine, amplified in the confined structure, bounced off the walls.

"I can't outmaneuver that Los Chacales rider. Not in this tunnel with those lane dividers," the driver said.

They were pinned, for all intents and purposes. Caught in the wave of traffic, the driver couldn't even slam on the brakes and pull a smooth defensive driving tactic.

The motorcycle roared up alongside them. They had stayed down, but the windows weren't tinted, and the light was dim, not nonexistent. They weren't invisible.

Gunfire pinged, smacking into the trunk of the Buick. Bullets sparked off the metal lane dividers and ricocheted.

"Get lower." Jagger shoved her head toward the seat.

She ducked down, trying to make herself as small as possible as he dug into the bag of supplies on his lap.

Bullets peppered the rear windshield, splintering it into a web of a thousand cracks. If the glass had been tempered, it would've shattered with the first slug. The only thing holding the windshield together was the laminate in the composite, but it would give under a barrage of more bullets.

She'd learned enough about cars from Jagger during the time they'd lived together to qualify as a mechanic's assistant.

Another volley of measured shots quickly followed, striking with plenty of force, and brought the rear windshield flying into the car in sharp chunks. Jagged pieces of glass stuck to reinforced plastic rained over her.

Wendy swallowed a gasp, wincing from the cuts on her hands, which were covering her head, but she was smart enough to stay low and out of the direct line of fire.

More bullets pinged into the side of the Buick.

The driver was shifting gears when a tire burst with a loud

pop. He wrestled the steering wheel and tried to prevent the car from swerving, but the Buick slammed against the lane dividers, scraping the steel posts, and scrubbed along the tiled wall. Metal squealed at an ear-grating pitch. She imagined the sparks from the rim grinding against the asphalt.

The rising roar of the motorcycle combined with the incoming gunfire stretched her nerves rubber-band tight, pulled taut on the brink of snapping. Given the acoustics of the tunnel and the broken windshield, the shots rang out despite the sound suppressor.

Shivering, Wendy closed her eyes. She quelled the panic. Quelled the fear rising in her throat and tamped it down before she screamed.

"Don't let him hit the gas tank," the older man said. "He's coming up alongside us."

In that instant, she didn't know which would be worse, drowning in the Lincoln Tunnel from a freak leak or being burned alive in a car explosion inside it.

Both were outcomes she wanted to avoid at all costs.

"I know. I've got a bead on him." Jagger drew a double-barreled shotgun from the bag, plucked out a box of ammunition and slid cartridges into the chamber.

Clicking his tongue in a sound of satisfaction that she'd long missed hearing, Jagger drew up the cocked and locked shotgun. He pumped the 12-gauge, rolled down the window and shifted the sawed-off barrel through the opening.

She covered her ears with her hands. Plenty of hunting trips with her brother and father had taught her precisely how loud a gunshot could be at close range from a 9 mm pistol, an automatic rifle and especially a shotgun.

Boom!

Wendy flinched, an uncontrollable reflex from the sound.

"Damn it!" Jagger muttered.

He must have missed. Perhaps the driver had swerved in anticipation.

This time, Jagger waited. With a stoic expression, his body tense and poised, he held the 12-gauge upright. Once the man on the bike shot at them again, Jagger swung the gun out the window and opened fire.

Boom! Boom!

She sat up and hazarded a glance at the scene unfolding.

The motorcycle wiped out. The bike flipped, bounced— once, twice—and rolled, leaving a trail of steely-gray smoke in its wake.

She exhaled with an instant flash of relief that was short-lived. "Do you think he's dead?" she asked, not worried if the would-be assassin had lost his life. She had other concerns.

"If not, he's hurt too badly to come after us," Jagger said, answering her real question.

Metal from the rim scraped against the pavement, making an earsplitting noise.

"Stop the car," Jagger said.

"What?" the driver asked, looking at both of them in the rearview mirror. "Why? Three more minutes and we'll be through the tunnel."

Jagger shook his head. "Only God knows what will be waiting for us on the other side, and I'm not talking about the police."

The driver's gaze lowered. "Oh. I didn't consider Los Chacales might be over there."

"They've got people everywhere," Jagger said. "One phone call, that's all it takes, and they could have anywhere from two to ten people or a second mobile unit waiting to ambush us out there."

The older man nodded. The car gradually slowed, giving the vehicles behind them time to adjust accordingly without causing any fender benders. "What are you going to do?"

"Wing it." Jagger flashed a fearless grin.

On anyone else the confidence would come across as

cocky. On him the self-assured demeanor worked. He handled every problem without losing his cool.

He might be hurting, but he didn't appear close to bleeding out.

"I'm sorry about the damage," Wendy said. "If we manage to survive, I'd be happy to pay for the repairs."

"Don't worry about it. This old-timer has a perfect driving record and excellent insurance."

The Buick came to a full stop and the sound of squealing metal faded, but horns blared behind them.

Quickly Jagger stowed the shotgun back in the bag.

He threw open the car door. "Thank you," he said to the driver. Without waiting for a response, he took her hand and she followed him out of the vehicle.

They scrambled into the empty parallel lane as the Buick crawled off and traffic resumed with a few angry beeps.

Jagger looked around for a second as if he was formulating a plan of action.

Standing in the dead center of the tunnel was ten times worse than passing through in a car at thirty-five miles per hour, a speed that had seemed interminably slow minutes earlier. The creeping, prickling terror that started at the base of her spine and slithered over her mind like a shroud had her in its clutches. Her legs turned leaden. The air grew dense. And those tiled walls separating her from the deluge of the Hudson contracted along with her lungs. She could scarcely breathe.

"Hey," he said, and brushed her cheek with his knuckles. "I will get us out of here," he said, sounding so damn confident despite the fact they didn't have a car, there was nowhere to run, and the cartel was waiting for them on either end of this godforsaken tunnel.

"How?" Her heart thudded hard, her stomach rolling in a sickening wave. "What if you can't?"

"I will. Trust me."

This was Jagger during any kind of emergency. Once she'd sliced her hand open while cooking and was bleeding everywhere. He'd bandaged the wound, kept her hand raised over her head to reduce the flow of blood—something she never would've thought of—and gotten her to ER in record time. Jagger always kept his head, prioritized needs, threats, saw that things were taken care of and nothing fell through the cracks. Acted with such calm certainty it endeared him to her and, truth be told, frightened her a little, too.

"The sooner the better." Her voice was a whisper, but he nodded. It was a miracle he heard her over the din from the traffic.

Jagger headed over to the left-side wall.

She bit the inside of her lip so hard she drew blood. The pinch of pain helped clear her head. Wendy took a deep breath, summoning her strength, and forced her feet to move. Jagger pointed up at the emergency walkway for Port Authority personnel as she came up alongside him.

She hadn't considered it previously. Probably because she'd been too busy spazzing out over entering the tunnel in the first place.

Jagger flung the heavy duffel bag onto the footpath under the railing. Then he jumped, catching hold of the ledge, and hoisted himself onto it.

He grunted, but he quickly swallowed the sound of his discomfort.

Once he was situated on the walkway, he reached down for her.

If there was a way for her to get up without bringing him further pain she would've taken it in a heartbeat, but their options were limited, and time wasn't on their side. She hopped, grabbing hold of both of his hands. Putting her feet on the tiled surface for leverage, she walked up the wall the best she could. Her heels kept slipping, but she was climbing for her life, to survive, and each second put strain on Jagger's wound.

Scrabbling up the subway tiles, she gave it everything she had as he hauled her onto the walkway. She climbed to her hands and knees, found her bearings and stood.

"We can't go back," she said, a bit winded, "and we can't go forward."

"So, we improvise."

The stain of blood on his shirt had spread. All the exertion wasn't doing his injury any good.

"Can we take a minute to stop the bleeding?"

"Not yet." He grabbed the duffel bag and hurried along the walkway at a clipped pace.

She looked back toward Manhattan. Plumes of smoke from the motorcycle wreckage obscured her view of the entrance.

If the rest of the Brethren were as tenacious as Jagger, they'd send in reinforcements at any moment. They could have any number of people amassing to cross the tunnel and come after them. A mental image of that possibility made her shudder.

Please, God, don't let that happen.

Patching up Jagger would have to wait. They had to keep moving.

Wendy lifted the hem of her dress and jogged to catch up to him, wondering what his plan was. It made no sense to run to the New Jersey side when they could have gotten there faster in the car, and it wasn't as if they could go back the way they had come.

"Here we go." Jagger stopped in front of a door appropriately marked Exit.

"Where do you think it leads?"

He shrugged. "My best guess is to a security office with armed personnel, but I like our chances better with them than the Brethren."

She agreed.

Jagger gave the door a nudge. It was locked.

He held up his arm in front of her. "Stand back."

She shifted behind him.

He aimed his weapon at the lock and fired. The door gave way with a kick from him.

On the other side lay a steep stairwell leading to only God knows where.

With one hand, she pulled her dress taut and ascended the stairs after him.

In some ways, she preferred the narrow stairwell to the tunnel and in others she didn't.

The steps and walls were concrete. A material she'd take over tiles any day to keep her dry and safe from the prospect of drowning. Of course she *knew* there were layers of concrete in the tunnel on the other side of those flimsy porcelain rectangles, but logic never outweighed her fear. Not inside the tunnel anyway. Throw her into any other scenario and she kept her wits about her. It was embarrassing.

The climb was strenuous. Not as grueling as the 354 steps, or twenty stories, inside the Statue of Liberty from the ground to the crown. Jagger had taken her there on their third date. Raced her to the top and rewarded her with their first kiss and a view to die for.

In the stairwell, she was huffing, the dank air sawing in and out of her lungs. She was a runner, in good shape, but doing stairs was a killer workout she avoided. Her burning thighs were the proof.

Her mouth was dry, her throat tight. She kept swallowing, which didn't help. Though she silently cursed her heels, she wasn't going to be a slacker or complain. Not when Jagger had been shot, was carrying a bag that weighed a good fifty pounds and hadn't slowed since they had started this ascent toward the unknown.

Finally they reached the top landing and faced a door.

Wendy rested her hands on her knees and raked in oxygen.

Jagger dug back into his bag of tricks. "I'm going to need you to open the door on my mark and stay down low behind me," he said, pulling out the shotgun.

"Anticipating trouble on the other side?" she asked, still a little breathless.

"We've passed three security cameras since we entered this stairwell," he said, but she'd been none the wiser because her head had been down on the climb up. "I didn't want to say earlier, but you're right about the tunnels being a security risk for the city. They're heavily monitored with surveillance." He double-checked that the shotgun was loaded and stood in front the door, poised for action. "I fully expect an armed greeting."

Chapter Six

Drawing in a deep, steady breath, Jagger prepared to handle whatever was waiting for them on the other side of the door.

The use of lethal force would be a last resort with law enforcement. Most cops weren't the bad guys and were only doing their jobs. He had to treat each one like a combatant who didn't know he was friendly.

Jagger nodded his head once, giving Wendy the signal, and she yanked the door open.

"Freeze!" said an armed Port Authority police officer standing in a hallway. "Drop your weapon and put your hands in the air!"

The officer was standing too close. A good thing for Jagger, but bad for her. If she had been two feet farther back, he would've had no choice but to comply or take his chances with her opening fire.

Her proximity gave him a third option.

Rushing forward two steps, he turned the shotgun sideways. He thrust the long barrel up, knocking the officer's gun and sending the muzzle toward the ceiling. He stepped into her and shoved the shotgun again, catching her arms and chin.

Her head flew backward from the force, and her arms flailed as the gun clattered to the floor. Momentarily shocked, she stumbled back.

Jagger swooped in and seized the advantage, pushing the officer's face forward against the wall. He pressed the barrel into her spine, with his finger off the trigger, and kept her pinned. "Wen!"

Wendy peeked out, taking in everything. She jumped up from behind the door and hustled into the hall. She grabbed the officer's weapon from the floor without him prompting her, and she stuffed it into the duffel bag.

"Zip ties," he said. "Right pocket. Restrain her."

With shaking hands, Wendy took a zip tie and slipped it around the officer's wrists.

Jagger glanced down and checked it. "Make it tighter."

Wendy adjusted it until the officer grunted. Jagger didn't want the Port Authority cop to be in pain, but he also didn't want her getting loose before they made it out of the tunnel.

"How many others in the security office?" he asked.

"Just me. My partner left early."

That was convenient, and if it was true, he wasn't going to look a gift horse in the mouth. "Why did he leave?"

"It's his wife's birthday," she said. "He couldn't get off work, so I told him I'd cover for him."

Jagger took her by the back of the shirt and hurried down the hall, keeping her in front of him. "What time is shift change?" When she didn't immediately respond, he nudged her with the barrel. "What time?"

"In an hour."

Stopping at the small office, he visually cleared each corner before they went in. Jagger steered the officer around the desk and ensured no one was hiding behind it. The office was empty, as she'd said.

Monitors showed various parts of the tunnel, the stairwell they'd come up and a couple of other hallways.

A third Brethren motorcycle had entered the tunnel, and the driver was helping the injured man who had wiped out. They both got on the bike and headed toward the New Jersey side.

Standard protocol. They wanted to clear the crime scene with any surviving members before first responders arrived. No doubt, they'd linger on both sides of the tunnel, watching, waiting for a sign of him or Wendy and a chance to finish their job.

Jagger wasn't going to give them that chance. "When you saw us coming up the stairwell, did you report it?"

The cop shook her head. "No."

Once again, convenient. *Too convenient.*

"I want you to get on comms," Jagger said, "and change the report you made about us." After the gunfire in the tunnel, there was no way she hadn't reported two suspicious individuals heading up the stairwell. "Say we doubled back. That we're on foot in the walkway."

"Going in which direction?" the cop asked.

"West." He shoved her into the chair behind the desk. From her wedding ring, he knew she was married, but he needed more heartstrings to tug. "Do you have kids?"

"Yes. Three girls."

"How old?"

She took a shaky breath but remained calm under pressure. "Seven. Nine. Thirteen."

"I know you want to see your family again. I don't want to hurt you. So while you're on the radio, I want you to remember that I'm armed and dangerous and how much you want to get out of this without catching a bullet."

"Is she your hostage?" the officer asked, referring to Wendy, who was shivering in a corner.

"No. I'm trying to protect her. Save her from Los Chacales hit men. You have no reason to trust me, but on my life, I mean you no harm. I need to get her out of here and I don't have time to debate how that happens."

A single vein popped out on the officer's forehead. He could see her weighing the things he'd told her.

"Okay." She nodded. "Pick up the mic and hit that button," she said, hiking her chin at the one labeled Control Center.

"Play this smart and you'll have a story to share," he warned, just in case she got any bright ideas while on the radio. "A dead wannabe hero tells no tales. Think of your girls." He hit the button, opening the line of communication to the control center.

She licked her lips and sat forward. "Control, this is Morales."

"Morales, what's the status of those two suspects? Are they still headed your way?"

Of course, she had reported it. Any good officer would've, but now he had confirmation and it meant he had to doubt any answers she gave him.

"They doubled back. The woman was having difficulty climbing the stairs. They're on the walkway again, heading west. Over."

"Roger, that. Also, Nichols and Seung are both delayed. Traffic. One of them should be there within the next twenty to thirty minutes."

She'd lied about the shift change, too.

"Good to know," Officer Morales said. "I'll put on a fresh pot of coffee."

"Control, out."

Jagger disconnected and narrowed his eyes at the cop. "You did good, but don't lie to me again."

Wendy came closer and peered at the monitors. Then she flicked a glance at him. In her eyes, he saw she wanted to know what they were going to do.

He was sorting through that. "Where do the other hallways lead?" he asked.

"Two connect with the other tubes," Morales said.

The Lincoln Tunnel consisted of three vehicular tubes with two traffic lanes each. They were currently in the northern tube that had exclusive westbound traffic.

Jagger rifled through the desk for anything he could use. "The other hallways?" he asked, finding a roll of duct tape.

"They lead to topside. One door on the New York end and the other New Jersey."

"Which entrance will those two cops use? Nichols and Seung?"

For a second, her gaze dropped and shifted to the left, but he caught it. Whatever she was going to say next would be another lie.

"New York side," she said.

That meant Jagger and Wendy couldn't go toward New Jersey because that was the real side the other two cops would enter.

"What does topside look like?" Jagger had always wondered where those emergency doors inside the tunnel led. He'd never expected to discover the answer while on the run from the Brethren and now the police.

"It's a parking lot."

"Security?"

She shook her head. "No. The lot is gated."

"Walk me through the procedure to leave."

As she explained, he knew he was getting only the partial truth, but it was better than nothing. He turned to the wall of lockers in the back of the office. Six units.

Inside the first one was a Port Authority Police uniform, black, utilitarian. It seemed small enough to fit Wendy. He snatched the uniform from a hanger and handed tossed it to her. "Change your clothes."

She glanced down at the impractical dress she had on. Looking back up, she nodded, her eyes clear and full of understanding that they needed to blend in. Without saying a word, she unzipped her dress and started changing.

Jagger looked away, turning his back. He'd ached for Wendy for a decade and under different circumstances he might've been tempted to sneak a peek, but in the end, he wasn't the kind of man to steal anything, not even a glimpse.

He moved to the next locker. There was a long-sleeved

uniform top that was about his size. He swiped it and dropped the shirt, along with the shotgun, on the desk.

If he didn't get the bleeding from the gunshot wound managed first, he might lose too much blood due to the nature of his injury, risk infection, not to mention that he'd ruin another shirt. Inside the duffel bag, he found the small medical kit he had in case of emergencies. Nothing fancy, it didn't even have tools for a suture.

Jagger set the kit on the desk. Quickly he took off his bloodied shirt and shoved it into his bag. He doused antiseptic on gauze and gritted his teeth in anticipation of what was to come.

"Let me." Wendy was at his side.

She'd changed with the speed of a ninja. The uniform was a little loose on her, but the belt helped. Heels weren't going to work any better than her going barefoot, but one problem at a time.

Holding out her hand, she offered to take over.

He gave her the wet gauze.

She cleaned around the area of his wound. The closer she got to the open gash, the more gently she dabbed, and he appreciated the tenderness.

"I think you're going to need stitches," Wendy said.

"Not a possibility right now." He rummaged in the med kit and fished out the superglue.

"What on earth are we supposed to do with that?" Wendy's gaze flickered from the glue in his hand to his wound. "Are you crazy? I can't." Her voice was strained, sounded thin.

"It's actually not a bad idea to close a superficial wound with it, in a pinch," Officer Morales said. "My husband is an EMT. Seen and done a lot of things. But you should go to the hospital to have that treated."

He should, but Officer Morales hadn't suggested it out of concern.

A trip to the ER for a gunshot wound would be the quickest way for them to be apprehended and for the Brethren to find Wendy.

Needle and thread and a proper suture were his first choice, but it wasn't as if he had many options. He gave Wendy a determined grin.

"You're unbelievable. Stubborn to the core," she said, snatching the glue from him. "This is going to hurt like hell. Are you ready?"

No, which didn't really matter. "Get it done so we can get going."

Wendy squirted the sticky liquid right into his wound and squeezed the skin together.

Jagger sucked in a sharp hiss at the agonizing burn. He groaned through the bloom of pain that lasted for several moments. Then she released the skin and the cut had sealed.

"See. It did the trick." He flashed another grin, though this one was tempered by the sting in his side. "No more bleeding."

"It's not medical grade. The skin could get irritated," Wendy said, inspecting his injury further. "You might get sick or die of toxic poisoning from that stuff."

"Superglue won't kill me. Don't worry, I'm not going anywhere."

Her eyes flashed up at him and her expression changed, turned dark like storm clouds gathering. Something in his words had struck a nerve.

Then he remembered. The last thing he'd said to her in Sing Sing prison.

There is no us. I'm dead to you.

He lowered his head at the sudden tightness in his chest. They needed to talk, have the conversation he'd dreaded since he was released, but right this instant he had only the strength to concentrate on one thing, and it wasn't revisiting that ugly day.

"Thanks for the help. I'll stay on my feet long enough to get you through this," he said to her, recalibrating fast.

Grabbing the clean uniform shirt, he turned away and gathered himself. He threw on the shirt, buttoned it and stared at a Port Authority ball cap at the top of one of the open lockers.

He slipped it on and found another one for Wendy.

"Officer," he said, "we're going to need a few more things from you, starting with your shoes and your car keys."

While Wendy reluctantly took the officer's tactical boots and put them on, he placed a strip of duct tape across the cop's mouth and used more to secure her torso and legs to the chair.

The communications terminal might still be problematic. Disconnecting the unit would raise a red flag at the control center. For good measure and to play it safe, he wrapped duct tape around the communications terminal. Morales would have to be Houdini to access it.

Checking the time, he estimated they had ten minutes before the officers replacing Morales showed up.

Jagger threw the shotgun in the bag, trading it for the officer's weapon. After taking her holster and placing it on his hip, he stowed the Glock. The badge with a bar code swinging low, clipped to her shirt, was the last item they needed to open the outer door and get through the gated parking lot.

"Come on," he said to Wendy as he was already on the move into the hall.

She was close behind him and then at his side.

He hiked the strap of the duffel bag higher onto his shoulder when they reached the junction of five passageways.

"Which one do we take?" Wendy asked.

The only posted signs were for the connections to the other tubes in the tunnel. The two remaining unmarked corridors didn't indicate which way led west and which east. If they took the wrong one, they'd waste invaluable time and ran the risk of encountering the late officers. Going back to ask Morales meant there was a fifty-fifty chance they'd get a truthful answer, and it was a hundred percent certain it'd eat up time they didn't have to lose. He hoped his naturally strong sense of direction wouldn't falter and lead them astray.

Jagger gestured with his chin toward the left. "If we are dead center along the length of the tunnel, it's about thirty-nine-hundred feet to the exit, give or take." A glance at his watch confirmed they had seven minutes. "Do you still run?"

In high school, she'd been on the track team. A morning run was her thing, rain or shine, during the time they'd been a couple, shacked up in unwedded bliss in a studio apartment the size of a paper bag.

"I've kept it up. Six days a week," she said.

Sundays were for being lazy, making love, breakfast in bed and reading the paper. Not online, but an actual, physical copy of the Sunday *Times*. They always did the crossword together.

Those simple Sunday delights with her—as delicious as their regular daily ones—now belonged to Tripp Langston. That was the way it should be, the natural order of things, but imagining it, knowing it, didn't stop his heart from feeling sick and slow, throbbing like a fish out of water asphyxiating.

"Can you keep you up, injured and hauling that arsenal?" she asked.

"I can handle it." Once a solider, always a soldier. Pushing through the pain came with the territory.

They jogged lightly down the corridor.

He would've killed for a pair of soft-soled tactical boots like the ones on her feet. Once they got to their ultimate destination, there would be a pair waiting. A bigger concern was the possibility of his wound reopening.

Her face took on a hardened edge, her gaze darting back and forth, searching for danger. The cartel and the cops both posed a threat. They needed to lay low and devise a plan.

They continued jogging in silence until they closed in on a steel door. There was a card reader mounted on the wall with a tiny red light at the top.

He pressed the officer's badge to the card reader. The red light turned green, and the lock on the door disengaged.

They pushed through it and stepped outside.

His skin prickled, though not from the change in temperature. "Damn it to hell." Once again Morales had woven the truth with enough misinformation to catch them up.

Wendy looked at the same thing he was staring at. "This isn't what she described."

Yeah, tell him about it.

Chapter Seven

Hell's bells. The small parking lot was surrounded by a high fence with barbed wire at the top, and at the entrance/exit was a structure the size of toll booth—a manned Port Authority guardhouse.

Wendy ducked back under the overhang of the doorway beside Jagger. "Morales said there wouldn't be security."

"Only fifty percent of what came out of her mouth was true. I think she lied about her replacements coming from the New York side and hedged our bets they're entering from New Jersey, where she hoped we'd be caught."

They were still in Manhattan.

He peeked around the corner at the police officer sitting in the guardhouse. "The cop is facing forward. Maybe I can sneak up on him and immobilize him before he hits the alarm."

That was the first time Jagger hadn't sounded completely confident, like he was capable of conquering the world. Then she tracked his gaze to the reason.

There were cameras mounted on the top of the fence around the perimeter. Most of them pointed outward to detect incoming threats, but a couple of them were trained on the guardhouse and, she presumed, the immediate area surrounding it.

If there were monitors in the guardhouse, the cop might spot Jagger approaching. There was nothing for him to hide behind. The parking spots were set several feet back and only two vehicles were in the lot.

Wendy spotted another detail Morales had given them that happened to be true. Beside the guardhouse was a stand-alone proximity card reader. The badge had to touch the electronic pad to open the gate.

"I think I have a better idea," she said.

"I'm all ears."

She unzipped the duffel and pulled out her purse. Inside, she found the hairpins she'd removed before they left the library. "Morales wore her hair up in a bun. Hers is a little darker than mine," she said, putting her hair in a similar style, "but with the bill of the ball cap pulled down low over my face and it being dark…" She shrugged.

"Might work."

"You'll need to hide in the trunk."

"And you'll need to keep your face turned away and avoid any chitchat with the guard."

"Got it."

"If it doesn't work, for whatever reason, pop the trunk and I'll take care of cop."

What did *take care of* mean?

Jagger hadn't harmed Officer Morales when it would have been easy for him to shoot her. Wendy had to trust his judgment and hope that he wouldn't have to intervene with the guard.

He gave her the car keys and the badge. She stepped out into the lot first. A gust of wind whipped up, nearly snatching the cap off her head, but she caught it in the nick of time.

Holding the ball cap down with one hand, she picked up the pace till she was just short of jogging. She hit the unlock button on the key fob. The lights on a red compact sedan flashed. As the guard's head lifted and he glanced over his shoulder at her, she pressed the button for the trunk. The raised door hid Jagger's approach from plain view and would keep the guard from noticing any differences between her and Morales as she walked.

Wendy stepped behind the open door and waited for Jagger to catch up and climb in.

"You've got this," he said.

Praying that he was right, she gave a nod and slammed the trunk closed.

Her heart raced as she slipped behind the wheel and started the car. The engine turned over right away.

Before pulling out, she adjusted the mirrors. She checked her reflection in the rearview, making sure the bill of the cap was low enough and tucked errant strands back in her loose bun. The hairdo wasn't nearly as tight and tidy as Morales's, but it should pass given the circumstances. She threw the gearshift into Drive.

As she drew closer to the exit, she realized how bright the light was shining in the guardhouse. Even though she and Morales were women with similar builds and hairstyles, the difference between the cop's olive complexion and Wendy's warm ivory skin tone might be noticed if the guard paid attention.

She glanced around the car for anything that might help. A scarf to wrap around her neck. A jacket with a high collar to obscure her face.

In the console, she found a pair of purple gloves. Perfect. They'd hide her French manicure. She tugged them on and got the badge ready to scan.

She eased up beside the guardhouse, tapped the brake and rolled down the window in front of the card reader.

At the same time, the guard turned toward her and opened the sliding partition of the booth that had been keeping the wind out. "Hey, Rochelle."

Without responding, Wendy slid the badge across the card reader. The red light flipped to green and the gate slowly started rolling aside.

"I heard about what happened in your tunnel," the guard said. "Sounded like it was pure mayhem. Crazy night, huh?"

Wendy rubbed her hand across her forehead and temple as if she were exhausted, concealing the side of her face, and nodded. "Mmm-hmm." That was the most she dared utter.

"I heard there was gunfire," he said. "Is that true?"

Her heart pounded out a wild rhythm. "Mmm-hmm." Good grief. Could the gate be any slower?

"I can only imagine how backed up traffic must be."

She gave another nod, keeping one hand up near her face. Her arm muscles tensed as she gripped the wheel with the other hand.

"Are you all right?" he asked, peering over at her.

"Mmm-hmm." Adrenaline mixed with her anxiety. Staring through the windshield, she watched the gate finally clear the front fender of the car. She waved bye, still holding the badge and pressed the accelerator.

Wendy turned right out of the parking lot onto an unmarked road. Not knowing if there were more cameras in the area, she didn't risk stopping yet and kept her head low.

After a quarter mile, the road intersected with a major street. She put the car in Park at the stop sign and popped the trunk.

Jagger hurried from the rear, around the car to the driver's side, lugging the bag with him.

She had no idea where they were going, but she could follow directions well enough. "You're hurt. You should rest. Let me drive." He was doing too much as it was.

"I'm fine. Save your fight for those who want you dead." Jagger gestured for her to move.

Suppressing a sigh, she climbed over into the passenger's seat. "You're not invincible, you know."

"Yeah, I'm painfully aware of that."

Tension throbbed at the base of her head. He was overextending himself, putting himself in harm's way for her, and risking everything. She wanted to do whatever she could to help them both, and he wouldn't even let her drive.

"Now what?" she asked, clicking her seat belt in place.

"I considered taking a different tube through the tunnel," he said, turning onto the major street. "The center one will have a travel lane going in each direction, but traffic will be gridlocked anywhere near it now. It'll be a nightmare. We have to use an alternate route."

Fine by her. She never wanted to go through the tunnel in the first place.

Chapter Eight

Emilio Vargas would be in his ocean side villa, sipping on a twenty-five-year-old Scotch, instead of locked up in chains like an animal in the San Diego Central Jail if it weren't for one man.

US Deputy Marshal Horatio Dutch Haas.

Dutch was responsible for this soulless circle of hell Emilio was trapped in. And he didn't mean the hell of being held captive in a jail cell. The hell of wearing an orange jumpsuit with shackles around his wrists and ankles, awaiting transfer to a federal facility. Or the hell of being stripped of his dignity as officers performed a full strip search, including a body-cavity check. An ordeal that would be repeated at the federal detention center.

Prison was nothing. Emilio could handle the invasive physical procedures. Tolerate confinement in a six-by-eight cage. Forgo the extravagances his lifestyle on the outside provided.

He was still king of Los Chacales cartel. Prison wouldn't change that. Not on federal kidnapping charges. The feds couldn't touch his assets. He could rule from anywhere, especially with his son, Miguel, leading their East Coast endeavors as a free man.

For Emilio, hell was losing his daughter.

First, the FBI had meddled in his affairs. The mole they had embedded in his organization would pay for his betrayal, too, no doubt about that. But those pesky marshals went from protecting informants who sought to cripple his empire to crossing the line when they dragged his precious Isabel into the middle of things.

The US Marshals had sent Dutch to get close to Isabel, *seduce* her, persuade her to turn against Emilio. They'd dredged up secrets of the past, and Isabel learned terrible truths he'd never wanted her to know.

All her life, Isabel had grown up thinking she came from a wealthy family who owned legitimate businesses, that Emilio was her *uncle* and Luis was her *father*.

Emilio had had an affair with his brother's wife, something he was not proud of. The illicit relationship had torn the family apart. When Maria got pregnant, Emilio's own wife left him, and Luis suspected the baby wasn't his. Shortly after Isabel was born, Maria had been diagnosed with stage four metastatic cancer. She was gone in a blink. The disease had taken her too damn fast. The day they had buried her, Luis sat him down, told Emilio that Isabel was the last piece of Maria that he had left. He recounted a story from the bible. The judgment of Solomon. Told Emilio that Isabel was his and all would be forgiven between them and they would once again be brothers. Or Luis would cut Isabel in two like the baby in the story and they'd each keep half of her, and then there would be war.

Emilio regretted how he'd wronged his brother, hurt him, and he was no stranger to sacrifice. There was nothing he wouldn't do to protect Isabel. For many years, he'd kept his distance, playing the role of a doting uncle, stolen moments with Isabel when he could, loving her from afar.

He had paid the price for his mistake, for the sake of peace, for as long as he could.

No one had told him that when children were small, they needed their mothers most, but once they blossomed into teenagers, they needed their fathers in a million different ways. The older Isabel got the more she'd needed. More time. More one-on-one attention to feel special and cherished in a manner only a father could give. Emilio had felt that same call to be a part of her life. To be there for her. His only daughter.

War became inevitable, and Emilio had his own brother

killed. Not for worldly things, such as money or power. Not to rule the cartel. He did it to be in Isabel's life.

Thanks to the marshals, all his dirty laundry had been aired. He'd been forced into a position where he had to tell Isabel the truth about her parentage, about the family business. Dutch had poured poison in her ear, coerced her to turn on him and had taken her away. Ripped her from Emilio's life like a thief in the night.

Emilio never got the chance to explain his side of things to her. Comfort her from the vicious blows of the truth. To tell her how much he had sacrificed for her, how much he loved her and always would. The marshals even denied him the opportunity to say goodbye.

He risked everything to see Isabel again, went so far as to kidnap another marshal's son for leverage.

I failed once to get vengeance. I won't fail a second time!

That's how the FBI had finally gotten charges on him that would stick. Not because Emilio had been stupid enough to get caught red-handed. The mole had stabbed him in the back.

Special Agent Maximiliano Webb had infiltrated his organization, betrayed him and seen to it that Emilio was charged with a crime that could carry a life sentence.

But it was Dutch Haas, former Delta Force turned marshal, Casanova extraordinaire, who had been handpicked by the marshals to entice Isabel, charm her, sleep with her, turn her into a traitor.

A slow, simmering rage pumped through Emilio's veins. Still, he kept his face impassive and demeanor apathetic, with the guard on the other side of the bars scrutinizing his every breath.

A reckoning was due, and it was coming. Like a firestorm, his retribution would be violent and merciless, and nothing would stop it.

For Special Agent Max Webb, Emilio would take his life.

Since Isabel believed she was in love with Dutch, Emilio wouldn't kill him once he found him. Wouldn't hurt a single hair on the young man's head. But Dutch was responsible for taking his daughter away from him, someone Emilio dearly loved. Someone he treasured above all else.

There was a debt and it must be paid.

A life for a life. Emilio would take away someone Dutch cared for.

His men had Wendy Haas in their sights. Dutch's sister was the same age as Isabel. It wasn't coincidence. Emilio had taken it as a sign that it was her life he should claim.

If she wasn't already dead, she would be soon enough.

Wendy Haas wouldn't live to see sunrise. He wanted his men to mess her up before they killed her. Wanted Dutch to live with the idea that she had suffered. Just as Emilio was suffering. He didn't mean the physical torment, though the cops had laid into him last night, not missing their chance to pound out their anger on his body until their captain had stopped it.

No, he was in anguish over Isabel, of what she must think of him, how she must be hurting to have lost two fathers. First, Luis, the man who had raised her, and now him.

Emilio screamed on the inside, seethed from the unfairness of it. He'd done so much, gone to extraordinary lengths—murdered his own brother—to be in Isa's life... and all for what?

If it was the last thing he did, he'd make sure Dutch knew it was Don Emilio Vargas who'd set everything in motion.

Take what is mine and you must pay.

Keys clinked as two officers wearing tactical gear walked down the hall and stopped in front of his cell.

"It's time, Mr. Vargas," Officer Andreas said, unlocking the cell and opening the door. "Let's get this transfer over with."

Emilio stood and shuffled forward to the threshold in his inmate canvas shoes.

Each officer took one of his arms and hauled him down the back corridor. Officer Littleton squeezed harder than necessary on Emilio's arm, making the bruises flare with pain.

Emilio pursed his lips in silent contempt, but he refused to let his discomfort show with even a grimace.

His chains jangled as he plodded along. A throbbing pulse pounded in his temple. His bicep ached under the tightening pressure of Littleton's cruel fingers. His armpits were damp with perspiration.

"Step it up," said Officer Littleton, a big clod of a man, who jerked him forward.

Emilio stumbled and clenched his jaw at the fact that he was at the mercy of the cops to keep him from falling flat on his face.

He loathed being in this position, shackled and herded like a leashed dog.

Littleton punched Emilio's lower back, right in his kidney. The area was already sore and tender from the beating he'd received after being processed. Every blow had been below the neck, each bruise covered by the jumpsuit.

Emilio hissed in pain and his eyes watered, but he didn't cry out. He wouldn't give the cops the perverse satisfaction.

"I said to step it up, not slip up." Littleton snorted.

"Maybe you should back off," Officer Andreas said.

"Why? He's a cop killer and child abductor. This scum deserves it."

It was partially true. Emilio was a cop killer, and he had orchestrated the kidnapping of a child. He was many things, not the least of which was head of the most powerful cartel in the Western Hemisphere, and he wasn't ashamed of any of it.

But he was not scum.

The officers steered him down a flight of metal stairs, and

they pushed through a set of double doors that opened into a parking garage. The air was warm and muggy, stifling.

Four additional officers waited beside the armored van along with Captain Kevin Roessler.

Emilio's armed escorts ushered him to the open rear door of the van, but before they got him inside, Captain Roessler stepped in front of him.

"Good riddance, Vargas," the captain said. "Enjoy your new home."

Music to Emilio's ears. He'd been in that dump of a county jail for almost twenty-four hours and couldn't wait to leave.

It took Andreas, Littleton and two other guards to help Emilio up into the van with the constraints of the manacles. They sat him inside a cramped cage, locked it and took up positions on the bench seats with their weapons at the ready.

The other two must have been behind the wheel and in the passenger's seat in the front part of the van that was sectioned off by a steel plate.

The doors closed and the LED security-recessed lighting popped on. He noted no access to any lock, handle or opening device from the inside of the unit.

Fury tightened his gut over this process, but anticipation of what was to come next had him smiling.

"Hey, what are you smirking at?" Littleton asked. When Emilio didn't respond, the officer slammed the butt of his shotgun against the cage.

That drew Emilio's narrowed gaze.

"You had better wipe that grin off your face," the cop said. "This is no limo service and we're not taking you to a resort for a vacation." He hit the cage again, hard enough to rattle the sides.

"One day you're going to regret having such poor manners," Emilio said around the two soft items hidden in his mouth.

"Oh, yeah?" Littleton sneered at him. Then he hit the

cage again. "Can you believe the head of Los Chacales, the freaking *jackals*, is lecturing me on manners?" he asked his colleagues.

Three of the officers laughed.

Littleton was an idiot and lacked respect. He was going to get what he deserved soon enough.

"Let's just get through this peacefully and, I recommend, quietly," Officer Andreas said. He hadn't taken part in the beating last night and was one of the few cops who didn't seem to derive any pleasure from knowing it had happened.

"Yeah, whatever, man," Littleton said, but everyone quieted down.

In the silence, Emilio looked over the guards, took in their bulletproof vests, helmets with face shields, elbow and knee pads, shotguns, rifles, Glocks holstered at their hips.

He smiled again, this time inwardly.

Once the speed of the vehicle increased, he presumed they'd hit the highway. He estimated they were going fifty miles per hour. At this rate, the trip to the federal facility in LA would take three hours.

Fortunately, Emilio had no intention of going to LA. He had other plans.

Plans that were a go. Captain Roessler, one of the men on his payroll, had confirmed it.

Enjoy your new home. The captain had delivered the line with sarcasm, but the choice of words had been positive. If he'd uttered something like *rot in prison*, well, then Emilio would've been expecting a far different outcome.

He closed his eyes, tapping into his other senses. The van was gaining speed. Contained in the rear compartment of the secured vehicle, he wished he was able to see outside.

Music blared in the front, drawing everyone's attention. The officers in the back exchanged confused looks. A minute later static crackled over the speakers, then silence.

Muffled talking between the driver and front passenger.

Agitated voices were tinny threads through the steel plate, their speech hurried.

The rectangular window in the steel plate divider slid open. "We've got a problem," the officer in the passenger's seat said.

"What's up?" asked Andreas.

"We're gaining speed, but we're not doing it. The brakes aren't working, either. We can't slow down."

"What?" asked a different officer as he leaned forward. "How can that be?"

"We've got no clue. We tried to radio back to headquarters, but our comms are down."

Littleton let loose a string of profanity.

"That's not possible." Andreas scrubbed his hand on his leg. "Did you try your cell?" He withdrew his from a utility pocket.

"Doesn't work either."

That was because they were being jammed. By the time the officers realized what was happening, it would be too late for them to do anything about it.

"Damn it," the driver said. "I've got no control over the steering wheel now. I can't even exit the highway." He yanked the wheel, and nothing happened.

Panic broke out among the cops. Emilio lowered his head, took a calm, cleansing breath and let a grin sweep across his mouth. The officers were too distracted and frantic to pay any attention to him.

We'll see whose cage gets rattled now. A small laugh escaped him. He couldn't help it. Hell, he didn't want to help it.

"You think this is funny?" Littleton asked.

"Of course he does." Andreas glared at the other cop and threw up his hand in frustration. "He's probably responsible for it."

"What?" Understanding slowly dawned on Littleton's face.

"My phone isn't working either." Andreas shoved his

cell back in his pocket as two other officers echoed the same problem.

"No, no. Oh, no!" the driver said.

Wide-eyed with fear, the passenger faced forward, leaving the window in the steel plate open. "Oh, my God!"

The van swerved and hurtled toward a V-shaped concrete barrier. The speed ticked up. They must've been doing at least seventy.

Emilio slowed his breathing and anchored himself in his cage, bracing for impact.

"Try the brakes again," the passenger said.

"I am! Practically slamming my foot through the floor."

The urge to turn his head and look was overpowering, but Emilio didn't want to get whiplash. He did steal a quick glance at the officers in the back sitting on the bench seats. Without seat belts.

Chaotic energy swelled like a balloon about to burst. One officer swore while another started making the sign of the cross over himself. He didn't get to finish.

The van slammed into the barrier. The harsh impact was bone-jarring as metal squealed and crunched. Emilio's teeth chattered in his head. His brain swam. His vision blurred. The world spun round and round in a kaleidoscope of colors and shapes.

He breathed through the disorientation. Shook off the pain. Prepared for the next step—extraction.

His vision cleared. The officers in the back were on the floor, trying to gain their bearings.

Up front, the other two were starting to come to, regaining consciousness. The bulkhead of the vehicle was completely smashed in. They were probably pinned, but still alive thanks to their seat belts and the yellow barrels filled with sand that had cushioned the impact. The heads of both officers up front wobbled. Something drew their attention toward the driver's-side window. They reeled back in alarm. One threw his hands up in the air and shook his head.

Bullets punched through the window in a bright flash of light, making a terrifying sound, and tore into the two officers.

The windows were *bulletproof*, which meant resistant to small arms fire, 9 mm, .357, .45. Whatever his men were using was high caliber and powerful. His guess, a .50 cal machine gun with incendiary armor-piercing ammo.

A buzzing sound started at the back doors.

The remaining officers struggled to recover, groaning and floundering on the floor. They looked like blackbirds with broken wings.

Sparks burst in a swift, fiery arc across the reinforced aluminum of the door. His men were working quickly, doing their best not to lose their advantage and capitalize on momentum.

Emilio didn't know every detail of the plan. It was easy enough to surmise how his men would proceed based on experience. He spit out the two foam earplugs into his hand and stuffed them in his ears. Captain Roessler had slipped him the hearing protection in his breakfast.

Closing his eyes and turning his head away from the back door, he covered his ears with his palms, pressing hard against the plugs to help deaden any sound.

A boom thundered moments later.

Surely, a flash-bang grenade had been thrown through the hole his men had been cutting. The grenade emitted a blinding flash of light around six to seven megacandela and a deafening sound greater than 170 decibels.

A nonlethal device had to be used with Emilio trapped in the rear along with the cops.

He opened his eyes.

The officers were writhing on the floor, hands clutching their heads, eyes squeezed shut, too late. They couldn't see or hear and were in intense pain due to the rupture of their eardrums.

The back doors flew open.

Masked men holding automatic weapons entered. One made a beeline to his cage. Using a bolt cutter, his guy didn't waste time searching for keys.

Even with the mask, Emilio knew it was Samuel. A fierce and loyal lieutenant Emilio had brought up from Mexico after he was no longer sure who to trust.

Samuel made quick work of cutting the chains of the manacles and held out a hand to help Emilio up.

Technically, Emilio was a senior citizen, had endured a vicious beating at the hands of the police and had just been through a traumatic car accident, but he was no invalid. A hand up wasn't what he needed. "Give me a weapon."

Samuel swung the M4 carbine slung over his shoulder off and passed it to Emilio butt first. The weapon was a shorter, lighter version of the M16A2 assault rifle.

Emilio aimed at his target and pulled the trigger, pumping bullets into Littleton until the man stopped moving. "You dare to put your hands on me!" He needed to expel the words even though the guards couldn't hear him because of the grenade. He pulled the trigger again. "I am the head of Los Chacales!" *You idiot.*

A dead idiot.

As he made his way out of the vehicle, he put a bullet in the legs of the other officers. Except for Andreas. He had shown respect, and for that he would be spared any unnecessary pain.

Two of his men took his arms, propelling him out of the police van and into their own.

The rest climbed in and the side door slid shut.

He glanced at the high-powered rifle mounted on a tripod that had been welded to the floor bed. A .50 Browning machine gun. As he had suspected.

They sped off from the scene.

He anticipated they would soon exit the highway and change vehicles, where fresh clothes would be waiting for him.

"Where do we stand on locating Max?" he asked. His mouth filled with bitterness saying the name. Emilio had trusted Max with his life, and the man had been a rotten, stinking mole.

"I followed him to the FBI building after you were arrested last night. They flew him out. Chopper on the roof. His FBI handler is good."

"I need him." Not only for revenge, but to send a message to the FBI.

"Our insider at FBI headquarters in Washington, DC, tracked him in the system. He's in Denver, Colorado. Taking personal days."

"Good." Samuel was an excellent lieutenant. The perfect choice to have at his side in a crisis. "Is the Haas woman dead?"

Samuel lowered his head. Never a good sign. "No. She's getting help."

Help? "From whom?"

"I don't know him, but I've been informed." Samuel glanced up with a grave look. "Someone named Jagger Carr."

Shock widened Emilio's eyes, parted his lips. The vein in his neck throbbed painfully. For the first time in his life, he feared getting a ruptured aneurysm.

Hahaha! That was the sound of fate laughing at him. Coming back to bite him where it would hurt the most.

"Is it true, Don Emilio? His father had been your lawyer, your...consigliere? We trained this guy? He's one of ours?"

One of his best.

"Yes." His voice was a whisper and he had to swallow back the bile rising in his throat.

Warren Carr had been a trusted advisor. The talented

lawyer had gotten Miguel established in New York City. Had done many unlawful things to protect Emilio's only son from the law as well as other cartels.

In return, Emilio had Jagger trained. To be a warrior. To be formidable. And he was under no obligation to the cartel, the way Warren had wanted it before he'd been killed by a rival cartel in Venezuela.

Jagger had been free to live his own life and even served in the military until he murdered a man and got sent to prison. Inside, he needed Los Chacales for protection, and the cartel was there for him. They had his back. Not only to honor his father's memory, but also Jagger had always been one of them in spirit.

After he was released, he became part owner of one the car shops that did a lot of custom work for them. A natural fit, a welcome one.

Then he had gone to Miguel and asked to be indoctrinated. Jagger had chosen to join the Brethren.

Now he was betraying them. It didn't make any sense.

This was different from Max or Isabel.

Max had been a special agent undercover the entire time.

Isabel never knew about Emilio's dealings with the cartel. She had been sheltered and had no understanding of their code of honor, their ways. What loyalty meant. The price of betrayal.

Whereas Jagger had grown up in their world, had chosen to become one of them, had taken vows when he joined the Brethren.

Emilio didn't want to believe it. Not Jagger Carr!

"I understand there's someone we might use as leverage to flush him out. A sort of stepmother, Tina Jennings."

Warren's old paramour. "She was never Jagger's stepmother. Nothing more than a kept woman. There's bad blood between them. Jagger despises her."

"Why?" Samuel asked.

"Because she stole Jagger's inheritance."

"Miguel is still overseas doing business." Samuel leaned forward, resting his forearms on his thighs. "The *sicario* in New York who has taken the lead on this, Alaric, wants authorization to activate *repo*. What is that?"

Tension snapped through Emilio. "A fail-safe." An acrid taste filled his mouth. Repo was a last-resort measure. Only one or two in the Brethren knew about it and for good reason. If Emilio gave the green light, Alaric and the others would find Jagger and kill him unless… "The boy." Emilio caught himself. That was how he saw Jagger. As a boy, one of his boys. "Jagger wouldn't do this for money." Not honor a blood debt and go against the cartel. "Find his motivation."

"What difference does it make? We've issued kill orders for both him and the woman."

"If I take Jagger Carr's life, I need to know why I'm doing it. I sanction any means necessary to find him, but rescind the kill order on him. Hurt him. Wound him. Cripple him. But spare his life. I want to know why he chose Wendy Haas over me."

Chapter Nine

After navigating the snarl of traffic, it had taken Jagger forty minutes to drive clear across Manhattan and hit the FDR. Not for a single one of those minutes was Wendy able to relax.

Her head was on a constant swivel. The Brethren were out there somewhere hunting them, Jagger was injured, and the car they were in had surely been reported stolen by now.

She didn't want to consider what might happen if the cops pulled them over. They would be arrested. Booked on one, two…too many charges for her to count, and with Jagger's criminal record it would be an utter disaster.

In the end, a repeat of the first time he'd been arrested and railroaded through the system.

Too bad his father hadn't been alive back then. His dad had been a phenomenal lawyer, quite clever from the stories, and he would've done anything to protect his son.

But when Jagger was in the army, deployed overseas, his dad went to Venezuela on business. A travel warning had been issued by the State Department, something about aggression against Americans in the country at the time. His dad was the victim of a carjacking that had gone bad.

She knew that not getting a chance to see his dad one more time, to say goodbye, haunted Jagger.

Wendy wouldn't leave him in the hands of an overworked, underpaid public defender assigned to the case at the last minute. That's how he had gotten such a long sentence before. Wendy had the means now to ensure he'd have proper representation. She wasn't wealthy, but she wasn't hurting either and, more important, she had the right connections.

People owed her favors. A few of them were lawyers.

History wasn't going to repeat itself if she had anything to say about it.

The smooth ride coaxed her to settle back in her seat. Traffic was remarkably light on the FDR Drive at this hour. They were due for a break from the universe. A spot of good luck to cling to.

"We won't be able to stay in a stolen car for long," she said, not wanting to push their luck too far.

"I know. We only need it for another thirty minutes or so."

She glanced out the window at a barge in the water.

"I guess your boyfriend is probably worried sick about you. Sorry you can't call him."

"What boyfriend?" she asked, turning to look at him.

"The one with you at the party. Tripp Langston. Mr. Top Thirty under Thirty in New York City."

Funny enough, she'd forgotten all about Tripp. He was probably curious where she'd ran off to, but Tripp wasn't the worrying kind. If anything, he'd be upset that she hadn't posted another picture of him on her Instagram with the *right* caption and was consoling himself by finding someone to sleep with tonight.

"Tripp isn't my boyfriend."

Jagger's brows drew together. "You're not dating him?" he asked in tone that implied she was lying.

"*Dating* is a strong word, and I most certainly wouldn't use it regarding Tripp." Or any man for that matter. Not since Jagger, and with him, dating hadn't been a strong enough word to describe what they'd been.

It was not only a lack of a relationship since Jagger. She hadn't fully enjoyed sex with anyone, either. He'd ruined her in that way. Every time they'd been intimate, she'd felt a thousand different beautiful things. Desired. Special. Loved. Needed. Cherished. Like she belonged in his arms. In his life.

Being with him had spoiled her, made it impossible for her to climax with another unless she could reach that emotional safety zone, and losing him had made it unbearable for her to risk opening her heart to another. A vicious double-edged sword that kept slicing apart any chance of her being happy with some else.

"We hooked up a couple of times," she said, compelled to clarify for some bizarre reason. Immediately, she was uncomfortable and self-conscious, like she'd admitted to cheating. Which was preposterous.

Things with Jagger had ended ages ago, and he'd been the one to dump her. Freeze her out. Not the other way around.

"It was never anything serious." Why couldn't she shut up and stop talking about it? "We were both going to the gala, thought it'd be bearable if we went together, and it saved me the trouble of booking a car service for the night. Nothing more to it." Not that she owed him any explanation. "And you?" she asked, wanting to get focus off her relationship status. "Is there a girlfriend who is going to wonder what happened to you?"

"No." He was quick to answer.

"No, what? No girlfriend? Or no, she won't worry because you gave her a heads-up you were going to play hero fulfilling some ancient oath you made to my brother?"

He clenched his jaw. "No girlfriend."

She was tempted to ask if he'd dated anyone since he'd gotten out of prison, but it was none of her business and she wasn't sure she wanted to know the answer. He was a healthy guy who'd been locked up a long time. Of course he'd been with someone in the past three years. One plus one equaled two, but she didn't need to hear about it, think about it or visualize details.

Rain started falling. It drummed steady, pounding the car. The rat-a-tat sound mixed with the *whoosh, whoosh* of the windshield wipers, filling the strained silence between them as they headed north. The rain was so heavy it blurred everything else, but she made out Yankee Stadium on the right.

They had gone to a game there once. Another date. She didn't care about baseball, not like football, but the Jets and Giants played at MetLife Stadium in East Rutherford, New Jersey. Baseball had been more convenient.

She didn't recall the score, the snacks they'd eaten, the blistering misery of that Indian summer, the discomfort of the hard seats, the squish of her sneakers as they ran for cover when the sky had opened.

All she remembered was the feel of his arms wrapping around her. Moving into the warmth of his body and clutching his waist. The heady smell of him drawing her closer. How he ran his hand into her hair at the nape of her neck and guided her mouth to his. The brush of his wet lips over hers, a featherlight tease that weakened her knees. The kiss that was so deep and erotic it stole her breath, had heat pooling low in her belly. Left her quivering, aching, needing... She'd wanted him so badly it hurt.

The razor-sharp details sliced through her brain, but it was her heart that bled.

"Do you remember that day?" Putting her head back on the seat, she looked away from the stadium and at him.

Jagger tensed. His knuckles tightened on the steering wheel. His gaze flashed to hers, and in the depths of his stare she saw that he remembered every detail, but he didn't respond right away.

He glanced back at the road. "Which day?"

"The Yankees game. The day I asked you to make love to me." More like begged, believe it or not. She was probably the only seventeen-year-old girl in history who'd had to beg her twenty-one-year-old experienced boyfriend to pretty please take her virginity.

That had been the day he finally made love to her at his place after six months of dating, of kisses and foreplay, sharing themselves, falling deeply, hopelessly in love.

He straightened and stared straight ahead. "I was right.

We should've waited," he said. "Given you a chance to date someone your own age. Given you a chance to—"

"Love someone else." Before she was lost to him completely.

He'd warned her. *Once we sleep together, I think that'll be it. For both of us.*

Oh, really. She'd laughed. *Are you that much of a super stud in bed?*

No. I just know you're the one, Wen, and I don't want you to miss out on anything. To have regrets.

"You were wrong," she said.

"About which part?"

She never regretted one moment of being with him. Not one. "I wasn't your average seventeen-year-old."

"No, you weren't."

Her mom had thrown her into kindergarten at four and she'd been placed in the gifted track. Skipped the eighth grade and graduated high school early. Started college at sixteen. "If it hadn't been you, it would have been some other older guy. Some blockhead, probably, who I wouldn't have been in love with. Is that what you wish?"

He was the only man she'd ever trusted with her body and her heart. She'd loved him so much he was a part of her, the other half of her soul.

"I wish," he said, his voice a pained whisper, "that you'd never met me."

The idea was a sledgehammer to her chest, robbing her of the ability to speak for a minute. "If I'd never met you, I'd be dead." It was true, but she wasn't talking about tonight and the cartel.

She'd finished her Crisis Communication and Reputation Management class at NYU and was waiting for the F train. Earbuds in, listening to music, she was absorbed in her instructor's notes on one of her papers. A fight broke out between two guys. She'd been oblivious and hadn't noticed until one guy bumped into her, sent her pages flying up in the air, and her sailing toward the edge of the platform right as the train was coming.

Jagger had caught her, kept her from falling. As if saving her life hadn't been enough, he'd helped her gather up what was left of her paper that had been strewn across the platform. She bought him a thank-you lunch, and over the absolute best falafel she was hit by that thunderbolt—a tug of attraction stronger than gravity. Or maybe it had happened the moment they made eye contact.

"Perhaps that's the way it should be," she said. "Me dead and you free to live your life." She didn't mean it in a pathetic *poor me* way, only as a matter of fact.

"Don't ever say that," Jagger snapped. He turned off the freeway and drove through a town.

The rain came down harder if that was possible. She looked outside at the torrent. Considered everything that had happened between them and how they'd gotten there.

The crushing weight of guilt settled in her chest. If he had never met *her*, he'd be better off. Never would've gone to prison. Never would've gotten caught up with the cartel. Sure as hell wouldn't be on their hit list. He'd be happy, safe, might even be married with a kid or two.

Jagger drove down a dark unpaved path through a stretch of woods and parked. There was a house or a cabin in front of them "We're here."

She didn't even care where *here* was. "I'm bad news for you. Not the other way around. I ruined your life, and I'm doing it all over again."

"What's happening now isn't your fault."

But what happened ten years ago was. "You can't keep saving me. It's going to cost you your life one of these days."

"If it does, then it does."

She clasped his arm. "You have to know when to cut your losses on a bad bet. I'm not worth it."

"Something bad brought us together. Something worse separated us. Now this, but it's not your fault. And I'm never going to sit back and let someone hurt you."

"Because of some stupid promise you made to my brother?" Dutch had taken the vow to heart, seen how much Jagger loved her and pleaded with their mom to back off. But she hadn't, thinking their relationship was too intense, too all-consuming for someone Wendy's age. So, a month after Wendy's eighteenth birthday, two weeks before Christmas, she moved out of the dorms and in with Jagger, and her mother's fears became radioactive.

"No," Jagger said, "not because of your brother."

"Then why?"

He lowered his head. "I guess I can't help myself when it comes to you."

"Even though you hate me?"

His eyes cut to hers, and he fixed her with a fiery stare that made her belly curl and the insides of her thighs tingle. The next thing she knew, his fingers were tangling in her hair and he brought her mouth to his.

She put her hands to his chest in a kneejerk reaction to push him away, but a heartbeat later when his tongue slid between her lips and stroked deep, caressing hers, she tasted him. It filled her up, rendering her unable to think straight, and she found herself pulling him closer. Kissing him back. Her hands slid up his chest and her fingers curled tight into his shirt. It was like some dam inside her that had been holding back years of desire and need broke in a hot rush, and a surge of sensation flooded her body.

His arm locked around her, bringing her against the hard, rugged lines of the one man she'd never stopped wanting. Craving. She wanted to keep touching him, holding him. She wanted to kiss him for hours, the way they used to.

He moaned in her mouth, abruptly drew back, letting her go, and stared at her. "I don't hate you, Wendy. I never could."

That bombshell unhinged her jaw and had her reeling back in confusion.

Jagger reached into the back seat and grabbed the duffel bag. "Let's get inside," he said, the gravelly heat of his voice scraping low in her belly. Then he jumped out into the pouring rain and shut the door.

A million different clashing thoughts rioted in her head as traitorous tears filled her eyes. Jagger had said the words she'd imagined hearing, dreamed of him whispering to her countless nights, but instead of relief, it felt as if a colony of fire ants were under her skin, biting and stinging, full of venom.

Chapter Ten

Inside the cabin, the air was heavy and stale. He lit the kindling and tinder that he'd placed between a few logs. The fire started with ease in the wood-burning stove that was set back against the wall and situated between the living room and eat-in kitchen.

Why did I kiss her?

So stupid.

But man, that kiss…such a tame word for what that had been.

Heat slid through Jagger as he replayed it in his head, making him ache.

Her lips had been so soft against his, and the little sound of pleasure she'd made as he swept his tongue against hers echoed in his ears. He'd savored every delicious second until he broke away. The urge to hold her and do it again was strong. So strong that he knew if he went back outside to haul Wendy in from the car, his mouth would be on hers before they made it to the porch. The rain be damned.

Their chemistry was still there in a big way. Touching her had ignited more than sparks or a brushfire—it was napalm in his veins.

A string of curses churned in his mind.

Jagger welcomed the mounting heat as he shivered from the breeze through the open front door and his wet clothes. When the car door slammed shut, he turned his head in the direction of the sound, but he stayed kneeling by the fire with his hands up in front of the glass door.

Minutes had bled from one into the other while Wendy had sat in the sedan for what felt like forever. She ran up the porch steps and stood on the threshold, drenched, her chest heaving. A shell-shocked look was stamped on her face, as if they'd just escaped another near-death encounter with the Brethren.

"Come in. Close the door," he said softly.

For a moment, he wondered if she'd heard him over the pounding rain because she just stood still, staring at him. Finally, she stepped inside. Shut the door. Locked it.

"There's electricity," he said, "but I'd prefer to keep the lights off tonight."

Houses weren't packed in on top of each other in the wooded area, but they were close enough to see lights on, and he didn't want to draw unnecessary attention. After being released from prison, he visited the place a few times a year to chop firewood and make sure no critters had gotten in. Since he knew the neighbors, he also made the rounds for a quick chitchat.

Sometimes he started the wood-burning stove and lingered, remembering, thinking.

"I've got the fire going," he said. Which was obvious. "You should warm up."

In the amber glow of the firelight, she looked around the living room. Recognition dawned in her eyes.

This was his maternal grandmother's old place in Mount Pleasant overlooking the Hudson Valley. No one knew about the place, except for Wendy.

He had brought her here to escape the city whenever she was out of school and they could both take a couple days off. A two-bedroom, one-and-a-half-bath cabin, surrounded by hiking trails. They'd had a great time here, almost magical. If plain, simple happiness was magic. They always had fun together, regardless of the location or what they were doing. Washing the dishes with her had been fun. They hadn't been a perfect couple. Sometimes they'd argued, but the fighting never lasted long. Never outweighed the laughs, the love, the intimacy—and he didn't mean sex, though that had been sensational, too.

Wendy's gaze narrowed and swung to him.

He wasn't sure if she was upset over what he'd said in the car or that he'd chosen their former love nest outside of the city as a hideout. Maybe it was both.

"Jagger—"

"If you're angry, I understand."

"If?" The misery in her voice caused dread to flash through him.

She had a right to be angry and hurt, and he'd face it. Answer for the choice he'd made.

Nonetheless, his throat tightened. "We'll talk." He stood and eased toward her. "Let's get out of these wet clothes first. Dry off. Change. I'll make us some tea. Okay. I didn't go through all the trouble of getting you away from the cartel only to let pneumonia do you in." He wiped rainwater from his face. "You still have some things here. Upstairs in the bedroom." It had been easier to keep basics here and not worry about lugging a bunch of stuff back and forth. "I couldn't bring myself to get rid of it."

"You could've mailed me my stuff since you knew my address before tonight." Accusation knifed through her tone. "Didn't you?"

Guilty as charged.

What he'd meant was, he didn't *want* to get rid of her stuff. He still buried his face in her soft, delicate nightgown, even though it didn't smell like her anymore. That was one of the things he missed. Her smell. Her smile. He could go on and on. "Yes. I've known for a while."

A tremor ran across her face. She clenched her hands into fists, as though she might sock him in the jaw. He wouldn't blame her if she hit him. Hell, he deserved it, and if memory served, she had a solid right hook. He admired her strength and grit, but the hurt in her eyes was gutting him. It was a sharp reminder that although she was strong, she was vulnerable, too.

He lowered his head.

All the things he'd longed to share with her since his release bombarded his mind, but he didn't want to be selfish. Doing the right thing wasn't easy. He needed to measure his words before they left his mouth.

He took the flashlight from the kitchen table, switched it on and climbed the stairs quickly, taking them two at a time. Behind him there was silence. She hadn't moved. After a minute, there was the creak of floorboards in the living room, something rustled, and then the old wood stairs groaned as she came up.

Moonlight spilled in through the large window at the end of the narrow hall.

He entered the first cozy bedroom, the one they'd once shared. "Your stuff is in there." He gestured to the closet.

She stepped inside the room with her glittery purse under her arm and Corey's 9 mm with the attached silencer in her hand.

"Planning to shoot me?" he asked, half-joking.

"Not tonight," she said, her voice devoid of humor. She turned, facing him with a neutral expression. "I didn't want to be up here, getting changed, alone, without protection. Just in case." She shrugged.

He nodded. Things were calm, but emotions were running high. The adrenaline kick from earlier still had his heart pumping hard—or it could've been from kissing Wendy.

The need to be prepared for the unexpected was familiar. That was the only reason he'd kept the electricity going. He didn't come out here often enough to warrant it, but he had an alarm system installed, and sensors on the road leading up to the house and at various intervals around the house throughout the surrounding woods. Her having a gun was a good idea. She knew how to handle a firearm, but until now she hadn't seemed calm enough to use one.

Jagger handed her the flashlight.

She took it and walked to the closet.

While she looked around at the things hanging up and what he'd packed in a box on the floor, he grabbed a change of clothes from the dresser, along with a pair of dry socks.

On his way out of the room, he snatched his worn-in hiking boots. They weren't tactical, but they were ten times better than the soaked dress shoes on his feet.

"Take your time," he said, wanting her to decompress a bit. He knew better than to have a conversation with her when she was fire-spitting mad at him. "There should be plenty of hot water if you want to shower, but you'll need to let it run a minute or two."

"I remember." She kept her back to him as she fingered through clothes hanging in the closet.

"Do you want chamomile tea?"

"Earl Grey. I don't see myself settling anytime soon."

Neither did he, on edge and feeling he was missing some important detail. "Powdered creamer?"

"Yes, please, and a splash of bourbon if you've got any."

He did. A bottle of Buffalo Trace in the kitchen cabinet. "Sure." He hurried out of the room, shutting the door. Putting a little distance between himself and Wendy while she undressed was probably a good idea.

In the tight hallway bathroom, he grabbed a towel. Everything up at the cabin was old and comfortable. It reminded him of his grandmother. His mom had died from a hemorrhage while delivering him. With modern medicine and technology, you wouldn't think women in developed countries died during childbirth anymore, but it was alarming how many did.

His grandmother had filled in, helped his dad raise him. She'd bequeathed him the cabin and her jewelry. He'd forever be grateful to her for being the warm, maternal influence that he needed in his life. Taught him how to be tough yet tender. Patient. That sometimes you had to sacrifice for the ones you loved.

Downstairs, he put the kettle on for tea and set the bottle of bourbon on the kitchen table along with two mugs.

The rain was letting up, shifting from a downpour to a drizzle.

He set the alarm. On the security panel, the ten sensors around the property and on the path up to the house were a row of bright green dots. He undressed near the fire and toweled off.

The stairs creaked as he finished putting on his pants and socks, but he hadn't pulled on a shirt yet.

"That was fast," he said to her, shoving on his boots.

"I couldn't relax enough to take a shower." She walked over wearing a pair of jeans, a light blue long-sleeved pullover that clung to her curves and a pair of Keds. "Everything sort of fits." She gestured to her clothes. "Albeit somewhat tightly."

She wasn't as lean as she had been as a teenager. Her body was softer, sexier. No longer a pretty girl, she was a stunning woman.

"You look great," he said.

Wendy's gaze dropped from his face to his bare chest. She grimaced and closed the space separating them. "When did you get this?" she asked, tracing the lines of the dagger tattoo over his heart.

Her touch on his bare skin sent a flush of warmth through his entire body. She had him spinning, fantasizing about things he couldn't have.

Focus. "Got it as part of initiation into the Brethren."

"Why did you join the cartel?" Her fingertips lingered on the raised skin in the center of the hilt of the dagger. A permanent mark of the Brethren. An oblong scar, a brand that, unlike a tattoo, no laser could remove.

He turned her face back to his. "In prison, I needed protection. It was a brutal world behind bars. Push came to shove, and the safety of a group became essential to survive."

His mother had been a WASP with blond hair and green eyes, and Jagger favored her more than his Latino father in looks. In jail, his choices had been the white supremacists or the cartel. He was proud of his Hispanic heritage and didn't want to hide it.

Los Chacales were many horrible, questionable things, but at least they weren't racist, and he knew their world. Grew up in it. His father had been a part of it. Why or how his dad had first gotten involved with Emilio Vargas, Jagger would never know. But he would take a dagger over a swastika any day.

"Needing protection, I can understand." She dropped her hand, and he missed the heat of her hand. "But joining the Brethren? Choosing to become an assassin? I don't understand. That doesn't sound like the Jagger I used to know."

Didn't it? He'd killed for Uncle Sam. He'd killed for Wendy. But it was true that he'd never wanted to take the life of another. "It's complicated. I had my reasons."

The kettle whistled. He grabbed a pot holder and removed it from the stove. After making her tea, he opted for two fingers of bourbon neat.

He yanked on a T-shirt and put a button-down over it, leaving the shirt open.

They sat on the area rug in front of the fire, each holding their respective mugs.

She blew on her tea and took a timid sip. "There's a lot I don't get. In the car…" She looked up at him. "If you never hated me, then why did you send me that horrible letter and say those terrible things to me on my last visit to the prison."

Taking a healthy gulp of bourbon, he aligned his thoughts. To make her understand, he had to start from the beginning. "That night you had to work late and close the restaurant."

"The night that ruined us," she said, shaking her head.

"I should've quit when you asked me to. Never should've flirted with customers for bigger tips like the other girls."

After Wendy had moved in with him, her mom had cut her off, stopped sending checks to pay for tuition. So Wendy, being headstrong and just as determined as her mom, didn't go back to the dorm, and instead got a job. At a restaurant called Bazooms. She became one of their *girls* and had to wear a revealing outfit, skimpy shorts that barely covered her bottom and an unforgiving tight tank top. A smile and a wink at the mostly male patrons meant bigger tips, and he'd never faulted her for that. Sometimes, though, the guys got drunk and handsy. Wendy was a looker, and he wanted her to be careful.

Any time she had to close the restaurant, he swung by and walked her home.

That particular night, he'd been late picking her up, and she had taken out the trash alone. By the time he arrived, he found her in the alley adjacent to the restaurant. Two guys had her cornered behind the dumpster. One had a broken beer bottle to her throat.

Jagger had gotten there before anything had happened to her, but he'd seen red and lost it. His control had slipped for a moment, a heartbeat, and he'd killed the man with the bottle.

"What happened wasn't your fault." Jagger set down the mug and caressed her face.

At that, one of her eyebrows rose and she pulled back from him. "You wrote me a Dear Wendy letter stating the opposite. I still have it. Memorized every ugly word. I told myself that if you saw me, you'd take it back. Tell me you didn't mean it. But you didn't, did you?"

Separated by a plexiglass partition, he'd looked her in the eye and yearning, startling in its intensity, had clawed at him. All he'd wanted was to hold her, reassure her that he'd never stop loving her. Instead, he'd picked up the intercom phone and told her how much he hated being behind bars. How much he hated *her* since she was the reason he was locked up.

He'd make the same choice, utter the same words if given the chance for a do-over.

"Wen, you're so stubborn." She would've kept visiting twice a month, holding on to their relationship, living half a life and enjoying none of it. That was the last thing he wanted, and when her mom came to see him and begged him to put an end to it, he'd known what he had to do. "It was the only way to get you to walk away from me."

Not that any of his sacrifices had prevented her, him and death from colliding tonight. Now he'd attacked fellow Brethren and he was diving back down the dark rabbit hole he'd never truly escaped.

Wendy set down her mug, and her blue eyes found his. They were so pale in color, almost icy yet somehow also warm and vibrant. "*You* were my life, Jagger. I would've waited for you, forever."

He knew it. "That was the problem, honey. You were only eighteen." Not that it would've made a difference if she'd been twenty-eight or thirty-eight. He was facing a fifteen-year sentence. "I didn't want you wasting your life waiting on a murderer to get out of jail. I promised Dutch and your mom that I would always look out for you." Even if it meant that he had to cut out his own heart and smash it into a million pieces. There wasn't anything he wouldn't do for Wendy. "You deserved better. More. To be able to move on from a convicted felon. To be happy."

"Move on? God, Jagger, do you really think there was ever any moving on from you?"

"Yeah, I do. You're successful. Dating lawyers, business-men, doctors, that stockbroker, the Orca of Wall Street."

"Lawyers? Doctors? You've kept tabs on me?"

Jagger heaved a weary breath. Getting sidetracked wouldn't be helpful. "My point is you did it. I pushed you away so you could have it all—success, a relationship—and you do."

"Are you kidding me? I don't have happiness. And I haven't *dated* anyone since you. With all the walls I've built around myself so that no one would ever hurt me that badly again, I've never gotten close to another man."

"But on Instagram and the magazine—"

"It's all fake. Appearances. I've been with other people, but anyone else was a distraction. Every morning when I wake up and every night when I go to bed, *alone*, all I feel is empty." Tears filled her eyes. "We had everything together. What most people dream about, go their whole lives craving, and never find. Someone we loved so much we would die for them. Kill to protect them. You weren't a murderer to me. You were my soul mate. You were my heart. My everything. When I lost you, I lost a part of myself, too."

Mrs. Haas had cried, yanked on every heartstring he had. Demanded he prove how much he loved Wendy by letting her go.

Breaking up with her while he was in prison, telling her that he blamed her, hated her, had been the hardest thing in the world for him. He'd thought she'd heal, move one, forget about him. The selfless thing to do was to set her free. Wasn't it?

"Wendy, I didn't know." He cupped her face.

Sorrow passed across her eyes like storm clouds. "What's so awful is that you weren't honest. All this time I thought you blamed me, hated me for what happened."

If he had been honest, she never would've left him. "It wasn't your fault."

"You let me believe that it was. Do you have any idea how that guilt has eaten away at me? Changed me? I was devastated." Her voice broke, and so did his heart.

"I never thought you'd believe me." He loved her so completely he wasn't sure if their bond could be severed. After he'd sent the letter, he'd known she would visit him. A part of him thought that no matter what he said, she'd feel how strong his love was. That she'd keep coming to visit, but she hadn't. He'd reconsidered, thought about reaching out to her, apologizing. Telling her the truth. But he'd been resigned to do right by her. Even though it had shredded him, he'd forced her to walk away and had to live with it. "I tried hard to sell the lie because I thought it was the right thing to do."

He took her hand, lacing their fingers together.

The rain had stopped, not even the pitter-patter of a drizzle. Silence wrapped around them, and he longed to have those ten years back with her.

"I'm not sure which is worse." Her face was tight with pain. "The lie you told me, or the betrayal of pushing me away like that when we swore to be there for each other?"

Guilt was like a shard of glass in his heart. "I'm so sorry." Pressing his forehead to hers, he stroked the back of her hair. "I'm sorry I lost control." He'd been so angry, seeing that broken bottle at her throat, and everything had unraveled fast. One wrong move and he'd killed that guy. A complete accident. A cruel twist of fate. "I'm sorry for hurting you."

All he'd ever wanted was to love her and make her happy.

Many nights he had lain awake in his cell thinking how different things would've been if she'd never taken the job at Bazooms. If she'd stayed in the dorms. If his dad had left him more than a vintage car and a cryptic letter about legacy while his father's lady friend inherited millions.

Peering into his eyes, she lifted her hand to his cheek, and when she touched him something inside of him came alive. Something he'd tried to bury.

A desperate, soul-deep longing for her to be his again.

"Why didn't you come see me after you got out, instead of stalking me?" she whispered.

Great. She did think of him as a stalker. "Getting released didn't change anything."

As soon as he was out of prison, he'd looked her up, gone to her apartment. Saw what a successful power player she'd become. She'd been dating a lawyer at the time. Not that it had mattered. With her pristine, high-profile image, rubbing elbows with politicians and jet-setters, she didn't need the scandal of associating with an ex-convict. Not even on a casual level and certainly not an intimate one—and that was precisely where any acquaintance would've led.

She rebranded all sorts of people, but there was no making over a murderer any more than putting lipstick on a pig made it attractive.

Trying to pick up where they had left off and recapture the past still would've messed up her life. The paparazzi would have had a field day with it, and she would've lost big clients.

"You were free. That changed everything," she said. "Unless you fell out of love with me. Didn't want to be with me anymore."

As if that was ever possible.

He leaned in and kissed her, a warm press of his lips against hers. If he could've absorbed her pain and borne it in her stead, he would've without hesitation. He kissed the corner of her mouth, down to her chin, lower to her jaw, and up to her earlobe as she softened against him.

"Wen," he said, low in her ear, hyperaware of her body so close to his, "I've never stopped loving—"

The alarm chirped. They jumped apart and he was on his feet.

"What is it?" she asked.

Another chirp. Jagger cursed himself for dropping his guard.

He moved to the security panel on the wall near the door. Two of the sensors had been tripped and had turned from green to red.

Three more chirps and the lights changed in tandem.

"Damn it. They're here," he said.

Chapter Eleven

Oh, God! Wendy's whole body tightened, and she tried to tamp down the fear that was swamping every inch of her.

"They're on the path that leads up to the house and they're crawling all over the woods," Jagger said.

Wendy scrambled to her feet, her heart already thundering in her chest. "How did they find us?"

"I don't know." He shook his head, throwing her a bewildered glance.

Three more chirps sounded.

"We've got to get out of here." Jagger dug into the duffel bag, pulled out the Port Authority officer's service weapon and tossed it to her.

He looked down her body and his posture stiffened. She followed his wide-eyed gaze to her chest, and her breath caught. A red laser dot wavered over her sternum.

Jagger launched himself at her.

The window shattered. A whisper of bullets whizzed overhead.

With his arms tight around her, they hit the floor. He took the brunt of the fall, but the side of her head smacked against the hardwood. Pain mixed with blinding panic as a groan left her lips.

He rotated, tucking her beneath him.

Bullets slammed into the wall where she'd been standing. The thud on impact reverberated in her chest. The distinct sound bit through the shrieking alarm.

Jagger covered her with his body, protecting her face from the falling glass and flying debris. He rolled her onto her stomach. "We need to get upstairs to the attic. There's another way out." He grabbed the duffel bag and urged her to move.

Without voicing the questions that ricocheted in her mind, she crawled toward the stairs. Using her forearms and knees, she scooted forward with her belly on the floor.

The gunfire was coming from every direction. The cabin must be surrounded.

Jagger shot back through an open window. The crack of gunfire from the shotgun was ten times louder than the sound-suppressed barrage from the weapons targeting them.

Neighbors would hear the ruckus and call the police. Whether that would work for or against them remained to be seen.

"You need to make it upstairs to the attic," Jagger said, "before they get inside."

"Me? What about you?"

"I'll hold them back."

Emotion held her frozen in place. In her head, she knew that not following his instructions wasn't going to help either of them. But, in her heart, she couldn't leave Jagger behind.

For years, she'd been bitter and angry, struggling to recover from the fallout of loving him. She was grateful to have learned the truth. Knowing that he didn't blame her or hate her freed her to be herself. After everything they'd endured, she wasn't going to let him die for her.

They had to survive this together.

"I'm not leaving you." She couldn't bear to lose him a second time.

He glanced at her. Tension stretched across his face and then something changed in his eyes. A split-second decision was made.

Jagger dropped the bag at her feet and duckwalked deeper into the room, carrying the shotgun. When he reached the wood-burning stove, he opened the glass door and, using a fire poker, he knocked out flaming chunks of wood. He lobbed one piece onto the sofa. A second hit a curtain.

No, no. He was burning down his grandmother's cabin.

The smoke and the fire might slow down the Brethren from following them and help conceal their exit, but this was a place Jagger cherished.

Several red lasers cut through the air above his head. Another volley of rounds shattered the rest of the windows, spraying the floor with glass and boring into the furniture. Pieces of wood kicked up near her.

She lowered her head, while keeping Jagger in her sights.

He pivoted and snatched the towel from the back of a chair. Staying low, he crept across the floor to her.

"Take it." He thrust the damp towel at her. "Put it over your mouth and nose."

A man slipped through the broken window closest to them. Jagger spun on his heels only to be greeted by automatic gunfire.

Wendy ducked as Jagger squeezed off two rapid shots from the double-barrel shotgun, putting the intruder down. Just as quickly, another man climbed through a different window.

Jagger redirected the muzzle at the newest threat and pulled the trigger.

Click. The 12-gauge was empty. Jagger lunged for the man with the shotgun raised. He slammed the butt of the gun into the man's face. Once. Twice. Three times. Lightning fast.

Flipping the shotgun in his hands, Jagger gripped it by the barrel like a baseball bat and swung. Metal connected with the man's skull with a loud crack, and he dropped to the floor.

Incoming gunfire forced Jagger to crouch low.

"Here!" Wendy slid the 9 mm in her hand over to him.

He switched off the safety and aimed at the windows. "Get upstairs! I'll be right behind you."

Hot flames consumed the curtains on one window and swept up the wall. Fire licked across the sofa. Smoke suffused the room. The gray air clouded her vision and made her eyes water. But the moist breeze from the open windows sucked out some of the smoke while feeding the flames at the same time.

How much longer would Jagger be able to breathe in there? Smoke inhalation would kill him faster than the fire itself.

Already the smoke burned her throat, and the heat from the flames was mounting. Coughing, she put the towel over her nose and mouth.

Jagger didn't run or duck. He was in full-offense mode. "Go!" He shot controlled bursts of rounds at each window.

She coughed at the irritation in her lungs. The smoke was getting bad. She grabbed the handles of the duffel bag and dragged it up the stairs, one step at a time.

Two more dark figures slipped through the windows behind Jagger. He spun before she had a chance to warn him, and he pumped bullets into them both, taking each person down with a sickening thud.

The gunshots, the bloodshed, the fire—everything happened in seconds. Heart-clenching, panic-stricken seconds of sheer terror.

She made her way to the top landing with the rest of the weapons. It would save Jagger time, allow him to move unencumbered up the stairs. If only there was more she could do to help him.

Grunting, she tugged the bag across the floor to the bedroom. In the corner on the ceiling was the hatch door to the attic. She jumped up, catching hold of the handle, and opened the door. The pull-down ladder popped out and she unfolded the stairs.

Jagger. Where was he?

She reached into the duffel bag and took out the first weapon she touched. It was a lightweight submachine gun. Her hands were shaking. Fear threatened to overwhelm her and shut down her brain. One thing stopped her from spiraling—the thought of Jagger dying for her. She forced herself to calm down, her focus becoming razor sharp.

Breathe, aim, shoot. She'd been hunting with her family and to the shooting range with Jagger plenty of times. This was the same, she told herself. Except she was the prey going up against a deadly predator. This was do-or-die.

Switching off the gun's trigger safety, she hustled into the narrow hall.

Jagger reached the top of the staircase.

Exhaling in relief, she clutched her chest. He ejected the magazine of the 9 mm. It was out of ammo. He glanced up, shuffling toward her.

Footsteps thundered up the stairs, the old wood groaning from the heavy weight.

Jagger whipped around, shielding her. But his weapon was empty.

A large man bounded to the top step and charged him.

Jagger shoved her aside, sending her stumbling back into the bedroom.

The tall, burly man seized Jagger by his shirt and kept barreling down the hall.

Wendy scrambled out of the bedroom. Raised the gun the gun, her finger on the trigger.

Without a clear shot, she might hit Jagger.

The two men fought, wrestling one another, locked in a deadly tussle. Jagger struggled to break free from the man, who looked strong as an ox.

She aimed low, hoping for an opportunity to hit the man in the leg or foot.

No such luck. The guy didn't stop moving. He pounded forward with gut-churning force, driving Jagger toward the window.

With a vicious grunt, the man picked Jagger up off the floor and bulled him through the windowpane.

The glass shattered as both men plummeted.

No! Her heart nosedived to her stomach.

She dashed down the hall and looked outside. Jagger and the other man rolled on the roof of the wraparound porch, still grappling, and tumbled over the side into the darkness.

Horror rose inside her and washed over everything for a second. She stood there, a loaded gun in her hand, unable to do anything, and had never felt more powerless in her life. For too long she had been helpless to do anything for Jagger, and now she had to do something. He needed her more than ever.

She couldn't go outside the window after him and the first floor was on fire.

There was only one option.

The attic. Jagger would want her to find the way out.

She whirled to go back to the bedroom. Another dark figure was clearing the top of the stairs.

Without thinking, without hesitation, she lifted the submachine gun, aimed center mass and pulled the trigger. The recoil was stout, but she didn't stop firing until the body dropped.

She ran to the bedroom.

In the closet, she grabbed an old backpack and tore two windbreakers from hangers, stuffing them inside. The duffel was too heavy for her to carry so she threw a few things into the other bag. Ammo, a couple of weapons that'd fit, the small pack of what she assumed was plastic explosives, and her purse.

She shoved her arms through the straps of the backpack and climbed the ladder. In the attic, she pulled the folding staircase up behind her.

What was the plan? Why did Jagger want her in the attic?

Spinning around, she scanned past the sheets of dense insulation for something useful. There was a window that hadn't been there years ago. Jagger must've put it in.

She sidestepped slowly across a ceiling joist, holding her arms out for balance. At the window, she spotted the rigged contraption.

Jagger had installed a zip line.

They'd once had a blast on a zip line adventure tour in the Catskills at Hunter Mountain. The highest, fastest, longest zip line canopy tour in North America.

She opened the window and peered out. Cool, sobering air swept over her, bringing goose bumps to her skin.

The zip line Jagger had set up started at the house. Where did it lead?

Outside, there was only the foreboding darkness of the woods, stretching out in a jagged sea of black. She imagined slamming into branches or, worse, smacking into the side of a tree in the dark.

Trust him.

He had a plan, Mr. Always Prepared. She simply had to put her blind faith in him.

Then something stood out in the distance. A little less than a quarter mile away in a straight line of sight were pinpricks of tiny lights. A neighbor's house?

She slipped her legs through the holes of the harness and adjusted the strap around her hips. Sitting on the window ledge with her feet dangling, she grasped hold of the trolley handles. The smell of burning wood was strong. She saw the smoke, heard the crackling of the fire.

Was Jagger all right?

That tall, burly man was insane to have taken them both through window down two stories. Like someone filled with viciousness and anger and nothing to lose.

Bile rushed up the back of her throat, and she had to fight the urge to throw up. One step at a time, that's how she'd handle this. She blocked out the rest. Refused to allow doubt and worry to paralyze her. First, she had to get safely to the ground.

She released the brake and let the trolley rip.

The roar of the fire drowned out the familiar gritty buzz of the zip line. Sailing through the air, she glanced back.

Flames crawled up the side of the house and danced across the porch, but that's not what sent an icy chill shooting through her heart.

The big guy seized Jagger from behind with a snakelike strike that locked him in a choke hold.

Jagger was in trouble.

Chapter Twelve

Jagger struggled to get a lungful of air. His neck was pinched in the crook of Alaric's right elbow, crowded between the bulge of his bicep and his meaty forearm. The pressure was cutting off the flow of blood to Jagger's carotid artery.

In about thirty seconds, it would put his lights out.

There was one good thing in all this. In his peripheral vision, he caught sight of Wendy zip-lining away from the burning house and into the woods.

She was safe, but not out of danger.

Pivoting, Jagger forced Alaric to move with him, turning their line of sight away from the zip line in case he spotted it in the light from the flames.

His lungs strained for oxygen, feeling like they were going to burst. The heat from the raging fire was blistering. The alarm was screeching.

"Time to take a nap," Alaric growled in his ear over the noise.

And then Jagger would be as good as dead.

He stepped forward with his left foot, stepped back with his right while throwing an elbow into Alaric's solar plexus—knocking the wind out of the guy—and rotated out of the hold.

Still in motion, Jagger reached for Alaric's weapon, but a fist smacked into the side of his face. Surprised, he stumbled back and before he recovered, Alaric was on him.

The man was large and heavy with muscle, but he moved with the speed of a lion.

Alaric drove Jagger back and down to the ground with his thick hands wrapped around his throat. They'd gone from a choke hold to a stranglehold, from bad to worse.

"If it weren't for the old man, I'd snap your neck," Alaric said.

The words rattled through Jagger's head. Don Emilio wanted to spare him? He didn't have time to make sense of why.

He slammed the heels of his palms against Alaric's temples. The striking blow would disorient him.

The guy grunted, and the death grip loosened just enough.

Jagger grabbed Alaric's shoulder with one hand and his forearm with the other in a cross grip. At the same time, he slammed his foot into the Alaric's hip, and rotated, flipping the guy over.

Now they were both down on their backs, perpendicular to each other, but Jagger had his legs around Alaric's throat and the man's arm locked in a game-changing position. Jagger thrust his hips up and he yanked the thick arm backward, breaking the bone.

Alaric roared in pain, but his cry was lost beneath the earsplitting sound of the blaring alarm.

This would've been the perfect time to question Alaric and get much-needed answers that could help them survive. At the top of his long list—how did the Brethren find them?

Jagger had been careful. Taken all the necessary precautions and made certain they weren't followed. This was no fluke, no coincidence, but he couldn't risk taking the time for an interrogation, even a speedy one.

There was no telling how many more *sicarios* were out in the woods or if any had seen Wendy escape. He had to take this win for what it was worth. Temporary, but appreciated.

Jagger snatched Alaric's weapon, jumped to his feet and hightailed it into the darkness.

The stretch of land along the path of the zip line was a thousand feet long and densely wooded, with heavy growth even this early in the year.

When he joined the Brethren, he had decided it would

be wise to have a backup plan. A hideout. But it was only safe if he had a contingency in the event the backup failed. He'd installed the alarm and sensors. Cleared a narrow path through the woods, trimming tree limbs where possible and chopping down maple and oak trees when necessary.

The hard preparation was paying off.

Jagger ran down the path, hard, at an all-out sprint. He didn't know if anyone had spotted Wendy fleeing the cabin and pursued her into the woods. Tearing through the night across damp soil and over a stream, he didn't slow for a second. His heart raced, damn near beating out of his chest.

The roar of the fire and the blare of the alarm grew more distant.

Alaric had been in charge. One of the most senior members. Tough. Shrewd. Unrelenting. An excellent choice to have leading the proverbial troops unless you were the target.

Jagger had gotten lucky in more than one way. The roof of the wraparound porch had broken their fall, sparing his spine. Then quick thinking and faster reflexes had gotten him out of the choke hold, but the reason he was still drawing breath was because Don Emilio didn't want him dead, yet. Not that the temporary dispensation had stopped the Brethren from shooting up the cabin.

Dread had him in a viselike grip until he burst through the tree line onto the Nelsons' property.

Dr. Evander Nelson, a retired veterinarian, stood on his lawn in pajamas and wellies, pointing a rifle at Wendy. She had her hands up in the air and looked like she was trying to reassure Doc that she wasn't the enemy.

Relief at seeing Wendy unharmed hit Jagger so hard that the air whooshed from his lungs. It was all he could do not to go running to her.

With the snap of twigs, Doc swung the rifle in Jagger's direction.

"Hey, Doc! It's me." Jagger's grandmother had been close to the Nelson family, and he maintained a cordial relationship.

Doc pushed his glasses up the bridge of his nose. "Jagger?"

"Yeah. It's me and that's Wendy." Jagger resisted the urge to double over, resting his palms against his thighs, and catch his breath. "You remember her, right?" He walked toward Wendy, taking slow, steady steps.

Doc lowered the rifle. "She told me her name, but she looks so different." He squinted at her. "You can never be too careful."

In his defense, he was pushing eighty. Ten years had passed since he'd met Wendy once and it wasn't as though his eyesight had improved during that time.

"Is all that commotion coming from your place?" Doc asked.

"I'm afraid so."

"That's what I figured. I called the cops."

"Thanks, but we can't stick around. I think it's best if you went inside, took your wife down to the cellar and waited for the trouble to pass."

"You did warn me this might happen someday." Doc made his way to the porch, slowed down by the arthritis in his limbs. "I'll get Gloria and we'll keep our heads down."

"Sorry about the inconvenience, Doc."

The screen door squeaked and slapped shut behind Doc, and then the storm door locked.

"I tried to tell Doc that you needed help, but he didn't remember me," Wendy said, rushing up to him, and he brought her into his arms. "Thank God you're all right." Her fingers tightened around his biceps. "I thought that man might kill you." She cupped his face with both hands and looked him over.

Alaric had come close to hurting him, but Jagger didn't want to find out why Don Emilio had spared him. They had dodged a bullet at the cabin, literally and figuratively.

"I'm all right. You did good, finding the zip line and taking it here."

"I was going to go back for you, but Doc held me up."

A good thing he had, too. If she had returned to the cabin to try to help him, it only would've put her back in the Brethren's crosshairs. "Next time, don't ever think about going back for me."

"To hell with that. We get through this together or not at all." She pressed her forehead to his chest. "But let's hope there's not a next time."

He loved her fire and determination though sometimes that stubborn streak of hers drove him crazy. "We need to keep moving."

Jagger guided her to the detached garage that had tiny string lights hung around the edge of the roof. After entering the code on the combination padlock, he opened the roll-up door. Inside was the vintage car his father had left him. A 1970s Mercedes-Benz SL-Class Roadster.

"What's your car doing here?"

"It's a long story."

They hurried into the garage and climbed into the two-seat pagoda coupe. He pulled down the visor and the keys fell into his palm.

Jagger cranked the engine and the car purred to life. He backed out, sped down the drive to the road and made a bee-line for State Route 117.

"Once I had the security system installed at the cabin, I realized I needed another exit. After I came up with the idea for the zip line, I needed someplace safe to attach the other end. The Nelsons are good people. My grandmother trusted them, and they were within range. Doc was happy to help. I've been renting the garage. It kept this old gal out of the elements," he said, patting the walnut dash. "Prevented anyone from sabotaging her. Doc started her up once a week for me."

"*Smart* always was sexy on you." She reached out and

put her hand on his cheek, then ran her fingers through his hair, stroking his ear.

He could say the same about *brave* on her. When Alaric had shoved him out the window, his greatest fear hadn't been for himself—it had been for Wendy. Not knowing how many others had gotten inside the cabin, anything could've happened to her while he was powerless to get her to the attic and out of the house.

With the fire and the Brethren attack and the gunfire, it would've been natural for her to freeze, but she'd saved herself. She had the fortitude of a warrior.

"Do you have any idea how they found us?" she asked.

He'd been racking his brain over the same question. "No. I've run through the possibilities, and I keep drawing a blank for the answer." The name on the deed was an LLC his grandmother had established, and no one knew about the house, except for Wendy. Not even Jagger's father.

"What are we supposed to do now that our safe house is toast?"

A sudden heaviness filled Jagger's chest. Their options had shrunk to one.

One he hoped they wouldn't regret. He'd made a deal with the devil three years ago and now he was going to have to call on that devil again.

"Did you get my burner phone by any chance?" he asked.

Wendy squeezed her eyes shut and swore. "I grabbed what I could—ammunition, weapons—but…no. Wait." She opened the backpack and, with a smile, took out her purse. "I still have my cell phone."

Making a call from her phone was dicey, but staying on the move while using the cell before they reached the interstate going either north or south mitigated the risk. Even if the communication was tracked, no one would know which way they were headed or their destination. It was worth the gamble.

She removed the back of her cell, popped the battery in and powered the phone up.

Then he noticed that the SIM card was already in it, but he had taken out both the battery and the SIM card earlier. Told her explicitly not to put them inside the phone.

"Did you call someone back at the cabin?" he asked.

Wendy stiffened, not responding for a heartbeat too long. She glanced at him and her lips parted, but she didn't speak.

"You gave me your word that you wouldn't use the phone." He'd trusted her, believing she understood the possible ramifications. "I told you they can track us through your phone. What were you thinking?"

"It was only for a minute. Less," she breathed. "Not long enough for a trace."

"Thirty seconds. That's how long it takes to trace a call."

"I wasn't on the phone that long." She lowered her head. "He didn't answer. It went straight to voice mail."

"Who didn't answer?" He glanced at her, hiking an eyebrow. "Tripp Langston?"

Her head snapped up. "Are you kidding me?" She pursed her lips and her eyes narrowed. "Tripp is a cold-blooded reptile. He's probably having sex with someone from the gala as we speak instead of wondering what in the hell happened to me."

Jagger tightened his grip on the steering wheel and checked his mirrors. "Then who did you risk our lives to call?"

"My brother. I thought Dutch might be able to help us. This whole situation came out of left field, blindsiding me. At the very least, he could shed a little light on why Emilio Vargas wants me dead."

If anyone had answers, it was Dutch. Vargas was angry enough at her brother to want Wendy dead. The fact that Dutch's phone went straight to voice mail troubled him.

He didn't let his worry show, not wanting to add to her

list of concerns. "I shouldn't have jumped to conclusions, but you should have told me you made a call."

She let out a heavy breath. "I didn't think it was important since his voice mail picked up, which was full by the way. I couldn't even leave a message. He called me a few days ago and told me he was going on an extended vacation with his girlfriend, somewhere remote, and that it would be hard to contact him for a while, but I didn't think he meant impossible. Anyway, I hung up and took the battery out right after."

From the sounds of it, she hadn't been on the phone long. Slim odds that her call had led the Brethren to them, which still left the big question. How did Alaric and the others find them?

Her phone chimed once it was finished powering up.

"I need you to text someone." He gave her the number. "Write this. *It's JC. Need to meet ASAP.*"

She typed the message and hit Send. As she went to shut off the phone, a chirp from a replying text came through. "That was quick."

"What does it say?"

Wendy looked at the screen: "Usual spot. One hour."

"Respond with *okay*, and shut off the phone."

She did and then removed the battery and SIM card. "Who did we contact?"

"The FBI. Special Agent Eddie Morton."

Shock washed across her face and her eyes brightened. "You have connections with the FBI?"

"Unfortunately."

"Why didn't you call this special agent for help sooner?"

"Because his help always comes at a high price." Agreeing to work for Morton, signing away his soul, had been a mistake. "He's more trouble than he's worth."

"How long have you been working with the FBI?" she asked.

"Three years."

The surprise in her eyes morphed into understanding. "The FBI got you out of prison early."

He nodded. "Two days after I was sent to Sing Sing, Special Agent Morton came to see me."

"Why?"

There were things about his past and his family that he hadn't wanted Wendy to know—footnotes that he never thought would have a bearing on his life. He couldn't have been more wrong.

"My father used to be Emilio Vargas's lawyer. I grew up around the cartel."

Wendy gave a soft gasp of surprise. "What?"

"My dad never wanted me to do business with them, become one of them. He also didn't want me to be naive about that world. The lure of it. The dangers. Some parents protect their kids by keeping them in the dark, insulating them in a bubble. Not my dad. He had the opposite philosophy."

"You know Emilio Vargas?"

"I do." Very well in fact. "And his son, Miguel."

"Please don't tell me that the man who is trying to kill me is your godfather or that you call him uncle."

"I don't have a godfather." But if he did, it would've been Emilio. "And no, I've never called him *uncle*."

Wendy shook her head slowly. "We shared everything with each other. Or I thought we had. Apparently not. Why didn't you ever tell me this?"

"I possessed none of the things your mother wanted for you. No college degree, no future in business… I was a blue-collar worker."

"My mom didn't care that you were a mechanic. She thought our relationship was too intense and moving too fast, especially after we started living together. She feared I'd get pregnant, drop out of school and we'd get married. My mom didn't understand that we were both being careful, using protection, that we had a five-year plan. She couldn't see what we shared. How real it was."

The words pulled him back to when he'd been the happiest. It had been an intense year and a half. An all-consuming relationship. Wendy had been it for him. The one. "Let's not forget that it was also a problem for her that I was a lot older."

"Only four years."

"In your mom's defense, you were seventeen, and the age gap probably felt as wide as the Grand Canyon. I understood those concerns, respected them, and that's why I took things slow in the beginning." Slower than he'd thought himself capable of, considering he'd wanted her the first day they met and she'd never been shy about her desire for him. "The one thing I had going for me was that I'd been a Ranger." Not that it had mattered much to her mother, but it had made every difference with Dutch, who had been Delta Force, and with that brought a mutual respect. "My past association with the cartel would have added legitimate fuel to the fire."

Her shoulders fell. "I get why you didn't want my mom to know," she said, putting her hand on his leg.

That's all it took to have his body soften in response, aching to draw her closer.

"Why not tell me?" she asked. "It was a part of who you were...who you are."

"After I joined the army, I put a lot of distance between me and the cartel. It was behind me, and I didn't want you to have to lie to your family about me. To feel you had to hide something from them."

"Always protecting me." She gave his knee a squeeze of understanding and rubbed his thigh.

He soaked in the affection he'd missed for a decade, no matter how small the gesture. The longing had been an itch deep in his soul that never went away.

"What does the FBI want with you?" she asked.

"The FBI tried to get my father to flip on Emilio for many

years, and every time they failed. When I got convicted, I guess I came up on their radar. Agent Morton approached me. Asked me to get inside the cartel and help them bring down the Brethren. They figured if they got enough of the hit men, they could get them to turn on Miguel and Emilio. Bring down the entire cartel on that angle instead of drugs, money laundering or racketeering. In exchange, the FBI offered to commute my sentence."

"So you agreed."

"Not at first. My father never turned on Emilio. I was raised to value loyalty, even to the cartel, but violent things started to happen to me in jail. Other groups began targeting me for no apparent reason. Looking back on it, I think Morton instigated it somehow."

"Why would he endanger you like that?"

"It forced to me to go to the cartel for protection. Then my cell was changed, and they put me in with Sixty."

"You think Morton was behind that, too?"

Every instinctive bone in his body said Morton was the man behind the curtain pulling the strings. "Yeah, I do, not that I have any proof. I don't trust him. He's calculating, strategic. The kind of man who likes to play the long game."

"You were in jail for years, why didn't you take his deal sooner?"

"He finally offered me what I really wanted. To have my conviction expunged." Remove his criminal record entirely and make it look as if it never happened. "Give me a fresh start as a free man, a decorated veteran, instead of a convicted felon. Give me a real stab at a second chance with you. I could call you, knock on your door, without tainting your life and destroying your business."

That was the goal. Not an easy one. Jagger still needed to provide enough evidence to bring down the Brethren to have his record erased.

"Oh, Jagger. You've been so busy protecting me, trying

to make sure nothing hurts me. I wish you would've given me the chance to do the same for you," she whispered, her hand moving from his leg to stroke the back of his neck. "If you had called me, knocked on my door, and been honest, the way you were at the cabin, our second chance would've started right then and there. I don't need you to protect my career. I've done a pretty good job of taking care of myself since you've been gone."

"I didn't want you to sacrifice anything."

"You sacrificed seven years for me. I could stomach a little a bad press for you." A sad smile tugged at her mouth. "I know you don't trust Special Agent Morton, but he has to help us. Doesn't he?"

"I'm not holding my breath, but we're out of options."

"So… What's the usual spot where you meet him, and what's our plan?"

Chapter Thirteen

After parking the car in an outrageously expensive garage—
one reason Wendy had never owned a car while living in the
city—they swung by a drugstore in Midtown Manhattan.

Mr. Always Prepared picked up a couple of essentials
while she found temporary hair dye spray that transformed
her locks from caramel blond to raven black. Still, as they
hurried down Lexington Avenue, they both purchased ball
caps from a street vendor.

There was a light chill in the air. She was glad for the
windbreakers they wore. The air smelled damp and clean,
and the pavement was wet from the rain that had fallen earlier.

He took her hand in his, the way he used to when they
were a couple strolling the street, their fingers interlaced.

The action flipped a switch inside her that she didn't want
to turn off. Every day they'd spent apart, a piece of her heart
had been missing, and now that he was back she didn't want
to let go of him. Not ever again.

Inside Grand Central Station in the large vestibule, Jagger pointed out the seven different pedestrian exits on a map.

"Why do the two of you meet here?"

"It's open twenty-one hours a day and it's the largest train
station in the world."

To call it massive, with its grandiose structure, soaring
high ceilings and acres of smooth pink marble floors, was
an understatement. She'd been inside before but had never
really appreciated the scale until now.

"Hundreds of thousands of people pass through here
every day," he said. "Makes it easy to blend in and go unnoticed any time of day or night." Even now, the station was

bustling with foot traffic. He grabbed a train schedule and handed it to her. "You know what to do?"

Her job was to stay focused on the time and the departure schedule of the trains, giving him a chance to concentrate on the discussion with Special Agent Morton. In the event the Brethren showed up, Jagger was relying on her to get them out of Grand Central in the most expedient way possible.

"I've got it." Wendy's stomach grumbled.

Jagger looked down at her and grinned. "I suppose I'll need to feed you."

"I can't be the only one starving."

He glanced around, checking their surroundings. "You're not. After the meeting with Morton, we'll worry about food."

They walked through the main concourse, past corridors and nooks, and into the Graybar Passage. The arched corridor was lined with shops and kiosks that were open late. Jagger led her into the Central Market, and they turned into a café.

"That's him there." Jagger gestured to a man sitting a table, sipping a beverage in a disposable cup with a lid.

Special Agent Morton was in his early fifties. He had a soft middle section and a feathering of gray in his beard.

"Normally," Jagger said, "I sit at the table next to his and we pretend to read while we chat. I'd rather keep moving, but he's not going to like the change in protocol."

Considering the Brethren had tracked them down at the cabin and they were still none the wiser as to how, she was inclined to agree that they couldn't afford to make themselves sitting ducks.

"Wait here."

She hung back near the entrance, looking at a poster of the café's seasonal specials.

In the coffee shop, Jagger waltzed up to Morton and motioned for the middle-aged man to get up.

Morton's face tightened with suspicion as he looked

around. It took a bit more prodding from Jagger, but finally the agent grabbed his cup and started walking.

"This better be good, JC," Morton said as the two passed her in the corridor. "I got out of bed for this."

"It's about the cartel."

Wendy walked behind them, staying within earshot.

"Do you have what I need?" Morton asked. "Evidence to bring down the Brethren?"

"No."

Morton clucked his tongue. "This is a waste of my time."

"What I do have is her." Jagger beckoned to her and she came up alongside him.

Special Agent Morton peered over at her, studying her face for a moment. "Wendy Haas, as I live and breathe. I almost didn't recognize you from the pictures in his file. I'll admit, I'm surprised." He sipped on his drink. "Now, please explain how your ex-girlfriend's presence helps my case against the cartel."

"Emilio Vargas put a hit out on me," she said. "I'm only alive thanks to Jagger."

Morton nodded as if taking it in, with no hint of emotion on his face other than a look of boredom. "Elaborate."

"A kill order was issued on her tonight," Jagger said as they entered the main concourse. "A blood debt. The entire Brethren is after her." He scanned the area as they walked through the crowd of commuters.

"After *us*," she clarified. They both needed protection.

"They know I'm helping her," Jagger said. "Which means they're after me as well."

Wendy noted the time on the clock adorning the terminal's information booth and checked the subway schedule. The 4, 5, 6 and 7 trains were viable options with three different access points to the subway platform on this level.

"My interest is piqued. Did Vargas issue the order personally?" Morton asked.

"No." Jagger shook his head. "He's in prison."

"*Was* in prison," Special Agent Morton said.

Wendy glanced between the two men. "What do you mean?"

"He escaped and is in the wind," Morton said. "It's all over the news, and of course his son, Miguel, is conveniently out of the country, so we can't question him."

Jagger looked around the concourse as they strolled the periphery. "Yeah, well, we've been too busy running for our lives to watch television."

"You could always listen to NPR," Morton said, casually. "No excuse for not staying informed."

Wendy's patience frayed. "Are you going to help us?" she asked, painfully aware they'd been in one place far too long.

"Help with what exactly?" Morton sounded dismissive.

Wendy glared at him. "Help us stay alive. Put us in protective custody."

Morton chuckled. "If I did, how does that help me get a conviction that'll bring down Miguel Vargas, the Brethren or the cartel? All I'm hearing is what you think I can do for you and not what you can do for me or rather your country."

"I served my country." Jagger stopped in front of a news and gift kiosk and faced Morton. "Gave four honorable years."

"Thanks for your service, JC. I mean that from the bottom of my heart."

"Help her." Jagger pointed at Wendy. "Put her somewhere safe and I'll get the evidence you need."

"No, Jagger." She clutched his arm. "We stay together. He has to protect us both."

Morton tossed his cup into a trash bin. "That's where you're wrong."

"You have a civic duty, an obligation, to keep us safe." Didn't he?

"Not my jurisdiction." Morton had the audacity to yawn. "Go to the police. It's their job to keep you safe."

"You know as well as I do that if I take her to the cops," Jagger said, "the Brethren will kill her in less than twenty-four hours."

"You're absolutely right. I agree." Morton crossed his arms as if preparing to go on the defense. "If you bring me your cartel buddies after they kill her, I can put pressure on them to flip on Los Chacales."

Wendy had heard horror stories about FBI negotiations, agents playing hardball in a game of the end justifies the means, but this was unreal. "You can't be serious. Is this some kind of sick joke?"

"I never joke, Ms. Haas. My wife says I don't have a sense of humor."

She stepped forward, looking him in the eye. "How can you sit back and let them kill me?"

"The same way I stood by and let your boyfriend here kill people in the name of the Brethren to cement his cover story," Morton said.

The statement hit her like a bucket of ice water. "You're lying." Wendy rocked back on her heels as her gaze flew to Jagger's. "You didn't. You wouldn't." That was too ugly, going too far.

"I can explain." Jagger gripped her shoulders. "It's not how it sounds."

Oh, God. It was true.

"Think of yourself as a sacrificial lamb, Ms. Haas," Morton said matter-of-factly. "Your death would light a fire under him to give me the evidence I need to finally stop the Brethren and save countless other lives. I know that may sound callous."

"May?" She breathed through the bitter taste in her mouth.

"Los Chacales cartel has survived, no, has thrived and

grown and is now one of the top threats to national security. It is a massive thorn in the FBI's side as well as the president's. We have an entire task force dedicated to nothing but the annihilation of Los Chacales cartel. If I have to be callous to get results, then so be it."

Jagger's head turned toward the MetLife Building entrance.

As Wendy followed his gaze, a tingle of apprehension skittered across her skin.

Two men dressed in black came through the doors. One was holding a phone or a device and was staring at the screen. Then he looked up and pointed in their direction.

"Our time's up. Start walking toward the trains," Jagger said to her. "I'll be right behind you."

Although she didn't want to leave him, she followed his instruction.

"Thanks for nothing, Morton," Jagger said behind her and she missed the rest of his words as she turned down the Forty-second Street passage. Jagger caught up to her. "Which train?"

"The 6 is our best bet, going uptown, but we have less than two minutes. We'll miss it unless we run."

"Not yet. Once we make the turn for the platforms, I'll tell you when." He glanced over his shoulder as he tightened the straps on the backpack that he carried. "They're closing in."

Two more men stormed in through the Forty-second Street entrance.

They both lowered their heads and rounded the corner into the passageway that led to the trains.

Jagger stuck his hand into his pocket and took out the bottle of baby oil he'd purchased in the drugstore. "Now. Run," he said, discreetly squirting the mineral oil in a swath behind them.

Wendy took off down the passageway, sprinting toward

the platform. She sneaked a glance back before she hit the escalator and lost sight of him.

Jagger bolted after her, gesturing for her to keep going with one hand, while he emptied the full bottle.

The four men charged down the corridor, shoving people out of their way. Other commuters veered to the sides. As soon as the men hit the slick patch of marble, going at an all-out sprint, there was no time for them to adjust and keep their balance. They slipped and gravity did the rest, taking them down.

The slippery surface wouldn't stop them, but it slowed them down. A few precious seconds. Perhaps time enough for them to get away.

She reached the escalator and ran down the moving steel stairs. A train was pulling into the station.

A distinctive sound echoed behind her and screams followed, but she didn't stop. It was gunfire. Suppressed but loud enough to draw the Transit cops.

The doors of the train opened, and one stream of pedestrians poured out as another flowed into the subway cars.

At the platform, she looked back. Jagger was making his way down the escalator, cutting around those standing still on the moving staircase.

She hurried onto the train and waited. Her chest tightened, her heart pounding in her throat.

Come on, Jagger. Hurry. Seconds ticked through her. Nerves rolled her stomach, making her feel that she might be sick.

A chime sounded and the automated voice announced, "Stand clear of the closing doors please."

No, no, no. She wasn't going to leave Jagger behind. No matter the consequences.

Two more shots echoed, sending a chill up her spine. The doors started to close, and she thrust her arm between them, triggering the train's conductor to pop them open again.

Another chime and repeat of the automated message.

Jagger hopped off the escalator, dashed across the platform and darted onto the train.

The doors slid closed behind him and the train lurched, rolling forward, inching out of the station.

The four men spilled off the escalator and slipped across the platform. One fired at them, but the bullet pinged into metal as the train entered the dark tunnel.

Trembling, Wendy leaned against Jagger and pressed her cheek to his chest. He took her into his arms and held her as if he understood that she needed a minute for the world to stop spinning. His heart beat strong and fast, the steady rhythm a comfort against her cheek. His hands were warm on her head and her lower back, and his body heat did the trick of chasing the cold from her skin until she could breathe again.

"Wendy, I need to explain," he said, his voice a low rumble in her ear, "about the things Morton told you."

She stiffened at remembering. Jagger had willingly killed people for the Brethren.

His arms tightened around her as if he feared losing her, and suddenly nothing was certain. "I did what he said. But I chose the assignments I accepted with Morton. To make sure that the people the Brethren sent me after were bad. Criminals and scumbags the world wouldn't miss. It was the only way I could be part of the organization without raising suspicion." He stroked his hands down her hair, rubbed his cheek against her temple. "You know me. Please, honey. You *know* me."

He repeated the words, a mantra, over and over. A sob rocked through her, but she reined it in. The truth was, she did know him. His heart. His soul. He was principled and kind.

Jagger would never hurt an innocent person, much less take their life. Everything he'd done, from going to prison to getting tangled up with the Brethren had been for her. To find his way back to her.

With that came guilt, an inescapable sense of responsibility, because deep down there wasn't anything she wouldn't do to have a second chance with Jagger.

To get closer to him, she tucked her feet between his boots, pressed into him and looked up, meeting his gaze. "I love you. I've never stopped. Never will."

Relief was heavy in his eyes. Jagger dropped a kiss on her forehead.

The train emerged from the tunnel, pulling into the next station.

"We can't keep running like this," she said, low.

"We have to figure out how they're tracking us. I know someone who might have the answer."

The train stopped and the doors opened.

They hustled onto the platform and ran up the steps.

"If they're on motorcycles, they could be here any minute," Jagger said.

They made their way through the turnstile and raced outside into the fresh air. Jagger waved down a taxi. They climbed in and he gave the driver an address.

"Who are we going to see?" she asked.

"Pilar Zahiri."

Wendy's stomach knotted. The name was unusual and familiar. Very familiar. "Your ex-girlfriend?"

Jagger sighed. "She was never my girlfriend."

"You slept with her. She was your first."

Another sigh. "We were childhood friends. It was a one-time thing. A lifetime ago."

"She's in the cartel?"

He nodded.

"Have you seen her since you were released?"

Jagger lowered his head and the knot in her belly clenched harder. "Not in the way you think."

"How do you know what I'm thinking?"

"It doesn't matter. Whatever you're thinking, it wasn't like that. Not as old friends. Not as acquaintances."

"Maybe it was for another one-time thing. I'm sure you've been with someone in the last three years and there's nothing wrong with that." Even if it hurt that it hadn't been with her. "Just don't hide it from me."

"I was with someone. A one-night stand, but it wasn't with her. Pilar is in the Brethren, or rather she used to be. Now, she's with Miguel."

"Vargas?" she whispered.

"Yep. She's now his…lady. I've seen her because of my dealings with Miguel."

"Why on earth do you think she'd help us?"

"Not us. Me. We have history and I know she's not happy. Correction, she is a woman with an ax to grind, hiding it behind a smile. She hooked up with Miguel as a power play, hoping that he'd grant her his favor and move her up the ranks in the Brethren. It backfired. He pulled her altogether, claiming he loved her too much to have her soiling her hands or putting herself in harm's way."

"Isn't that a good thing? That he loves her enough to want to keep her safe?"

"Miguel loves her about as much as he loves his Ferrari. Actually, he might love his car more. She wanted power, and he put a leash on her ambition instead. It's turned into this sick game of control between them, and for her there's no winning. No way out. She's stuck. It's a shame, too, because she's smart as a whip, speaks five languages, strong, ruthless when necessary, keeps her ear to ground on everything. She'd make a good partner for him, but he's not willing to let her rule *with* him. Then again, maybe he's worried that if he gave her the power she wants, she'd slit his throat in the night and take the entire kingdom."

They were going to Lady Macbeth on steroids for assistance. "Do you really think that she's bitter enough to betray Miguel by helping you?"

He shrugged. "I hope so. You know what they say. Hell hath no fury like a woman scorned."

Chapter Fourteen

"Are you sure she'll be here?" Wendy asked, feeling self-conscious as they walked through the Hotel Duchand's swanky bar wearing jeans and windbreakers.

The idea of approaching Pilar hadn't grown on her. There were too many ways this could go wrong, but she didn't have a better alternative.

"She lives here on the top floor with Miguel in a lavish penthouse suite. When he's not in town, she has a tendency to drink at the bar."

Wendy wasn't going to dive back into the jealousy pool by asking how he knew that detail.

"I see her. She's with her driver." Jagger let go of Wendy's hand and walked up to a striking woman sitting at the bar, talking to a man in a suit. She wore a white one-shoulder leather dress that hugged her slender figure like a second skin and sky-high heels. She had long, toned legs that were evidence of serious commitment to the gym and shiny dark hair that fell to her waist.

Wendy trailed behind Jagger, giving him a little space while still staying close enough to hear the conversation.

"Pilar."

The woman turned, giving Wendy a chance to see how drop-dead gorgeous she was. Pilar slunk off the bar stool with the grace of a viper, hugged him and kissed both his cheeks.

A hot knife of jealousy stabbed Wendy at the show of genuine affection between them.

"Jagger? What are you doing here?" In her heels she was as tall as Jagger, and she looked like a damn swimsuit model. Not a former hit woman.

"I need to talk to you. It's urgent. Can we do it in your car? Now?"

The look of confusion crossing her face was fleeting. "Of course. Ronaldo," she said, motioning to her driver.

The man got up and led the way out of the bar.

As Pilar snaked her arm around Jagger's, she gave Wendy a sidelong glance. "Is she with you?"

He held out his hand to Wendy and brought her in close on the opposite side of him. "She is."

A smirk curved Pilar's glossy red lips. One of her perfectly plucked eyebrows lifted, and her nose crinkled in an expression of curiosity.

"Time is of the essence," Jagger said.

Pilar straightened, letting him go, and strutted off in front of them.

"Still sure about this?" Wendy whispered. "She looked a little possessive of you."

"It's nothing. She respects me, cares for me, but like a sister. I promise." He wrapped an arm around her shoulder and squeezed—a bit of reassurance, also maybe a warning. They were working against the clock and desperately needed answers.

They piled into her car, which was parked out front. If you could call a fully loaded four-hundred-thousand-dollar extended Maybach that seated four in the back simply a car.

"Can you ask him to drive around? Keep us moving?" Jagger asked, seated beside Wendy and across from Pilar.

"Certainly." Pilar relayed Jagger's instructions and then rolled up the tinted privacy partition.

Jagger waited until the car was in motion on the road. "Where's Miguel?"

"Overseas. Doing business. I suspect you already know that if you came looking for me at the bar."

"Why didn't you go with him?" Jagger asked.

She flashed a smile and let out a throaty chuckle. "Isn't

it pathetic enough that I'm arm candy in the States. Must I be reduced to a useless sexual trophy in Europe as well? Besides, it gives Miguel an opportunity to do his on-the-side gallivanting without rubbing my face in it."

A scorned woman, indeed. Pilar might help them after all.

Jagger leaned forward. "Do you know about the recent kill order?"

"I'm aware that something big came down the pike."

"Do you know why Emilio claims a blood debt?"

Pilar crossed her legs. "Why does it matter?"

"This is the target. Wendy Haas. The Brethren have been tracking us. Everywhere we go, they turn up."

"So, you come to me!" Outrage washed across her face. "Sorry, I can't help you."

"Pilar, you're the only person who can help me. Please, wouldn't you love to get back at Miguel? Feel like you have the power to do something. Exercise that God-given free will unless you're happy being a pretty puppet for the rest of your life."

"Don't try to get in my head, *guerrero guapo*." She called him *handsome warrior* as she pointed a finger at him. Her long, manicured nail looked like a talon.

"I just need you to answer a couple of questions. I'm begging."

"That's a first. You never beg." She let out a heavy breath and pulled a flask from her purse. "Make it fast."

"Why does Emilio want her dead?"

"Quite a few radioactive bombshells have dropped in the Vargas household recently." She unscrewed the top on the flask and took a long pull. "Emilio doesn't care about you," Pilar said, looking at Wendy. "He's angry at your brother. More like spitting mad really."

"This is about Dutch," Jagger said. "I knew it."

"But why?" Wendy asked. "What did my brother do?"

"He went undercover for the US Marshals to get close to Emilio."

Wendy shook her head. "That doesn't sound like him. He works in fugitive recovery."

"Listen, sweetheart, we don't have time for all the interruptions as you wrap your brain around what I'm saying."

Wendy stiffened, and Jagger patted her leg and cast her a pleading look to let it go.

Pilar caught the look and his hand on Wendy's leg, and there was a flash of something heated in her eyes.

"As I was saying," Pilar continued, "your brother went undercover and seduced Isabel."

That was the name of Dutch's new girlfriend, the one he mentioned taking an extended vacation with. Was this story true?

"Isabel? Emilio's niece?" Jagger asked.

"Turns out, Isabel is his daughter. And that marshal, your brother, made her believe she was in love and convinced her to turn against Emilio."

"What?" The alarm in Jagger's voice told Wendy the situation was worse than he'd anticipated.

"Miguel is hot under the collar about not knowing Isabel was his half sister all this time and about some old affair being the reason his mother left. *Boo-hoo*, I say, but Miguel refused to help break Emilio out of prison. That's the real reason Miguel is overseas. Hiding from daddy and having a tantrum." Pilar rolled her eyes. "So, I graciously stepped up to facilitate arrangements for Emilio outside of El Paso."

"But why does he want me dead?" Wendy asked.

"Emilio feels that since Dutch stole his daughter and stirred the proverbial pot, he's going to punish him by killing you." Pilar swung a talon in Wendy's direction. "It's an old-school underworld way of handling a grievance. An eye for an eye. In my opinion, it's overkill. No pun intended. But no one gives two flying figs what I think."

Wendy folded her hands, resisting the urge to scrub her sweaty palms on her thighs. "How do we get Emilio Vargas to rescind the kill order?"

Pilar turned her dazzling fake smile on Wendy. "You're cute. Your naivete works for you, like a beautiful accessory." Her gaze bounced to Jagger. "I can see the appeal," she said, and then looked back at Wendy. "The kill order will only go away if the Brethren completes their task, or…you two kill Emilio first."

A fresh wave of nausea rolled over her. Both options were unfathomable.

"How are they tracking us?" Jagger asked.

"Why are you helping her?" Pilar turned the flask up to her lips again. "Disloyalty isn't a good look on you."

Jagger sat back. "It's none of your business."

"You made it my business, *guapo*, the second you came to me. Now, either you tell me, or I have Ronaldo stop, let the two of you out, and you'll never know how they keep finding you." She glanced between them. "It's rude to waste my time. Not to mention dangerous for all parties."

"My murder charge," he said, taking Wendy's hand. "She's the woman I was involved with at the time."

Pilar's dark eyes lit up like hundred-watt bulbs. "This is the love of your life?" She licked her red lips in a predatory way that made Wendy's skin crawl. "My, the plot thickens."

"How do they keep finding us?" Wendy asked, wanting to get the hell out of the car and as far away from Pilar as possible.

"Remember the rumors about repo?" Pilar took another swig.

"Yeah." Jagger nodded. "That if anyone in the Brethren stepped out of line, they would be repo'd."

"As in repossessed, like property?" Wendy asked.

"Exactly. Turns out, it's not a rumor. It's real. Before they tattooed us, when they gave us our brand," Pilar said, tapping a spot on her chest, over her heart, which was covered by her dress, "it was to hide the fact that they were implanting a GPS tracker in us. That's only one of the more horrifying things I've learned as Miguel's *woman*. They don't want the Brethren knowing about the fail-safe, but you going rogue has forced them to tip their hand."

"I've got to cut it out." Jagger rubbed his chest.

"Good luck with that. It's below the hypodermis layer of skin and could've migrated anywhere in your chest at this point. There's only way to circumvent it."

"Care to share?" he asked.

Pilar put the flask to her lips, and down the hatch went another sip. "You have to die."

"What?" Wendy asked, horrified. "No. There has to be another way."

"It sucks. I know. Imagine how I feel. Everywhere I go Miguel knows it. He's probably tracking me this very moment." Pilar stilled, her gaze roaming as if she was thinking about something. Then she swore in Spanish and French. "If he's tracking both of us, then he knows we're together." Pilar had the driver pull over. "If Miguel questions me about it, I'll say you came to me for help, but I tried to kill you and you got away. Understand."

"How do I disable the tracker?"

"Four hundred volts of electricity should do the trick, but make sure you stay on the move." Pilar kissed Jagger on the lips and opened the car door. *"Buena suerte, hermano."*

Chapter Fifteen

Jagger hailed the first taxi he spotted. "Central Park," he said to the cabbie, and the taxi cut into traffic.

"Why the park?" Wendy asked.

"I only told him that to get us going until we know our next step."

"You have lipstick on your face." Wendy frowned and wiped it from his lip with her thumb. "Do you trust the information Pilar gave us?"

Going to see Pilar had been a gamble, but worth the risk. "She had no reason to lie. It would've been easier for her not to speak to us at all and she told us more than she needed to."

In fact, he now saw a way to save Wendy. What had once been impossible had become feasible, but first he had to deal with the GPS tracker.

"She did spill her guts, but I can't believe Dutch would seduce someone for his job."

"I agree, it doesn't sound like him. Maybe he really fell for Isabel. Sounds as if her feelings for him might be genuine if she betrayed Emilio."

The idea that Isabel was Emilio's daughter still made Jagger's stomach turn. The infidelity, the magnitude of the betrayal and the years of lying boggled his mind. He understood why Miguel was upset, and rightfully so.

Jagger had been in the army when Luis, Emilio's brother had been killed. He'd always assumed it had happened in a turf war with a rival cartel. What if it had been something altogether different, perhaps infighting between the brothers?

This would also explain Emilio's desire for a blood debt. No one messed with his family. Especially not his son or his daughter. That was probably a secret Emilio had planned to carry to his grave.

A dangerous, powerful man with a vendetta was on the warpath, making life-ending decisions based on hot-blooded emotions.

"It can't be easy to lose the ones you love. First, his daughter and, based on what Pilar said, his son is turning his back on him," Wendy said, showing the depth of her compassion, even for a man who had put a hit out on her.

"Maybe the discord between Emilio and Miguel could be used to our benefit somehow. If Miguel refused to help break his father out of jail, that's big." An indication of a major rift between them.

This was such a mess.

Wendy rubbed her forehead on a sigh. "That brings me back to Pilar. Why did she tell you so much?"

"She still has a soft spot for me. I would've helped her if the situation had been reversed."

"I don't trust her."

"You don't like her. That's not the same thing."

She straightened with a jerk. "You're right. I don't like her, any more than she likes me. I also don't trust her."

Green was not Wendy's color. "You can't seriously be jealous." Though this fiery, territorial interest in him was something he was glad she hadn't lost.

"Cut me some slack. It's hard not to be jealous of Pilar Zahiri."

The sentiment wasn't a foreign one to him. He'd always wanted Wendy to be happy, to move on with her life, live it to the fullest. But when he had seen her with Tripp Langston—the stockbroker's arm draped around her waist, holding her close as they posed for pictures—tightness had threaded Jagger's chest, as well as a ringing in his ears worse than fingernails on chalkboard.

"Sure, Pilar is beautiful," he said, "in the same way a sword is. A work of art capable of slitting your throat. Miguel probably sleeps with one eye open. There's no competition between the two of you, believe me. You're warm, kind, and you love with your whole heart. That takes a type of courage someone like Pilar will never understand."

Wendy's love, so fearless and undeniable, had been the air he breathed, and for the past decade, he'd been suffocating without her. She was still everything he wanted. Needed. His ideal partner. Once you had experienced *ideal* it was damn near impossible to settle for anything less.

Her fingers found his, and they did a little intimate dance as he enjoyed the feel of her beside him.

"I'm sorry," Wendy said. "It was the first time I've been face-to-face with someone you've slept with and still care about. Does Miguel know that you and Pilar were once together?"

"No. It wouldn't do either one of us any good if he knew. Besides, it's ancient history. Our feelings for each other are fraternal, not romantic."

She blew out a breath. "My personal feelings aside, she strikes me as the type of person who would only help if she was getting something in return. Is thumbing her nose at Miguel with her little act of defiance enough for her?"

"Pilar put herself on the line for us when she didn't have to."

Wendy tipped her head back and looked up at him. "Not us. You, *guerrero guapo*."

Jagger wrapped his arm around her shoulder. "Thanks to her we know how they're tracking us." Without that tidbit, they'd still be running around the city clueless while being stalked, and then it would've only been a matter of time. Pilar might have saved their lives.

"But what are we supposed to do about it? Use a Taser on you, or a stun gun?"

"I don't think that has enough juice. The voltage is high enough on one of those, but the amperage is way too low. We need to think in terms of electrocution to short circuit the GPS tracker. Maybe we use a car battery and jumper cables."

Wendy's face twisted in horror that he too felt but didn't show. "Are you insane? What if something goes wrong? What if you actually die and I…" Her voice trailed off.

"You what?"

"I know where we need to go." Wendy leaned forward and tapped on the plexiglass partition. "Excuse me," she said to the driver. "Change of plans. Instead of Central Park, we need you to drop us somewhere else." She gave him an address Jagger didn't recognize.

"You want the hospital?" the cabbie asked.

"Yes."

"There's a closer one," the driver said.

"No, take us to the address I gave you."

"It's your money, lady." He put on the turn signal and changed lanes.

Jagger sat up. "We can't go to a hospital, remember."

"We can't be put in the system, but the hospital is exactly what we need. I know an ER doctor. He was a client."

"What's his name?"

"Fitz. Fitzgerald Gilmore."

That was a mouthful.

The doctor was a client she had gone out with. He'd been in her dating lineup after the lawyer. Voicing that knowledge would only support the idea that Jagger was a stalker, but Wendy didn't want him to hide things.

"I know you had a fling. I don't care. Ancient history, right? And it'd be great if you didn't care how I know."

Wendy glared at him and shook her head. "I don't care that you kept tabs on me," she said, and he silently thanked her for not using the creepy *S* word. "I care that you didn't contact me. Three wasted years when we could've been fighting for our second chance."

She made it sound so simple when it was anything but.

Still wasn't as long as he was a convicted felon. The emotional baggage between them was heavy and real. Every time they dug below the surface of it, they found bruises—on their hearts, on their egos.

For now, he'd focus on the doctor.

If memory served, Fitz had been sued for malpractice and beaten it with a settlement. His reputation had taken a major hit, according to the papers, and it looked as if the hospital was going to let him go. In swooped Wendy, a PR superhero, and transformed Dr. Code Blue into The Doctor Who'll Pull You Through.

Maybe Dr. Code Blue was who they needed after all.

"My phone." She held out her hand. "It'll be faster if I call him and give him a heads-up."

He fished her phone and battery out of the backpack on the floor between his legs and gave it to her.

She powered it up and made the call. "Hi, Fitz, it's Wendy. This isn't a social call. If you could just hear me out before you say anything. I'm with a friend, someone very important to me. We're in danger, but you can help. I need you use a defibrillator on him and make sure that he doesn't die."

Her gaze dropped as she listened.

"I can't explain why," she said, her words low and fast, "but if you don't do this, then my friend and I are both as good as dead. You'll be responsible for two deaths for certain. If you don't help and I do survive, a certain story about you and black-market organ transplants might get leaked to the media. Before you know it you'll find yourself neck deep in bad press, and that'll be the end of your career."

That nugget hadn't been in the papers. The doctor had a dirty past and a lot to lose.

"Please, don't think of it as blackmail. I'm giving you an incentive to help me. I would never do this unless I had no choice. Fitz, please, I need you." She was quiet for a moment. "Thank you. There's one other thing. You'll need to do it in an ambulance because we have to keep moving. Don't ask, it'll only raise more questions." A long pause. "Okay, we'll see you in a few minutes."

THE TAXI DRIVER stopped by the Emergency Room entrance. Jagger peeled off two tens and paid the cabbie, letting him keep the change.

"Wendy!" A man in blue scrubs waved them over to a different part of the parking lot, where three ambulances were parked.

They ran to the back of the ambulance that had the engine running and an EMT sitting behind the wheel.

Fitz greeted them and helped Wendy up into the back. He was average height, fit, designer stubble, intense eyes, curly brown hair. Radiated calm control. A good trait for an ER doctor. He looked younger in person than he had in the paper. Maybe late twenties, early thirties.

It occurred to Jagger that Wendy catered to a specific demographic. All her clients were millennials.

"You're going to have to pay the tech." Fitz gestured to the driver as they pulled out of the hospital parking lot.

"Will a hundred do it?" Jagger asked.

Fitz's mouth flattened into a thin line. "You better make it two to be on the safe side. I don't need his loose lips damaging my ship."

Jagger dug in his wallet and counted out the money.

Fitz passed the wad of bills to the driver, who stuffed it in his pocket. He directed Jagger to sit on the gurney while he sat on the bench seat beside Wendy and folded his hands. "I understand you can't or won't get into specifics, but in order to help you, it'd be good to know why you need me to hit your bosom buddy with a defibrillator. I take it there's a point and this isn't for recreation."

Wendy stared at Jagger. "It could mean the difference between success and failure if he knew."

"There's a GPS tracker inside me." Jagger took off his windbreaker and pulled up his shirt. "Three years ago, it was inserted here." He pointed to the brand on his chest. "But it could have migrated. We need you to short-circuit it with an electric current. Someone recommended four hundred volts. I honestly don't know if that's enough."

Wendy rested her hand on Fitz's forearm. "We need to be sure that you fry it. There are dangerous people after us. Tracking us as we speak. I also need you to keep him alive."

"Trust me, that's in my best interest as well," Fitz said flatly, not seeming the least bit rattled by the situation, like this was an everyday occurrence.

The doctor's bedside manner inspired confidence.

"The lowest possible voltage is one-forty. It also carries the lowest risk, but if we want to eliminate any doubt about shorting out the device inside you, we should go with five hundred."

Jagger was willing to go as high as necessary, but they had to be sure they fried the GPS tracker. "Five it is."

"Remove your shirt and lie back." Fitz put on latex gloves as Jagger took off his top. "What do we have here?" Fitz asked, inspecting Jagger's patched up wound.

"Gunshot. Superficial. I used superglue on it."

"Looks like you two are having quite the evening. In the future, I don't recommend using superglue. It contains toxins that can be harmful to tissue. Best left in your toolbox and not your medical kit, but if it was the only option to keep you from bleeding out…" Fitz shrugged. "I'll give you a shot of antibiotics so you don't get an infection, just in case."

"Thank you," Wendy said.

Jagger nodded. "Yeah, thanks."

"If you survive this, then you can thank me." Fitz reached over and turned on the defibrillator. "Do you understand that as a healthy individual, you run the risk of cardiac arrest and possible death by proceeding with this?" he asked in an infomercial tone.

The latter was a guarantee if he *didn't* do this. "I understand."

Fitz glanced at Wendy. "Do you understand that if he dies and I can't resuscitate him, the disposal of the body is on you?"

Her face paled and her gaze fixed on Jagger's. The mask slipped. Anguish filled her eyes. It was immense, startling, and seeing it made him ache with regret.

"It won't come to that." In prison, he'd done a lot of reading and come across a myth about how the sun loved the moon so much that he died every night to let her breathe and to put an end to her misery. That's how he thought of his time in jail. He died every day so Wendy could live. Now she needed him to survive. To help her. The universe had messed with him plenty. He had to believe this wouldn't end horrifically. Not for his own sake, but for hers. "I'll get you through this."

She took Jagger's hand and brought it to her lips. Kissed it. Stroked his arm. "If you die on me, I'll never forgive you," she said, her voice shaking, as was her body.

There was so much woven in that statement, simmering beneath the words. He heard it, felt it. All those years ago he thought he was doing the right thing. That if he set her free, it would liberate them both, but all it did was bind them together in an unimaginable way.

She had hurt every day they'd been separated, and it was his fault.

"I can't have that, can I?" He tried to smile but only managed a grin. "I won't leave you alone. I swear it."

"Very touching," Fitz said, deadpan. "Can we get on with it? I'm on call."

"Okay," Jagger said.

"You need to keep your hands off him while I do this," Fitz warned Wendy.

She leaned over and gave Jagger a kiss. It was quick and hard, but he tasted her, got to slide his fingers into hair, absorb the warmth of her touch. For ten damn years, he'd dreamed about lying beside her, holding her, and he wanted it all back. She was the light in the darkness that had saved him from drowning in despair. He wasn't giving up now.

On a gasp, her lips parted and she was about to say something. He put his fingertips over her mouth, stopping her.

"Tell me after," he said. Because they needed to believe that they'd get the chance.

Wendy nodded, her eyes glistening with emotion. "After."

She let his hand go and he stared at her, wanting to hold on to the image of her gorgeous face, no matter what happened.

Fitz adjusted the setting and picked up the defibrillator paddles. "Clear," he said, and pressed them to Jagger's chest.

A searing jolt of agony gripped him, tearing through his body.

Then Wendy and the world slipped away into darkness.

Chapter Sixteen

"Jagger!" Wendy clenched her fists, wanting to shake him until he opened his eyes. When the defibrillator pads had touched him, his whole body had convulsed and popped up inches from the gurney.

"You've got to calm down and be quiet," the EMT said from behind the steering wheel. "Let the doctor work."

Fitz started chest compressions. Jagger's heart had stopped, and he wasn't breathing.

Her anxiety skyrocketed with each passing second that he remained unresponsive.

Fitz checked Jagger's airway, put an oxygen bag mask on him and squeezed. "Hold the bag," he ordered. "Squeeze twice when I tell you."

Wendy scooted forward and held it in her trembling hands as Fitz resumed chest compressions again, much longer than a five count.

Wake up, Jagger. I need you. She prayed for him to open his eyes.

If she lost him a second time, she didn't know if she'd be able to pick up any of the pieces again.

"Squeeze," Fitz hissed at her as he withdrew a syringe from his pocket, tapped it and flicked off that cap. He felt Jagger's left side, pierced his chest wall between his ribs and depressed the plunger, injecting the contents of the syringe.

She swallowed the panic rising in her throat. "What is that?"

"One-milligram epinephrine. Adrenaline. I was hoping we wouldn't need it, but…"

Jagger wasn't responding. They were losing him. The breath in her throat tightened like a fist, refusing to fill her lungs.

Stay with me! Please, God, help him.

Memories crashed over her. Good. Bad. Ugly. Every one of them tied to Jagger. Pent-up grief and loss punched through the surface, shattering something inside her, and tears spilled from her eyes. "Don't leave me," she whispered. "Please, don't leave me again."

Not like this. Cheated out of more time together. It was so unfair.

Fitz began another round of chest compressions, moving faster, pushing with the heel of his palm. He kept pumping to a furious count of thirty as her heart wilted.

Her turn. She squeezed the bag, giving him oxygen.

Holding up a hand for her stop, Fitz put the stethoscope hanging around his neck to Jagger's chest and listened. "We've got a pulse."

Jagger's eyes fluttered and opened. He hauled in a deep breath, glancing around.

Wendy steeled herself to keep from sobbing and clutched his hand. She was too choked up to speak. All she could do was caress his cheek, giving quiet thanks he was back with her.

He looked as weary as she felt. She wished she could give him what little strength she had left.

His gaze settled on her face. "See. I'm not going anywhere. If I make you a promise, I'll keep it." He said it like the vow came straight from his soul.

The words arrowed right through her chest. A whirlwind of emotion stormed inside her, pain from the past, gratitude for this moment, the uncertainty of the future, but one thing burned clearly. "I love you." Her voice trembled. "I'll always love you."

"Good. Because my heart still belongs to you."

He was hers and she was his.

There was no way in hell she was going to lose him again.

Not a chance that she would ever walk away or give up on him. Never again.

Fitz sighed. "Speaking of your heart. I'm glad we got it restarted. You'll need to rest, as much as possible for the next twelve hours. That means no more getting shot and drink plenty of fluids." He looked through the upper cabinet for something. "I'll start him on an antibiotic drip. Do you think you'll be able to keep the IV going for him wherever you're headed?"

The truth was she didn't know, but she'd find a way to make it happen for him. "I'll take care of it."

"Great."

Wendy helped Jagger put on his T-shirt and buttondown. They had to go someplace safe, where no one would find them. Give Jagger a chance to recover. A hotel was out of the question. They'd have to use a credit card that could be tracked. There was also the possibility that footage of them from the Lincoln Tunnel had made the news, and so anyone in a crowded hotel might spot them and call the police.

She was glad her mom was safe and out of town with her new husband, Eric. Not that she would have been able to turn to her if she had been in the city. Friends and close associates were out, too.

That left only one place for them to go, and Jagger was going to hate it.

Fitz started the intravenous drip of antibiotics and regular fluids. They attached the IV bag to the top of the backpack after Jagger slipped it on. She would have preferred to carry it for him, but the tubing wasn't long enough.

"Thank you, Fitz," Wendy said. "I appreciate this."

"We're even," he said. "This will never happen again. Right?"

Out of desperation, she'd crossed the line. She felt awful for coercing Fitz. Even though they'd short-circuited the GPS tracker, which gave them a chance to survive, and Jagger was on the mend, the ends didn't justify the means. "Right. Never again."

TWENTY MINUTES LATER, it was nearly eleven thirty.

In the lobby of the Upper East Side apartment building, Wendy smiled at the doorman, who was seated behind the front desk. She had one arm wrapped around Jagger's waist, holding up some of his weight.

"Can't we go somewhere else?" Jagger asked her in an irate whisper.

"No." She turned back at the doorman, pretending that this wasn't a bizarre situation. "We're here to see Tina Jennings."

The doorman's gaze bounced from her, to Jagger, to the IV bag hanging from his backpack. "Is she expecting you?"

"I doubt it unless she's clairvoyant." She broadened her smile.

The doorman showed no reaction to the joke. "Who can I say is calling?"

She wasn't comfortable using their names, but she had to give the man something to work with. "Tell her that Warren's son is here, with his girlfriend."

His eyebrows creased and his eyes narrowed, but he picked up the phone and rang her apartment. He relayed the message, listened briefly, and said. "Yes, ma'am." Rising from his seat, he hung up and looked at them. "You're both welcome to go right up."

He came around the desk, walked to the elevator ahead of them and pushed the button. The doors opened right away, which was a relief. She was ready for this tense, awkward moment to end.

Once she helped Jagger inside, the doorman pushed the button for the top floor.

"Thank you, for the assistance," Wendy said.

He nodded. "Have a good evening."

The doors closed.

"We shouldn't have come here," Jagger said.

"We have nowhere else to go." They were lucky Tina was even letting them come up.

"If it weren't for her stealing my inheritance, none of this would have ever happened. I would've had the money to pay your tuition. You never would have gotten that stupid job. I never would've gone to prison." He grunted in frustration.

"It's time to bury the hatchet. We need someplace safe for you to recover. You said she hasn't had anything to do with the cartel since your father died. Everyone knows how much you—" she swallowed the word *despise* "—dislike her. No one will think to look for us here. We'll leave in the morning."

The elevator doors opened. They walked off and made their way to the apartment.

An elderly woman with a welcoming smile opened the door before Wendy could ring the bell or knock. Her hair was snow-white, her frame thin and a bit frail, but her blue eyes were radiant. She wore a simple cotton blouse and loose-fitting black pants.

Wendy had never met Tina. Jagger had cut ties with her after his father's death. Based on his description, Wendy had assumed his father had been in a May-December relationship with a younger woman. But Tina appeared to be in her late sixties, possibly early seventies, making her Warren Carr's senior by at least ten years.

"Jagger. Come in." She stepped aside, letting them in. After she locked the door and put the chain on, she turned back to them. "Hi, I'm Tina."

Wendy shook her proffered hand. "I'm Wendy."

A curious expression crossed Tina's face. "Wendy Haas?"

"Yes. How did you know?"

"How many Wendys could there be in Jagger's life? When

he was on trial, I went to go see him once to offer any assistance I could."

"I asked her to get me a good lawyer," Jagger said, "and she didn't even do that much for me."

"It wasn't that simple." Tina lowered her head. "Jagger shared the details of his case with me. It was a good thing your name was kept out of the paper and you didn't have to worry about reporters hounding you." Tina looked Jagger over from head to toe and frowned. "Why don't you two take a sit?"

The apartment was spacious by Manhattan standards and tastefully decorated. Dark hardwood floors. Comfy-looking leather furniture, also dark. The walls were painted in light, airy neutral colors. There were pictures of Warren everywhere, one with him and Jagger in his military uniform, several of him with Tina.

The place was a shrine.

They shuffled to a sofa and plunked down.

Adrenaline had bled out of Wendy and fatigue was setting in. All she wanted to do was sleep. "We're sorry to intrude on you so late."

"I don't turn in until well after midnight and appreciate the company. I've told Jagger that he's welcome to come here anytime."

"How gracious. I can come to the apartment you stole from me anytime."

Tina pursed her lips and sat in a wingback chair across from them. "To what do I owe this unexpected pleasure?"

"We're in trouble, with the cartel," Wendy said, cutting to the heart of it. Tina had a right to know this if they were going to stay the night.

"Oh, my." Tina blanched. "Is there anything I can do to help?"

"Is this another offer of impotent assistance?" Jagger asked.

Wendy leaned over to Jagger. "Stop it. You're embarrassing yourself and me," she whispered in his ear. "If she kicks us out, you'll have to rest on the subway."

Drawing in a deep breath, Jagger went to fold his arms, but thanks to the tube from the IV, he straightened them instead.

"Could we spend the night?" Wendy asked. "If we had someplace else to go, we wouldn't ask. We'll leave first thing in the morning."

"Of course," Tina said, without expressing any concern for herself or whether she was in danger. "Stay as long as you need."

Wendy's stomach growled in an inconvenient break in the conversation. It was loud and mortifying.

"Can I get you two something to eat?" Tina asked.

Wendy shook her head. "No, thank you. We don't want to impose."

"Yes," Jagger said. "We're starving."

Wendy elbowed his right side lightly.

"Please. Thank you," he added through clenched teeth.

"How about steak and asparagus? And I have an extra baked potato. It can all be ready in ten minutes. Is medium rare all right?"

"That would be lovely," Wendy said, starting to feel a little light-headed from low blood sugar.

"I can also whip up a molten lava cake in the microwave. Homemade, not from a box. It's delicious and gluten-free. I have sugar-free vanilla frozen yogurt to go on top."

"Please don't go to any trouble on our account," Wendy said.

Tina beamed and waved a dismissive hand. "It's been a long time since I've had the pleasure of cooking for anyone. No trouble at all. Why don't I show you two to the guest room?"

"Do you mean my old room?" Jagger asked.

Tina's bright smile faded. "Yes. Your old room."

"I know the way." Jagger stood, and Wendy went to put his arm over her shoulder to help him, but he brushed her away and headed down the hall.

"He's a Carr man, through and through," Tina said in a low voice. "Fortunately, I have a lot of experience. You wipe that pitiful look off your face and go in there after him. I'll let you know when the food is ready."

"Thank you," Wendy said. "I appreciate your kindness."

"Think nothing of it. This is Jagger's home as much as it is mine. He is always welcome here. That's the way Warren would've wanted it."

In the first bedroom down the hall, Wendy found Jagger. He was sitting on the bed, looking drained and irritated, staring at the drawn curtains.

Taking a deep breath, she shut the door behind her and sat beside him. For a long moment, there was only silence between them.

"Hey," she said softly, caressing his face and tilting his gaze to hers. She studied him for a heartbeat. Saw the anger and the pain lurking deeper. "Your father loved you. I love you. Let the rest of it go."

He leaned in and kissed her. A deep, long, melt-her-into-a-puddle kind of a kiss. Breaking away, he put his forehead to hers. He stroked her hair and ran a hand up and down her arm. It was so familiar, so intimate, dragging her back to when they had been together. He used to touch her all the time, always tender, always passionate, like he couldn't keep his hands off her, and it wasn't until that moment she realized how terribly she'd missed his affection.

"If I could let it go, I would," he whispered across her lips. "I can't reconcile what my father did."

Leaving Tina millions when a small portion would've changed Jagger's life. Both their lives.

"It's not Tina's fault. You can be angry, but *mean* is beneath you. You're better than that."

There was more to Jagger Carr than met the eye. She loved that about him, but she also needed to make sure he remembered that he was a good man, with a big heart. It hurt her to see him like this.

Tina knocked on the door.

"Come in," Wendy said.

The door opened and Tina stepped inside, carrying a coatrack. "I thought this would be handy for the IV bag."

"That's considerate of you." Wendy took it from her and attached the drip bag to one of the hooks.

"The food is ready."

Wendy and Jagger followed her into the dining room off the kitchen. Jagger insisted on carrying the coatrack himself. The color had returned to his face and he was already looking stronger.

Tina plated the meals and set the food down in front of them. As they dug in, she made herself a cup of tea and joined them at the table.

"This is delicious," Wendy said. The steak was tender and juicy, with a buttery texture, and the asparagus was crisp. It hit the spot. "Thank you."

Jagger stuffed food into his mouth, keeping his gaze lowered to the plate.

He'd gone from indignant to mute when she was hoping for cool politeness.

"You look so much like your father," Tina said. "Though you have your mother's eyes."

He responded by clearing his throat and taking a sip of water.

"I'm happy you're here," Tina said, making another attempt at conversation. "The circumstances are regrettable, of course, but I'm always here for you, Jagger."

His gaze slid up to Tina, and hostility rolled off him in waves. "I appreciate that you're allowing us to stay the night, but let's not pretend that we're ever going to be friends."

"Why can't we be friends?" Tina asked in a gentle tone. "What have I done to offend you?"

Jagger set down his fork and knife. "Maybe it has something to do with the fact that my father left you everything."

"No. That's an excuse," Tina said pointedly. "You were like this when your father and I started seeing each other. I have always welcomed you with open arms. Treated you with kindness and respect. I can't say that I've ever received the same in return. I'd like to know why."

Jagger had never shared with Wendy details about his relationship with Tina before his father's death. Everything she'd heard had been colored by the will and his anger over the inheritance.

"You came along at a difficult time for me and my father," Jagger said. "I needed more from him, and everything he had went to the cartel or to you."

"You were the apple of his eye. He loved you more than anything else in this world. More than me."

He laughed in bitter disbelief, and Wendy's heart sank. "Then why did he leave you millions and give me a car and a stupid letter filled with the ramblings of a crazy old man? One hundred thousand dollars to cover her tuition and my life would've had a different trajectory."

It was true. But the same could be said if Wendy had never moved out of the dorm, had never pushed her mother to cut her off. In so many ways she was responsible. Tina wasn't.

Tina rubbed her palms along the side of her mug. "I should've told you this years ago, when I came to see you in jail, but I was embarrassed, and the truth wouldn't have changed anything."

"What truth?" Jagger asked.

"I didn't steal anything from you. Your father didn't leave me millions. His estate owns this apartment. The whole building, in fact. I'm *entitled* to live here, the utilities are paid, and I receive a modest stipend once a month for expenses."

Wendy cringed inwardly as an awkward silence settled around the table like a bad smell. Jagger sat frozen, unblinking. He must have a million questions—she certainly did.

"Who does his estate belong to?" Wendy finally asked when Jagger remained speechless.

"It's in a trust. For Jagger's kids. If he ever has any." Tina's eyes turned glassy. "If he doesn't, then it will go to charity."

Jagger shook his head. "I don't understand. Why wouldn't he leave it to me?" His voice was low, barely audible.

"Your dad knew you so well that he believed you were the type of person who would do better on his own. Top of your class in high school, full scholarship to Columbia University that you turned down to join the army. He never worried about you. Warren so admired you for joining the military and becoming a Ranger. He thought your star would shine brighter if his money didn't influence who you became." She looked down at her cup. "I should've told you that day I came to visit you, but you were so angry at me and I was ashamed that there was nothing I could do to help you. A good lawyer wanted a ten-thousand-dollar retainer. To start with. That's three months of my stipend." She pressed a hand to her cheek. "Whatever I can do to help you now, please let me."

"Why didn't dad's estate planning lawyer explain all of that to me? Why leave me in the dark with a stupid car and that crazy letter about how his legacy would always be there for me, to protect me?"

"I think Warren was trying to be secretive about whatever is inside the Legacy."

"*Inside* the legacy?" Wendy asked. "What do you mean?"

"His safe, that's hidden in the office. It's a Legacy safe. I can show you."

Chapter Seventeen

In his father's office, Tina went to the built-in bookshelf behind the desk. She ran her finger along a seam and hit a button. The upper portion popped loose. She swung the bookcase out, revealing a safe that had been inserted into the wall.

"I never knew there was safe hidden behind the shelf," Jagger said.

"I thought you did." Tina looked at him. "Considering that, other than your father, you're the only person who can open it."

"You're mistaken." How could he open a safe he never knew existed?

"No, I'm not. Warren told me that you could."

"Is it possible your father left a code to unlock it in the letter?" Wendy asked.

He didn't recall any numbers, but the whole letter had been in code. All this time he had thought his father's words didn't make any sense, rambling on about his legacy, when he'd been referring to a safe in his office.

"There's no code. It's a biometric safe." Tina stepped aside, pointing to it. "Your dad was such a long-term planner, always prepared. I'm sure there's a way for you to open it."

Jagger moved closer, carrying the coatrack with the IV bag dangling from a hook. He peered at the safe. There was a biometric fingerprint scanner on the door. Engraved on the top was the brand name, *Legacy*.

A quick burst of nerves sent his pulse skittering.

"Your dad used his thumbprint," Tina said.

His father had used a device to scan Jagger's thumbprint when he was about fourteen or fifteen, but his dad had never deigned to explain why. Since before Jagger had been born, his father had been involved with the cartel. Secrets came with the territory, and at an early age he'd learned to walk on eggshells and follow orders without question. Maybe that was part of the reason he'd made such a good soldier.

Too many secrets and unresolved misunderstandings had brought him here. To this safe. With no clue as to its contents. Had he ever really known his father?

Wendy came up alongside him and put a hand on his back between his shoulder blades, as if sensing he needed support. "You don't have to do this right now. It can wait until the morning, after you've rested."

A trail of hateful little breadcrumbs and a violent shove from fate led him here. To his father's *Legacy*. The prospect of waiting was unbearable. "I have to do this. Now."

He pressed his right thumb to the scanner. A red light on the safe blinked green and the lock disengaged. He pulled the door open.

Inside the safe was a flash drive.

Jagger picked up the USB stick and turned to the computer on the desk. "Do you mind if I use it?"

"Go right ahead. Make yourself at home," Tina said. "Whenever your dad got that same gleam in his eyes, I could tell he was going to pull an all-nighter. Should I put on some coffee?"

"Yes, please," he said.

"No. Thank you." Wendy's gaze shifted to him. "Your heart." She placed her palm on his chest, the gentle heat stirring something tender and bone deep in him. "You need rest. Not caffeine."

As much as he hated to admit it, she was right. When the defibrillator paddles had touched him, it had felt like an electrified mule had kicked his damn chest. He was still fatigued, but curiosity had adrenaline firing through his veins again. "I'll pass on the coffee."

Tina nodded. "I leave you to it then." She headed for the door.

"Wait." Jagger met her eyes. "I'm sorry. For the assumptions I made. For not being nicer to you over the years. You made my dad happy. I should've been grateful to you for that instead of resentful."

"There were times I could've tried harder, too. You were just a kid who wanted more attention from his father. I wish I had encouraged your dad to tell you how he felt about you. He was so guarded about his feelings. Private."

His dad was a tough man, harder on Jagger than any drill sergeant or four-star general. Better at giving an *attaboy* than a hug.

"Don't ever doubt that he loved you." Tina gave him a sad smile and left the room, closing the door.

Jagger sat in front of the computer and turned it on. "I never thought I'd say this, ever, but I feel sorry for Tina. I wasn't fine with her having the bulk of his estate, but for her to only be left with a monthly allowance." He shook his head. That couldn't have been an easy pill to swallow after devoting herself to someone for years. "She deserved better. More."

Wendy kissed the top of his head. "Now that sounds like the man I know and love."

He inserted the thumb drive. "I can't believe my dad didn't want his millions to influence me, but he had no problem turning any children I have into spoiled-rotten brats."

"Isn't that a grandparent's sacred prerogative? Spoil their grandchildren and have their kids clean up the mess. Sort of like feeding them as many homemade cookies as they want, and then sending them back home to their parents to have their sugar rush."

"Well, we're talking ten million dollars' worth of a sweet rush."

"Wow. That's a lot of cookies."

Jagger clicked the folder on the screen for the drive linked to the USB stick. There were multiple files. Holdings. Property, residential and commercial. Every compound and safe house was probably listed. After a quick perusal, he found one in Texas, on the outskirts of El Paso.

"What's that?" Wendy asked, indicating the file labeled Layers.

He opened it and scanned the paperwork. "Documentation on shell companies. These are the layers the cartel uses to hide their money, their drugs, their businesses. It puts distance between them and their illicit activities." If Morton saw this, he'd be drooling right now. "Without the shell companies, they're exposed."

"So this is proof of what they've been doing?"

"If you connect the dots, yes." It was a silver bullet straight to the heart. He opened the next folder called Accounts. "Do you know how long the feds have been looking for this?"

"Bank accounts. Offshore. Overseas."

"The assets they've been hiding can be frozen with this information. Without money to conduct business as usual, keep the pipeline of drugs flowing, for bribes, it would cut them off at the knees."

"What do you think Transport is?" she asked, pointing to the last folder.

Something his father had once said to him came back. *Transport is the bloodline of the cartel. Their carotid artery. They live or die by it.*

He clicked on the file. "It's a list of the cargo ships they use to transport their drugs in shipping containers. With the names of these vessels, serial numbers and container identifiers, they could be tracked, stopped, searched. Seized. These files show the entire network of Los Chacales. How they transport their drugs, hide their money, the locations of their homes, their safe houses, their properties. This flash drive is the end of the cartel."

She looked up at his IV bag, which was now empty, and removed the needle that had been taped down on his hand. "Are you going to give the thumb drive to Special Agent Morton?"

A part of Jagger wanted to. He'd crush the cartel and have his record expunged, but Morton couldn't save Wendy's life.

Only one thing could.

Jagger went back to the folder of residential properties. He scrolled through until he came across the one in Texas. He'd been to the house in El Paso once, but it had been a long time ago. At first, he thought he might have to recall exactly where it was from memory, but the address was right here in front of him. "Going to Morton is the wrong play. We need to go Texas."

"Why?"

"To see Emilio."

Wendy reeled back, her eyes wide, her mouth open in shock. "You *are* insane. The chicken doesn't pay the fox a visit."

Jagger wasn't a chicken, or a fox. He was a wolf. Trained by jackals and the US Army. "I always knew there were two ways for this blood debt to end. You die or Emilio dies, but I couldn't get to him because he was in jail. Thanks to his little prison break he's not anymore."

"You want to try to kill him?"

"No." Not now that he had these files. "I want to negotiate. Your life and mine for this information."

"The FBI already has Emilio on kidnapping charges that aren't going away, probably a life sentence according to the news. Why would he care about these files?"

"Because of his legacy. If I hand this over to him instead of the FBI, it'll keep his only son, Miguel, out of prison and the Los Chacales stay in power in North America. This file in FBI hands means no safe houses for him, no money for the cartel, no power while he's in prison. He'll negotiate."

"What if he doesn't agree?"

"Then I'll kill him."

"Do you hear yourself?" She sat on the edge of the desk and cupped his face in her hands. "This isn't logical."

Love wasn't logical. It made people crazy. Made them do beautiful things. Terrible things that they wouldn't otherwise. And Jagger would do anything to protect Wendy. "It's the only way."

"We can go to Special Agent Morton. He gets his win and you get your record expunged. The cartel loses power and I stay safe. Then we get our second chance."

Jagger wanted that more than anything, a clean slate and to be with Wendy, but that might not be possible. "There's a blood debt, Wendy. That won't magically disappear. Emilio can be apprehended and sent back to jail. Miguel can be arrested, brought up on charges based on these files, and that blood debt will still exist. The Brethren will seek to carry it out. They will honor it if it's the last thing they do. You'll be looking over your shoulder for the rest of your life. Is that what you want? To know your days are numbered and to spend them waiting for a *sicario* to show up?"

She dropped her hands from his face. "Stop it."

"Because they're going to keep coming until you're dead."

"I said stop." She stood and moved away, but he caught her wrist.

As individual hit men, each person in the Brethren was formidable, but the whole was greater than the sum of its parts. United, they were a terrifying force, and they would honor the code of the blood debt.

"This is the only way. Emilio rescinds the kill order. Or he dies." He got up from the chair and brought her into his arms. "If Morton was a realistic option to keep you alive, I'd take it."

"Witness protection. That's realistic."

"You'll never make it into the program." He nudged her chin up with finger, forcing her to look at him. "Do you know how many steps there are, how long it'll take? The information on the flash drive would put an end to the cartel, but it'd be a slow death. Months, years of red tape in the legal system just to have a trial. Los Chacales won't go down without a fight. Feds will die. Prosecutors will have accidents. Their families will be terrorized and threatened. While that's happening, the Brethren will find you, they'll find *us*, before Emilio or Miguel ever see the inside of a courtroom."

"I don't like it."

"If it's any consolation, neither do I." He also couldn't escape the certainty that this was the right course of action, the one he was always meant to take.

A call to serve led him to become an army Ranger, trained to do precisely what he was proposing. A direct-action raid in a hostile environment to kill a high-value target. Or, if he got lucky, negotiate. His history with the cartel, his father's legacy, was the only thing giving him the chance to pull it off. Out of all the US Marshals who had to seduce Isabel Vargas and persuade her to betray Emilio, it ended up being Dutch Haas.

This was a serious alignment of planets. A once-in-a-lifetime grand trine, but whether the end result of this conjunction would be positive or negative was anyone's guess.

Wendy slid her hands up his chest and linked them behind his neck. "I want you to be safe instead of risking yourself for me again."

"There is one unbreakable moral line above anything else for men like Emilio. Protect your children, no matter the cost." That was why his own father had left him those files. "I can get him to agree to a deal. I know I can." If he was wrong, then he'd put a bullet in Emilio. "I know where I need to go in El Paso, I just don't know how to get there. It's not like I can fly, and that'll be two to three days in a car."

"Are you sure about this?"

He brushed his knuckles across her cheek. "I am."

"Then I might be able to help."

"How?"

"My newest client is Chase Rothersbury. He happens to own a private plane, or rather his family does. That means bypassing TSA, no ID check and no baggage search. We've signed the contract, but I haven't been paid yet. Maybe he'll let us use his plane as payment."

"Us?"

"Wherever you go, I go. You're not leaving me behind."

Getting her out of New York was probably safer anyway, and flying private would be ideal. He wouldn't have to leave any of his gear behind. "Okay." He brushed his lips across hers. She leaned back in his arms, her softness yielding to him, but he didn't mistake her soft body or concession for weakness. She was the most determined, headstrong woman he'd ever met. "Do you think this Rothersbury might help?"

"There's only one way to find out. I'll make the call and ask."

Chapter Eighteen

Wendy held the receiver of the landline phone to her ear. "Chase, thank you for agreeing to this. I know allowing me to use your family's plane instead of paying me is an irregular arrangement."

"It's a win-win. My parents will foot the bill and I'll reap the benefits."

"I appreciate your discretion," she said. It was a done deal. Despite the horror of the past few hours, a smile pulled at her mouth and entered her voice. "I'll be at the hangar at noon sharp and will give your pilot the exact destination then." She had to give him a city within a hundred miles to file the flight plan, but Jagger didn't want Chase or anyone for that matter to know where they were going until they were in the air.

There was a knock at the door and Tina hurried into the office. "You're on TV," she whispered. "The authorities have identified you from the incident in the Lincoln Tunnel, but they still don't know who Jagger is."

Wendy swore at the timing. Then again, this gave her a chance to manage it. "Chase, before you go, I need you to turn on the news for a moment."

"What for?"

"There's something you should see."

Jagger stood. *What are you doing?* he mouthed.

She covered the receiver. "He's going to find out. It's better to face it now." Over the line, she heard the television in the background.

"Wendy, I'm speechless," Chase said. "As my mother can attest, that's rare."

"I haven't done anything illegal, but the authorities have

questions for me." She deliberately made no mention of Jagger. "In twenty-four hours, the optics will have changed."

"Hmm."

With that being his only response, she wished she saw precisely what was being reported.

"I'm no longer comfortable with our arrangement," Chase said. "My current predicament is bad enough as is." A second DUI and property damage in the Hamptons. "I came to you to make it better. Not worse."

"Not helping me will only hurt you."

"How do you figure?"

"You chose me out of the other PR firms for a reason. Do you remember what that was?"

"Everyone else wanted me to hide behind the Rothersbury coattails and do community service. You saw more than my bloodline. You saw me and had great ideas to reform me in the public eye. Your proposal was nothing short of electrifying."

She hadn't even gotten into the nuts and bolts of how she would do it. During a proposal, you had to be impressive without giving the cow away for free. "I'm going to make you a household name. A role model who will inspire young people. Others can learn from your mistakes. You're going to glamourize clean living, a healthy state of mind, supporting the environment." Putting his name and money to worthwhile causes. If other celebrities could get DUIs, resist arrest, assault a police officer and turn that into a popular cabaret show, everything she promised Chase was more than feasible. "I'm going to make you an influencer. I'll be working on rebuilding your image even while you're in rehab."

"That all sounds great, but—"

"I have a contact who is willing to collaborate with you on a mobile app." It was a booming sector of the tech business that Chase was keen to enter, but his profile as a bad boy was toxic and no one wanted to take a chance on him.

"A well-known video game developer. I convinced him that you're perfect for the project, but you'll have to give up your old circle of friends. Consider it a gesture of goodwill that you're serious."

"Isn't rehab a gesture?"

"No. That's court mandated. You'll have some creative input, and I can set up a preliminary meeting before you leave for rehab." It was the biggest carrot she had to dangle. If he didn't bite, they'd have to drive to Texas. "You have very little to lose and everything to gain. What do you say?"

"Okay, but to reduce my risk you leave in three hours. There's hardly any personnel at the Westchester airport at that time, and because the on-call flight crew will get paid time and a half they'll gladly turn a blind eye."

"Sounds good. Thanks." She hung up and looked between Jagger and Tina. "We're taking a red-eye flight."

"That's so soon," Tina said, "but it's probably for the best. The doorman won't say anything about you two. A resident, on the other hand, will call the police in a heartbeat. It'll be easier for you to slip out of the building unseen in the middle of the night."

"Are you sure the cops won't be waiting for us at the airport?"

"Chase has been living in his family's shadow his entire life. The spotlight has only been on him for negative press. Another PR firm can deflect the dirt for a little while with community service photo ops, but I'm the only one who is offering him a way to carve his own path. Not to hide what he's done wrong, but to use it to change the narrative to his benefit."

She was worried about Chase relapsing down the road, but the more invested he was in himself, with things like the mobile app, blogging about his journey—another one of her ideas—forcing him to take public accountability of his lifestyle choices, the better his odds for success.

"He likes my proposal," she said. "Likes the person that he can become with my plan. Calling the cops on me isn't going to turn him into a hero or give him what he wants. Deep down, he knows that."

"Okay," Jagger said.

"I want you to get some rest. We'll leave in two hours."

"You could use a nap, too. Why don't you come lie down with me?" He pulled her close, wrapping his arms around her.

Tina excused herself with a coy smile, closing the door.

Jagger kissed Wendy, really kissed her as he ran his hands down her back and to her hips. Hot and deep and full of need. A familiar hunger burned through her, racing over her skin.

This was everything she wanted and not enough, at the same time. She loved the feel of his lips, the taste of him, the way he touched her with the right mix of tenderness and roughness.

Her plus Jagger together in bed wouldn't equal rest. Kissing, touching, him inside her... She'd thought about it. Wanted him, craved him. Pictured him when she closed her eyes. Remembered the intoxicating pleasure and knowing without a doubt that she belonged with him.

But he was planning to go up against the head of a cartel and had to be at the top of his game, needed his strength.

She eased back. "You died a couple of hours ago. You need to sleep."

"I didn't die. My heart stopped for a second. There was no tunnel. No bright white light. And I still felt you with me."

He owned a piece of her that she prayed would always be with him. In this life and the next.

"Don't fight me on this because you'll lose. If you want to face Emilio, you need to get your strength back. I'm glad Fitz thought to give you the IV, but you also need rest. As much as possible for the next—" she glanced at the clock "—ten hours. Doctor's orders."

"Yes, ma'am." He kissed her nose. "What are you going to do?"

"I need to email my game developer contact and get the ball rolling for Chase." In the event of a worst-case scenario, she wanted to make good on her promises and have Chase poised for success. "Then I'll catch a few winks on the sofa."

"Want to tuck me in?" He waggled his eyebrows, but she saw the fatigue in his eyes.

Smiling, she hauled him into the hallway. "Not a good idea, mister." She nudged him in the direction of the guest room. "Rest."

"Will do." After another kiss, he disappeared into the bedroom, shutting the door.

She went back to the desk and sent the email to the video game developer.

Her gaze fell back to the files on the thumb drive. The folders were still up on the screen.

Even if the negotiation with that madman panned out, they should have copies of the information. What if Emilio decided to double-cross them later? Jagger believed in the code of the cartel, but she didn't trust any of those jackals.

She right clicked on the main folder. The total size of all the documents were over a hundred megabytes. An email attachment supported twenty-five megs. It wasn't as sleek and sexy as having a duplicate flash drive but emailing herself copies of the folders would suffice.

The only problem was if Emilio killed them both, how would justice be served?

Jagger's plan was dangerous, and a million things could go wrong.

The cocktail of hormones and adrenaline must have dulled her common sense if she was going along with this. Not that he'd back down.

When Jagger made up his mind, there was no changing it.

It wasn't that she didn't think he couldn't pull it off—she

knew he was capable, had witnessed it firsthand tonight. He backed up his confidence with lethal action. Put himself in the line of fire and protected her again and again.

Maybe it was time for her to protect him. If only she knew how.

Picking up the landline, she punched in her brother's cell phone number. Once again it went straight to voice mail and the box was full. She still couldn't leave a message.

Dutch, where in the hell are you?

Her brother would drop everything to help her, if only he knew she needed him.

Wendy got up and left the office. She tiptoed down the hall past Jagger's room and found Tina in the living room, watching the news.

"Any more updates?" Wendy asked.

"No. They're clueless as to Jagger's identity." Tina stared at her a moment. "I don't think anyone will recognize you with that black hair."

Wendy had forgotten about the hair dye spray. As soon as she showered, it would be gone. "I know we've asked a lot of you tonight already, but I'd like to trouble you for one more favor."

"Sure. What is it?"

"Jagger and I are going to El Paso to negotiate with Emilio Vargas. There's a chance that things could go sideways."

"Emilio is dangerous. Warren always treaded with care around him. They seemed to have an understanding, but to this day I wonder if Emilio is the reason my Warren died in Venezuela. I traveled with him on his business trips all the time. That's the reason I didn't work while we were together. I had to be able to pick up and go at a moment's notice. But he didn't want me to go to Venezuela."

"Did Emilio go on that trip?"

"Yes, I believe so."

"Does Jagger know?"

Tina shrugged. "We really weren't on speaking terms when Warren died. It was a tough time." She took a framed picture of Warren from the side table and stared at it with fondness in her eyes. "What was the favor, dear?"

"Oh, I wanted to email you a copy of the files we found on the thumb drive. If you don't hear from us in two days, I'd like you to send the documents to my brother. I'll include his email address and phone number in the body of the message."

Wendy could have simply sent the files straight to Dutch right now, but if Jagger managed to pull a white rabbit out of his bag of tricks and Emilio agreed to the deal, her brother would act on the information and the truce would be null and void.

Tina reached over and took her hand. Her skin was paper-thin and soft as cotton, but warm. "I'll do it. For you. For Jagger. For Warren."

"Thank you."

"I do have one request in return. If you two make it through this and come out on the other side, I'd like to see Jagger. At least once a year. A day of his choosing, though I'm partial to the anniversary of Warren passing."

Tina didn't have to say it, the loneliness in her face spoke volumes. No husband, no children. All she had were these pictures, memories and a connection to the man she'd loved through Jagger.

"I'll make sure he visits."

"You'll come, too?" Tina patted her hand. "You seem to have a calming effect on him."

Wendy laughed. "We'll both come visit." And they could do better than once a year.

First, they had to survive.

Chapter Nineteen

On the patio of his safe house, Emilio turned his face up to the Texas sun and stretched after his long nap. Basked in the warm light and the fresh air as a free man. He gazed out at the vast Chihuahuan Desert surrounding the property. Many people assumed that Texas was a hot, dry, barren region, but this was shrub desert, sprinkled with grasses, where many things thrived. The rocky landscape was dotted with cacti and yuccas and agaves, the Guadalupe Mountains not far in the distance.

He loved El Paso. Plenty of space for privacy, and he could count on the sun shining for three hundred days out of the year. That was more than San Diego by double.

There was nothing much around for miles. Set fifty feet from his house were three trailers. Two were for his men. Room for them to unwind and sleep. To bring women for a little fun when they got bored.

The third was reserved for a special purpose.

There was the clack of cowboy boots across the wood floors, growing louder, coming his way. "Lunch is ready, Don Emilio," Samuel said, stepping outside.

"I wish to eat here in the open air."

Behind him, Samuel snapped his fingers and spoke hurriedly to the cooking staff. Dishes and glasses clinked. There was the distinct ting of silverware being set.

"As you wish," Samuel said. "Everything is prepared."

Emilio spun on his heel and looked over the table. Lobster salad with roasted corn. A champagne flute had been set out along with a bottle of Krug Grande Cuvée in a bucket of ice.

His mouth watered as he sat. "Take away the champagne. I'll drink it after I have Special Agent Maximiliano Webb shackled in that trailer." He pointed to the third one. "Receiving his punishment for his betrayal."

Samuel beckoned to one of the cooks, who stood by waiting to make sure everything was up to snuff. "Remove the champagne. Bring him a Scotch."

Good lieutenants who anticipated his desires were hard to find.

The young woman bowed her head, came around the table, and took away the champagne and flute.

"You'll have Max soon. He'll be here tonight."

"Excellent." Emilio took a bite of lobster. The sweet, tender meat practically melted in his mouth. Cooked to perfection. He would've invited Samuel to join him, but that was the mistake he'd made in the past with other lieutenants. Allowed them to get too close. Permitted the line between professionalism and friendship to blur.

That's what burned him down the marrow of his bone. Not only had he trusted Max, but also he thought of the man as a friend. A confidant.

"I want him to suffer," Emilio said. "Make it slow and painful, but when I'm finally ready to kill him, I want him to be conscious enough to know that I'm the one pulling the trigger."

Delicate business keeping a prisoner alive and aware through hours of torture. It needed to be planned with care and executed with finesse. He had the utmost confidence in Samuel's skills.

"*Sí*, Don Emilio. It will be done."

The young woman returned, carrying a bottle of Scotch. Thirty-year-old Isle of Jura. His favorite. She set the bottle on the table and Samuel poured his drink.

Emilio swirled the amber liquid in his crystal tumbler. Inhaled the scent of vanilla and guava and toasted oak. He sipped it, letting the full-bodied flavors roll over his tongue.

Moaning his satisfaction, he smiled. Everything tasted better after being released from captivity.

He pierced a fat piece of lobster on his fork and was about to savor another bite when Samuel's cell phone rang.

"It's Pilar Zahiri. She called while you were sleeping. She wanted to speak with you directly, but I told her you gave orders not to be disturbed."

Pilar. Intelligent. Beautiful. Deadly. Loyal. Everything he wanted in a daughter-in-law. She'd be the perfect mate for Miguel. His equal. Perhaps even his son's better in some ways.

Lowering the fork, he extended his other hand for the phone. "Yes, Pilar," he said, as one of his other bodyguards came outside, whispered in Samuel's ear, and passed him another phone.

Samuel stepped away, taking the call.

"Don Emilio, you're awake. Good. I'm calling with news. I found out why Jagger Carr is protecting the woman."

If anyone could, it was her. "Tell me, my dear. Apparently, you're the only one capable. My men are still in the dark about Jagger."

"That's because they've been looking in the wrong place. Digging into his present when they should've been looking into his past."

"As titillating as you make the suspense, my patience is thin."

"Wendy Haas is the reason Jagger went to prison. She was the woman he was living with at the time. The one he got into a fight over and killed a man."

At the time of Jagger's trial, her name hadn't been mentioned in the newspaper and Jagger had never discussed the incident with anyone in the cartel to his knowledge.

"How can you be certain?"

"I saw him last night," Pilar said. "He came to me desperate for help and spilled his guts. We fought. I injured him, but he got away."

Emilio picked up his glass and took a gulp of Scotch. The sweet burn slid down his throat, taking the chill away from his belly. Jagger had already gone to prison once for the woman. There was no way he was going to throw her to the jackals.

Jagger Carr had drawn a line in the sand.

"Is there anything else, my dear?"

There was a pause. A long, deliberate pause because Pilar never did anything by accident. Every move, every word, was calculated. The way she was able to think on her feet was astounding.

"No, Don Emilio. I only wish to be of service."

Pilar was young, but she understood what it took many others a lifetime to learn. The people who were useful and could do something for you got respect, curried favor, and the ones who were useless lost it.

He had no time for useless things. Or people.

"You have been. Good job." He disconnected and handed the phone back to Samuel.

The pause from her taunted him. She wanted to say more, but hadn't. Perhaps she was concerned about Jagger. They had once been close friends.

Friends were a liability in this business. Most of the time. There were always rare exceptions. Emilio missed Warren. The one true friend he had and considered to be like family. That man had stuck with him through the highs and lows, thick and thin. They didn't make them like Warren anymore.

It was a shame he was going to have to kill his son.

Samuel finished his phone call and took a seat. "That was Alaric. Late last night they lost the signal on Jagger's GPS tracker. They're not sure why. No one has confirmed a kill. They were hoping his body would turn up in a morgue."

Samuel shook his head. "No luck. It's still possible that he's dead."

That would be too convenient.

Emilio didn't like it. Something was off about the situation. Not the least of which was that both Pilar and Alaric had waited hours to update him. "It's also possible that Jagger figured out somehow that we were tracking him and found a way to neutralize the signal." Emilio never underestimated someone's will to survive. "Tell the others to assume Jagger Carr is alive and when they find him, he's fair game."

JAGGER HAD PARKED the beater vehicle they'd rented using cash behind a rocky mound.

Looking through the binoculars, he watched Emilio Vargas eating on his patio. The man had just broken out of prison and was dining on lobster and drinking Scotch, the good stuff, like he was on vacation at a resort.

It was too bad Jagger didn't have the training or proper rifle to be a sniper. This range was doable. They were less than twelve hundred yards away.

Security was light. Five bodyguards. Two vehicles. A couple of household staff.

Sweat rolled off his forehead. It was hotter than Hades. The temperature had climbed to record-breaking ninety and he couldn't wait for the sun to go down for multiple reasons.

He lowered the binoculars. "Are you clear on the plan?"

"We'll come back after nightfall. I'll hang back here while you go do your Ranger thing, taking out the men in the trailers and around the perimeter first. If I see anyone coming up behind you," she said, and tapped the package of Bluetooth intercom earpieces they'd purchased in the El Paso airport, "I've got you covered and I'll let you know. Once you're in the house, you're on your own."

"I'll ditch the earpiece inside. I don't want Emilio to know

I'm communicating with anyone. No matter what happens, once I'm in the house, you do not follow me in."

Wendy nodded.

"Honey, I need to hear you say it."

"I won't follow you inside. I promise. No matter what."

"Don't forget to remain aware of your surroundings. There are mountain lions, snakes and other predators in the area."

"As long as there are no jackals, I'll be okay."

He kissed her forehead. "We've got eight hours to kill. Let's get out of here."

They climbed into the old pickup truck, and he eased away from the spot he'd scouted.

He turned the truck around and went at a slow speed, twenty miles per hour. More of a crawl. It helped prevent kicking up dust in the air as they drove away, which would draw dangerous attention. The rocky terrain helped mask their leaving the area, but he needed to do all he could to maintain the element of surprise.

"I really owe Chase Rothersbury one," Wendy said.

"He came through. I guess you're pretty good at reading people."

"I have to be for my job."

He finally reached the main road and pressed down on the gas pedal. They zipped off along the asphalt. "I always pictured you at some high-powered PR firm. How were you able to start your own company and compete with the big dogs?"

"So you don't know everything about me." Wendy smiled. "I was at a big, high-powered company for a while. I'd built up my client list and was starting to make a name for myself. One of the partners invited me to dinner at a restaurant in a hotel to discuss my future. I went. Like an idiot."

Jagger tightened his hands on the steering wheel. "He put the moves on you?"

"He did. His approach was very transactional. If I slept

with him, I would do well. If I didn't, I would never advance. *The choice is yours*, he'd said to me."

"Did you slap him? Throw a knee to his groin."

"No, Jagger. Although, sometimes when I think back on it, I wish I had been brave enough to throw a drink in his face."

"You are brave. Don't ever let some idiot make you think otherwise." He took her hand and squeezed. "What did you do?"

"I quit and took a couple of clients with me. About week later, a different partner came to see me. The only woman in the firm. She knew what I had been through without me telling her the story, and she didn't share many details of what had happened to her. After she apologized for not being a mentor to me, she informed me that she had threatened the other partners. If they invoked the noncompete clause in my contract, which would've made me liable for taking those two clients, she was going round up all the women they'd harassed and encourage them to file a lawsuit. Then she offered me seed money to start my own company. She's my silent partner. From time to time, she floats clients my way, ones that would be a better fit for a young progressive than the other firm."

"It took courage to quit and go out on your own. I'm proud of you. You're a trailblazer."

A blush rose to her creamy cheeks. "Thanks, but she's the reason I was able to make it and become so successful so fast."

"You're the person who puts in the hard work and convinces clients to sign on the dotted line. You made your company a success."

He turned into the small motel off the I-10 Interstate, outside the city, where they'd gotten a room. Forty bucks a night. Unlike Manhattan, here they could pay cash and leave a little extra for incidentals. Nobody cared and no one questioned that they didn't use a credit card.

Parking in front of their room, he shut off the engine. She unlocked the room door while he gathered up their gear.

"Next time we go out, it'll be dark. Do you think it's okay if I wash this dye out of my hair? Every time I touch the stuff, it gets on my fingers."

"It should be fine," he said, dumping everything on the desk. "When we leave, wear your hair up and put the ball cap on." He wiped sweat from his forehead with the back of his hand. "I'll shower after you. Feel free to use as much hot water as you need."

A cold shower would do him good. Since they had been at Tina's, he'd been thinking about tearing off Wendy's clothes. Touching her on the bed. Making love to her on the plane. Even when they'd first arrived at the motel in El Paso, but she'd been more focused on the mission than he was.

Ten minutes under the cold spray of water would reset his mind.

Wendy kicked off her shoes and pulled her top overhead, revealing her lace bra. "Or you could join me?"

"In the shower?"

A ghost of a smile curved her lips and she stepped backward into the bathroom. "Yeah." She turned on the water and her gaze returned to his. "We used to shower together all the time. Remember?"

More like make love together in the shower all the time because he couldn't control himself being within reach of her naked body, with water sluicing over her curves. Getting her soapy and clean, just to have the pleasure of dirtying her up again, had been…irresistible.

How could he ever forget? "I remember."

She unzipped her jeans, slid them down her hips, past her thighs and took them off.

His gaze toured over the swell of her breasts, down her

slim waist, to her shapely thighs and back up to her face. "You're still the most enticing woman I've ever seen."

"Is that a yes?"

"No," he said, and her smile faltered. "That's a *hell*, yes."

WENDY HELD OUT her hand to Jagger and he went to her without hesitation. She tugged his shirt off and said, "Let me look at you a minute."

Even with excitement blazing in his eyes and his fingers twitching from his crumbling control, he stood still. There were times she used to tease him with her fingers and mouth until he was a quivering, begging mess. That's what they did, gave their bodies to each other. With complete trust.

She took in the sight of him, let her hands explore his chest. Strong, sculpted, solid, thicker with muscle than before. Gently she traced around the wound on his side. "Are you going to be okay if we do this?"

His heavy breathing filled the heated air between them. "I'll be better than okay. Probably the best I've ever been. Trust me."

She reached for his belt, struggled to unclasp the buckle, and unzipped his jeans. "Condoms?"

"I picked some up in the airport when we got the earpieces."

"I missed that. You're sly." She slipped her hand inside his pants, palmed his growing erection in one hand and felt the hammering of his heart under the other pressed to his chest.

A husky growl rumbled in his throat, and it was the sexiest sound, spurring her on.

"I'm not sly, I'm just always prepared," he said, and whipped out a condom from his pocket.

"Indeed, you are." This was the quiet before the storm. Their chance to love each other. To be bold and honest. Not hold anything back. "I want you."

When his lips touched hers, she sighed, melting against

him. His hand cupped her breast, tugging down the front of her bra, and he dragged his thumb over her nipple. A needy sound from the back of her throat spilled from her lips into his mouth.

Easing away, he looked down at her and licked his lips. He unhooked her bra, letting it fall to the floor. She glanced at her bare chest. The tight, rosy points of her breasts declaring how aroused she was made her cheeks heat.

Smiling, he gripped the thin waistband of her panties and pulled it down.

On his way back up, he shed his jeans and boxer briefs and showered her legs with kisses and licks and nibbles. His eyes finally met hers. "You're so beautiful I can barely stand it."

She dragged him into the shower under the warm spray of water. A thrill rushed through her.

"Hang on." He grabbed the tiny bottle of shampoo, poured some in his hand and worked up a thick lather in her hair. Massaging her scalp with slow, sensuous strokes, he made her whole her body soften.

He put her back under the water and rinsed her hair. He brought his soapy hands to her shoulders and rubbed them, skimming his fingers over her throat, down her back, up to her breasts.

All of it was more intimate than sex somehow and required a level of vulnerability she'd never had with anyone else.

Turning, she ran her hands up his chest, brought his head down and kissed the hell out of him.

Their hands roamed over each other, her body sliding against his in the water.

"I want you inside me?" she whispered.

"Where do you want me? Here." His thumb skimmed her lips, dipping into her mouth, and she sucked his finger. "Or…" His hand drifted down her body, caressing every inch along the way, and his fingers slipped between her thighs, diving inside her while hers stroked the thick length of him. "Here?"

"Do I have to pick and choose?" she asked around a needy whimper.

"I would never be that selfish."

She laughed, he laughed, and they kissed. She'd missed this. The affection and the fun. How playful they'd been together. His mouth, that tongue, his hands, his chest pressed to hers.

Their attraction was visceral, the heat building around them like a cocoon. The rest of the world disappeared. Nothing else existed but the two of them, locked together in that bittersweet moment, and she wished the sun would never set.

Chapter Twenty

A dark thrill coursed through Emilio as he stood in the trailer reserved for his guest. "Special Agent Maximiliano Webb."

With his hands and ankles handcuffed to a steel chair that had been bolted to the floor, Max stared at him. His long hair had been shorn. His beard was gone, and his face was clean-shaven. He looked like Samson after he lost his strength. A different man. Of course, that was the point. Once he finished a deep cover assignment, the FBI would want him to change his appearance.

Max's face was bruised, bottom lip split, knuckles bloody from fighting back.

He was still in fairly good condition, barely harmed, but Emilio's men were just getting started.

"Don Emilio," Max said.

"Still you use the title of respect for me. Why?"

"Respect?" Max spit blood onto the floor. "For me, don means scumbag, miscreant, swine. And those are some of the kinder definitions."

"I'm above the law, Maximiliano. Haven't you learned that by now?"

"No one is above the law."

"Yet, here I stand. Free. On American soil. I didn't crawl through a tunnel back into Mexico like a rat trying to escape a sinking ship." Emilio shoved his hands into the pockets of his linen pants. "While you are in *my* trailer. Chained like an animal to *my* chair. And before you die, you will know *my* brand of justice in excruciating detail."

"You've got it all planned out, huh?"

"As a matter of fact, I do. After you're dead, I'll track down your loved ones and make them suffer, too. Your ex-wife and your son."

"They're not a part of this." Max struggled against the handcuffs like he wanted to tear Emilio to bits with his bare teeth.

"You made them a part of this. By gambling, playing against me instead of for me. Don't get upset when the house wins. And the house always wins."

"That's all you understand. Violence. Anger. Revenge. Isn't it?"

"I do know these things, intimately." His life had been hard, and if he had not become a brutal man capable of unspeakable horrors, he wouldn't have survived. A man like Max would never understand the things Emilio had survived, endured, so he would not waste his time or breath explaining it. "I also know love and joy and mercy."

"Yet, you still lost Isabel because she saw you for the monster that you really are."

His heart suddenly felt brittle and squeezed painfully in his chest. His mind shouted at him to silence Max with a bullet, but he would not be overcome with rage. Instead he would take pleasure in this man's punishment.

"If you so much as whisper her name again," Emilio said softly, "I will have them cut out your tongue."

There was a flicker of something in Max's eyes—fear, panic, Emilio couldn't be sure. Whatever it was, he very much liked seeing it.

"You may think you have a monopoly on justice and that you're above the law," Max said, "but karma is coming for you. It's just a matter of time."

A smug smile tugged at Emilio's mouth. "When my men are done hurting you, I will come back to send you on your way to hell." Pivoting on his heel, he moved toward the door.

"Do you hear that?" Max asked.

Emilio glanced at him over his shoulder. "Hear what?"

"Ticktock."

Emilio felt his smile slip away as his jaw hardened. A

cold niggle of dread stirred in his belly, but he quickly dismissed it. "Soon the only thing you'll hear is the sound of your own screams."

JAGGER HANDED WENDY the binoculars. "Emilio is heading back inside the house."

"There's a lot more activity than earlier."

"Two more vehicles showed up. Extra men. By my count there are now ten."

He laid out all the weapons from his pack on the hood of the truck. After taking inventory for the third time, he geared up. Two 9 mm guns with silencers went into holsters. Extra loaded magazines and his garrote were in his pockets. He had already rigged a detonator to six ounces of C-4, to be able to use it quickly.

The timing of when he set it off had to be right, because once it blew everyone would know he was there, and the element of surprise would be lost.

The last smoke grenade he stuffed into a utility pocket of the cargo pants he'd picked up at a thrift store near their motel.

After he attached the sound suppressor to his Heckler & Koch MP5 submachine gun, he slipped the strap over his head and one shoulder. It was too bad he didn't have his sophisticated laser sight. Wendy had done the best she could, packing in a hurry. He was lucky to have this much gear.

Jagger picked up his switchblade. He pushed the release button and the blade flashed out with a harsh metallic click. Flipping the knife in his palm, he handed it to Wendy, handle first.

She took knife and hit the button, retracting the blade.

"Please take one of the guns," he said, wishing he had the shotgun to leave her.

"No, you'll need them. I'll be way back here, safe."

"The wildlife in the area can be dangerous. Maybe you should wait in the truck. Or better yet, go back to the motel."

Her beautiful eyes gleamed with stubbornness. "I'm not leaving you. And I'm not staying in the truck. I won't be able to see the house, and the very least I can do is cover your back."

"What are you going to do if you see a mountain lion?"

"Stay away from it."

"What if it doesn't stay away from you?"

She hit the button on the knife and the blade glinted in the moonlight. "Satisfied?"

Hardly. Shaking his head, he went around to the back of the truck and pulled out the emergency road kit. When he'd checked it earlier, he'd seen a flare gun. Not uncommon to have one out here in the desert in case you got stranded.

He handed her the flare gun. "It'll scare off a predator, but if you get into trouble, tell me."

A beat of hesitation. "Okay, I will," she said, and he knew she was lying.

"I won't be able to focus if I'm worried about you. That's the kind of distraction that could get me killed. I need to trust that you'll tell me."

It was a test of sorts. If she lied again, he was hauling her back to the motel and duct taping her to a chair until this was done. She'd hate it. He'd hate doing it. But she'd be safe, and that was all that mattered to him. The thought of her in danger sent his heart into free fall every time.

She brushed her thumb over his forehead, down the side of his face, rubbed his bottom lip, and his brain misfired, his thoughts careening back to the motel room, under the water with her, in the bed, falling asleep with his arms wrapped around her, holding her as close as possible. Feeling like they were one again.

What was she doing to him? Turning him to mush when he needed to steel himself for battle.

"You owe me more kisses and showers, and I intend to collect," she said, her voice firm and sure. "So, put your mind at ease. If I'm in trouble, you'll know."

He believed her.

She handed him his earpiece and put hers in.

He pulled her to him, needing to kiss her, but she put her fingertips up to his mouth.

"After," she said, and he thought back to being in the ambulance, preparing to die. "For now, get your head in the game, soldier." She shoved back, slid the knife into her pocket, put the flare gun on the hood and grabbed the binoculars.

She. Was. Right.

His sole focus had to be getting to Emilio. The man was going to cancel the blood debt or Jagger would kill him, effectively putting an end to it anyway. Either way worked for him.

He headed out in a slow jog under the cover of darkness and didn't look back. "Testing. One. Two. Three."

"I've got you loud and clear," she said, her voice husky in his ear.

He used the terrain to mask his approach. Quick and quiet, he stayed low, dropping to the ground when necessary, using the shrubs as concealment. The wind whistled across the land. Noises grew louder the closer he got. People talking. Music playing somewhere. He crept up to one of the trailers without incident and peeked through a break in the curtains.

A guard was inside with a young woman Jagger had seen earlier in the house. She was sitting on his lap with a look of disgust, which didn't stop the guy from touching her.

"The door to the first trailer closest to the house just opened," Wendy said.

Jagger crouched low, pressing up against the side of the third trailer.

"A man left. He's walking into the house. One of the guards out front followed him inside, but two guards are still patrolling the perimeter."

He didn't respond verbally, not wanting to alert anyone that he was there, but gave her a thumbs-up.

"I see you," she said, as if reading his mind.

Jagger pressed on to the next trailer. A radio was playing. The lyrics were Spanish. Three men were sitting around drinking beer and playing cards.

He put the C-4 against the wall where the sofa was on the other side. This would kill three birds with one stone, but he didn't set the timer, leaving it set to explode with a manual trigger. He had the detonator tucked away close.

Drawing the MP5 up at the ready, he darted to the last trailer, the one closest to the house. Unlike the others, there were no windows. He had no idea how many men were inside, but he made out the sound of flesh hitting flesh. Grunts of pain interlaced with profanity.

The only door faced the house. That meant he'd have to take out the two guards on patrol first and hope no one spotted their dead bodies before he detonated the C-4.

He edged around the side of the trailer and sneaked a quick glance.

One guard was vigilant, his head on a swivel, his rifle in his hands. The other was smoking, and had his weapon slung over his shoulder. As soon as the wary guard turned away, Jagger was up and pumped two bullets into the back of his head.

Moving forward swiftly, he nailed the smoker, who had a deer-in-the-headlights look. Two bullets center mass. His body fell backward with a soft thump.

"You're all clear," Wendy said. "No one is looking out the windows or outside on either patio."

Still, he scanned the area as he hustled to the first trailer. Force of habit. He grabbed the handle and flung the door open.

Two guards were taking turns beating on a third man who was handcuffed to a chair.

Jagger aimed and shot, dropping them before they screamed for help. He swept inside, shutting the door behind him. "Who are you? Why does Vargas have you here?"

"I'm FBI. Max Webb. I was undercover in his organization. I'm part of the reason he was going to jail."

"Good enough for me." Jagger searched the pockets of the other men for the keys.

"Who are you?"

"Jagger Carr."

"Why are you here?"

Bingo. He found the keys and hurried to release the guy. "Emilio put out a blood debt kill order on my girlfriend." The word sounded so small and insignificant to describe what she was to him. "I'm here to resolve the issue." Although the FBI agent's presence complicated the matter. That resolution was looking more and more like it would come in the form of a bullet.

"Who's your girlfriend?" Agent Webb stood, rubbing his wrists.

"Wendy Haas."

The agent froze. "Haas? Any relation to Dutch Haas?"

"Yeah. You know him?"

"I do. Small world. I helped Dutch and Isabel Vargas once." Agent Webb pulled a Glock out of one of the dead guy's holsters. "You should get out of here."

"I can't. Besides, I think you could use the backup. I've got C-4 rigged to the middle trailer. Three guards inside. There's a fourth with a woman in the trailer farthest from the house. She looks to be innocent, maybe household staff. After I blow it, you take out the fourth guy and go call the cavalry."

"What are you going to do?"

"I've got unresolved business with Vargas." There were

four more men inside the house standing between him and Emilio. Jagger was putting an end to the blood debt, come hell or high water. Nothing was going to stand in his way. He grasped the door handle. "Is it clear outside?" he asked Wendy.

"You're good."

"Ready?" Jagger asked the special agent, gun in his hand.

Webb gave a curt nod, holding the Glock.

They swept outside going in different directions. Jagger went around the side of the house to a patio door. It was unlocked.

"Headed inside," he said.

"Got it." Wendy's voice was a whisper. "Stay safe."

He took out the earpiece, shoved it into one of his cargo pockets and hit the button on the detonator.

WENDY JUMPED BACK as the middle trailer blew.

The explosion was startling, rocking the quiet. The fireball roared up into the dark sky. She'd nearly dropped the flare gun under her arm.

Swinging the binoculars back to where Jagger had been, she searched for him, but he was gone. Disappeared inside the house.

She pulled out the earpiece, and her body sagged with worry for Jagger. There was another man helping him now, but Jagger was still on his own in the house. By her count that left four more guards.

A chill slid down her spine, drawing her shoulder blades tight. It was the eerie feeling she had when someone was watching her.

She spun around and came face-to-face with Pilar and the barrel of her gun. Fear choked her as air backed up in her lungs.

Pilar came right for her. No hesitation. No banter. She seized the flare gun from under Wendy's arm and tossed it away. "Run and I shoot you. Scream and I shoot you." Pilar's cold eyes were narrowed in focus, her long dark hair was drawn into a slick ponytail, and she was dressed in black, blending in with the darkness. "Get in the truck, behind the wheel."

Wendy struggled to think, but the panicked rush of blood through her head made her brain cramp.

"Now!" Pilar said in a harsh whip of anger that got Wendy moving.

She got in the truck as Pilar climbed into the passenger's seat, keeping the gun pointed at Wendy's face.

"Drive to the house."

Wendy started the truck and threw it into Drive. Nerves took off in a wild dance in her stomach. "What are you doing here?"

"I got on the first flight this morning, at the crack of dawn. Last night, I baited Jagger. Dangled the lure of Emilio in El Paso. With your life on the line, I figured he couldn't resist. So, I came to reel in my catch and get the credit I'm due."

Wendy tried to control the anxiety welling inside her, but her whole body was shaking. "But why? You're friends. He trusted you."

"We are friends, but it doesn't serve my interests to remain friendly. I'm tired of my arrangement with Miguel, waiting for him to give me control of the Brethren. If I want the position, I have to take it. Show Emilio what I'm capable of. My value."

What a snake. "How did you know I was out here?"

"I've been lurking around the property all day. Spying on you while you scouted the place."

Oh, God. Her stomach clenched under a wave of nausea. "Emilio knows we're here? Jagger's walking into a trap?"

"No. If I had warned Emilio, then I would've had to ask permission to come. I'm more of a beg-forgiveness kind of woman. If Emilio had welcomed me with open arms, he would've let his men handle the situation, while pawing me, trying to turn me into his diversion in the desert." Her mouth twisted in revulsion. "No, thank you. That doesn't serve my interest either." Pilar's voice was pure steel. "But this little surprise does. These men… They look at me and see a mistress. It's time I opened their eyes to what I really am."

Panic slid through Wendy's veins. "What's that?"

"A cold-blooded mercenary."

JAGGER'S SIDE ACHED. He'd taken out three guards inside the house. One had hit him right in his wound, but he'd still managed to snap the man's neck.

There was one more guard. Jagger suspected the man was being a dutiful lieutenant and protecting his don.

Jagger was low on ammo. The submachine gun was empty. Only one 9 mm was fully loaded and the other was down to two bullets. At least he still had the smoke grenade.

He headed down the hall toward the office.

The door was closed. Most likely locked. He stopped in the doorway of a supply room short of the office.

After he squeezed off a couple of rounds, aiming at the lock, he ducked into the supply room just as the barrage of gunfire he expected came his way.

Hot slugs tore through the hallway. He got down on his belly, peered around the frame and smiled. All those bullets were eating up the door. It had already swung open partially and only chunks were left hanging from hinges.

Jagger popped the smoke grenade and rolled the canister down the hall. It clanked as it tumbled, landing in the office as the white phosphorous dispersed.

The hail of gunfire stopped.

Jagger hopped up and was on the move. He stormed down the hall, staying light on his feet so as not to make a sound, and charged into the office.

Through the smoke, he made out two figures shuffling into an adjoining room.

Determination fired through Jagger. He hustled forward, refusing to let them get away. Emilio Vargas was a disease, a cancer that brought misery and death.

It was time for this to end.

A lieutenant helped Emilio toward the patio doors in a small private living room. Jagger rushed them. The guard whirled around, jumping in front of Emilio.

Jagger pulled the trigger. The man stumbled backward, and Jagger squeezed the trigger again, punching another two rounds into the man's chest, sending him falling to the floor.

As Jagger shifted the muzzle to his true target, Emilio raised his own weapon, finger on the trigger, and pointed at Jagger's head.

They were locked in a standoff. If Jagger fired, Emilio would also be able to squeeze off a shot. Without a bullet-proof vest, the gamble wasn't worth taking. Jagger needed to get him to lower the weapon first.

"This is over," Jagger said. "You're finished."

"I'm just getting started."

"The FBI agent is loose. He's in the wind, calling his buddies to come haul you back to jail."

"They'll have to find me first. I won't be sitting here waiting for them." Emilio edged toward the patio door.

"They will eventually find you. But I don't care about that. I care about Wendy Haas."

Emilio smiled, then his grin turned into a snarl, with teeth bared. "The blood debt must be paid. And you must answer for your betrayal."

"Or I give you the flash drive in my pocket. Records my father kept. Bank accounts. Documentation on your shell companies. Every detail of how you transport your drugs. It'll send Miguel to prison as well. For a very, very long time."

Emilio paled. "No. Not Warren, too." His gun wavered, but it didn't lower.

The muzzle was still pointed at Jagger's face. A shot would be fatal.

"Can no one be trusted?" Emilio said. "At least I'll no longer feel guilty about what happened to him in Venezuela."

Jagger's racing pulse slowed as the words sank in. "What really happened to him?"

Emilio's eyes hardened. "You'll never know."

The taunt was meant to throw Jagger off, have him spinning. His father was dead, and the truth wouldn't change it. He had to focus. No distractions.

"The flash drive is in my pocket. You agree to release Wendy from this debt and spare me, and I hand over all the evidence that would destroy the cartel. Miguel will stay safe." Jagger waited for an opening, for the gun to drop in the slightest. "Do we have a deal?"

Emilio's gaze flashed toward movement coming from the office.

Jagger pulled the second gun that was low on ammo and aimed at the newest threat.

Pilar emerged from the smoke. She had Wendy in front of her with a gun pressed to the back of her head.

Jagger's heart lurched.

"I have a better proposal," said Pilar. "Don Emilio gets the flash drive. I kill Wendy. He kills you. Then I take my rightful place as head of the Brethren." She yanked Wendy's head back, positioning her as a shield.

Even though Pilar's grip on Wendy's hair must've been painful, she didn't cower or cry.

"I'm sorry," Wendy said, her voice low but firm.

"Aww." Pilar's tone was mocking. "That's so adorable."

The situation was a powder keg. From this angle, Jagger's options were limited, but he had to get Wendy through this.

He had to kill Emilio, even if it meant that Jagger wasn't walking away.

"What are you doing, Pilar?" Jagger asked, his gaze bouncing between her and Emilio, keeping a gun trained on each of them, knowing how vulnerable the position made him.

"Earning a promotion," Pilar said, full of ego. "No hard feelings. This is business." Her gaze swung across the room to Emilio. "What do you say to my proposal? You know how I love to be of service."

Jagger had been such a fool to trust her. She was using the discord between Emilio and Miguel, and exploiting Jagger's situation with the blood debt, to get what she wanted.

"Later, you'll tell me how you arrived in the nick of time. For now." Emilio smiled. "You have a deal."

One second everyone held their position, and the next, the room erupted into chaos.

A flash of movement on the patio caught Jagger's eye. Then a gunshot rang out. Don Emilio's body spun from the impact as he dropped the gun and staggered back.

Jagger glimpsed Agent Webb on the patio.

Pilar redirected her weapon outside, keeping a hand on the back of Wendy's neck, using her as a human shield while returning fire.

Jagger didn't have a clear shot. Damn it.

During the commotion, he caught Wendy moving her hand. She whipped out the switchblade from her pocket, pressed the button and jammed the knife behind her into Pilar's leg.

Pilar roared in pain as Wendy dove for the floor.

Before Jagger could seize the opening and pull the trigger, incoming gunfire from the window slammed into Pilar's chest, throwing her body backward.

Pilar hit the wall and slid down. Dead.

Wendy's eyes flared wide, filled with fear, but she wasn't

looking at the dead woman. Jagger followed her gaze to the other side of the room.

Emilio had picked up his gun and was taking aim, with Wendy in his sights.

Jagger's heart clenched in his chest. In a blink, he raised his weapon and opened fire. At the same time, Agent Webb pulled the trigger, too.

Emilio took bullets from both men. Jagger didn't stop shooting until his weapon was empty. Emilio crumpled to the floor in a lifeless heap.

For a surreal second, Jagger was in shock. It was over. Don Emilio Vargas was dead.

"Wendy," Jagger called out, his eyes burning. He reached her, dropping to his knees beside her, and pulled her into his arms. "Are you hurt?"

Wendy shook her head. "I'm fine." She cupped his cheek. "I was so scared."

"I'm sorry I let Pilar get to you." God, the thought of what could have happened to her made his blood run cold.

"I wasn't scared for myself. I was scared for you. That you might be walking into a trap."

Pilar had had a gun to her head and Wendy's concern had been for him. Not herself. She was an amazing woman with the biggest heart.

He kissed her. "That was quick thinking, using the knife."

"My brain shut down somewhere in the truck with Pilar. I just reacted."

"Still, you have impressive instincts."

"I can say the same about you, Carr," Agent Webb said, coming in from the broken patio door. "You took out a ton of men. Saved me a lot of pain, not to mention my life. I owe you. Big. What's your background?"

"US Army Rangers."

Webb nodded. "You did good." He knelt and checked Emilio's pulse, ensuring he was dead. "I called the police using one of the guard's phones. They've already mobilized and are on the way here with the local US Marshals." Webb went to Pilar and confirmed she was down permanently.

"But how?" Jagger asked.

"I don't know, a tip-off. Maybe good old karma." Webb looked around. "We should wait for them outside. Preserve the scene so we don't move anything by accident." He led the way out.

Jagger pushed to his feet and helped Wendy up from the floor.

"Thank you," she said.

"For what?"

"Everything." She wrapped her arms around waist and put her head to his chest.

With his arm around her shoulder, they made their way out to the front of the house.

"Jagger, now that I'm out of danger, do you plan to stick around?"

"I'm still a convicted felon. Being with me could complicate your life."

"Give the flash drive to Special Agent Morton. Better yet, we know a special agent that owes you big." She hiked her chin at Max Webb. "I'm sure he'd help you. After all, you did save his life."

Flashing police lights from a long line of cars were coming down the road.

"If for some reason, it doesn't work, and my record remains?" He leaned back, eyeing her, a frown tugging at his brow.

"Record or no record, we work. We've been through so much. Don't we deserve this, to be together, to have our second chance."

"Even if the cost is a major hit to your career?"

"I love you and I want to be with you. No matter the

cost." She cupped his face and pulled him down for a kiss that made his knees grow weak, and his heart ache with joy.

They'd already paid such a high price. He wanted to start a future with her right now. "I do owe you a lifetime of kisses."

"And showers. Breakfasts in bed while we do the crossword puzzle." She laid her head on his shoulder and he soaked in her warmth. "You once promised to get me a dog."

He had. Made lots of promises, and he wanted to make good on all of them.

The police and the marshals pulled up. Agent Webb spoke to them and directed one of the marshals over to them.

"Hello, I'm Deputy Marshal Laura Kirby, are you Wendy Haas and Jagger Carr?"

"Yes," they said in unison.

"Good. Your brother is going to be relieved to know that you're all right."

"Dutch?" Wendy straightened. "I haven't been able to get in contact with him."

"He was traveling, flying back from Alaska. When he landed, he was briefed on the situation with the cartel. He saw that you had called him, but he couldn't get a hold of you."

They had never turned her phone back on, not wanting to take the chance.

"But he had a missed call from a New York number he didn't recognize and called it back. He spoke with Tina Jennings. She gave him information that led us here."

Jagger looked to Wendy. "What did you do?"

"I wanted to help you and to see justice served if things went south."

He picked her up in a bear hug, kissed her cheek and then set her down. "Good instincts, honey. Don't ever doubt yourself."

"Let's get you two down to our marshal's office," Deputy Marshal Kirby said. "Your brother is expecting a phone call."

"I also need to speak to Special Agent Webb," Jagger said. Wendy's idea was great. He'd probably have better luck with Webb than Morton.

"You'll get a chance. They're going to bring him down to our office once he's finished here."

They followed Kirby to her car and climbed into the back.

He held Wendy's hand, and she put her head on his shoulder. The sense that everything was right in the world and the scales had been rebalanced came over him.

"Do you think the Brethren will leave me alone now?"

"Once they get word that Emilio is dead, yes, and after Miguel is arrested and his assets are frozen, they'll do what they can to help him avoid a conviction. But we should probably lay low for a bit, until the dust settles."

"Dutch will help us figure out the next step." She stroked his legged and he relaxed. "This whole thing has made me believe in fate. Like we're destined to be. As long as we're together, we'll be all right."

He tucked her in closer against his side. His heart was so full of love and something else he hadn't known in a long time—hope. "Well, we can't fight destiny."

Epilogue

Wendy walked through her town house in Arlington, Virginia, arm in arm with Isabel.

"It's gorgeous," Wendy said, holding up Isabel's hand, letting the sunlight streaming through the bay window reflect off her diamond engagement ring. "I'm surprised Dutch did such a fantastic job."

"I heard that!" Dutch called from upstairs.

"It was a compliment," Wendy said. "Not that you should be eavesdropping."

"I love how your wedding band matches your engagement ring," Isabel said. "It's gorgeous."

"Come up and take a look at it," Dutch said. "It's almost finished."

"Do you guys want some beers?" Isabel asked.

"It'd be kindly appreciated, sweetheart, after all our hard work," Dutch said, and Jagger grumbled loudly.

Wendy and Isabel both laughed.

"Go on up," Isabel said, "I'll grab the beers from the fridge."

"I could use the head start." Wendy stretched her back. She was so slow these days.

Taking her time, she ambled up the stairs and strolled down the hall. She turned into the room where the guys were. Dutch stood, leaning against a wall while Jagger was on his knees tinkering away.

She went to her brother and gave him hug. *Grateful* didn't even come close to expressing how she felt.

Dutch had paved the way with Special Agent Max Webb to have Jagger's record expunged in exchange for turning over evidence that not only put Miguel Vargas behind bars, but was also put the proverbial nail in the coffin for Los Chacales cartel.

As if that wasn't enough, he got Jagger a job at the US Marshals headquarters in Arlington, outfitting the government vehicles that they used for prisoner transport and fugitive apprehension. Jagger wasn't making the kind of money he had with Sixty, but it was an honest living and he was proud of his work, which would help keep marshals safe.

Wendy had relocated her PR firm to Virginia, and she had decided to do a complete one-eighty in how she approached things. No more social media. Her private life was private. Most of her clients were from Washington, DC, now, and by referral only. Less stress. Less hustle.

The change was good. Looking back, it was as though she'd been pretending to be someone she wasn't. Now she was more herself, the woman she was always meant to be.

Rising on her toes, she kissed Dutch's cheek.

Isabel came in with the beers and handed one to Dutch.

"Thanks, beautiful," he said, and Isabel beamed. They made such a great couple.

Isabel was beautiful and warm and kind, even though her father had been Emilio Vargas. Most important, she made Dutch happy, and her brother looked like he'd do anything for her.

Wendy sat in the rocking chair, watching Jagger tighten the last screw on his latest project.

"It's finished," Jagger said. "No thanks to you." He glared at Dutch. "I thought you came here to help."

"No, I came to visit my sister and supervise you."

Jagger stood up and tested his handiwork, shaking it to make sure it was sturdy. "Supervise? How many cribs have you put together?"

"None, but that's beside the point. I'm a natural-born leader, and I can see when things are going off the rails and corrections are needed."

Jagger rolled his eyes as Isabel laughed and handed him a beer. "Thank you."

Wendy rocked in the chair, looking around the nursery. They'd chosen a constellation theme. A starry night painting hung on one wall. Another was painted dark blue and had constellations drawn in glow-in-the-dark acrylic. She and Jagger both felt like the stars had aligned, or rather conspired, to give them a second chance and the baby boy growing inside her.

Orion, the hypoallergenic labradoodle they'd adopted from a shelter, crept in, even though he knew he wasn't allowed in the baby's room. He lay down beside her and curled up at her feet.

"You guys should consider getting a guard dog," Dutch said. "Like our Doberman, McQueen."

"McQueen is such a cool name." Jagger took a long pull on his beer. "But Steve McQueen was the king of cool."

"Amen," Dutch said.

Chuckling, Isabel shook her head. "He was named after Alexander McQueen."

"Who?" Jagger asked.

"The fashion designer," Wendy and Isabel said in unison. Everyone laughed.

Wendy listened to the banter and laughter around her and had never been happier. This house, the dog, the crib, the life growing in her belly was all a manifestation of her deepest desires.

To have Dutch and Isabel to share it with them overwhelmed her with emotion. Tears filled her eyes and streamed down her cheeks.

"Honey, are you okay?" Jagger rushed to her and knelt in front of her. "Is it the crib? Do you not like it?"

"No, the crib is wonderful. You did a wonderful job." She whisked away her tears. "Ignore the pregnant lady. I cry at toilet paper commercials these days."

Jagger smiled at her, compassion and love gleaming in his eyes. Putting his hands on her round belly, he rubbed in circles. His touch was instantly soothing.

Later, he'd give her a foot rub and she'd sing his praises.

Before she started crying again, she looked up from Jagger and her basketball-shaped belly. "Are you guys coming for Christmas?"

"Definitely," Isabel said.

"Mom and Eric are also coming," Dutch said.

"And so is Tina." Jagger kissed her stomach. "It'll be a full house with baby."

"So, does your kid inherit ten million when he's born or when he turns eighteen?" Dutch asked.

Everyone chuckled.

"Either way, I'm going to be his favorite uncle," Dutch said.

"You'll be his only uncle." Wendy smiled at her brother and silently repeated her current favorite word. *Gratitude.*

Hard to believe it had been almost a year and a half since the ordeal with Los Chacales cartel. The horror of it was a distant memory, but she wouldn't change a thing because her life was fuller and happier than she had ever dreamed possible.

* * * * *

COLTON'S
COVERT WITNESS

ADDISON FOX

For Olivia, Izzy and Callin.
With love.

Chapter One

Evangeline Whittaker stared down the main street of Grave Gulch, Michigan, and wondered when the whole world had gone sideways. Although her eyes were protected from the early-evening sun by oversize sunglasses and a floppy hat, no amount of shielding her gaze could stop what she saw through the lenses.

The citizens of Grave Gulch, now protesting outside the city's police department—a common sight over the past few months, due to an increase in local crime—with signs and heavy shouting, eerily audible even though she was several blocks away.

Protesting…and the subtle yet unrelenting pressure from the knowledge that a killer was in their midst.

Although the GGPD was doing its job, people were fed up and anxious by the latest details pouring out of the news cycle. Only, instead of the news showing a random family dealing with a bad situation in a faraway place, this time, it was local. *As local as you could get*, Evangeline admitted to herself as she stepped aside to allow a couple to walk past her on the sidewalk.

There had been three dead bodies discovered in Grave Gulch in a matter of six months. All found with a gunshot to the chest and all seemingly random until you searched beneath the surface.

But once you looked below, it was easy to see the similarities, Evangeline thought on a hard shudder.

All male. All shot while alone walking their dogs. All in their fifties.

Enough similarities that the GGPD had been forced to admit the one thing that was guaranteed to send people into a panic: Grave Gulch had a serial killer on its hands.

Add on the trauma of discovering a well-loved grandmother, Hannah McPherson, was a toddler kidnapper, the GGPD's lead forensic scientist, Randall Bowe was assisting criminals he deemed "worthy," and the discovery and subsequent takedown of a drug kingpin running his business in town, and all of Grave Gulch's residents were scared. The fear either they or a loved one would be next on a killer's list swirling deeply beneath it all.

Hadn't she felt the same sense of concern? Sure, she might be eternally single, but she had a family. And while her mother was quick to lock up good and tight each night, her father often had a mind of his own when it came to how he wanted to live his life. Or worse, his unique brand of screaming obstinacy whenever he felt the world around him wasn't bowing to his wishes.

A persistent worry, the two of them, but one she couldn't overly concern herself with now. She had enough to contend with on her own. Forced leave from her job. That doggedly odd sense that she was being watched—even in her own home—that hadn't let up in weeks. When you added on the mess that was currently the Grave Gulch County DA's office—one she'd managed to find herself smack in the middle of—life was on an out-of-control roller coaster at the moment.

How had it happened so quickly?

She'd spent well over a dozen years in the district attorney's office, keeping her head down and doing her job. Doing it damn well, as a matter of fact. Yet somehow, she'd failed to see a problem right in front of her face.

And now she had tangible responsibility for a serial killer out on the streets and preying on innocents.

Evangeline had spent innumerable sessions with her therapist over the years, dealing with the ever-present twin feelings of despair and responsibility. She'd worked long and hard to ensure that those feelings, a leftover gift from her father's parenting failures, didn't veer into her professional life.

But there was no help for it now.

Three people were dead and a killer was on the loose because she'd not properly prosecuted him. Not on purpose—she let out a frustrated breath—but still on her watch.

On her work.

Damn Randall Bowe and his mishandled—and *criminal*—approach to evidence keeping. And damn her for not digging harder.

Round and round she went, on the endless circle of arguments in her mind. Yes, the GGPD's forensic scientist had often tampered with evidence or flat-out overlooked it, but as a prosecutor she shouldn't have simply assumed a GGPD employee was acting in good faith.

Yet she had.

The blowback had been awful. The cases where she'd used Bowe's evidence—or lack thereof—as part of her legal argument had put them all in this mess. Even worse, she'd failed her boss, Arielle Parks. Arielle was both mentor and friend and it was an endless source of embarrassment and pain to Evangeline that her mistakes reflected so poorly on the district attorney.

And underneath the roiling thoughts in her mind was a bigger one. The lone thought she never seemed able to get past.

How could the world be full of so many awful people?

At this stage of her life, she should know the answer. She'd learned the lesson young, hadn't she? So, in a lot of ways, it should have stuck by now. Yet it hadn't. She lived a life steeped in reason and lawfulness and it still amazed her how many people saw the world as a place to get away with things.

A place to take their anger out on others.

Or selfishly reap whatever benefit they could derive for themselves, no matter the cost to others.

On another hard sigh, Evangeline blew out a breath. *Maudlin much?*

She'd come out because her condo had begun to feel stifling and, at those persistently odd moments, creepy. She couldn't explain it, but even in the confines of her own home, she'd been aware of a relentless sense of being watched.

She'd sensed it for about a month, the feeling growing stronger by the day. At first it was just a fleeting sense, that someone caught her eye too long on the street or a strange sense someone was lingering in the parking lot of her condo complex, even if she couldn't define why she felt that way.

But it had grown worse.

A persistent scraping at the base of her neck, rippling the nerves to her scalp, had become a regular occurrence.

She'd initially blamed it on the pressure at work, the mishandled evidence causing any number of errors in her caseload. Finally, though, Evangeline had had enough of sitting home feeling stuck and decided to head out for a bit of fresh air and some dinner. Yet as she walked, watching the people and trying to appreciate some of the early summer warmth, the fresh evening air wasn't doing much for her mood. That strange sixth sense continued to crawl up and down her spine.

A feeling that had done nothing for her already dour mood.

It was early June, which meant the days were getting longer and longer. And here she was, the space between her morose thoughts getting smaller and smaller so all she focused on was her mistakes. She'd left her home because she needed dinner and a reprieve from the increasing claustrophobia induced by her own four walls, but she'd find no break if all she did was keep covering the same ground over and over in her mind.

With a glance at one end of the street at the protesters, Evangeline turned and headed the opposite direction. She briefly toyed with the idea of going to sit down and have a bite at Mae's Diner, but the last few times she'd gone out, someone had inevitably recognized her from the news. Something dark and uncomfortably swirly had settled in her thoughts today and she didn't want to risk adding to her bad mood. A slice at Paola's Pizza would be the better bet. Hot, gooey dough and cheese was always a mood lifter, and the entire transaction at the counter would take no more than five minutes, ten tops.

She might have to head back to the glum quiet of her condo but at least she'd have pizza.

As she headed in the direction of the restaurant, that strange sense skittered over her once more. It was subtle and if she weren't so on edge she'd likely have ignored it, but was it possible she was being watched?

The public had recently made no secret of its disdain for the DA's office, and while she believed she'd acted in the best interests of the residents of Grave Gulch County, that didn't mean everyone saw it that way. She and her colleagues received threats from time to time. It was unpleasant, but it was a part of the job.

Evangeline crossed the last block for Paola's, once again trying to shake off the miserable mood. Pizza. *Pizza*, she kept reminding herself as she put one foot in front of the other.

It was only as she crossed the last alleyway before the row of storefronts that led to Paola's that something caught Evangeline's attention in the distance. Two people, struggling at the end of the alleyway. The fading summer sun backlit them both so that Evangeline couldn't clearly make out their faces, just snatches of their features as they fought.

Downturned, angry mouths as they shouted.

Slashed eyebrows.

Waving hands.

What she could clearly see was the larger form of the man struggling to hold the arms of the smaller, slender figure—a woman, dressed in a white blouse and dark slacks.

An urgent need to help rose up inside of her and she'd nearly started toward them when the distinct shape of a gun filled the man's hand. Before Evangeline could utter a word or even gurgle the start of a scream, the unmistakable sound of a gunshot rang out.

From where she stood she could see the clear stain of

red spread across the white blouse, just before the small woman fell to the ground in a heap.

Rooted to the spot, Evangeline stared down the mouth of the alley in horror at what she'd just witnessed. An overwhelming urge to help warred with an innate sense of self-preservation.

It was only when that large, still-faceless figure turned toward the woman on the ground and lifted her by her feet, dragging her through the alley, that Evangeline pushed herself into motion.

Digging into her oversize bag, she fumbled through the endless depths until she finally got a grip on her cell phone. Hands shaking, she ran back in the direction of the protesters she'd seen earlier. What had felt menacing a little while ago now seemed like a haven of humanity. Scores of people who could help her and keep her safe from the dark, faceless threat at the end of that alleyway.

She clumsily fingered the screen of her phone, whose face remained locked no matter how many times she tried to swipe and enter her password. It was only as the comforting sound of voices grew louder that she finally managed to get her phone open.

With the desperate hope that she wasn't too late, she jabbed 911 into the phone and tried to summon up a calm she didn't feel.

"Nine-one-one. What's your emergency?"

As the operator's voice flowed through the line, Evangeline wondered if she would ever find that calm again.

DETECTIVE TROY COLTON listened to the dispatch coming over the loudspeaker in the conference room where he and a fellow detective, Brett Shea, had holed up for a work session. As he comprehended the urgency of the summons, he tossed his pen onto the table. The move offered no comfort, but the endless screaming outside the Grave Gulch Police Department had grown tedious in the extreme and his patience had increasingly waned as the afternoon wore into evening.

And now they had a witness claiming someone was shot in an alley downtown?

He stood and pulled on his sport coat over his weapon harness. Brett had already snapped to attention, along with his K-9, Ember. The black Lab was a tracking specialist. She'd come to full alert and moved to stand beside Brett in the span of a heartbeat, despite Troy's previous assessment that she'd been fast asleep in the corner of the conference room.

"Let's swing by and ask Mary if she has any other details." Brett was already nodding as he and Ember followed Troy to the door. "We'll have her notify Melissa, as well."

The GGPD's front desk clerk was young but her sweet face and endless excitement at being a newlywed didn't diminish her ability to be both serious and on her game at every minute. "Detective Colton," Mary Suzuki addressed Troy as he and Brett walked up. "Dispatch is still on the line. Should I patch them through?"

"Sure." Troy nodded. "And get Melissa on this, as well. I know it's the chief's day off and she's earned every bit of it, but she's going to want to know something's going on. I'll call her after Brett and I figure out what's happened."

He loved his cousin Melissa and respected her implicitly as the head of the GGPD. He'd never keep her in the dark, but it killed him to think that all her years of hard work couldn't even give her a reprieve on a night off with her fiancé, Antonio Ruiz.

"It's the job, Troy," she'd say back to him. He could already hear her voice, threaded through with responsibility, thrumming in his head.

But he still hated to ruin her evening.

Wasn't that why he and Brett had volunteered to take the late shift? The entire department had been working tirelessly to get serial killer Len Davison off the streets. He and Brett figured they'd tag-team it and see if they could spark any questions between them that might push them all in a new direction.

Mary watched him with alert eyes as he took in the details from the 911 operator. A female caller had seen another woman shot in one of the alley entrances in downtown Grave Gulch. He shifted the phone back to Mary, instructing her to stay on the line as he and Brett headed out. The affirmation from the operator that an ambulance was en route rang in his ears.

"It'll be faster there on our own two feet," Troy said as he headed for the exit. "But we need the cruiser."

He knew it was the best choice, especially if they needed to give chase. But the time it would take to get through the melee outside the precinct and into town would cost precious seconds a shooting victim didn't have.

Brett nodded. "Let's go."

Troy ignored the protesters as they ran for their vehicle. He well knew the reality of how badly the woman shot in an alley needed them. And if the thought of an innocent person lying in a pool of blood set off an unpleasant string of images of his own mother, he'd just have to push them down.

He and his sister had been much too young to have actually seen the evidence of Amanda Colton's murder.

It was only years later, as a GGPD rookie cop, that he'd had access to the crime scene photos. They were painful, but a confirmation that finally put to bed what had lived in his imagination since childhood. Even with that terrible reality, his mother's sudden and violent death was a constant presence in his mind. It drove him to enter law enforcement, and he knew it did the same for all of his Colton family members in the field, as well. Sometimes bad things happened. And even worse, there were times when the bad person who did those things was never caught.

The cop lived with the cautionary tale.

The son lived with the painful reality that was his life.

EVANGELINE PACED THE SIDEWALK, still on the phone with the 911 dispatcher. The voice on the line was soothing and calm, but Evangeline felt neither. All she could do was stare down the mouth of the alley, imagining the dead body lying just beyond view.

She'd suggested that she go down to check for a pulse but the dispatcher had remained adamant that the police were on their way. Evangeline should remain in place or, even better, seek shelter in a nearby shop. The operator had already scolded her for leaving the sea of people farther down the sidewalk and cautioned Evangeline against going anywhere near the crime scene. A terrible sense of cowardice filled her, even as she knew the reality of the situation and the logic in the dispatcher's orders.

The victim had taken a gunshot at close range and likely hadn't survived, she knew. Add on that Evangeline had no medical training to help, and she had to face the bigger risk that the woman's assailant was still there, trapped in the alley and waiting to make his move to escape.

"Police are in range," the other woman reassured her just as the sight of two men and a K-9 came into view.

Evangeline had lived in Grave Gulch for most of her life and recognized one of the cops on sight. She'd known Detective Troy Colton for years, even though they'd only spoken a handful of times and then only in relation to cases Evangeline was prosecuting.

But oh, goodness, the man was a looker.

Tall and broad, he moved with purpose. He was fit and competent, his large frame as impressive for the solid, muscular build as the kind-hearted soul who lived inside. His eyes were a tawny, golden hazel that had the ability to actually weaken her knees and his skin was a warm brown.

Yes, she'd always had a bit of a crush on Troy. But what were the odds he'd be the one to show up here in her moment of horror and need?

"Police are on scene," Evangeline relayed to the dispatcher. "I'm going to hang up now."

The operator seemed inclined to argue but Evangeline cut the connection before she could be persuaded otherwise. The adrenaline that had pumped so fiercely through her system hit another uptick as she waved on the men now running toward her. "There! Down the alley. Hurry, please!"

"Stay here, ma'am," a man she didn't recognize ordered her as he and his dog raced down the alley.

"Please stay here, Evangeline," Troy said, no less urgently, even as he slowed. "Don't follow us."

"The killer might still be down there."

"All the more reason for you to stay put."

Troy was already off, following the other cop, so that all she could do was holler at his back. "Be careful!"

A quiet voice brought Evangeline back to the moment, even as her gaze still lingered on Troy's retreating back. "Sweetie, are you all right?"

She turned to find an older, kindly-looking woman. The stick holding her protest sign was dangling from her hand, and her eyes were full of concern. "I couldn't help but overhear you mention a killer. What's going on?"

Although Evangeline saw nothing but support and help in the woman's rheumy blue gaze, she eyed the sign warily. As an officer of the law, she believed deeply in the right to protest in peaceable assembly. As one of the objects of those protests, however, she found her inherently broadminded nature wavering.

"Um, I needed some help."

"You said 'killer.'"

"It's—" She broke off, struggling for the right words. "I thought I saw something. The police are investigating."

"Willie!" The older woman hollered to someone across the street, waving the man over with her free hand. "Get over here!"

Whatever kindness Evangeline believed she'd seen in the woman was nowhere in evidence. Instead, she saw the obvious thrill of being in the thick of things coupled with an already heightened sense of purpose that had brought her into the streets in the first place.

"Get Evan and Sally, too!" she added before the man had a chance to cross the street.

The dispatcher's words echoed around in her mind, warning her to keep her distance, while this person dragged more innocent, vulnerable people closer to the threat.

"What are you doing?"

"If a killer's on the loose, you can be damn sure I want a front seat to his arrest."

Chapter Two

Ember let out a series of hard, sharp barks as Troy crossed the last few feet into the alleyway. He stopped short at the T-shaped entrance; the sidewalk alley that fed into the broader area running behind the various shops and buildings was empty. With the precision honed over years of training, he lifted his service weapon, sweeping the area, only to find his initial assessment was correct.

"No one's here." Troy gave the alley one additional sweep before dropping his gun.

"Nope," Brett said as he ordered Ember to his side, the two of them trotting back from the end of the alley-way that gave access into downtown.

"But dispatch said a woman had been shot. There's no one here. No body." Troy reviewed the ground, quickly taking in the area that would have been visible from Evangeline's position on the main street. "No blood."

His gaze roamed the alley again, even though he knew what he'd see. He'd lived in Grave Gulch his entire life and while he hadn't spent that much time walking the town's alleyways, he knew how they were structured. The long, thin corridors served the functional aspects of the town's businesses, just wide enough for delivery trucks and garbage pickup to pass through.

A killer could have escaped through one end of the alley or the other, but dragging a body through the area would still have left a mark. Not to mention that it would have captured the attention of people back out in the main walking areas of town. Only there was nothing. No shell casings, no blood. Not even a sign of a struggle in overturned trash cans or knocked-in recycling receptacles.

"I don't understand." Brett moved close, Ember at his side. "The call was legitimate. And I realized we passed by her quick, but Evangeline looked scared out of her mind as she pointed us down the alley."

Troy had seen it, too: the black eyes, even from a quick glance, that were obviously wide and terror-filled. The strong, straight pose that had seemed crumpled up on itself somehow. Defeated, almost.

He'd known Evangeline Whittaker for quite a while now. She was strong, smart and tough as nails. Her reputation as a fair but tenacious member of the DA's staff had taken a serious hit over the past few months. A situation he could appreciate since the GGPD's had taken a hit, as well. But fair or not, their citizens had a right to be upset.

And Evangeline's actions in the courtroom sat squarely in the midst of their unhappiness.

Was it possible this was some sort of stunt? A way to drum up sympathy and to take the heat off the bad press directed her way?

As a trained detective, Troy knew he had to consider all the angles. Yet even as he did consider the very real possibility Evangeline had made the entire thing up—a situation only corroborated by the lack of evidence and indication that anything had even happened—something in him fought the suggestion. Hadn't he learned that lesson the hard way? Randall Bowe had tampered with evidence, ensuring things weren't what they appeared on the surface.

Recent events aside, he'd also spent years observing that she was incredibly good at her job. A role that, if done right, required honesty, thoroughness and overall decency. He'd always been impressed by her, on the occasions where he was part of a case she was prosecuting.

And she's gorgeous.

That lone thought whispered in, hardly subtle and completely inappropriate for the moment. Yet even as he couldn't deny the images of her that always sprang to mind when he heard mention of her, Troy pushed them aside. Especially when he considered the scared woman, shuttered behind a large floppy hat and big sunglasses, that he'd spoken to on the sidewalk.

The long waterfall of dark hair he normally pictured, along with the eyes that were the color of her hair and the firm cut of her cheekbones had no place in this situation.

Nor did they have any bearing on her possible guilt or innocence.

Which meant it was time to talk to her and find out what was going on.

Brett had already started for the alley exit with Ember, and Troy turned to follow.

Which made Brett's heavy shout, along with Ember's corresponding bark, deep and angry, that much more jarring.

Especially when his fellow detective and his K-9 partner took off at a run, straight for Evangeline.

THE CROWD PRESSED in around her. The anger Evangeline had only heard from a distance earlier as she'd observed the protesting residents had an entirely different quality as it hemmed her in from all sides. Snippets of fuming remarks and heated utterances grew louder and louder, the frustrated citizens' anger reigniting at the chance to focus on a new object.

No longer a person, she thought frantically. She was increasingly not a person to them, but rather, a target for all that ire and fear.

That's the one from the DA's office that put a killer on the streets.

I thought she was fired.

What right does she have to stand out here talking about killers when she's the reason Len Davison's on the loose?

Over and over, the remarks flew, picking up steam along with the head nods and the angry faces and the stifling press of bodies.

She hadn't told the older woman what she was waiting for or why she'd mentioned a killer to the police, but the crowd had made up a story of their own. That and the continuing fear, coursing through all of Grave Gulch, that a serial killer was on the loose.

"Excuse me! Break it up!" An authoritative voice rose up over the comments of the citizenry.

That voice was joined by a second, ordering everyone to move on and disperse.

The whirling blur of humanity slowly stood down, the individuals' movements too sluggish for Evangeline's taste. But even in the lingering panic, she couldn't deny that they were moving along. As her panic receded, she could make out faces again. Some she recognized, some she didn't, but the whirling rush of fear had stopped spinning quite so quickly.

"Evangeline. I mean, Ms. Whittaker…" Troy Colton started in. "We'd like to talk to you."

"Did you find her? Is she okay? Did you find the man who shot her?"

"Shot who?"

The other man she didn't recognize posed the question and it only managed to re-spike her waning reserves of adrenaline yet again. "The woman! The one I called nine-one-one for!"

"There's no woman, Ms. Whittaker."

She whirled to look at Troy, the face she'd so recently thought sexy and competent now set in hard lines. "What do you mean, there's no woman? I saw it. A man and woman were fighting. Right there at the end of that alley." Her hand flung out toward the entranceway between the two buildings. "He shot her. I saw the spread of blood all over her white shirt myself."

A hard shaking settled in her bones, rattling her body as the adrenaline faded, leaving nothing behind, not even the reserves of strength she'd been subsisting on for the past few weeks. "I saw it."

Troy's gaze hadn't left her face and she saw the pity that shifted his mouth from grim to something far worse. Doubt.

"There's no one there?"

He glanced at the crowd that still surrounded them. The protesters had moved back to give them room, but they hadn't left the area. And they were all within earshot of everything taking place.

"Why don't you come with us? We'll take your statement and try to figure out what's going on."

What was going on?

And why did she suddenly feel as if the world had fallen away beneath her feet?

MARY HAD RADIOED for additional backup and the two officers on duty who'd taken her call helped disperse the rest of the crowd. Another team was sent to scout the entire downtown area, checking for anyone on the run or bearing any resemblance to a beefy man in a hat.

Troy commandeered use of the police vehicle while the pair working the crowd stayed to make sure everyone went on their way, promising to send someone back for them. The other cops on duty only nodded, even as they assured him that they could walk, based on their proximity to the precinct.

Brett and Ember took the cruiser they'd driven over from the precinct to cover off the area around the alley and corresponding routes that fanned out from there. So it was only a matter of settling Evangeline in the back and heading to the GGPD.

He'd been deliberate and careful in his movements and she was obviously uncuffed, but it still struck him that having to sit in the back of a police cruiser might make her feel like a prisoner. She remained quiet on the quick ride, and every time he glanced at her through the rearview mirror her face remained wan and pale, her wide eyes determinedly focused on the still above-average-size crowd out and about downtown Grave Gulch on a Sunday night.

Troy considered what he knew about her, beyond his knowledge of her prowess in the courtroom.

She had been a part of the Grave Gulch County DA's office for a number of years, her case record impeccable up until the issue with the town serial killer, Len Davison.

Davison's actions had caught them all off guard, his escalation a situation the GGPD was trying desperately to manage. The entire department had gathered as much information as possible and were all working around the clock to catch the man, but his methods so far had been unpredictable.

So had his connections.

What their chief, Melissa Colton, had originally assumed was mere sloppiness coming out of the CSI department had taken a dark turn earlier in the year. Their chief forensic scientist, Randall Bowe—responsible for working some of the most challenging cases the GGPD managed—had been falsifying evidence. Or flat-out not collecting it.

Troy had seen that truth himself when he worked with Melissa to comb through Bowe's files. Or what little they could get their hands on, seeing as Bowe had fled with his hard drive and hard copies of his work back in January. The GGPD's tech guru, Ellie Bloomberg, had managed to recover quite a bit and it all supported what they'd already come to suspect: Bowe had been mishandling and destroying evidence.

They'd spent the ensuing months combing through all of Bowe's cases, searching for inconsistencies and falsehoods. All while going after a serial killer, as well as dealing with the normal amount of crime in Grave Gulch. His cousin Jillian, a junior member of the CSI team and Bowe's scapegoat prior to his skipping town, had been putting in serious overtime, trying to find whatever she could in the files. She'd done an amazing job working through the evidence, but the department still had a lot of holes.

Holes, Troy thought as he walked Evangeline into an

empty conference room, holes that had caused problems for the DA's office, too. Belief in Bowe's evidence had caught all the prosecutors short and had resulted in several mishandled cases, including Len Davison's.

And it was that mishandling that put a serial killer on the streets. A fact she would be well aware of and, likely, feel some responsibility for.

"Can I get you anything, Ms. Whittaker?"

"It's Evangeline, Troy. We know each other. And no, thank you. I'm okay."

Troy recognized the shock and fear that still mixed beneath her gaze. He walked over to the small fridge in the corner of the conference room and snagged two bottles of water despite her polite decline. "Why don't you have some water anyway."

She accepted the bottle with a quiet thank-you before her gaze tripped around the room. It was covered with notes, maps of Len Davison sightings and crime scene photos. Concern for her rode low in his gut. "I'm sorry you have to see these things."

"No, it's fine. And they're all images I've seen already."

"I guess you would have."

Although the DA's office had to request crime scene photographs through normal legal channels, it wasn't a surprise that she had seen the images of Davison's victims.

"I still can't believe this is happening in Grave Gulch." She murmured the words before firmly turning her back on the photos and taking a seat at the long conference room table.

"I'm sure people say that everywhere. Any crime is a shock, but something of this nature is what people expect to see in movies or experience in books that keep them reading late into the night. They don't expect it in their backyard."

"I guess you're right."

Although Troy, Melissa and his fellow officers had all been dealing with a lot—along with the town's considerable ire at how the evidence for Davison's case had been handled—he knew they weren't alone. He'd heard plenty of rumblings that the Grave Gulch County DA's office was having a hard time, too.

Troy's cousin, Stanton, and Stanton's new love, Dominique, had seen it firsthand. Dominique's connections as an investigative journalist, along with her contributions to the local prison with creative writing skills courses, had led her to realize one of the convicts she worked with hadn't gotten a fair trial. Charlie Hamm's case was more testament to Bowe's shoddy work, but it had been one more mark against the DA's office, too.

Well aware that blowback was pressing hard against Evangeline, Troy asked, "How have things been at work?"

"I wouldn't know. I've been on enforced leave for a few weeks now."

News traveled quickly, especially in the county's police and legal circles, but this one had been kept close to the vest. He'd heard the barest whisper Evangeline was on leave, but when he hadn't heard it over and over as a continued item of gossip, he'd assumed that she was cleared. "For how long?"

"They haven't put an end date on it yet, but my boss is quite sure I will be back in a few more weeks." Evangeline opened the bottle of water and took a long, draining sip. "I'm not so sure she's right."

"Why is that?"

"Because the good citizens of Grave Gulch County don't appreciate ADAs who put serial killers back on the streets."

"They don't appreciate police departments who keep corrupt forensic specialists on the payroll, either."

Troy wasn't quite sure why he said that, because it smacked of disloyalty and the airing of dirty laundry. As a Colton, he avoided doing both. Yet there was something about her. Something in those big eyes and slim, fragile shoulders that spoke to him and made him want to offer her some comfort.

It was interesting, because in all the time he'd known her—and, admittedly, they didn't know one another well—Troy had always seen Evangeline Whittaker as strong and capable. She was slim, but there was a core strength to her that infused her very essence.

The woman sitting opposite him looked defeated.

Which made what he had to do that much more difficult.

"Are you ready to talk about what you saw in the alley?"

"I already told you what I saw. You don't believe me."

"I didn't say that."

For the first time since he came upon her on the street, he saw a spark of fire light the depths of her eyes. "No, you don't."

"We didn't find a body, Evangeline. No sign of a struggle. No shell casings. No blood."

"I know what I saw."

"Then why don't you take me through it. Step by step, tell me what happened."

He pulled a blank notepad from the table and took notes as she began to speak. Her legal training had obviously kicked in, because she shared the information in clear, concise terms and with minimal embellishment.

Troy wrote it all down. Her decision to go out and get dinner, just to get out of her condo for a bit. The waning light as the summer afternoon turned into evening. Even the tone and tenor of the crowd protesting down near the GGPD. She captured it all.

It was only when she described what she saw in the alley that Troy's doubts crept back in. He wanted to believe her. The fear in her voice and the rising tension as she described the man and woman struggling were real. Just as real as the tremors that gripped her voice when she recounted that man pulling a gun.

"She was wearing a white shirt, Troy. I saw the blood spreading on it. I know what I saw."

"Can you describe what he looked like?"

"Had a ball cap on and he was arguing with her. Yelling. He looked so angry. He was bigger, and clearly male from his size and build. And in the way he had a grip on her, I could tell they were fighting."

"Could you hear what they were fighting about?"

"No." She shook her head. "I just knew they were fighting."

Troy flipped through the pages of notes. The steady cadence of her voice still whispered in his ears as he reread the words. Again, he took in the clear, concise descriptions. Her consistency in narrating the scene as well as what had transpired before she happened upon the alley. Even her account of the altercation had the distinct marks of someone who was skilled at noticing other people.

Abstract recognition of clothing. A sense of proportion between the two people having an argument. The ability to read and recognize they were fighting, without hearing their actual words.

She had been an observer. An astute one, too.

So where was the blood? A body? Or a sign one had ever been in that very spot she described?

His phone buzzed and Troy dug it out of his pocket. Brett's name filled the screen above his text.

Headed to precinct. Ember never found a scent.

It figured.

One more odd detail in an evening full of them. He'd spent some time in his career around K-9s but hadn't been in such close proximity to one on active duty until Brett joined the GGPD a few months prior. He'd easily seen the bond between Brett and Ember. Even more, he'd come to understand just how well trained the animal was. If she didn't pick up the scent of blood or gun residue it was because there wasn't any to find.

"What's that look for?" Evangeline's voice was low but he heard the threads of suspicion and doubt all the same.

"My partner's K-9 wasn't able to scent any evidence in the alley or in the streets surrounding the area."

"I know what I saw."

Troy stared down at his notes again, surprised to see where he'd abstractly doodled on the words. The phrase "white shirt, blood spreading" was underlined and he'd written and rewritten the word *blood*, emphasizing its presence on the page.

Much as he wanted to believe her—and he knew himself well enough to know that somewhere deep inside, he did believe her—it wasn't that easy. Nor was it going to be easy to convince his fellow officers as well as his chief that this was a lead they needed to follow.

But as he sat there, staring into the dark depths of Evangeline Whittaker's eyes, Troy recognized the truth. This woman needed his help. He'd spent his life wishing there had been someone there to help his mother in her moment of need.

He'd be damned if he left Evangeline alone in hers.

Chapter Three

He didn't believe her.

Over and over, that truth bored into her thoughts. Evangeline wanted to scream with the frustration of it all. She knew what she'd seen.

What she'd witnessed.

That woman had been shot in the alley, in a way that left no question murder was the intended outcome.

But there was no evidence. No sign of a struggle. Nothing that would indicate what she had seen had actually happened.

Although adrenaline still pumped through her in heavy, syrupy waves, Evangeline forced herself to focus. Yes, she had been edgy over the past several weeks. That feeling of being watched had become oppressive and cloying. Not to mention scary.

She also had to acknowledge that she was under a tremendous amount of stress with work and with the chilling reality of knowing Len Davison was out on the streets. She had always taken pride in working hard at her job and being a model employee. Yet over the past few months, all of that hard work and all of that effort had felt like it was for nothing.

The questions she had seen other people's eyes. The questions that had rattled around in her own mind.

And now, the questions she saw in Troy Colton's serious, hazel gaze.

He was a good cop. A good detective. She had worked around him long enough to know those things were true. She had to trust him, even if his initial response left her feeling vulnerable and alone.

"The dog didn't pick up any scent at all?" she finally asked.

"No, not based on Brett's text."

"It doesn't make sense. Any of it. I know what I saw. And even if the woman did survive, there would be some evidence of it. Troy, the man shot her at point-blank range."

Despite that weird sense of being followed and the oppressiveness of feeling trapped in her own home, Evangeline *knew* what she had seen. She didn't doubt herself. How did you doubt watching two people fight and another one pull out a gun and shoot the other?

Yet as the minutes ticked past, the inevitable questions crept in.

Was there some sort of stain already on that white shirt? Something she hadn't noticed at first glance.

Had that fight been some sort of strange role-playing between the two of them?

Or worse, was it just two people, fed up and irritated with all that had been going on in Grave Gulch, simply having a fight? But even then, the dog would have found a scent.

"Why don't we look at this from a different angle?" Troy said. "Was there anybody else around you when you saw the altercation in the alleyway?"

"No, there wasn't. I was avoiding the protest happening at the opposite end of town and decided to go a different direction to get a slice of pizza."

"So, no one was near you?"

"No, not at all," she said.

"What made you look down the alleyway at all?"

Evangeline recognized the tactic. She had used it herself, many times, questioning a witness. It was an effort to get her to re-create the scene, and also give Troy an opportunity to see where there might be holes in her story.

"I understand how suspicious this looks. But I know what I saw. You're not going to trip me up or get me to say something different."

"That wasn't my goal," Troy said.

"Oh no?"

"No, actually I'm trying to see if we can find anyone to corroborate your story. Because while I recognize we haven't found a lick of evidence, I saw your face when Brett and I arrived. And I know you, and I don't believe you're making up fake calls to nine-one-one about women being shot in alleys."

"Oh."

"Yeah. Oh."

Evangeline considered his words, and that small moment of heat that had risen in his eyes when she had suggested he was trying to trip her up. Was it possible he *did* believe her?

Or more to the point, that he was on her side?

It had only been the past few weeks, since she was put on extended leave, that Evangeline had realized just how alone she was. Her job was consistently busy and she took a deep pride in doing it well, but the time spent with her own thoughts had been rather revealing.

She talked to her mother regularly, on their twice-weekly calls, but those remained light and airy, with Evangeline unwilling to say anything that might ruffle her. Her mother had spent far too many years dealing with the fallout of her father's behavior, and Evangeline had no wish to add to the now stress-free life she led post-divorce.

Her father was different. They exchanged bland, cordial emails and the rare phone call to celebrate an annual holiday. A decision that suited them both but kept her life somewhat stress-free, as well.

Or, it had.

The Davison case and the truth that had come out of Randall Bowe's deception had upended every bit of order she had managed to create in her adult life. Order that she now realized was dependent on keeping others at arm's length. A fact that made the creepy sensation of being watched or the long, endless days with nothing to do suddenly overwhelming.

"Why don't I drive you home?" Troy's offer interrupted the direction of her thoughts and she was grateful for it.

"You don't have to do that."

"Sure I do. I can swing by and get you something to eat, too. You never did get dinner."

The offer was thoughtful and a reminder of all she'd always believed about the good and upstanding Troy Colton. He was a consummate professional, focused on his job, but also unfailingly kind. A man who took care of others with a simple ease that often went unnoticed.

Only, she had noticed.

She'd noticed him often, burying her little crush on the attractive detective with a focus on work and a line of questions on whatever case they might be discussing. It would never do to show that side of herself. The one that was woman first, lawyer second.

She had been raised in a home that had proven women couldn't have it all. She'd taken that learning into her own life and career and had never deviated from those beliefs.

It was only now, when she'd been forced to question all she held close, that she had to wonder if she'd been wrong all along.

Because it felt incredibly good to have a nice, thoughtful man to lean on.

TROY WAITED UNTIL Evangeline was buckled into the passenger seat of his SUV before he turned on the ignition.

Although there were still a few things he wanted to look into on the Davison and Bowe cases, based on the way his evening had gone Troy knew it was time to call it a day. He had connected with Brett shortly before heading out of the precinct to let him know he was done for the day, and Brett's response was all Troy could want in a partner. After asking after Evangeline, Brett had promised he was going to put another couple of hours in on the Davison case and would follow up with an email on any notes he made.

They weren't formal partners yet, Brett's recent arrival in Grave Gulch ensuring he was still getting the lay of the land in the department, but the two men had found a good, working rhythm with each other. Troy knew the addition set Melissa's mind at ease and his own thoughts had improved since he'd realized he had such a qualified person to help work through various cases.

It made it easier to leave tonight and take Evangeline home. He'd decided it was important to do that in his own car instead of in a police vehicle. As he pulled out of his parking spot, he briefly glanced at her face. She looked considerably less tense than when she had sat in the back of the cruiser.

"What are you hungry for?"

"You really don't have to get me dinner."

"I think I do. Especially since I'm stopping for something myself."

"Okay. Well, what do you want to eat, then?"

He fought the smile at the ease with which she'd shifted the conversation—*just like a lawyer*—and went with honesty on his part. "A burger is always a good idea."

"That is an excellent point. A burger sounds great."

And he knew a local place that did pretty good carryout. Troy dialed them from his in-car dash, his phone quickly connecting. In a matter of minutes, he'd ordered two cheeseburgers and added the fries for good measure.

Based on the directions she'd shared, it wasn't far to Evangeline's condo and he was grateful for the extra time needed on the food prep to observe her a bit more. After navigating his way out of downtown, Troy turned into the parking lot of the burger joint. Cutting the ignition, he turned to face her.

"How have you been holding up?"

She hesitated for the briefest of seconds, as if weighing how much she was going to say, before she spoke. The trembling, upset tones he'd heard back at the precinct had faded, replaced by a layer of something he could only interpret as resignation.

"I'm fine. It's been a bit jarring not waking up on a schedule every day, but I'm doing okay."

"Honestly, I was a bit surprised when you mentioned

that you were still out of the office. I heard the lightest rumblings when you went on leave but since I hadn't heard anything else about it, I'd assumed you were cleared to return."

"You did?"

"Yes. Which is good because it means your personal business is being kept private. As it should be."

"It doesn't make it any less embarrassing."

Troy heard those notes of frustration once again lining her voice and he had to admit he would feel the same if the position was reversed. For him, being a cop was a calling. He had worked so hard to make detective and strived every day to make sure that he lived up to the responsibility of the badge.

While he knew a lot of his professional drive came from emotionally processing his mother's murder, it wasn't just Amanda Colton's premature death when he'd been just a child that had affected him. The Coltons believed in justice, honesty and the value of hard work. It was important that they conveyed back to the public that their trust was placed in capable hands.

He wore the badge with honor and he had learned early in his career that others in the GGPD felt the same. He had certainly always believed that of his counterparts in the DA's office, as well.

It was what made the situation with Randall Bowe so terrible. Yes, the man might be CSI, but he still had the responsibilities of a cop. Of protection. Of honesty. Of integrity.

And he'd betrayed all of them.

Evangeline let out a light sigh. "Embarrassing or not, thank you for telling me that. I assumed everyone knew about my situation."

Her words pulled Troy out of the angry thoughts that always accompanied any mental wanderings about Bowe. The man had proven himself scum and it was Troy's biggest wish to see him arrested and prosecuted to the full extent of the law. "You're welcome."

"You look sort of upset for a guy who's about to eat a juicy cheeseburger. You want to talk about it?"

Troy shifted in his seat to look fully at Evangeline. She still had the big floppy hat on but had tucked her sunglasses away somewhere. The look didn't diminish her beauty. Instead, the long waves of dark hair that had escaped her hat now fell down her back, soft, enticing and eminently touchable.

Shaking off the thoughts he had no business having, he keyed in on her observation. "Was I that obvious?"

"Kind of. Your face got a little squinty and your lips fell into a straight line. I figured something upset you."

"What isn't upsetting lately? Something is happening in Grave Gulch and it has been since the start of the year. My sister's little boy, Danny, was kidnapped. Twice." Troy shook his head, the mental anguish that Desiree had lived through not once, but twice, still fresh in his memory. "Then there's the obvious situation with Davison and with Bowe. But even beyond the two of them, there have been some incredibly strange things that have happened to my cousins, too. There's this general sense of unrest and unease and it's becoming increasingly difficult to process."

It felt good to say the words. To actually let out all of the things that had been bothering him the past several months. But it was because it felt good that Troy realized he should say nothing.

Police business was one thing. Family business was

another. And the Coltons had certainly dealt with their fair share of both. His nephew's recent kidnapping as well as his cousin's run-in with a drug kingpin. It had all felt overwhelming at times.

Evangeline's voice was gentle and pulled him back from the dark direction of his thoughts. "Although I haven't been as closely in the loop as usual, I was very happy to hear that everything worked out okay for your sister. And also happy to hear she's engaged."

"Thank you. Desiree had a tough time there for a while. Her son, Danny, was at the heart of it all, at serious risk as a kidnapping target. Stavros has changed her life. Both their lives."

"I can't imagine anything scarier for a mother. Or for your family."

He saw the genuine compassion in her face and recognized that even in the midst of her own troubles that day, Evangeline could still think of others.

Wasn't that one of the things he was struggling with?

Of all the things they had discovered about Randall Bowe over the past few months, his lack of compassion for others had been the worst.

Recently, some of the GGPD had noticed a pattern— that Bowe's behavior appeared tied to the ending of his marriage. Although they were still technically married, the relationship was now over. Melissa's discussion with Bowe's wife had confirmed that, his wife confessing that things had gone bad after her infidelity.

The GGPD had determined that it was that betrayal that indicated which cases Bowe played with in the CSI files. A cheating spouse or a relationship gone sour? Consistently, Bowe tampered with those files.

It indicated someone who not only lacked compassion

for others, but who could only assuage his own feelings of anger by hurting other people.

Danny's initial kidnapping, from the wedding of Mary Suzuki, had been the first clue that ultimately broke the case wide open. The note that came after his nephew's kidnapping had been very clear. The GGPD needed to reopen a case that had been handled improperly if they wanted the boy back. The kidnapping was an act of desperation by the grandmother of a woman whose case had been mishandled from the start. Everleigh Emerson had been innocent of her estranged husband's murder, but the evidence had been fairly clear-cut against her.

Or it had *appeared* clear-cut.

In the rush to get Danny back, Troy and the rest of the GGPD had listened to the warning in the note and done what was asked of them. From there, it was only a matter of reading Randall Bowe's files more closely, and then they'd begun to find inconsistencies.

As tactics went, Troy was still seething over the approach taken to use his nephew as bait, but no one could argue with the outcome. Bowe's crimes had been uncovered. Everleigh was innocent of murdering her husband, had never cheated on the man as Bowe had believed, and remained equally innocent of any involvement in Danny's kidnapping. A fact that had brought her even closer to his family.

When the man who had actually murdered her husband came after Everleigh, Troy's cousin Clarke had put all of his PI skills into finding the real killer and keeping her safe. So safe that Everleigh was about to become a Colton, her and Clarke's intense time together having led to love.

He couldn't help but compare that situation to Evangeline's.

Confused at the direction of his thoughts—she was hardly a victim like Everleigh—Troy brushed them aside with brisk efficiency. It was fine to think this woman was attractive. It was another to let those thoughts of her cloud his judgment when it came to handling cases.

Instead, he fell back on his training and the polite veneer he used in any and all situations. The "Colton polish," as he'd heard fellow townsfolk refer to it, never failed. "Thank you for that. I know my sister really struggled to find any sense of peace and normalcy for a while. It helped that the motive for kidnapping Danny was discovered and dealt with."

"How? I mean, I know he was kidnapped but I never heard the reason why."

Troy was surprised Evangeline didn't know the story. "I guess the GGPD and the DA's office aren't talking as much as I thought."

"Maybe that's part of the problem," Evangeline muttered.

"You think?"

For the first time since he came upon her outside the alleyway, Troy saw a spark of the Evangeline he knew and admired. It lit the depths of her eyes and framed her voice in a layer of passion and determination. "We're matched resources, right? Law enforcement captures the criminals and the DA's office prosecutes them. Yet here are two very intimate issues that neither of us knew details about. You barely knew I was on leave, save for a few light whispers. And I had no idea your nephew's case had been solved. Twice."

"I'm sure Arielle was trying to give you your privacy with respect to your leave." Arielle Parks, the well-respected Grave Gulch County DA, was under a ton of scrutiny herself. He could only imagine she wanted to shield her staff as much as possible.

"And I am more grateful for that than I can say. But it still doesn't change the fact that our organizations should be talking more."

He was prevented from saying anything by the ping on his phone that said the order was ready.

As he got out of the car to go retrieve their burgers, Troy couldn't help but take Evangeline's impassioned words to heart. It had meant a lot to him to sit and talk with her, openly and honestly, about all that had happened in Grave Gulch since the new year.

More than he would have ever thought possible.

EVANGELINE DIRECTED TROY through town and back toward her condo complex. She'd lived in the elegant building for about three years now, her home a product of years of saving as much as possible and then the satisfaction of building a place in the world that was all hers.

She directed him to a parking area in front of her building and then quickly got out of the car before he could come around to help her. It was hard to explain, but she felt as if they had reached some sort of intimacy as they sat and talked while waiting for the burgers. She knew Troy Colton, obviously, but didn't actually *know* him. To talk the way they had, in the car and before, while they sat at the precinct, had meant something. Even there, he was in full cop mode but he never made her feel badly.

That ability to talk, engage and, ultimately, to understand—that was a skill. One she knew was incredibly valuable for someone in law enforcement. Because in the end, wasn't that all anyone wanted? A fair shake. The feeling of being listened to.

The feeling that they mattered.

Of course, she acknowledged to herself, it also helped that she wasn't accused of anything.

Yet, a small voice whispered in her ear.

"Evangeline?"

She turned to see Troy's expectant face staring up at the building. "Sorry, I was woolgathering. I'm right down this way. The third door."

"I guess I've been a bit presumptive." Troy held up the brown paper bag. "But I assumed we would have dinner together."

"Oh, yeah, sure, that would be great."

It's not a date. It's not a date. It's not a date. She mentally whispered those words to herself over and over as she unlocked the door, flipped on the lights and invited him into her home.

"Here, let me take that."

"Oh, no, ma'am, this is door-to-door service. Just direct me to the kitchen."

She smiled at that and pointed down the small hallway that led to her kitchen. "Right down there, then."

It was simple, but his silliness was enough to set her back at ease. This wasn't a date and she was perfectly capable of sharing a meal with a man. But that didn't mean it couldn't feel nice to have a houseguest. Someone to talk to.

Something that would break the monotony of what she had been living with for the past few weeks.

Evangeline followed him into the kitchen, heading for the cabinet where she kept plates. Troy had already torn open the bag, the scents of cheeseburgers and fries filling the room with a delicious aroma that had her stomach growling.

"That smells amazing. Burgers were an inspired idea."

"They usually are." Troy smiled. "I also find they help on the days when I had a really big adrenaline rush and need an energy pick-me-up. Are you doing okay?"

The concern was completely unexpected. "Yeah, I'm okay."

"All right. I just wanted to check." He turned back to the burgers, busy setting the wax paper–wrapped halves onto plates.

"I can tell by your tone of voice that you don't believe me." The words came out more accusatory than she'd intended, yet Evangeline found she couldn't quite pedal them back.

"I believe you. My question is if you believe yourself."

"What is that supposed to mean?"

"You've been under a lot of stress. It's okay not to have all the answers, or to be perfect."

Although she had appreciated the sharing of confidences in the car, this felt like a bit too much intimacy. And it cut a little too close to home. "You don't know anything about my life, Troy. I'm telling you I'm okay, because *I am* okay."

She eyed him but refused to engage any further. She'd spent her life trying to one-up her father in conversation and when confronted like this, all she wanted to do was back off and curl up into herself.

In the courtroom, she never backed down.

In her personal life, she backed away so quickly she left proverbial tire tracks in the dirt.

"All right, then." He shrugged before handing her a plate. "You're okay."

The "damn right" was on the tip of her tongue but she held it back, refusing to give him any satisfaction.

Settling in at the table, she had just pulled a napkin onto her lap when his phone went off. He set his plate on the table and dug his phone out, frowning as he stared down at the face. "Excuse me."

Troy left the kitchen, all signs of the lighthearted dinner companion who'd followed her into the house vanishing.

All she saw was the stiff and stoic back of a cop.

How had their conversation turned so quickly? One minute he was teasing her about door-to-door service and the next she was backing away like she'd been stung by a rattlesnake. Of course, she couldn't quite forget the personal snapback in between.

Way to welcome your guest, Whittaker.

She left her burger on her plate, unwilling to start eating before he came back, but she did sneak a fry as his words drifted toward her from the hallway.

"What did CSI say about the alley?"

CSI?

He hadn't mentioned putting CSI on anything. Sure, Detective Shea and his K-9 had looked into the surrounding area but they'd sent more cops down there, too?

And what would they have back in hand so quickly? She understood the processing of evidence took time. No matter how riveting a TV crime drama, securing evidence simply didn't work the way it was portrayed in entertainment. Add on the fact that Sunday night at the

GGPD wasn't exactly crawling with CSI experts on duty and his questions to whomever was on the other end of the phone were a puzzle.

It was only when he walked back into the kitchen, grim-faced, that Evangeline felt those frissons of fear she'd finally managed to force back on the ride home rise up again in full force.

"What happened?"

"CSI combed the alley for evidence."

"You didn't tell me that." The accusations were back but Evangeline didn't care. Was this the way he operated? A few nice words and dinner, all while keeping a suspect on the hook?

For the first time, she saw the heat and sparks of anger fire up under her direct gaze. "I didn't need to tell you that. It's part of my job and as an assistant district attorney, you're well aware of that. In fact, if I hadn't sent out a CSI team your office would be on my ass for violating proper protocol."

He was right.

Damn it all, he was 100 percent right.

And still, she felt a tiny sting of betrayal she couldn't quite define.

"And suddenly CSI works overtime on a Sunday night?"

"They do when a serial killer is on the loose in my jurisdiction."

Damn. Once again, he had an answer. And once again, she had to admit it was the right one. More than right. It was proof the GGPD was determined to take any and all action to get a killer off the streets.

"Our jurisdiction, Troy. We're in this together."

He nodded, even as his face remained grim. "Yes. Ours."

She appreciated his ready agreement, even as she couldn't get past the broader issue at hand. "Killer or no killer, CSI can't process evidence that quickly."

Troy sighed but his gaze never left hers. Never dropped in the split second before he delivered bad news. "They can when there isn't any evidence to process."

Chapter Four

Troy hated to have such irrefutable proof, but he knew the
investigators and was sure they had done a thorough job.

He'd always believed in them, but Randall Bowe's betrayal had lit a fire under the entire team. Even though
no one else in Grave Gulch's CSI division was suspected
of colluding with Bowe, they all had something to prove.

And they'd all been working overtime to prove it.

"It's just like Detective Shea said. Before." Evangeline's voice was low, the distinct notes of defeat lining
her words. "His K-9 didn't catch a scent, and CSI is saying nothing is there, too."

"Yes."

"Which means you think I'm lying."

"No, I didn't say that."

"You're thinking it, which is the same thing."

Her burger and fries still sat on her plate, untouched.
Dark circles rimmed the fine skin beneath her eyes and
a defeated slump rounded her shoulders.

"No, I'm not. Quit putting words in my mouth and quit
assuming you know what I'm thinking."

"What else could you be thinking?" she asked. "I
called in a murder and not only did you not find a body,

but you haven't found a bit of evidence that suggests there ever was one."

She was right. Empirically he knew that. Yet bodies didn't suddenly disappear. And well-respected members of the community who worked in positions of authority simply didn't go around seeing murders where none existed. "Then something else is going on."

"What else could possibly be going on? I know what I saw, Troy. I know what murder victims look like. And I saw one. Yet there's no one there."

"Then we figure out the angle."

"What angle? There is no angle."

He sat down as if he hadn't heard her. She was on edge and he'd spent enough time around people to know that part of defusing a tense situation was to avoid further engagement. This woman had a great legal brain and sooner or later it was going to get its way past her anxiety.

In the meantime…

Well, in the meantime he had a new focus. And that started with getting some food into her.

"You're going to eat right *now*?" Her high-pitched voice was just shy of a screech, which only reinforced his tactic.

"Yes, I'm hungry. You should be, too."

"How am I going to eat?"

He shoveled in a fry and kept his tone light. Irritatingly so, if he had to guess. "One bite at a time."

"Why?"

"To keep your strength up," he said around a mouthful of burger.

The wariness never left her eyes but she did sit back down at the table. With a small headshake she reached for a fry. And he didn't miss the way her eyes fell to half-mast as crispy potato and salty coating hit her tongue.

Good.

Hell, it was damn good. And getting some food into her was a step in the right direction.

He figured they might be out of the woods when she picked up her burger and took a bite.

"It's good, isn't it?"

She eyed him narrowly over the burger, before nodding. "Yeah, it is."

"Never underestimate the power of food."

"Is that a rule of the law?"

"No, it's a rule of my stepmother." He couldn't help but smile as he pictured Leanne Palmer Colton standing in the middle of the family kitchen. "She always says very little can't be helped by a bit of food and a good night's sleep."

"She's a wise woman."

"Yes, she is."

Leanne was amazing. She had come into their father's life, and by extension, his and Desiree's, before they even knew they needed her. But she found a way to reach them—all of them—through the nearly paralyzing grief of Amanda McMahon Colton's horrifying murder.

A big heart and love that overflowed from it had been Leanne's secret. She'd fallen in love with all of them, she'd told Troy once, and knew that her life had become complete when he and his father and sister had come into hers.

It was a lesson he'd carried with him. That even in the midst of sadness and tragedy, something good and meaningful could flourish and grow. It never diminished the pain of losing his mother, but through Leanne's love, he had found a way through it. They all had.

Even now, she was the first to call him on the anniversary of his mother's death and she'd made sure that photos of Amanda and his father, Geoff, were in the family home, and on the mantel. They sat alongside photos of the family they'd raised together. Troy and Desiree, Geoff and Leanne's two biological daughters, Annalise and Grace, and their adoptive son, Palmer, had all grown up knowing they were loved.

They were a family, Troy thought with no small amount of happiness and deep-seated pride. One that had been born as much as made.

Through love.

His father was a good man and Troy had always known Geoff would do anything to keep him and Desiree safe. But finding Leanne had made all the difference. Her generosity of spirit was a gift and Troy knew that he was beyond fortunate for it. All his siblings were.

"You speak of her with such love. You're quite lucky. Not everyone speaks of a step-parent in that way."

"I am lucky. Desiree and I talk about that a lot. How we kind of hit the stepmom jackpot with Leanne."

His mother's murder was something that was well known around Grave Gulch, and he had no doubt that Evangeline knew the story. Yet Troy still felt compelled to add, "There are times I think my mother sent her straight to us. That somehow she knew we never would have survived without Leanne's love."

"That's a very beautiful way to look at it."

"I think it's true."

"I think you're right." Evangeline opened her mouth, then closed it again, as if she were hesitant to say something. Troy waited, giving her a moment, curious to see if she'd continue.

He was pleased when she started in on her story. "When I was little, my grandmother from the Philippines came to visit. She told me a story of a small bird that lived in her village growing up."

She stopped again, seeming to question herself, but Troy waved her on. "Please. I'd like to hear it."

"She said the bird was little but very beautiful, its feathers plumed in rich shades of blue and purple. And she often heard it singing."

Troy set his burger down and reached for a napkin to wipe his fingers. He sensed this conversation was important to her and felt that she needed his full attention.

"A rash of crows had come to the village and one morning she found the small bird on the ground, hurt and on the verge of death from an attack of the larger birds." Evangeline played with one of her fries, taking a small bite as she summoned the words of her story. "My grandmother took the bird in, terrified it would die but unable to leave it alone. She cared for it and nursed it back to health."

"That's very caring of her." And not a surprise based on what he knew of Evangeline. She was known for her strong preparation in the courtroom. She fought hard, but fairly and compassionately, seeking outcomes that would help someone find the road back to society, instead of away.

"It was caring, but in a lot of ways it wasn't enough. The bird grew strong again, but it wouldn't sing, and its feathers faded, their brilliance turning a mottled, grayish color.

"It was as if the attack had taken away its spirit. I remember being so sad when she told me that story. Because I could picture the bird in my mind and could feel his pain."

"It's part of life."

"I suppose it is, but I still thought it was sad. That even after being saved, the bird couldn't quite find its way." She took a deep breath. "But fortunately, that wasn't all. My grandmother cared for the bird for many months. She never heard it sing again, but she did see it was healing. And one day she was on her morning walk and found another bird, not nearly as broken as the colorful one, but still in need of help."

Although he had a sense of where the story was going, Troy was captivated, and wanted to hear to the end of her tale.

"She nursed the new bird, splinting its wing and giving it the proper time to heal. Through it all, she kept the two birds near each other in side-by-side cages. As days passed, the bird with the broken wing got better. And so did the colorful bird who needed to heal."

She leaned forward and laid a hand on his. "It's a gift, that sort of love. Companionship. Understanding. And the time to heal. So I believe you when you say that your mother sent Leanne."

"Thank you for that. And I agree with you."

Evangeline sat back in her chair, her eyes far away with a memory.

"Is your grandmother still alive?"

"No." She shook her head. "She died the year after that visit. My mother was devastated to lose her. Even more devastated when my father wouldn't allow her to go to the funeral."

"Why not?"

He saw it then. Despite the myriad of emotions, he'd seen cross Evangeline's face throughout the evening, that one was new.

And the sign to back off was crystal clear.

"Not everyone is fortunate to have an understanding companion like that colorful bird."

Although his mother's death was a painful subject, because it had happened when he was a toddler, he'd spent his entire life dealing with it and discussing it. Troy recognized in Evangeline's quiet the truth of her situation, as an adult living with the aftereffects of trauma. For her, there existed a desperate need to keep that suffering buried, because it lived much too close to the surface most of the time.

He was curious about her experience but respected her privacy all the same.

And wondered what had made her feel comfortable enough to tell him the story of the bird and her grandmother's passing in the first place.

ALTHOUGH SHE'D INTENDED to only eat a few bites, Evangeline stared down at her now-empty plate in wonder. She had no idea how he did it, but Troy had managed to get her talking, weaving from one subject to the next, and enjoying her meal throughout.

There were those few strained moments, when she'd spoken of her family. Why she'd even brought up her grandmother's death she had no idea. Grandmother's passing had nothing to do with the story of the two healing birds, yet she'd blithely followed that story with another even more personal one.

Why?

Even as she mentally berated herself, she couldn't

deny his kindness in moving their conversation on to something new after she'd so obviously shut down. Her father's mercurial anger and unfair edicts over her mother weren't something she discussed with anyone. She didn't even discuss them with her mother any longer, the years of living with that unprompted rage having done their fair share of damage to Dora Whittaker's nerves.

And to her own.

Yet something about sharing a meal with Troy and the words seemed to spill out, almost of their own accord.

Was it because she felt a kindred spirit in him?

She knew the story of his mother's death. There were few in Grave Gulch—and certainly no one around law enforcement—who were unaware of the terrible tragedy. Not only was Amanda McMahon Colton murdered when her two children were small, but her killer had never been found. It was a reality that haunted the family and something she'd heard spoken of more than once.

Amanda's death had somehow galvanized the Coltons. It was as if they all understood that justice wasn't always served and it was essential to do everything you could to work for that outcome. As a result, most of them had gone into law enforcement of some sort. And still, despite every effort, there were cases that remained open and cold, a frustrating reality for the loved ones left behind.

"So Danny is enjoying being spoiled even more than usual," Troy continued their thread of conversation, pulling Evangeline back from the wayward direction of her thoughts. "My father and Leanne do a darn fine job with their grandson, but now that Stavros is in his life he's a very happy toddler."

She knew Troy spoke of Stavros Makros, the ER doctor who was now engaged to his sister. He'd talked of the man throughout their dinner and it was easy to see Troy genuinely liked his sister's fiancé.

"And Uncle Troy doesn't spoil his nephew?" Evangeline said with a smile. She could only assume what a wonderful experience it was to have nieces and nephews. She didn't have any as she had no siblings, but the way people talked about the little ones in their lives had always made her wish for some tiny relatives of her own to spoil.

Or even children of her own. A fact she quickly shut down at the reality she had no partner to make a family with. Something she'd always hoped would change but, as of yet, hadn't.

"You found me out." He lifted his hands and shrugged his shoulders, the move enough to pull her from her dour thoughts. "I just can't resist that little guy."

"Although you and I have known each other through work for a long time, I can't say the same about your sister. Is she in law enforcement, too?"

"Desiree is an artist. She does some part-time sketch work for the GGPD. She was essential to catching the kidnapper last month who went after Danny."

"How so?"

"It was all in the eyes."

"Desiree was able to capture that in her sketch?"

Troy nodded. "Amazing, isn't it? But yes. Although the woman had a face covering on, Desiree could see her eyes before she tried to grab Danny in the park. When it happened again, during an incident in the hospital, Desiree was close enough to capture the look in her sketch."

"And that saved your nephew?"

"It was Stavros again. He recognized the instability in the woman and understood they were dealing with someone battling mental illness. It was scary, but his

medical training and his own personal experience ensured he knew the signs."

"His own experience?" It felt like an intrusive question, yet it also seemed right to ask. Natural, even, as their
conversation had unfolded throughout dinner.

"Stavros lost his own child several years ago. His ex-
wife was unstable, a situation made worse when Stavros was awarded full custody. She kidnapped their child
while in the middle of an episode, killing them both in
a car accident during a snowstorm."

"I am so sorry." Those words often felt so useless,
yet she meant every bit. "To live through that must have
been awful."

"I don't think anyone ever gets over that. But I think
the fact that he's moving on with his life—" Troy hesitated "—and living again…it matters."

"It does."

Before she even realized his intention, Troy stood,
dish in hand, and reached across the table to take hers.

"Oh, you don't have to do that."

"It's my pleasure. I haven't had such a lovely dinner
companion in a long time. It's been nice to sit and talk
for a bit."

"I know what you mean. I've been—" She broke off,
not comfortable with how sad and lonely she sounded.
Or how sad and lonely she *would* sound if she expressed
how desperately she'd craved conversation these past few
weeks. So instead, Evangeline settled for polite platitudes.
They were safe. Easy. And they didn't smack of those
overtones of neediness that were about to come roaring
out of her mouth once more. "It's nice to have a professional discussion that can also blend with the personal."

"I agree. And although I didn't want to spoil your dinner, I would like to get your take on Len Davison."

"You mean the psychopathic criminal I let go free?"

And there they were, right back to desperate and needy.

Troy had obviously keyed in on her words, his eyebrows slashing over that magnetic hazel gaze as he turned toward her after snapping the water on at the kitchen sink. "You didn't let him go free."

"I was the one who prosecuted him. Ineffectively. That rests on me."

"Actually, it rests on Randall Bowe. In the information he falsified. In the records he deliberately didn't keep."

"Then I should have dug deeper."

"On what? A man who had no history of criminal activity? One who also hadn't shown signs of nefarious behavior?"

He twisted the water off, his economical motions tense. "Tell me, Evangeline. Dug deeper how? You relied on the information that was given to you. Information from the GGPD you should have been able to trust."

"It's not enough. I hold myself to a higher standard."

"And you think I don't? You think the rest of the GGPD doesn't? You think Arielle Parks as the DA of Grave Gulch County doesn't?"

There it was again. That flash of temper that suggested Troy Colton wasn't at all fine with the way things were going in his jurisdiction.

"I know you hold yourself to a very high standard. My comments weren't about you, nor were they meant to insult you."

"I know that, Evangeline. That's my point. We are all up against an enemy we never expected. A snake that got inside our garden. It's humbling and it's frustrating. But that doesn't mean you stop fighting."

All the internal struggles she had battled since going on leave from her job had made her feel so lonely. She'd been dealing with those accusations of failure all along, struggling with the consequences of her legal decisions and their impact on the community. And other than a few conversations with Arielle, not once in all that time had she experienced any kind of kinship with others. But here, now, talking to Troy, was different.

For the first time in quite a while she felt understood. And that meant more than she could say.

"Thank you. I needed to hear that. And I needed a perspective other than my own. More than I think I realized."

She stared up at him, the two of them now standing side by side at her sink. He'd somehow managed to wash and rinse their dinner plates, all while delivering the raw truth of what the entire police and law enforcement community was dealing with. It was only as she handed him a towel from the counter, turning so they faced one another, that Evangeline realized just how physically close they were.

She was a tall woman, but he was still taller, and she had to look up at him as their eyes met. Whether it was a trick of the light or the quiet tenor of reflection after their heated words, she had no idea. But in that moment it was so nice to simply be.

With him.

The quiet tension spun out, Troy's gaze never leaving hers. And it was only as she was about to move away that his hand came over her shoulder, pulling her close. He bent his head, his lips finding hers on a quiet sigh.

The kiss was unexpected and lovely, that sigh feathering over her lips on a warm exhale of breath. She leaned into it, moving closer into his arms, surprised at the immediate flare of desire that filled her. Yes, she'd been attracted to him. For a long time she'd both admired him and had a small crush on him. But this…

It was incendiary.

The immediate spark to flame of heat and need that flowed effortlessly between them.

The feel of his large hands as they gripped her shoulders, pulling her even closer.

The touch of his tongue to her lips as he sought entrance to her mouth.

It was overwhelming and heady, a fantasy coming to life.

And as she opened her lips against his, Evangeline knew this moment in time was everything.

TROY FLOWED WITH the waves of desire that battered him, head to toe and back again. He felt their power in the press of his lips against hers. The feel of her body as her lithe frame fit against him. The softness of her skin as his fingertips ran, featherlight, against her nape.

She was beautiful.

And, for the moment, every fantasy he'd ever had about Evangeline Whittaker was coming true. Right there in the middle of her kitchen.

Which was…a problem.

Troy stilled before dragging his lips from hers.

What was he doing?

She'd had a terrible night and he'd brought her home. There were still a ton of questions about what she'd seen in that downtown alleyway. And—

And she was a *colleague*. Yes, a distant one, but one he was sworn to protect, not kiss senseless in her kitchen.

"Troy?"

Her dark eyes were wide with desire, her pupils dilated despite the overhead lights above her sink.

"I'm sorry, Evangeline." He dropped the hands that still cupped her shoulder and upper back as if suddenly singed by the heat through the thin material of her summer blouse. "I'm so sorry. That was forward and inappropriate of me."

"No, I—" She took a few steps back, before pressing her hands together in a tight fold against her waist. "It's fine. Really it is. Thank you for dinner." Her gaze alighted on the sink. "And for doing the dishes, which you didn't have to do."

"It wasn't a problem. Look, I should be going."

He saw the tight, tense smile fall before she nodded, seemingly reassuring herself. "Of course."

"I'll call you tomorrow to check in." On a frown, he pulled out his phone. "I don't think I have your number and I want to make sure you answer if I call."

"The dreaded robocall. I never answer those."

"Me, either. So this will be easier. What's your number?" Troy tapped it into his phone as she rattled the ten digits off, sending her a quick text once he had it in place in his contacts. "There. Now you have mine, too."

He heard a distant ping from the direction of her purse, settled on a chair in the corner of the kitchen, and was satisfied he'd at least be able to reach her again to update her on the progress with her case.

"Troy." He glanced up from his phone, well aware he was using technology as a distraction from the suddenly tense atmosphere in the kitchen. "Thank you. For everything. I needed a cop. But I also needed a friend."

At her honesty, the awkwardness between them seemed to fall away. Yes, he was attracted to her, but he actually *liked* her, too. They had known one another for a long time and while they didn't really cross social circles, they were friendly acquaintances. Kiss or no kiss, that meant something.

"I'm glad I could help." He tucked his phone into his pocket and headed for the hallway. "Why don't you follow me and lock up? I'll call tomorrow to check in on you."

"Will you promise me you'll give me updates? Even if they continue to be inconclusive. I'd like to know what's going on."

He stilled, unwilling to give too many concessions on an active investigation, yet unable to fully say no. With that in the forefront of his thoughts, Troy stopped in the hallway, turning to look at Evangeline fully. It was only when he had her gaze, direct on his, that he spoke.

"I'll share whatever I can, when I can. I meant what I said before. I believe you. But I won't go against protocol and I won't break the rules of an active investigation."

"I'm not asking you—" She stopped herself, a small smile—the first he'd seen since dinner—settling over her face. "I guess I was asking you to do that, so let me amend my answer. Go be Detective Colton and do your job. And I promise to remember that I'm not ADA Whittaker right now, barreling through any and all red tape to get the answers I want."

"There she is. The fighter we all know and love." Troy headed for the door, satisfied they'd hit more even ground. "And I still promise to call tomorrow."

It was only when he stepped through her front door,

waiting on the other side until he heard the snick of the lock, that Troy realized the words he'd used to reassure her. One big one in particular. *Love.*

As he got into his car and started the ignition, it continued to linger in his thoughts, keeping him company on the drive across town toward home.

EVANGELINE WALKED BACK to the kitchen, surprised to realize Troy's light scent still lingered in the air. Just as his kiss still lingered on her lips. The subtle hints of leather from his holster stood out, as did the remembrance of how warm his skin had felt through the material of his shirt beneath her fingers.

She'd kissed him.

The thought dazzled her as she put their now-clean dinner dishes back in the cabinet. Right there, in front of the sink. And it had been amazing. Yes, she'd been lonely when she'd headed out that night, but wonderfully enough, the kiss hadn't been about loneliness. Or sadness. Or any sense that she was failing at life.

Oh no, this kiss was about passion and interest and mutual need. And for the first time in more months than she could describe, she felt something other than fear or gloom or disappointment.

The cabinet door slipped from her fingers, hitting the frame with a thud. It was only when she heard an answering noise, much harder, from the back of her condo, that something dark and cold ran down her spine.

Even as her mind whispered, warning her to calm down, Evangeline fought it. She knew what she'd heard. And while she'd felt the lock in the front door turn beneath her own fingers mere moments before, she hadn't been anywhere near her back door.

As an owner on the bottom floor of the condo complex, she had two entrances to her home. The front door she normally used and a door that led to the grassy public area between buildings. Hadn't she locked it earlier?

She remembered checking it, but had she actually turned the lock in the door? Felt the hard snap of the dead bolt beneath her fingers?

As that fear kicked in again, knocking her heart against her chest with heavy thumps, she fought for a deep breath. It was an odd night wrapping up a tiring and difficult stretch of weeks. That was all. It was summertime and people enjoyed the common area of the complex long into the evening, barbecuing, or it could be neighbors sitting around talking. Maybe someone tried the wrong door heading back to their own home.

Yet even as she tried to talk herself out of what she'd heard, Evangeline reached for the sharp kitchen scissors in the small caddy she kept near the stove. With the handle-end wrapped tightly in her fist, she left the kitchen and headed for her back door. Even from this distance, she couldn't see any sign of entry. The door was closed firmly. She kept her gaze trained on the hallway and the small powder room that speared off near the back door.

Could someone be hiding in there?

Tightening her grip, Evangeline moved closer. Just shy of the bathroom she twisted so her free hand could swing around the doorframe and flip on the lights, even as her body remained physically protected by the wall.

Only no one was there as light flooded the small space.

The heavy thump of her heartbeat calmed slightly as she took in the area. The back door was closed and she could see from where she stood that the dead bolt was still thrown. No one was in the bathroom. There wasn't any other place to hide on the back side of the condo. And Troy had been with her for the past hour, walking through the front of her home.

They'd have both heard if anyone had gotten by.

Satisfied it was one more weird occurrence in a night full of them, Evangeline rechecked the dead bolt for her own comfort and walked back to the kitchen, dropping the scissors back into their rightful place.

"Skittish much, Whittaker?"

The sound of her voice did little to comfort the tangling, jangling nerves that still twisted beneath her skin, but she was determined to ignore it.

What was it Troy had said? Very little couldn't be helped by a bit of food and a good night's sleep.

She'd had the burger and now it was time for rest.

The lovely image Troy had painted of his stepmother's kind warmth and genuine caring kept her company as she walked into her bedroom. It was only as she hit the light switch and saw the book on her nightstand, propped up and facing her, that she screamed.

She had never purchased a travel book about the state of Michigan.

Nor had she left one in her room.

Chapter Five

Troy answered the call on the first ring, his in-dash Bluetooth lighting up with Evangeline's name.

"Hello?"

"Troy!" A hard sob muffled his name but nothing could hide the agony in her tone. "Someone's here! Or was here!"

He had just turned into his neighborhood and was already swinging around the nearest cul-de-sac as her frantic words continued spilling from the speakers. Something about her back door and a book and her bedroom, all running together in a rush of words.

"Evangeline." When she continued sobbing, he pushed harder. "Evangeline!"

"Yes?"

"Are you still in the house? Have you called nine-one-one?"

"No one—" She hiccupped. "No one is here. I checked."

She checked?

White hot anger filled him at the thought of her being in the house by herself, walking around looking for an intruder.

And what the hell was an intruder doing in her home

in the first place? He was just there. Hell, he'd left less than ten minutes ago. And while he'd own being somewhat distracted, especially there at the end with their kiss, he'd have known if someone was in her condo.

Wouldn't he?

He might not have seen her entire place but he hadn't missed how the bedrooms had been tucked away off a hallway on the opposite side of the living room. The layout was well done, keeping the bedrooms separate from the kitchen to allow for privacy while entertaining. Would that have given someone time to get inside? Or more to the point, to get out while he and Evangeline had been enjoying dinner?

He raced through several lights leading into downtown, retracing the route he'd just driven.

He needed to get to her.

That lone thought accompanied him as he navigated through the last mile to her home. As the various landmarks that made up his hometown flew past, Troy considered all he knew.

Evangeline's initial 911 call earlier this evening. The strange, empty alley even CSI couldn't decipher. And now a possible intruder.

What was going on with this woman?

Did someone have an ax to grind? Or worse, was she targeted in some way? As an image of their latest case file on Len Davison came up, Troy's blood ran cold.

Was it possible Davison was changing pattern?

He wasn't that well versed in serial-killer behavior but he'd had enough police training to understand the basics. The adherence to pattern. The odd comfort the killer found in repetitive actions, matching some internal motive only he or she understood. And the even more dangerous points of tension when that pattern escalated.

It was Len Davison's escalation that had put the GGPD in their current situation, facing off against the man's devious mind. But another change in that pattern? That would be akin to a bomb going off in the middle of Grave Gulch. They had some sense of what they were up against based on Davison's approach to his victims. Men of a certain age, out alone after dark. A kill every two months.

But if that pattern changed?

Then no one in Grave Gulch was safe.

Troy swung into Evangeline's parking lot, pulling into an empty space in front of her home. He raced for the door, his hand lifted to pound on the thick wood just as it swung open. She stood there, still in the outfit she'd worn through dinner. If he'd thought she looked peaked and scared when he met her on the street in Grave Gulch, it was nothing compared to the pallor that now filled her face.

"You're here." She said it on a breathy sob before throwing herself into his arms.

Troy held on tight, his gaze already roaming over her head and through the open door beyond. He couldn't see anything out of place but she'd sobbed into the phone about her bedroom and a book.

Pulling back, Troy stared down at her. Her dark eyes were wild in her face, the pupils blown wide with another burst of fear-pumping adrenaline. But in the midst of that panic, he saw something else.

Terror.

And the man who'd spent his life imagining his mother's last moments simply couldn't walk away.

"Let's go inside and I'll check everything out."

"I already did."

"I'll do it again. And then I want you to tell me what happened."

They walked back into the house, his arm around her shoulders. With deliberate motions, he turned and closed the door, flipping the lock as he did so. Pointing toward the sofa, he directed her there. "Why don't you take a seat for a minute and I'll check everything out?"

Evangeline nodded, taking the seat as he instructed. Her shoulders trembled and he walked back to her, grabbing a blanket off the back of the couch and settling it around her shoulders.

"It's the dead of summer."

"And you're shaking like it's February." Troy nestled the blanket around her shoulders. "Warm up a bit. I'll be right back."

He walked through the entire house, itching to pull his service piece out of its holster but holding back. Evangeline had already confirmed her own visual search and it felt like an unnecessary step that carried more risk of scaring her instead of protecting them. But he remained conscious of its heft and weight as he combed her house, room by room.

Enter, sweep, review.

He did the two bedrooms off the living room, checking closets, the en suite bathrooms and even under the bed, before moving on. The book she'd mentioned—what looked like a travel guide on her nightstand—was there and Troy eyed it but didn't touch it. He'd ask her about that after he cleared the rest of her home.

He glanced at her briefly as he moved back through the living room. Evangeline was still huddled on the same chair where he'd left her, the blanket wrapped around her. The haunted look still rode her dark gaze but he could see some color returning, erasing the pallor of her skin. Satisfied she was warming up, the fear of an intruder fading, Troy headed for the kitchen and then on down the small hallway to her back door.

That door wasn't as formal as her front entrance, but its thick wood was serviceable. He'd gotten a good sense of the layout of the condo complex, with front doors facing the parking lot and any back entrances to the homes facing a common area. He opened the door now, bending to search the locks and the area beyond. The dead bolt seemed sturdy enough and he saw no sign of scratches when he looked at it. Still, he'd like to check it in the light, as well, to look for anything that might be out of place.

Stepping through the door, he kept his gaze on the small spread of poured stone that made up her back patio, two overstuffed chairs set up around a wrought iron coffee table. The area was pretty, he noted. Simple but cozy, with the inviting chairs giving a place to curl up and enjoy a book on a summer afternoon. The nearby firepit ensured she could use the space well into the fall, even as the Michigan nights grew crisp.

Executing a full turn, Troy surveyed the space. Looking to his left and right, he could see matched patios spreading down in both directions, Evangeline's neighbors having various furniture setups of their own. Everyone had managed a sense of privacy, even without formal fencing separating each home. It was only as he gazed on past the patios to the shared lawn beyond that Troy recognized how easy it would be to sneak around behind her building.

The furniture did provide a layer of cover and if no

one was in the yard—or the reverse, if there were a lot of people milling around and enjoying the day—it wouldn't take much to walk up to the back entryway of any of the first-floor homes.

He headed back into the house, closing up and locking the door. He saw nothing to indicate an intruder had been in her condo or had used aggressive means to gain entry. A flag that was too close for comfort to the incident earlier in the alley.

A frantic call with no body.

Now a frantic call without any evidence of a break-in.

Troy stared down the hallway toward the living room.

It was time to talk to Evangeline.

EVANGELINE FINALLY FELT the warmth return to her limbs, the achy trembling that had suffused her body fading. Although the blanket had seemed silly overkill for June, she was grateful for Troy's quick thinking.

And his even quicker arrival.

She'd been tempted to follow him as he searched the house, but he seemed insistent that she wait in the living room. And the few quiet minutes gave her a chance to gather her thoughts.

What was someone doing in her home?

Over and over, she'd sought some sort of explanation but had none. That book wasn't hers. And even more jarring, other than going out this evening for a bit of a walk, she'd been home nearly nonstop for two weeks. She had gone out the day before to get some groceries while the cleaning woman was in, doing the house, but Kathy hadn't reported anything odd when Evangeline had returned home.

Although she hadn't made much of a mess over the

past few weeks, tidying to keep herself busy, Evangeline didn't have the heart to call Kathy off and not pay her for a service. Because the house was spotless, she had finished earlier than usual, heading out a few minutes after Evangeline had unpacked her groceries. They'd exchanged a few pleasantries before Kathy headed off to her next job.

No mention of anyone even knocking on the door. No delivery of a package. And while Kathy was an avid reader and could have left something behind as a pass along, her tastes trended toward popular fiction, not travel guides to the state where she had already lived a lifetime.

The book made no sense. And certainly not perched on her nightstand, the cover facing out.

"I've checked everything," Troy said, his large, competent form seeming to fill the living room by his very presence. "The house is secure and I can't find anything out of place."

The house is secure.

Not "no one is here," Evangeline thought.

Just a quick, clinical *The house is secure.*

Secure implied safe. And she felt neither.

"Thank you for checking. And for coming back."

Troy took a seat on the couch, facing her. "Why don't you take me through it? From the point I left until the point I got back here."

Evangeline considered the best way to start. The slamming of the door? The book? Or maybe she should just start by pleading with him to believe that she had her sanity firmly intact.

In the end, she did as he requested—at the beginning—and went straight through to the end. Troy never interrupted, but a whirl of emotions crossed his face, from anger to grim resolve, with a stop at fury along the way.

"Have you had any issues with your back door before? Anyone unwanted?"

"My neighbor made a mistake the first week she lived here. She'd gone down to sit out in the common area and tried the wrong door when she came back up, confusing which condo was hers. It was totally innocent and she apologized profusely. It also gave us a chance to meet each other."

"You've had no other problems since?"

"Troy, it was hardly a problem." She sat up, pushing the blanket off her shoulders. "That was a mistake."

"And I'm trying to understand if it was possible it could happen again."

"It wasn't like that."

"How was it different?"

Just like the series of questions earlier, she recognized his patience and appreciated it. Yet even as she knew his questions were fair, Evangeline couldn't fully fight the tense knot of embarrassment that kept screaming he didn't believe her.

"It was—" She hesitated, well aware how the next words would make her sound. She told herself to hold it back, but something pushed her forward. "It was different tonight. There was a sinister quality to it I can't explain. Just like I haven't been able to explain why I feel like I've been watched for the past few weeks, even though it's been there all the same."

"You what?" Troy leaned forward, his forearms perching on the edge of his knees. "You've been watched?"

"I feel like I've been watched. I can't prove it."

Troy had been on high alert since racing up to her front

door, but at the admission she'd felt watched, his entire demeanor changed. "Watched? Where?"

"Everywhere. It's been going on for a few weeks now. I felt it a few times before I went on leave from my job and now that I've been home it's happened more frequently. Even sometimes when I'm in the house."

That sense of someone looking at her through the window. Or the feeling of a *presence* on the few occasions she'd gone to sit on the back porch, trying to divert her mind with a book or magazine.

"When was the last time it happened?"

"Earlier. Tonight." The same fury she'd sensed earlier was back in full force, darkening his hazel eyes to a fiery amber. "When I was walking around downtown."

"And you didn't think to mention it?"

"I forgot. And when I thought about it again it didn't seem relevant to what I saw in the alley."

"It's all relevant, Evangeline. And when you add on that we've got a serial killer on the loose, ignoring your instincts is the worst thing you can do."

Without warning, a long-forgotten memory rose up to the forefront of her thoughts. It had been one of her biggest cases to date at the DA's office and she'd had to depose darn near half of the county in the process. A beloved, well-respected teacher had been embezzling from the district, siphoning money off over a span of nearly two decades. Administrators, fellow teachers and the PTA were all up in arms that they'd had no idea what had been happening just under their noses. But it was an older woman who worked in the administration office whose testimony about the guilty teacher had resonated. *Something was off from the day she started. I couldn't put my finger on it and I'd never have guessed she was doing this, but I knew something wasn't right with her.*

That testimony had stuck with Evangeline through the years. The woman's absolute conviction something was wrong. And the reality that she'd been right all that time.

It felt stupid to say it out loud, with no obvious evidence to back her up, but she had felt off. The world around her had felt off. And her instincts had been clamoring at her for weeks now.

Maybe it was time to start paying attention. Real attention. The sort that caught criminals.

"I wasn't ignoring anything. Or more to the point, I wasn't trying to," Evangeline added. "It felt silly to admit it. To say it out loud."

"It's not silly and it's something you should be admitting. It's one more piece I need to look for. Anyone lurking around here that doesn't belong is a good place to start."

"Troy, you don't need to make this your problem. The GGPD is dealing with a whole lot worse right now."

"You are my problem. The moment I took the call to come help you tonight, you became my problem. You're also the prosecuting attorney directly tied to Len Davison's freedom. Which only further reinforces my point."

She wanted to be his partner, not his problem. That thought came on her swiftly, the memories of their kiss winging right back along, as well. The noise in the house and the scare from the book—about Michigan, of all things?—had erased their kiss from her immediate thoughts, but now that Troy was sitting here, looking like the very source of safety in his big, broad shoulders and large, capable hands, the memory was back.

Her lips still tingled from the feel of his. Her body

was still warm in all the places that muscular form had pressed against her. And for the first time, Evangeline had to wonder if she was in real danger. She believed in the GGPD's ability to watch out for her and keep her safe.

But she had no idea how she was going to hide the very real feelings of attraction she had for Troy. Feelings she'd kept tamped down for so long, which she now had a glimmer of hope about.

TROY POURED BOILING water from the teakettle into two mugs. He hadn't gotten much more out of his discussion with Evangeline. Any questions he posed about her feelings of being watched were met with vague descriptions.

How did you use that? The reality was that you couldn't.

While he didn't disregard her feelings, the sensation of being watched was different than actually being able to describe someone. Height, build, possible weight. All of it was needed to go find a suspect.

Again, his thoughts swirled around the subject of Len Davison. Was the man escalating? Did he have Evangeline in his sights? His initial concern—that Davison was breaking pattern—was still there, but Troy knew it wasn't the only answer. If Davison had put his focus on Evangeline, it could also be out of a desire to remove an obstacle from his path.

Yes, she'd been instrumental to ensuring Davison stayed out of jail, but now that she knew the truth, she was a voice for putting him away. It could be enough to break pattern.

And what about Bowe?

Troy nearly bobbled the mug, as his hand tightened on the handle, his anger at Randall Bowe a living thing.

Damn, but the man had done damage. Terrible damage that had cost people their lives.

Righting both mugs in his hands, Troy walked back to the living room. That peaked look had left her features, but Evangeline still appeared wrung out from the day's events, her legs curled under her on the large oversize chair that sat offset from her couch. Had it only been a matter of hours since she put that 911 call into the precinct?

Yes, he thought with no small measure of surprise, it had.

In that time, he had been forced to question her motives more than once, and yet still managed to kiss her. An act that was so far out of line he was still upbraiding himself for the personal slip.

"Here's your tea." He set one of the mugs down on the small coffee table before taking his own seat on the couch.

"Can I ask you a question?"

"Of course," Troy said.

"Do you believe me?"

"I believe you believe what you're telling me."

As answers went, he knew it was unsatisfactory, but he had nothing else to give her and he wasn't going to prevaricate on an answer to make her feel better. The reality was, this was an active investigation barely six hours old.

"I guess that's something." Her tone was flat as she stared into her mug.

"It *is* something, Evangeline." Troy leaned forward, setting his mug on the coffee table. He wanted her to understand his perspective, even if it wasn't what she wanted to hear. "I'm not going to lie to you. And I'm not going to give you information that is untrue. But just as I told you before, I can't tell you everything. And I take my job seriously enough to do it the right and proper way."

Even if I did kiss you.

It continued to haunt him. He'd *kissed* her. Really kissed her, the sort that had mouths and breaths and bodies mingling as they joined. And it had been all he had ever imagined. All he'd hoped, really.

It was funny, Troy realized, that all this time he'd admired her from afar, keeping his professional distance, he'd known deep down that he had feelings for her. Feelings that, if he were to give in to them, could be so much more.

Only now, the timing was off. He needed to protect her, not romance her. And wasn't that the real surprise?

"I'm not lying to you, Troy. I'm not making this up."

Grateful for the distraction from his errant thoughts, Troy keyed back into Evangeline's plea. "That's why I said I believe you."

"But if I'm being fair, I can also understand why you think the way you do. I realize there isn't any evidence. I know how outlandish it sounds to tell you things happened, when there's no proof that they did. All I can tell you is that I know what I saw earlier in that alley. I know what I heard in my own home. I know for a fact that book on my dresser is not mine."

At her mention of the book, Troy stood. "I left the book where it was when I swept the house, but I'd like to look at it again. I'd like to understand what it was about this particular book that upset you."

As if pleased there was something to do, Evangeline stood, those dark eyes a little bit brighter. "It was the book itself, as well as where it was placed. Standing up, face out, so that I wouldn't miss it."

She made a good point, especially the fact the book was standing. Even if the travel guide was her own, some forgotten impulse purchase, no one left books standing up face out.

He followed her into the bedroom, the entire experience much more intimate than when he had done the sweep of her home earlier. This was where she slept. He felt surrounded by her scent in here, the light swirl of mint and jasmine a sensual feast.

Determined to ignore that thought, and the hints of impropriety it smacked of, Troy followed her to the nightstand. "A travel guide to Michigan?"

"Yes. I don't have a book like this. Nor do I have any interest in owning a book like this, so it's not like I forgot that I purchased it at some point."

"Is it possible anyone left it behind?"

"I thought about that, earlier. Other than the woman who cleans my home, no one has been here. And she's hardly diving into books about Michigan travel, either, or leaving them as a present for me to read."

He considered saving the book for prints, but knew it was a bit frivolous, based on CSI's already overworked caseload. Still, it was worth keeping, especially with his suspicions about Davison.

He snagged a tissue from the box on the corner of the nightstand, gingerly lifting the book but not putting his own fingerprints on it. With careful movements, he turned it over to read the back.

Thoughts of Davison filled his mind once again. Was this some sort of clue? So far, they believed all of the man's crimes had been concentrated in Michigan. Was this meant to be some sort of taunt? A sign that he would strike again? Or more, a sign that he could do his deeds anywhere across the state and not just in Grave Gulch County?

"Have you prosecuted any cases that could be tied to this?"

"Not that I can think of. Nothing I've done, or the crimes I've handled, have screamed 'travelogue.'"

Gingerly, Troy set the book back down, leaving the tissue lying on top of the cover. He would come back in with a plastic bag and take it in for evidence. CSI may not be able to prioritize the fingerprints, but at least they would have the book in evidence. They couldn't afford to overlook any and all things that might relate to the Davison case.

If there was something nefarious afoot, processing the book would need to be prioritized on CSI's exhaustive caseload.

Hadn't this evening suggested as much? He was well aware he couldn't divert his focus from the problems currently plaguing Grave Gulch. But as he stared down at that book, Troy knew he was in this now.

Evangeline Whittaker needed help. And he'd be damned sure she was going to get whatever she needed.

"I'd like to stay here tonight. I'll take the couch or your spare room, but I don't want you here alone."

"You don't have to do that. Especially because I'm starting to feel really silly sobbing into your ear over a travel book."

He saw the false bravado and couldn't stop the impulse to reach out and brush a wayward lock of hair that had fallen over her cheek. Tucking it gently behind her ear, Troy insisted, "You weren't silly and you need to stop saying that."

"It was silly."

"You were scared. And I'd like to take a look at that lock in the fresh light of morning anyway."

"It's silly and—" She broke off on a deep exhale before turning to face him fully. "And I'd really appreciate having you here as backup."

Chapter Six

Troy took another big sip of coffee and navigated his way through the seemingly ever-present protesters outside the police station. He respected and admired the right to peacefully assemble but it was getting increasingly difficult to hear the shouting reverberating throughout the precinct. He was as frustrated as the protesters with the current situation in Grave Gulch and their waving signs felt like a visual reminder of the GGPD's failure to protect them.

The added pressure of a sleepless night, his proximity to Evangeline more challenging than he would've anticipated, had him feeling like a tired grizzly bear this morning.

And of course, he had Melissa's staff meeting first thing.

Heading into the precinct, he waved at the team on the front desk with the second cup of coffee he had in hand for Brett. "Is Detective Shea in yet?"

The earnest young man riding the front desk nodded his head, Mary Suzuki's Sunday shift earning her a day off. "Yes, sir. Detective Shea has been in for about an hour."

"Thank you." Troy avoided the inwardly disparaging

thoughts that threatened, well aware he was entitled to an evening off, even if Brett had stayed. And it was not like his time with Evangeline was a date. Her involvement in the Davison case meant her situation needed to be watched and monitored. Evaluated.

Evaluation that includes kissing? his inner voice piped up.

Ignoring the mental taunts, Troy headed straight for Brett's office, not even stopping at his own to drop his workbag off.

"You look like you had a night," Brett greeted him with a hearty smile as he looked up from his desk.

"Then I'm keeping the extra coffee I picked up for you all to myself."

"Gimme." Brett held out a hand as Ember perked up from her large pillowed perch beside the desk.

"I'm sorry, girl, I didn't bring anything for you." Troy said to the pretty, black Lab, who thumped her tail in response.

"Don't worry," Brett said. "She's got her after-practice bone coming her way in another hour or so."

"It's a full-time job, isn't it?"

"Ember's training?" Brett looked up from his coffee at the question. "It is, but it's time we both enjoy."

"Is there any chance that training could've overlooked something in the alley last night?"

As questions went it was certainly loaded, and more than a little fraught with hope. But he had to ask anyway.

"I'd like to tell you no, but unfortunately I don't think I can. And if it just rested on her training, I wouldn't be so confident. But the CSI report was pretty clear."

"Damn it, I know. I read through it this morning before heading in."

He had done a quick scan first for the basics and then a second time through to get all the nuances. The report was clear and irrefutable. No sign of any violent activity or blood.

"Look, you know you've got backup on this," Brett said. "I saw that woman's face last night when we arrived on scene, and I don't think the sheer terror that paled her skin was made up."

"Thank you for that. I appreciate it. And the support."

"I only have one question for you in return."

"What's that?" Troy replied.

"Are you prepared if the answer doesn't come back in her favor?"

It was a fair question, and one that he'd asked himself more than once through the long hours in Evangeline's spare bedroom until dawn. He believed her and thought that she was telling the truth as she knew it. Yet even with that confidence in her, he couldn't deny that there were doubts. In the lack of CSI evidence as well as any trace a K-9 could pick up.

Both sat at the top of his list.

"I'll do what needs to be done. You can count on that," Troy assured his partner.

"All I need to hear."

Brett stood at that, Ember coming to immediate attention at his side. "It's time to head into the chief's meeting."

When Troy and Brett walked into the main conference room, Melissa was already putting together her notes at the head of the table. She turned to look at both men as they entered. "Sounds like you two had quite an evening last night."

"One more frustrating dead end in a year that's been

full of them," Troy said, hearing the ready annoyance in his own voice.

"Is that all?"

Troy loved his cousin Melissa and had absolute respect for her as their chief of police, but it was never very comfortable to be on the receiving end of her questions, especially the ones that ended in raised eyebrows. "I think so. The investigation is open and active, even if initial results are inconclusive."

"Can you have the full report to me by this afternoon?" she asked.

"Yes, absolutely." Troy would have it done by lunch, unwilling to let the situation with Evangeline rest. They had too much riding on this, both for Evangeline's own safety as well as the potential connections to Len Davison and Randall Bowe. "I'm also happy to give an update during the meeting, as to what I know so far."

Melissa nodded. "See that you do."

Troy took a seat and settled in. He enjoyed their staff meetings. He'd come to look forward to the camaraderie and partnership he felt inside that conference room.

While their collective sense of team spirit had never been higher, their work had become more challenging of late. Grave Gulch wasn't small, per se, but its share of violent crime had always been at manageable levels. Unlike their counterparts in Grand Rapids or even larger metropolitan areas like Detroit, they'd always found overall crime here to be somewhat subdued.

Until the start of this year.

The things that had happened since January—his nephew's kidnapping at Mary's wedding almost a catalyst of sorts—had been on the extreme end of what law enforcement would experience in an average year.

And nothing about this year had been average so far.

It was like he'd said to Evangeline the night before. Things just felt *off*. And while that was hardly a term he'd use with his colleagues, it was one that fit.

Within minutes, the rest of the squad had taken seats around the room and Melissa called the meeting to order. They would hit the high points of their ongoing investigations, but Melissa usually started by asking about any late-breaking or important details they needed to know.

This morning was no different.

"We have an update on Davison." Melissa broke her typical pattern by launching into their most pressing case herself.

Troy opened his mouth, before snapping it shut at the dark look from Melissa.

"Saturday, Davison broke into the home of an elderly couple here in Grave Gulch. They are thankfully unharmed, but terribly scared. He tied them up while he went through their home, used their shower, stole their food and ultimately cleaned them out of all money and valuables inside the house."

"Son of a bitch," Brett muttered under his breath.

"That he is, Detective Shea." Melissa eyed him from where she stood at the front of the room, her comment both the signal that she had heard him regardless of how quietly he spoke, and that she agreed with her newest detective wholeheartedly.

"He is armed and dangerous, proof from the fact that he held that couple tied up and at gunpoint for almost thirty-six hours. And while we remain pleased that he didn't take the situation any further, and both the husband and wife have been checked out and released at this point with a clean bill of health, Davison continues to prove himself a dangerous criminal."

Troy considered the timeline, as he listened to the rest of Melissa's overview. Work had already begun to notify any pawnshops who might get some of the jewelry described by the couple, and additional K-9 resources were being brought in to comb the area around the couple's home. "Detective Shea," Melissa continued, "we need you and Ember over there with the rest of the team today."

"Of course." Brett nodded, shooting the dog a quick glance over his shoulder where she rested behind his chair.

"Melissa? When did Davison gain entry into the home?" Troy asked.

"Sometime Saturday, best the couple can tell. They were out earlier in the day and he was there in the afternoon once they had come back in from running errands. He departed late last night. The couple finally worked themselves free from the ropes he'd used to tie them up around three this morning. They immediately called for help."

Troy backed his way through the timeline. Davison had been in Grave Gulch for at least thirty-six hours as he held the couple hostage. Possibly longer since there was no telling exactly how early he'd gotten into their home while they were out. But if the man had been in Grave Gulch throughout the weekend, it was very possible he could have also orchestrated the situation Evangeline saw the alley. Especially if he was on the run and fighting with some sort of female helper.

It could fit.

Yet even as he considered it, Troy knew the scenario rang false. The timing was a possible match but little else. Davison was a suspected lone wolf. From all they'd learned, the man continued to bear the grief of losing his wife to cancer after more than thirty years of marriage and it was that spark—the death of his wife—that pushed him into killing.

Additionally, Evangeline might not have clearly seen the man at the end of the alley, but based on her description of his height, weight and overall physical heft, the assailant she observed wasn't a match for Davison.

Which meant it was very possible they were dealing with someone else altogether.

A reality that didn't sit any better on his shoulders.

He meant his promise to Brett. He would do whatever needed to be done. He'd never let his partner, his chief or his department down like that.

But he'd do what needed to be done for Evangeline, too.

He just hoped like hell those promises weren't at odds with one another.

EVANGELINE FINALLY QUIT roaming around the house about an hour after Troy left. She'd already taken a walk around the condo complex, talking for a while with her upstairs neighbor, Ella, and trying to clear her mind of the cobwebs that seemed to have settled there. She was restless and anxious, despite the exercise, but enough was enough. It was only when she'd settled on the idea to sit down with a legal pad that she'd finally felt a bit like her old self.

With a pen and paper in hand, she was the problem solver. The strategist. And the woman who knew how to take charge and use the legal system to its full benefit. A woman who made lists, reviewed evidence, wrote briefs and understood that the truth didn't come in waves, but as a series of revelations and approaches that got you to a successful outcome. It was how she'd argued cases for years and it was time to apply that same logic to her own life.

With renewed energy coursing through her veins, she wrote down her first question. What did she know?

Randall Bowe had falsified evidence in numerous cases. A situation Arielle's office had been combing through, trying to determine where falsely imprisoned individuals needed their cases reviewed.

She knew the DA's side but needed Troy's additional details there through a cop's eyes. Best they currently understood, the disgraced CSI leader had tampered with evidence for reasons only he seemed to know and, once discovered, gone on the run. He wasn't a killer but he'd enabled one in Len Davison.

Which brought her to her second note. Len Davison was responsible for the murder she'd prosecuted; thanks to Bowe's tampering with the evidence, he'd been acquitted. He'd gone on to kill again, his pattern focused on men in their fifties, out alone, walking dogs in the park. Each victim had died with a single gunshot to the chest. He'd struck three times and while Troy hadn't said much the night before, she knew enough legal psychology to know that the third murder meant Davison had graduated to serial killer.

Interestingly, the dogs hadn't been harmed. Evangeline tapped the back of her pen to the paper, considering the angle. Did it mean something?

She got up and padded to her spare room to retrieve her laptop from the small desk she maintained in there. It was only as she entered the room that she stilled. The bed was neatly made, no sign that Troy had ever been there. Unless you counted the lingering scent of him and the knowledge that his head had lain on the very pillows now propped on the bedframe. Something warm filled her stomach, suffusing out to her limbs, and she couldn't hold back the smile.

He'd been the soul of propriety last night, but he'd also insisted on staying. It had been sweet of him and incredibly caring. And it added one more dimension to their kiss. Was it possible he cared?

She'd always been attracted to him, and she knew many women in the county's legal system felt the same. Troy Colton was an attractive man, his broad shoulders and slim hips always sure to garner attention. But when you added on the competence in his work and the innate kindness in his eyes, that attraction had nowhere to go but up.

Unwilling to let her thoughts move too closely toward her quietly held fantasies, Evangeline snagged the laptop quickly off the desk and left the room. And if those hints of sandalwood and fresh summer sunlight still lingered in the room—scents she had reveled in as she'd kissed Troy—well, she needed to shut that part of herself off.

He'd come to help her, not date her. She'd do well to remember that.

Back in front of her legal pad, she opened the laptop and tapped in the details of the Davison murders into a search bar. Just as she'd already known, news reports confirmed he'd killed three times, the pattern the same. All men in their fifties, all out walking dogs in the park. And in each case the pet was unharmed.

A positive situation to be sure, but it seemed significant somehow. As if the dog was the conduit to get to the man in the park but not the object of the attack.

She enjoyed a good thriller as much as the next person and recognized her serial-killer knowledge was heavily steeped in the books she'd read or the movies she'd watched. But there was something about animals... Many future killers escalated over time, having hurt animals as their initial targets.

Yet Davison hadn't touched the dogs. The beloved pets of his victims. That meant something.

With that as her focus, she added more questions to her notepad.

What was his motive? Why these men? And why now, after what seemed like a crime-free life? What had driven Davison to his actions?

Hadn't that been one of the things that made her legal argument seem so clear? Davison didn't have a history of violence and had been considered a good, upstanding citizen. At the time of his trial, she'd had no reason to think the evidence had been tampered with because the man on trial hadn't exhibited any bad behavior—and they hadn't yet known of Bowe's crimes. It didn't excuse her role in his trial, but it was one more item in the "it doesn't add up" column on her notepad.

Nor did it really explain what she was personally dealing with.

Davison might be unstable and increasingly violent, but he had a pattern. One that didn't at all match what was happening to her.

The ongoing sensation of being watched.

The events that had unfolded at work.

Even the incidents the night before felt off.

She knew what she saw, yet there was no evidence to

suggest it had ever happened. Crimes just didn't work that way. Humans left forensic trails, no matter how hard they tried to suppress them. So did guns and ammunition. Yet despite what she'd seen, a trained K-9 and a well-honed team of CSI experts had found nothing in that alley.

It just seemed…impossible.

Which only led to more questions.

Was she overtired and hallucinating? She'd slept terribly over the past few months, the situation at work all-consuming. While she took deep pride in her work ethic and willingness to give her job her all, including late nights and long weekends if necessary, was it possible she'd imagined her fears into existence?

A dark shudder ran the length of her spine and Evangeline stood, heading to the kitchen for a glass of water. She needed to shake this off. This negative thinking that suggested she didn't know her own mind.

Wasn't that the root of her parents' difficult marriage for so many years? Her father had issues controlling his rage, so he'd lash out at the most minimal of offenses or situations. Her mother would cower and cry and he'd apologize later, telling her that his behavior wasn't nearly as out of proportion as her reaction suggested.

A constant game of push-pull on her mother's emotions, suggesting she didn't know her own mind or understand what she'd experienced. That she somehow didn't understand Cecil Whittaker's rage issues and their serious consequences.

For years, Evangeline had observed the problem, helpless to make it change. Her mother protected her as best as she could, bearing the brunt of the emotional abuse and demanding Evangeline stay out of it.

But how did you stay out of it, even as a child?

It wasn't a situation that could be ignored. The roiling anger that seethed beneath the surface in her home had been a steady companion throughout her childhood. It was only once Evangeline was out of the house, off to college, that Dora Whittaker had finally made a change. Had finally left, satisfied that her daughter could no longer be a pawn in a divorce settlement.

Or worse, have to face the same consequences if she were to spend time with her father in a shared custody agreement.

It was no way to live. And while she was grateful her mother had finally gotten out—that they both had—it didn't change the lingering damage her first eighteen years had done.

She took another sip of water, willing the cool liquid to ease her suddenly tight throat. The memories of her parents' marriage always upset her and nothing good ever came of reliving that time in her life. The helpless feelings. The anger at her father, even as she continued to love him as her parent.

It was hurtful and confusing and had left an incredibly dark mark on her life.

The heavy knock on the door pulled her from her musings and Evangeline was grateful for the distraction. She'd go answer it and then make some lunch. She had some of her mother's *sinigang* in the fridge and it would make a soothing antidote to the painful memories. The tamarind soup had always been a favorite and she was already anticipating the rich flavors that had only grown stronger as it spent a few days as a leftover in her fridge.

The knock came again and Evangeline headed more quickly down the hall. She had no idea why whoever was out there hadn't rung the bell but disregarded it as she swung the door open.

And looked down to find a bloody white shirt on her front entryway.

TROY SCROLLED THROUGH the notes he'd jotted down on his phone, confirming he'd included everything in his report for Melissa. He'd already added in the notes he'd taken down in the conference room the day before as Evangeline walked him through the events she witnessed in the alley and now sat back to reread through the report one final time.

He'd nearly finished his read-through when the knock came at his door. "Melissa." He sat back, not surprised his cousin had found her way to his office. "Come in."

"I wanted to discuss the Whittaker case."

He'd figured as much but didn't say it, giving her time to settle in instead. Melissa was a good chief because she innately understood the places that required more of her attention versus the cases that her team had well in hand. She shifted her attention as it was needed and was able to pivot quickly, taking in new information and feeding back theories to her team that they might not have considered yet.

She was also engaged and planning a wedding *and* dealing with the department's troubles. It was that reality that Troy couldn't disregard. The sheer pressure on her shoulders, upholding justice for the citizens of Grave Gulch, all while trying to keep her large, extended family safe.

"Come on in and sit down."

Melissa came fully into his office but she remained standing, her hands clasped behind her back as she stood in front of his desk. "You held back there in the conference room. I got the very clear sense you didn't share all you knew."

"I did share all I knew. My report will support that."

"But?" She left the word hanging there and in that moment she was 100 percent his chief. Their common last name and family connection had zero bearing on her hunt for information.

"But nothing. Detective Shea and I responded to a nine-one-one call last evening. We investigated the scene and were unable to find a body or any indication there'd been a violent incident."

"And you questioned the witness?"

"Extensively. Her story remained unchanged from what she reported to the nine-one-one dispatcher or in her initial feedback on site to Brett and me."

"She's been put on leave from work, you know." Melissa's vivid blue gaze was direct as she said it, that look adding to the undertones in her comment.

"A point Ms. Whittaker and I discussed."

"You don't think that's suspicious?"

"Suspicious how? It has no bearing on witnessing a crime."

"What crime? There's no body and no evidence, Troy."

It was the reality he kept slamming into, no matter how much he wanted to ignore it.

"Tell me you understand that," Melissa pressed.

"Of course I understand it."

"Good. Because I can't afford to have you distracted off the Davison case. He's struck twice since January, and based on his pattern, we need to stop him before he hits again soon."

"I know what we're up against."

Melissa dropped into Troy's guest chair, her strong, capable shoulders deflating. "I know you know. That's what's so tough here."

And just like that, he saw the Melissa he'd grown up with sitting before him across the desk. "I'm running out of answers here, Troy. The man's in his mid-sixties and until his first murder is so squeaky clean he's barely rated a speeding ticket. How does the death of a spouse—even if she was so beloved—make someone do this? To change course so badly? And worse, because he isn't a criminal and presumably has never run in those circles, how has he managed to get away with it all for this long?"

"I don't know, Mel. I really don't."

And wasn't that the worst part of it all? They knew exactly who they were up against. They'd discovered his guilt, the assistance he'd gotten from Bowe, and they'd even built a relationship with Len's daughter, Tatiana. Yet despite all that progress, they were no closer to getting the man in custody.

"How's Tatiana holding up?" Troy asked. Although they'd initially questioned how Davison's daughter could have been unaware of her father's actions, they'd come to learn that she was as shocked and hurt by the news as the families of the man's victims.

Their cousin Travis had had a fling with Tatiana, his co-CEO. They'd soon fallen in love while both were working at Colton Plastics, but her surprise pregnancy had become public around the same time she was being questioned by the police about her father.

It was an extraordinary set of circumstances, but the Colton family had quickly closed ranks around Len's daughter, unwilling to paint her with the same brush as they did her father.

"As good as can be expected," Melissa said. "Travis keeps a close eye and the two of them are busy with Colton Plastics and planning for the baby's arrival. It's keeping her occupied, which has to be good in this situation."

"Does she know this latest news? About the home invasion?"

Melissa nodded. "I called her myself this morning. She handled it. She didn't ask a lot of questions, but she held it together. And Travis has been a rock for her."

Troy thought about what his cousin and his fiancée had dealt with over the past several months and was glad they had each other. He'd always believed he could handle whatever life threw at him—and had little interest in dragging a romantic partner into the risks that came with his work—but he also recognized the power of love.

Although he'd lost his mother when he was barely old enough to remember her, his father had always talked of the great love he shared with Amanda Colton. Geoff also spoke of how lucky he was to find a deep and lasting love with Leanne, long after he'd believed he would never find that sort of companionship and affection again. Lightening had struck twice, as it were. A special circumstance few were fortunate to experience.

"It's good they're together." Troy nearly expanded on the point when his phone went off. Evangeline's name registered on the readout. "I'm sorry, Mel, I need to take this."

She waved him on, even as her gaze narrowed.

"Evangeline. What's—"

"Troy! Someone was here. Outside. The shirt!"

Just like the night before, deep panic vibrated through the phone like a living, writhing entity. "What shirt?"

"The white shirt. It's a bloody mess on my front step."

Chapter Seven

Evangeline huddled on the same living room chair as last night, the air conditioning blowing through the room making it feel like a tomb. She wanted to act—wanted to do *something*—but no matter how often she told herself to move, all she could do was huddle on the chair.

What was wrong with her?

That question frittered and flowed through her mind, at moments an insistent banging and at others quiet and meandering. It was the only one she could seem to conjure, even as fragments of thought kept telling her she should wait outside or at least stand near the window, keeping an eye on that shirt.

But the blood. It was so red. So real. And so…vicious.

The killer must have left it on her front door, a taunting tease that not only reinforced the fear of last night, but ensured something else.

He *knew* where she lived—and had been in her home, too.

The urgent sound of sirens suddenly filled the room. Troy had come.

He was close. He was here. And that meant she was safe.

It was the only thing that could get her moving, she realized, as she stood and walked to the door. The sound of sirens was nearly overpowering as police cars pulled into the parking lot of her building. It was only when Evangeline heard the shouts through the door—and Troy's reassuring voice—that she finally felt ready to open it again.

The door handle was heavy in her hand and she needed to grip it with both hands to turn it. Slowly, slowly it turned and she pulled on the door.

Only to find Troy standing across the threshold, a line of officers behind him.

"Evangeline!" His voice sounded far away as she stared down at the front stoop of her home.

The concrete was empty, no sign of anything even having been there. Frantically, her gaze shifted to the lawn that stretched out to either side. Had the shirt blown away? The summer air felt still around her, not a breeze in sight, but it wouldn't take much to move a shirt, right?

Wind could have blown it from the front porch.

Only, as her gaze roamed the lawn on either side of her and further down the length of her condo building, Evangeline had to accept the truth.

There was no shirt.

No blood.

And no evidence it had ever existed.

THE MAN WATCHED from across the parking lot, a casual observer of what was taking place through his windshield. To anyone who saw him, including the rash of cops, he knew he'd just look like another guy waiting for someone in his car. The book in his lap would be a handy excuse should anyone knock on the window and question what he was doing there. Not that he was planning on sticking around.

But oh, how he'd wanted to see her face.

He'd been hiding down the yard when she opened the door to find the shirt and hadn't had a chance to enjoy the stark shock that would have covered those angelic features.

But he heard the scream.

Loud and pure, it practically reverberated off the bricks of her condo building. And damn, was it a fitting punishment for all she'd failed to do. Because it turned out the angel had a pair of broken wings. And she deserved what she got.

A fact he was more than happy to prove to her by removing the shirt after she'd slammed the door on the evidence. Again, more proof that she couldn't be trusted with the truth.

If she were a good lawyer working for the citizens of Grave Gulch County, she'd never have run in fear like that. She'd have picked up the shirt, no matter how much it bothered her, and brought it inside until her precious cop showed up.

But no.

She did just what he expected her to do. Slam the door on the truth. Just like she'd believed all the evidence from that phony, Randall Bowe.

Oh yeah, he thought as he slowly pulled out of his spot, circling the back of the parking lot to steer clear of the cops. Those wings were mighty broken. And she deserved every single thing that was coming her way.

TROY FELT THE HARD, unyielding gazes of his chief and two fellow cops as he watched Evangeline, stare sightlessly from the chair in her living room. The scene felt way too much like the night before and he was struggling to find any sense of equilibrium as he considered the shuddering woman in the chair.

How did he reconcile her with the strong, competent lawyer he knew?

And what in the hell was going on with her?

She hadn't faked the dread in her voice when she'd called him, nor was she faking the situation now. He'd bet his badge on it.

But still, something remained overwhelmingly off. How was it possible she'd had three panic-inducing scares in a matter of twenty-four hours, yet there was no evidence any of them had taken place? They would get the security footage of the building and several uniforms were already fanning out to canvas the property for witnesses, but the lack of a bloody shirt was a problem.

He'd been so focused on thinking Davison was responsible, but was it possible Randall Bowe had targeted her somehow?

"Troy. Can I speak with you?" Melissa's question was really a request and Troy shot a look at one of the deputies who'd arrived on scene, their silent exchange an order to keep watch on Evangeline.

Melissa waited at the front door of Evangeline's condo and gestured Troy outside. The midday sun was high in the sky, summer making its presence known in the sticky heat. "You want to tell me what's going on here?"

"She called me in distress, Mel."

"I can see that. And you responded in kind." His cousin spread her hand wide to take in the four police cars and scattering of cops milling around the small yard and parking area that made up the exterior of the condo complex. "What I can't see is any sign of evidence."

"I have an idea about that. Is it possible Bowe's trying

to exact some revenge? Planting evidence on her, then taking it away."

"Troy—"

"He could do it. He's already proven he knows how to tamper with evidence, and he's enjoyed making taunts when he can. Wouldn't this be an escalation?"

"Troy!" Her voice was clipped and any sign of the family member and friend he knew and loved had vanished. Right now, she was fully his boss. "Are you listening to yourself? You're making up reasons which, while fair, remove any and all responsibility off Ms. Whittaker."

"But she's scared, Mel."

"And also currently on leave from a high-stress job. A leave that was directly related to letting a very guilty man go. A man who has murdered two more times in a serial fashion since her legal arguments got him released from our custody."

"You're blaming that on her?"

"Some of it, yes," she admitted.

"Because she used evidence our department improperly handled?"

"Where are your loyalties, Troy?"

"Where are yours?"

In all the years he and Melissa had worked together, Troy couldn't ever remember a harsher disagreement between the two of them. In addition to their familial bond, they had a close working relationship and had always been compatible.

But on this he simply couldn't agree with her. He'd seen Evangeline's face. Had watched her tremble in fear. Hell, he'd held her himself, and felt that bone-deep anxiety ripple through her.

He just couldn't walk away from this.

"This isn't about loyalty. This is about doing the job," he said.

"Doing what job? Running at the drop of a hat to placate a hysterical woman?"

"That's not fair."

"The truth isn't always fair." Melissa shook her head before extending a hand in frustration. "Look at it out here. I've got damn near a third of the department stomping around this condo complex while a serial killer roams loose."

"Other crimes haven't stopped because Davison is out free. The Coltons know that better than most." Troy saw the moment he might have gotten through to her. "Drew Orr tried to kill you in January, at the same time we were discovering the depth of Randall Bowe's deception."

"I know that. I lived it." She had had to shoot the man dead herself when he attempted to kill her and her now-fiancé, Antonio.

"Clarke and Everleigh, too," Troy pressed. "Everleigh was nearly killed by her ex-husband's lover, the woman was so hell-bent on revenge."

"You going to give me the whole list of Colton cousins, Troy? Because Travis and Tatiana are still reeling from that creep at Colton Plastics who had his twisted eye on her for far too long. Stanton and Dominique helped us uncover a drug ring operating right here in Grave Gulch County. And Desiree is finally able to sleep at night thanks to getting Danny back and living with the security and protection of Stavros's love. You think I haven't understood the pain my family has gone through these past months?"

"I know you have."

"Then why are you tossing it in my face?"

"Because we Coltons know it better than most. We can't ignore an upstanding citizen right here in Grave Gulch who needs our help."

"What if she's making it up?"

And there it was. The one piece of the puzzle he didn't have an argument for. Because in each of his family's experiences, there had been a clear problem. Escalating violence. Kidnappings. Serious threats.

Where was that here?

Other than what Evangeline claimed to have witnessed, there was nothing he could go on as tangible proof. And unlike his family situations where those terrible incidents had still somehow led to his family finding love, he and Evangeline weren't a couple. Nor did interfering in her life as if he had a right to be there meet his personal standards as a member of the Grave Gulch PD.

In the end, all he could go on was his gut. And the continued feeling that something was going very, very wrong around Evangeline Whittaker.

"What if she isn't?" Troy finally asked Melissa. "Can you honestly say we would have done our job serving and protecting this community if we ignore her?"

Melissa's steady gaze finally dropped, that brilliant blue going cloudy when she lifted her eyes to him once more. "No. That's not what I want."

It was why Melissa was a good cop and an even better chief. She always did what was right and put the health and safety of her constituents above everything else.

"Let me ask you one thing, though."

Troy nodded, already anticipating the warning.

"We've worked long and hard to have a good relationship between our precinct and the DA's office. Randall Bowe's actions have put a serious dent in that relationship."

"Has anyone said anything to you? Has Arielle called you?"

Arielle Parks had a stellar reputation as Grave Gulch County's district attorney but the pressure she'd been under could get to anyone.

"Arielle and I talk regularly about any number of things. We respect each other and also respect the offices we each represent. We've each taken our collective ownership for the damage Bowe has done."

"Why do I sense a *but* in there?"

"I'm giving in on this a bit because Evangeline is one of Arielle's best and most well-respected ADAs. And I trust Arielle's opinion." Melissa glanced around once more. Troy's gaze followed and he couldn't deny the way his fellow officers appeared to be done with work, the lack of evidence leaving them with little to do. "But I also can't allow resources to be used this way."

"I understand."

"Why don't you go talk to Evangeline? See if you can't figure out what's happening. She doesn't have a door camera, which would have been a huge help in this situation."

Troy had noticed the same and was already making plans to ensure Evangeline addressed that problem. They'd get the footage from the parking lot but he already knew there would be gaps in what area of the large parking lot the cameras reasonably covered.

In the meantime, his concern was more narrowly focused. He needed to get Evangeline calm and then get her thinking who could possibly be behind this rash of incidents.

Assuming, of course, it wasn't her.

EVANGELINE HADN'T MISSED the skeptical looks tossed her way for the past hour. But the one she couldn't dismiss from her thoughts was the serious once-over she'd gotten from Chief of Police Melissa Colton.

She'd met the other woman on several occasions, just as she had Troy. They had a cordial, professional relationship and Evangeline had always respected what Melissa had accomplished. While there were some women in law enforcement, Melissa's ascension to chief—and well before forty—was a significant milestone. It was proof, Evangeline had always believed, of a department that truly championed the best person for the job.

It wasn't a position a person attained resting on their laurels. And that sort of person—dogged, committed and absolutely competent—was rather intimidating when they stared you down like you were a common criminal.

Evangeline had finally escaped to the kitchen, puttering around and cleaning the grout around her already-clean sink for something to keep her occupied.

"The team's wrapping up outside." She stopped mid-scrub and turned to see Troy as he stepped into the kitchen.

She'd seen him just that morning but he'd clearly stopped home before going into work. He was now dressed in a crisp, blue button-down shirt and dark slacks. The look was professional and efficient and did nothing to diminish the lethal addition of the holster strapped across his back, his sidearm resting against his body.

"Is everyone gone?"

"Nearly everyone. There's a team finishing up out front, and then they'll head on out."

"Look, Troy, I know how this must look and I'm sorry I called you over here. Sorry that all these people had to come out on a false alarm."

"You have nothing to apologize for."

"Nothing? I called you in hysterics, again, and yet there's nothing outside. I know how that must make me look. I can imagine what your colleagues are thinking. What Melissa is thinking."

"Melissa and my colleagues and I all want to do the right thing. For this investigation and for you."

The right thing? What was the right thing in this situation? She was a lawyer. She dealt in facts. And everything she'd encountered in the past twenty-four hours suggested otherwise.

It was why she had to convince him to leave. To just step away from whatever it was that was going on. Her own career had faced a significant hit these past weeks. She had no desire to do that to someone else. "I'll understand if you just need to walk away."

"Evangeline." Troy moved closer to her, stepping fully into the kitchen. "I'm not walking away. From this, or from you."

"I'm putting you at risk. Your career."

"Clearly *you* are the one at risk." The emphasis he put on the word *you* was pointed. But what that emphasis meant was more than a little scary.

Pushing that away and unwilling to have him dissuade her from doing the right thing, she dismissed his concern. "I'll be fine."

"With bloodied clothes on your front porch and strangers somehow sneaking into your house?"

"Who can even say that happened?"

"You can! You say it happened."

"What if—" She broke off on a hard, unexpected sob. The truth was too horrible to even say. But it haunted her, the idea that her mind could be playing tricks on her like this. "What if I'm wrong?"

Troy pulled her into his arms and as those tight, warm bands wrapped around her, Evangeline allowed herself to give in. She wanted to be strong. More, she believed it was required of her, to stand on her own two feet and handle whatever life threw her way.

But this was too much.

The anger and self-recrimination she'd carried for months now, over the case that let Len Davison go, had weighed heavy. The families who now suffered because he'd taken a beloved father, husband or brother away, haunted her.

What could she have done differently?

There hadn't been any answers. Not since the day Arielle had called Evangeline into her office to tell her the news. The mishandling of evidence that had allowed a guilty man to go free had become public, and with it, the reality of what they'd contributed to the situation by not conclusively proving Davison's guilt.

Despite her desire to stay on the job, she'd accepted the enforced leave. Had understood it as her due, a time to stop and reflect on her work and understand where she'd made missteps.

If that was all she'd had to live with, she'd have accepted it. A legal career was fraught with the cases that haunted you. Evangeline accepted that reality as part of the job. Even when it felt bad.

But all that had come since?

It was terrifying and maddening, all at once.

She clung to Troy, grateful for both the physical support as well as the emotional. He had been such a surprise in all this, almost as if he had come to her rescue. The idea of a rescuer wasn't language or imagery she particularly cared for, especially with the way she had grown up, yet she couldn't quite shake the image, either.

Troy Colton had, literally, come to her aid. He had shown up after the 911 call when she believed she had seen a murder. He had come here to her home, taking care of her with food, understanding and protection. It was humbling, to know someone could care that much. Would give of themselves that freely.

"Are you doing okay?"

She lifted her head, unable to look away from his deep hazel gaze. "Not yet, but I'm trying."

"For starters, you need to stop doubting yourself."

"How can I do that? The things that keep happening, they're impossible."

"They can't be impossible. Which means they have to have a reason. A possibility, if you will, for why they're happening."

"They have a possibility. It's that I'm hallucinating."

His eyes darkened at that, his mouth dropping into a deep frown. "Don't say that."

"What if it's true?" she argued back, the idea taking root. "If there has to be a reason, that is as good as any other one."

"Okay." He tilted his head, considering. "Let's play that idea out. Have you ever hallucinated before?"

"No."

"Not once?"

"No, not that I'm aware of."

"So why did you suddenly start now?"

She let out a frustrated breath, perked up by his reasoning even if she still questioned her own mind. "For people who experience hallucinations, they have to have one for the first time."

"Yes, that's true. But what would be the reason you suddenly have one? One day, randomly walking to get some dinner, in the middle of downtown Grave Gulch."

"Stress. The situation with my job. A serial killer on the loose. Take your pick." The reasons were endless. He had to know that as a law enforcement professional. Heck, he lived with stress every day. Lived with the consequences of criminals that got away with crimes they perpetrated, no matter how well-intentioned the police.

"Fine, let's play that out, too. You've been under stress at other times in your life. Law school's pretty tough and works you intentionally hard to make sure you've got the mental fortitude for the job. The difficulty keeps up as no sooner do you graduate then you have to study for the bar. And now, working your professional career in the DA's office. Is that a piece of cake?"

"No."

And it wasn't easy. She and her fellow ADAs handled a caseload that would fell most people. But it was the life of someone in the district attorney's office. Too few lawyers for far too many cases.

But as she contemplated the picture Troy painted and weighed the truth of his words, Evangeline did feel some of that oppressive load of fear recede a bit. The Davison case might be on a level no one in the county had seen or experienced, but she had lived with stress. Professionally, absolutely.

And if she also considered how she'd grown up—in

a highly emotional atmosphere with her father's behavior—she could add additional stressful situations to the tally of examples Troy had provided.

Yet in every one of those situations, hallucinations had never been a part of how she handled things. With any of it. Instead, she just put one foot in front of the other and tried to work through the answers.

"You've been coping with everything, Evangeline. There's no reason to think otherwise."

Troy's kind words—and the sudden realization she was still in his arms—had her pressing her hands against his chest. It felt so good to stand here with him, surrounded by his gentle strength. But there was no way she could come to depend on this. She'd already taken up far too much of his time.

And he was increasingly taking up too much space in her thoughts.

"Thank you."

She knew she should back away. It was the right thing to do, here in the midst of an emotional meltdown. Yet as she stood there, feeling both safe and confident for the first time in weeks, Evangeline found she couldn't move away.

Instead, she lifted her head as her gaze never left his. And when her mouth met his, she found that same quiet strength in the press of his lips to hers.

Chapter Eight

He needed to walk away. Troy knew that. Felt it down to his marrow. Yet as Evangeline's lips met his, soft and warm, he could no sooner move away from her than he could stop drawing breath or force his heartbeat to still.

He wanted her.

It was the wrong time in the wrong place, but he couldn't quite find it in himself to care.

Where their kiss the night before had been tentative movements and a dive into the forbidden, this time it was different. This time, he knew how good she'd taste and how badly he'd wanted to kiss her again.

To hold her in his arms.

Even if he shouldn't.

Actions that should have been motivated solely by a protective urge had turned on him. He knew she needed comfort and he'd believed himself capable of giving it. Only now, he knew a hunger he couldn't deny.

Yes, he wanted her safe. And increasingly, he believed himself the only one who could keep her that way.

But he also wanted her.

Mouths merged, a soft sigh—his? hers?—mingling between them. Troy trailed his fingers down her spine before settling at the enticing curve of her lower back.

Pleased with the way his hand fit there, nestled in the arch, he found his need turning wanton, and in seconds he'd fisted the material of her blouse in his hand.

Had he wanted like this before?

And how had he waited this long to taste her? To feel her?

Could he have known how neatly they'd fit together, her tall, lithe figure pressed to his? She was strong. He could feel that in the long lines of her body, in the firm sweep of muscle down the back of her arm, in the play of subtle strength beneath her shoulder blades.

He wanted.

In the end, it was really that simple.

And in the simplicity of that knowledge, Troy knew he needed to stop. To step away from Evangeline and the increasingly desperate desire to be near her.

Lifting his head, he stared down at her. Her thick eyelashes swept up from lids that were half-closed, the irises underneath dark with desire. "Troy?"

"I'm sorry. I've come into your home—" he glanced around "—your kitchen no less, and taken what I shouldn't have." He held onto her shoulders to keep her from swaying, but took a firm step back. "I'm sorry."

"For kissing me?"

"For taking advantage when you're vulnerable and scared."

"I'm fine."

He kept his gaze on hers, sharing the only truth he had. "I'm not."

"Oh."

She stepped back and he let his hands drop, satisfied she had her footing. He sensed that a wholly unnecessary apology sat on her tongue before she seemed to think better of it. "I'm going to go check if the remaining cops are still outside."

"I'll do it. And then I'd like to talk about something. I had an idea earlier, talking to Melissa. I wanted to run it by you."

It wasn't an out-and-out lie, exactly, but it was a slight prevarication. One that, while a bit spur-of-the-moment, increasingly made sense as Troy turned it over in his mind. He followed Evangeline to the living room, then moved to look out the front windows toward the parking lot.

"Is anyone there?"

"No. They're all gone." He let the curtain fall back in place in front of the large window framing her living room.

"Good. I can't begin to imagine what my neighbors must think."

"Let them think. Maybe it'll get them to pay attention a bit more, too."

Her head tilted, a soft waterfall of black hair skimming down over her shoulder. "I hadn't considered that."

"Maybe it's time to. The challenge of living in a complex like you do is that it's not quite as easy to notice strangers. But the benefits are that there are a lot more eyes, all focused on the same places. Someone lurking around your home should get noticed if they do it too often."

He hated using scare words like *lurk* and *stranger*, but there was no help for it. And more to the point, he wanted to stress those things so Evangeline would understand she wasn't alone. The quicker she understood that and recognized it, the better off she would be. She lived in a crowded housing complex and it was time to try and use that to their advantage. Especially since the threat to her seemed so ephemeral.

"What was your idea?"

"Before, when I was talking to Melissa, we talked about my cousins."

"What does your family have to do with today?"

"I might have mentioned it yesterday, but my sister, as well as various Colton cousins, have had some strange experiences so far this year. Run-ins that have necessitated law enforcement involvement."

"We do have crime here, Troy. I see the caseload that regularly comes into the DA's office and while we're not rolling in it, we're hardly crime-free."

Her quick assessment was a good sign that her earlier fear had receded and Troy was pleased to see how deftly Evangeline questioned his points. It was a far cry from the shaken woman he and Melissa had found less than an hour ago.

"It's disappointing," she continued, "but we live in a big enough jurisdiction with a big enough population that we deal with our fair share of bad things happening."

She sat down, clearly engaged in their discussion, and Troy took his first easy breath since their kiss. While he would like nothing more than to keep kissing her, he knew they needed to stop. More, he knew he needed some physical distance from her. The easiest way to get back on common ground was to talk about a subject they could both wrap their heads around.

A subject that her legal brain would quickly assess in a way he might be more likely to miss.

"I heard about Melissa. When something happens to the chief of police, that's big news. She and Arielle are friendly, as well, so my boss shared some of the details as she knew them, too."

"The stalker that went after Melissa was pretty big news." News that still shook Troy down to the marrow. It wasn't something he liked to dwell on, but knowing his cousin had experienced that situation had lit a fire under him to catch Len Davison. "And a cop discharging their weapon, even in self-defense, is even more news. Ever since, the Davison case has consumed us all. It's also given her the head space to work through her act of self-defense with a bit of distance."

"That's good. I'm sure it helps that she's planning a wedding, too."

"You do have a pulse on the Grave Gulch grapevine."

A light blush colored her cheeks. "Like I said, Melissa and Arielle are friendly. And there's little a group of women love to talk about more than wedding plans. With Antonio Ruiz owning the Grave Gulch Hotel, well, it's hot gossip."

"Well, if we're talking weddings, personally, I'm a tulle guy."

The joke was enough to get a quick laugh before her smile faded. "That's not news to me about Melissa but you said 'cousins' as in plural. What else has happened?"

In careful detail, Troy walked her through all his family had experienced. Other than the few details intersecting with the ongoing Davison investigation, which he skipped, he gave her the unvarnished truth.

"How is your family holding up?"

"We're managing. We're Coltons and when bad things happen, we tend to close ranks and watch each other's backs. They did that years ago for my father after my mother was killed. And the next generation is committed to doing the same."

"Her death impacted all of you."

"It did."

"I don't mean that in an offhanded way, either. Obviously, losing your mother at any age is hard. What you and your sister had to endure is unimaginable."

He'd lived with it for most of his life: the knowledge that a stranger—one who had never been caught—murdered his mom. He had coping mechanisms and the love of his father, sister, half siblings and stepmother, as well as his extended family, to manage the grief. But until that moment, Troy hadn't realized how much it meant for someone who was basically a stranger to simply acknowledge his mother.

Her value.

Her worth.

Even her death.

"Troy, I'm sorry. I said the wrong thing."

"No, actually you didn't. You said the exact right thing. Thank you."

Her direct gaze was as skeptical as Melissa's had been earlier. "The right thing? Really?"

"Yes, really. My sister and I have talked about this through the years. People don't typically know what to say when you tell them that your mother has passed. That is only more real and more acute when the reason for death is murder. It's out of the ordinary and people don't know how to handle it."

"She was a person, Troy. She mattered. She doesn't deserve to be erased."

"No, she doesn't."

To the Colton family, Amanda McMahon Colton had

never been erased. Her memory and the desire to seek justice for others drove all of them. But that still didn't mean that others outside the family understood it.

But Evangeline did.

The ever-present knot of grief that was usually tied so tightly around his heart eased at that revelation. And for an impossible moment, he was able to sit with another person and celebrate his mother's memory fully, instead of simply trying to erase the pain.

EVANGELINE STILL WONDERED if she'd said the wrong thing about Troy's mother, but couldn't find any hint of anger in his face. She knew how to read anger. She'd gotten good—very good—at reading her father's anger cues until she could pinpoint what would put him into a rage.

But Troy seemed calmer, somehow. As if talking about the horrible death of a loved one could calm instead of enrage.

It made little sense and she still mentally braced for some blowback, but as their conversation shifted once more, this time as Troy spoke of his sister and her wedding plans, Evangeline began to suspect he wasn't upset at all.

Although she had listened to everything Troy said, that clamoring sense of the threat faded. As it did, she keyed in more closely to what he was saying, only to be surprised once more when he stood up, crossing the room in two long strides. "I don't know how I missed this. Why I didn't think of it sooner."

Before she could even ask what he had missed, Troy had his phone in hand. "Dez, it's me."

Evangeline listened to Troy's side of the discussion, but it wasn't hard to piece together his sister's responses.

"I need you to do a sketch for me." He paused as he got some answer before adding, "Can we come over?"

We? Come over? Troy wanted her to come to his sister's house?

"Me and Evangeline Whittaker." He nodded, adding, "Yes, from the DA's office." She heard the hard laugh as well as a more distant one through the phone before he pressed on. "Yes and yes. I will bring dinner. See you at six."

Yes to what? Dinner was one yes, but what was the other?

Troy shoved the phone into his pocket, the rapid-fire call obviously at an end. "We're going to my sister's for dinner."

"We can't. I mean, I can't. I mean, why?"

"She's a sketch artist. I don't know why I didn't think of this sooner but I want you to work with her to sketch out the man you saw in the alley."

"But I didn't see him. I have impressions of him, but I never saw his face."

"That's Desiree's job. She'll pull out of you what she needs for the sketch."

"But we're intruding." Evangeline looked at her watch, frantic for some excuse that would keep her from meeting the no-doubt practiced—and discerning eye—of Troy's sister. "And it's four already. She wasn't expecting company."

"She is now."

"But she's got a little one. And a new fiancé. She doesn't need a stranger intruding on her personal time."

"It's fine."

"But I can't. What if I don't remember anything?"

What if that makes you think I'm an even bigger phony than you already do?

The fear was irrational—it had to be. But the idea of sitting with someone and trying to scrape her brain for any memory of a man whose face she'd never seen anyway felt tantamount to losing any and all credibility.

Troy had already dropped back onto the couch, his pose relaxed. Confident, even. And why wouldn't it be? He had nothing to lose.

"This isn't going to work."

"It will work."

"But I didn't see his face."

"But you saw something. Likely more than you realize, actually. Desiree is trained to do this. She has a way of bringing an image to life. You just have to trust the process."

Trust it? How?

THE SENSE OF looming disaster didn't fade, but strangely, as she and Troy walked up the front walkway of Desiree Colton's home, it wasn't getting worse. Maybe, Evangeline thought, it was the small scattering of toys on the front lawn that calmed her. Or perhaps the warm, welcoming smile on the face of the woman who held the door open for them.

"Troy." Desiree Colton held out her hands to her brother, enfolding him in a tight hug before turning to face Evangeline. "I'm Desiree. It's wonderful to finally meet you."

Evangeline took the proffered hand, and Desiree's slim fingers—what Evangeline thought of as artist's fingers—clasped hers. "I'm glad you're here. I'm sure my brother railroaded you into this seeing as how we only spoke a few hours ago. So come on in, we'll have a glass of wine and some dinner and relax a bit."

"I'm on the clock, Dez," Troy said as they followed her into her home, his hands full of the tray of lasagna they'd picked up in town.

Without skipping a beat, Desiree tossed a look over her shoulder for her brother. "No wine for you, then." She reached out and gave Evangeline's hand another squeeze. "More for us, then."

In a matter of minutes, Desiree had taken the hot tray into the kitchen, poured two glasses of wine and a seltzer for Troy and settled them all in the living room. Evangeline had no idea how the woman had done it, but everything moved seamlessly. Effortlessly, really.

And Desiree managed this all while looking picture-perfect at the end of a long day and keeping up with a toddler.

One whose toys were all over the room but who was nowhere in sight.

Before she could ask, Troy beat her to it. "Where are Danny and Stavros?"

"Danny had a late nap and if we don't wear him out a bit he'll be up until midnight. Stavros ran him down to the park for a bit to run out the wiggles."

Evangeline could only assume she'd given Desiree a blank stare, because the woman smiled and added, "Also known as some serious two-year-old energy."

"Ah." Evangeline nodded, the picture in her head of an energetic child suddenly making much more sense.

"I'm also not above admitting I had another motive, as well."

"Subtle, Dez," Troy said, glancing at his sister from where he sat beside her on the couch.

"Subtlety went out the window with this whole year." Desiree leaned forward, her expression eager. "Troy mentioned some of the things that you've been dealing with. I'd like to help however I can."

"I appreciate that." While she had initially said the words as a platitude, as they came out, Evangeline quickly realized they were completely true. She did appreciate the help. More, she appreciated the idea that someone besides Troy might believe her. Especially since her own doubts had begun to waver since that afternoon with the incident on her front porch. "You need me to tell you everything that's happened?"

"Yes, that will help. I'd like to get a sense of what you're dealing with. It will also help you later, when we try to work through the images."

Evangeline took a sip of her wine, Desiree's kind eyes and steady manner more of a relief than she ever could have imagined. "I've only ever been on the other side of it, looking at police sketches after they've been generated. But Troy said that you'll be able to pull images from me, even if I can't remember what the man I saw looks like."

Desiree nodded. "That's mostly true. The mind is fascinating in the way that we capture and snag fragments of images. My job to take those fragments and put them together into a complete picture."

The process as Desiree described it made sense and Evangeline was surprised to realize how excited she was to get started. "That's an interesting way to describe it. I never thought of what you do in that way, but I can see how a picture could come together, piece by piece."

"It feels like it shouldn't work, but it does. I've done hundreds and hundreds of sketches through the years, and I'm always amazed to see how a face comes to light on the page."

"Dez is one of the best," Troy said with pride. It was clear the siblings were close—Evangeline saw that from the moment they'd arrived—but it was equally nice to see how he supported her.

Yet one more experience she'd never had as an only child. Nor had she seen much pride in her parents' eyes. Especially her father's. Oh, sure, he was proud the day she graduated from law school, but that emotion never seemed to last. Never seemed to overcome the anger and disillusionment he carried around for life.

Shaking the bitter memories off, Evangeline focused on Troy and Desiree. She wasn't here to be maudlin and it was actually nice to be out for an evening talking with other people. "How long have you worked for the GGPD?"

"Almost ten years." Desiree took a sip of her wine, considering. "I've been an artist my whole life, and I got interested in all things police procedural as part of processing the loss of my mother. Doing the police sketches seemed like a natural fit."

"It's a tremendous way to use your talents."

Once again, the discussion she had with Troy about his mother filled her thoughts. How sad that both Troy and Desiree had often felt they couldn't celebrate their mother's memory. She was a person. One that they loved. There was nothing about those memories that should be erased or diminished.

"Thank you. I like to think it makes Mom proud."

"I've no doubt it does."

Before Evangeline could say anything else, a delighted giggle filtered in from outside. She heard a deeper laugh and then another chuckle and saw Desiree's eyes alight with excitement. "My boys are home."

The next half hour flew by in a blur. Evangeline hadn't spent a lot of time with small children. She'd babysat when she was younger, but since becoming an adult, kids hadn't been a big part of her life. And in a matter of minutes, little Danny had her wrapped around his finger. Or, she thought with a rueful smile, his chubby little fist.

Although he took a few minutes to warm up, by the time Evangeline took a seat next to him on the floor, nodding to his mix of words and baby babble as he showed her his toys, he had become her chattering little best friend.

"Vange. Lean. Here—" He held out his hands, full of a fuzzy teddy bear. "Bear."

Evangeline's heart melted a little at the way he said her name. *Vange. Lean.* It had a sweet little ring to it coming from the mouth of a two-year-old. "What is your bear's name?"

"Mike."

"His favorite character from his favorite movie," Desiree was quick to add as she joined them with a seat on the floor. She shot Stavros a saucy smile as she did. "A movie that has quickly become Stavros's favorite, too."

Stavros shrugged, his smile equally cheeky and even more smitten than Desiree's. "I like little green sidekicks, what can I say?"

Evangeline had warmed to Stavros as quickly as she did to Desiree and Danny. The handsome ER doctor had an easy way about him, confident and competent, yet still warm and approachable. He'd extended his hand as soon as he walked in the door, introducing himself around a wiggling armful of toddler, and immediately putting her at ease. She imagined it was the skill that came in handy as he dealt with people in some of their most challenging personal moments.

The warm welcome made her glad she had come. Or, more to the point, glad Troy had suggested they visit with his sister and her family. She was still a little spooked at the idea of doing the police sketch, but had enough confidence that Desiree knew what she was doing that it would be a worthwhile experience.

It was only as she glanced up from her careful perusal of Mike's fur and button nose that she caught Troy's steady gaze. That sensual hazel had turned golden in the late afternoon light filtering into the living room and, for an unguarded moment, she felt herself caught up in it. Caught up in him.

She was captivated.

And while her life might be upside down at the moment, going wrong at every turn, it was increasingly difficult to think of Troy Colton as anything but absolutely right.

Chapter Nine

"You most certainly did walk past her house every day for a solid month," Desiree shot back across the table, tossing her wadded-up napkin for good measure. "Little Lisa Baker. I remember it like it was yesterday."

Troy felt the heat creeping up his neck but made one, final valiant effort to redeem himself. "You make me sound like some sort of hopeless fool."

"You *were* a hopeless fool!" Desiree cackled, her glee at his expense more than evident. "A sixth grader in love with an eighth grader. Like that ever works."

"That's some serious pining," Evangeline added.

Troy turned to her, deliberately ignoring his sister's eye roll. "You're picking on me, too?"

Evangeline shrugged, her smile wide. "If the shoe fits."

Although his overt intention had been to bring Evangeline to Desiree's to do the police sketch, as the evening wore on, he couldn't deny how helpful the time had been to simply allow her to relax.

He could watch it happening, too. Her smile came easier, and the haunted look he had seen in her eyes had vanished around the same time she got on the floor to play with Danny.

What was funny was how neatly she and his sister turned the tables on him. Desiree's love of telling embarrassing stories—most often with him as their subject—had rung true this evening. But those stories had delivered the added benefit of putting Evangeline at ease. Maybe at his expense, but it was wonderful to see her smile all the same.

Which was the exact opposite reaction he should be having. He'd brought her here to get his sister's professional help. Not to notice the easing stress in Evangeline's shoulders or her smile. Even if that smile was beautiful.

He'd battled those wayward thoughts all evening. Even on the drive over here, as they stopped to pick up dinner, he had to force himself not to think of the evening as a date. Yes, he was bringing a woman to his sister's home. And yes, he had an interest in her that went well beyond the platonic. But this wasn't a date.

So why did it feel like one?

Embarrassing sixth grade stories aside, it amazed Troy to realize how comfortable he felt. On most dates, he worried about what to say or how the evening was going or how the evening might wrap up. But right now, sitting here with Evangeline and his family, he was at ease.

And he reminded himself as he reached for his glass of seltzer, this wasn't a date.

Was. Not. A. Date.

Without warning, Evangeline's comments about his mother filtered back into his thoughts. He meant what he had said to her earlier. Most people found it hard to talk about Amanda Colton and the way she had died.

Only Evangeline hadn't shied away from it. Instead, she had shown compassion as well as a willingness to speak of the dead. It was so simple. For something so complex as grief and loss and all the ways you coped with childhood trauma well into adulthood, the simplicity of just speaking of his mother was humbling.

And somewhere deep inside, he was grateful.

"Do you think it might be time to get started?" Evangeline asked the question of Desiree, but her gaze quickly shifted to Troy.

"I'm ready if you are," his sister agreed, her tone easy and warm.

Desiree had excused herself about a half hour before to put Danny to bed. After returning, she had sat back down at the table and continued with the discussion as if she'd never left. Troy was pleased to see how she quietly allowed Evangeline to pick the time instead of interrupting their after-dinner conversation.

It was one more thing about his sibling that he admired. Not just her compassion, but her ability to acknowledge where someone else was coming from. Desiree hadn't missed Evangeline's wide eyes and nervous demeanor when they had arrived earlier at the house. But in her own inimitable fashion, his sister had looked past it all and brick by brick, helped Evangeline take down the emotional wall that had locked her in. It was a skill, and one he didn't compliment her for often enough.

"Troy and I will take dish duty," Stavros said with a big smile, standing and picking up plates.

"I say we take it and run, Evangeline," Desiree said. She stood and gave Stavros a smacking kiss before turning back to Evangeline with a wink.

At ease with the lighthearted moment, Evangeline smiled and nodded. "I think you're right."

In moments, the women had disappeared to Desiree's studio, leaving Troy and Stavros alone in the kitchen.

"She's going through a tough time." Stavros started right in while setting the dishes in the sink.

"She is. I hope Dez can help her with the sketch."

"If anyone can, it's your sister. That woman does the most amazing things with a pencil and paper. I'm lucky if I can draw a stick figure and even then, it's never in proportion to a house or a tree."

"I feel like I'm violating some sort of important brotherly responsibility," Troy said as dumped the rest of the plates in the sink before slapping Stavros on the back. "But you really love my sister. It makes me happy."

"More than my own life. I don't know how it happened, and as fast as it did, too. But yes, I love her. And I love Danny. And I love the life we're making. It's nothing I thought would ever happen for me. Especially not after losing Sammy."

It was sort of amazing how Desiree and Danny had come into Stavros's life, just as Leanne had come into his father's so many years ago. A blessing, long after it seemed there wasn't any good left to experience or feel.

Stavros had lost his baby daughter in such a horrible way. He'd thrown himself into his work and found a way forward, but he'd done it all alone.

Troy could still remember Desiree's concerns as she'd spoken of her growing feelings for the doctor. How she cared for him but wasn't sure if Stavros could find it in his heart to love again.

To live again.

Yet he had. They'd found their way and would continue to find their way. Together.

"You've got an eye for the pretty lawyer."

Stavros's quiet words hit him like a shot to the chest and Troy nearly bobbled the rinsed plate he was loading into the dishwasher. "It's not like that. She's in trouble. And I've known her for a long time. And she's—"

He broke off as Stavros grinned. "In trouble. Yeah. I get it. Doesn't mean she isn't pretty and pretty great, all at the same time."

"She is those things, but this isn't like that. I'm helping her. Protecting her."

"You can help her and protect her and still think she's pretty great."

"It's just not like that."

Stavros handed him a dish, his stare direct. "But maybe it could be."

"WAS THE MAN taller than the woman or shorter?"

"Taller. Much taller."

"Taller, like he loomed over her?"

Desiree's question stopped her and Evangeline closed her eyes, replaying the memory in her mind's eye. She'd believed the man a lot taller than the woman but now that she thought about it, had he been?

Her eyes popped open, even as the memory still lingered in her thoughts. "Well, maybe he wasn't as tall as I think. It was more that he had a big, hulking body to him. He had height on her, yes, but it was also the breadth and heft of his frame."

"Good. That's good," Desiree said as she sketched.

Evangeline waited as Desiree made some changes to the paper in front of her, using her pencil and eraser in equal measure. The whole process had been interesting, and far more methodical than she could have imagined. Each of Desiree's questions built on the one before, and many were things Evangeline wouldn't have immediately thought of.

The man's height was an example. Yes, he was tall. Definitely taller than the woman. She had seen that clearly while they struggled at the end of the alley. But now, being forced to think about it, she realized that some of that feeling of height was also tied to his solid form. It wasn't like there was a foot's difference between him and the woman. Instead, his physical bulk had given her the perception he was so much bigger.

Height hadn't been the only revelation, either. The man had worn a hat and Evangeline had struggled to see his eyes. But with Desiree's questions, she realized she had gotten a solid look at his chin and neck. When pressed, she could bring that image back in her mind's eye. The rounded chin, and the fleshy throat beneath it. He had a heavy, bulldog-like look that now took real shape in her mind. Like it had been there all along, but she just needed to think about his face in pieces instead of as a single memory.

Desiree continued making tweaks to the paper and Evangeline used the lull in questions to look around the room. Desiree's studio was just a converted bedroom within the house, but it had her artist's stamp on it in every way.

While the artistic components were expected, she hadn't counted on the pin-neat desk or the state-of-the-art computer mounted on the surface. Desiree had excitedly showed her the sketch program she'd use later, after the initial session, to work and refine the images Evangeline had provided. The tool was brand new, an investment the GGPD had made in expanding its capabilities, and Desiree was like a kid at Christmas, she was so excited to use it.

For her part, Evangeline was amazed by the entire

process. The computer program was just the icing on the cake. It was a fascinating blend of art meeting science and she'd marveled at how truly functional Desiree had made her talent.

Not that it diminished anything from her art. There were several pencil sketches framed on the walls, some of them of Danny. She could see his progression, from infant, to baby, to the toddler he was now. Although each image was beautiful, it was the love that came through so clearly that truly captured Evangeline.

"There are times I can't believe he was so little," Desiree said, her gaze skipping over the various prints.

"He's still pretty little, but I do see what you mean."

"He's my miracle."

Evangeline briefly weighed not bringing up the kidnapping, but it had come up a few times during dinner and Desiree seemed able to handle discussing it. "I'm so glad he's unharmed and doing so well."

"Thank you. It's been a difficult time, but so much good has come out of it, too. Every time I wake up in a cold sweat, I try to remind myself of that."

Evangeline knew that Desiree meant finding Stavros, when she referred to the good that had come about, and she was happy that things had worked out so well. "It always amazes me how things come into our lives when we least expect them."

"Well, since you brought it up—" Desiree let the comment hang there, before she continued. "I'm glad that you're spending time with my brother."

"Oh no, no. It's not like that."

"Are you sure?"

"He's been so kind to me. Looking out for me as he works this case. That's all it is. Really."

Was that all?

If the situation was different and she wasn't afraid because of the weird, violent happenings in her life, would she consider Troy differently? Think about a relationship with him? Yet it was exactly *because* of what was happening in her life that he'd walked into it.

"Maybe it's like you said. Good things come into our lives in unexpected ways." Desiree's tone was casual but it was impossible to miss the woman's point underneath. And the belief that there could be something going on between her and Troy.

Which was why she had to keep pressing against that fantasy. It was wonderful that Desiree and Stavros had fallen in love, especially in such an extremely tense and challenging time in her life. But that didn't work for everyone. And Evangeline had no reason to assume she and Troy would have the same sort of outcome.

"It's a difficult time for the GGPD and for Grave Gulch overall. I feel like I'm only adding to the problem, with whatever it is that's happening to me." She shook her head. "If there even is anything happening to me."

"Of course something happened to you."

"But that's the problem. What if nothing *did*?"

She hated saying the words, especially to this woman, who had done nothing but open her home and offer her kindness. But no matter how hard she tried, Evangeline could not shake the continued feeling that the things she thought were happening somehow *weren't*. That phantom killers in alleyways and invisible intruders who left travel books behind didn't exist.

"You don't really believe that." Desiree set her sketchbook down, her gaze as direct as her brother's. "What happened to you is real. You saw something in that alley."

"But the police didn't find anything. CSI hasn't found anything. Even a K-9 tracker came up with nothing."

"Then there has to be different reason. But you saw something. What you just shared with me, when you walked me through your images of the man in the alley? That's real."

Desiree's conviction went a long way toward making her feel better, even if it couldn't quite erase the lingering doubt.

"Here. I'll show you how real." Desiree picked up the sketchbook, turning it around so that the image was facing outward.

On a hard gasp, Evangeline leaned forward in her chair, reaching out to touch the edge of the paper. As promised, the man she'd seen struggling with that woman in the white shirt was facing her from Desiree's sketchbook. Her disparate memories of his features had somehow, some way, coalesced into the image of a person.

A real person.

One who'd murdered a woman while she stood and watched.

TROY CONTINUED TO mull over his conversation with Stavros long after the two men had settled back in the living room. Danny's toys had been moved into a neat pile in the corner and there was once again room to sit.

It was surprising, on some level, to have his feelings read so easily. He didn't date much, but he had been in relationships off and on throughout his adult life. Never before had his sister keyed in so quickly on a woman he was interested in. And while Stavros was a recent entry into the family, it was equally unsettling to have another man pinpoint the feelings Troy was working so hard to deny.

Although he probably shouldn't be surprised. Stavros and Desiree had only recently gotten together, and the lingering pain of losing his child had colored Stavros's world for many years. Love and relationships weren't a part of that. Maybe Stavros was having an easier time recognizing attraction because he was still in the early stages of it himself, relatively speaking.

"Desiree didn't have a chance to tell me much, but it sounds like Evangeline has been having a difficult time coming to terms with this crime she witnessed."

Grateful for the break from his thoughts—and any and all musings that suggested he was talking about feelings with Stavros—Troy grasped for the conversational lifeline. "She has. We all have. Detective Shea and I arrived on scene last night to investigate her nine-one-one call, and all signs of a crime scene had vanished."

Stavros frowned at that. "What you mean vanished? Humans shed far too much DNA in day-to-day life, let alone in a violent situation, for it to simply vanish."

"That's the problem. We didn't get anything from a visual review of the scene, but CSI hasn't gotten anything on a molecular level, either."

"It's just not possible."

"Evangeline is doubting herself because of it."

Stavros quieted, glancing in the direction of Desiree's studio. It was only when he seemed satisfied that the women couldn't hear them, that he spoke. "Is it possible she's having hallucinations of some sort? A mental impulse could make a situation seem real, even if it isn't."

It was the same question Evangeline had brought up and he had been quick to dismiss it. To tell her was impossible. But now, to have the same question come from a doctor? Maybe it was time to consider it.

"Is that possible, especially if she's never had any sort of struggle like that before?"

"Anything is possible. She's been under a tremendous amount of stress with work and we never know exactly what it is that can cause a lapse of that sort in the mind."

"It still doesn't make a lot of sense. I recognize she has been under stress with her job, but her record is impeccable. And being an ADA isn't easy in normal times. Wouldn't there be some sort of decline? Something that would've been recognizable, before a strong hallucination that lasted for several minutes?"

As Stavros considered the counter argument, Troy forced himself to reflect honestly on the man's points. Since his time in the GGPD, he'd experienced plenty of situations with individuals who had some mental or emotional break with reality. Mental illness or extreme stress brought on by life-changing situations or those times when life was simply too much. He'd learned to think more favorably of others in those moments, recognizing that he'd want—and more important, *need*—the same compassion in return if the situation were reversed.

And even with that understanding, he still chafed at the idea that Evangeline was experiencing some sort of emotional break with reality. Especially when it seemed like everything happening to her centered on some phantom threat.

A phantom threat that kept executing real, tangible actions.

Tangible actions that vanished the moment someone else showed up…

Was it possible? Troy mused.

He hadn't had many in his career, but he had seen people, often women, the victim of gaslighting. A sort of slow, steady drip of behavior from a hidden foe, making them believe there was a danger, then hiding it.

Was that happening here?

"I don't think you're wrong," Stavros finally said. "But I do think you need to be open to all possibilities."

Troy's mind still churned with the possibilities, even as Stavros's kind words gave him one more avenue to consider.

One more thread in what was becoming an increasingly complex knot.

Brett and Melissa had all shared similar warnings and it would be foolish to disregard a consistent theme from others he respected.

But he also respected Evangeline.

They might not have exchanged much in the past beyond the occasional hello, but he'd observed her plenty in the courtroom. Even now, he remembered a small incident she likely had no memory of.

She'd been prosecuting a hit-and-run case. Additional challenges had arisen when it was discovered a child was in the car that had fled the scene. The driver was eventually apprehended, and through the course of the deliberations, the man's daughter had been brought to court. Troy had been convinced at the time the child was being used as a prop for sympathy, but he knew his role and avoided editorializing when he gave his testimony. Even as he vowed to himself that he was going to look into his suspicions of abuse.

It was only during a recess, when the child and her mother were in the hallway outside the courtroom, that he'd overheard Evangeline. She wasn't supposed to approach the other side, the potential for judicial action against her a real possibility if she was discovered. But Troy had heard her all the same, telling the wife quietly that she and her daughter could get away from the woman's husband and get help. That Evangeline could find them a safe place.

He'd been even more surprised when Evangeline had reached into her bag to produce a card and, along with it, a small stuffed animal she'd handed over to the girl. It wasn't much bigger than her fist, the sort that was sold in the stationery and gift shop on the corner next to the courthouse, but the little girl had wrapped the plush cat in her arms as if it were a lifeline.

She hadn't seen him. Troy was sure of it, the spot he'd stood observing the exchange hidden behind a large pamphlet rack. But as the woman rushed away, leaving Evangeline alone in the corridor, he'd seen Evangeline drop her head and brush away a tear.

He'd always respected her and he'd thought her beautiful from the first moment he'd laid eyes on her. But in that moment, he'd seen the genuine care and concern in her actions and he'd never been able to shake that memory.

Or that quick rush of tears she'd brushed away before anyone could notice.

EVANGELINE STARED AT the parked cars underneath the lights in her condo's parking lot and tried desperately to ignore the wash of fear that suddenly roiled through her stomach. It had been a good night. A great night, actually. She'd spent the evening with nice people. She'd laughed, talked and had even played with a small child who reminded her that all the work they did, from law enforcement to the entire legal process, was worth it.

And she'd spent the evening with Troy.

For all the fear and confusion of the past few days, he had been a bright beacon of calm, caring and concern.

She was also becoming far too comfortable having him near.

"Thanks for this evening. I had no idea how badly I needed a night out and the company of other people. Your sister and her family are wonderful."

"Dez and Danny were great all by themselves. But I'm happy to see her have a new love in Stavros."

It was so simple. That he could accept others so easily. No frustration or anger at the disruption in his life by someone new. No distrust that someone had come along and captured his sister's heart.

"Who are you, Troy Colton?"

The question was out, weird and silly, and now hanging between them in the car as he pulled up in front of her door.

Troy put the car in Park and turned to face her. The light that filtered in from the overheads painted everything with a stark fluorescent glow, yet even in the neon haze of the illumination she could see the warmth in his eyes. "I'm just me, Evangeline. I'm a cop. A brother. A son. An uncle. A cousin. And maybe someday soon, a brother-in-law."

Although she heard no censure in his tone, something compelled her to keep going.

"But your family is so open. So welcoming. Your sister has a new love and just like that, you and he get along famously. Your cousins seem to number the stars and you have a relationship with all of them. You might think your nephew has you wrapped around his finger but you've got him equally wrapped around yours." She took a deep breath. "It's not anything I'm used to. And I just wanted to tell you how special it is."

"Thank you."

She saw the question before he asked it. It filled his gaze, his brow furrowing as he obviously weighed whether or not he was going to say something.

"I mean that thank-you. We never really know how our family situations look on the outside. I'm lucky to have mine and it's nice to hear that the affection we have for each other is obvious."

"Of course."

"But it does make me curious. Was your family different?" he asked. "Because you don't seem to just be observing my relationships—you seem surprised that they exist."

"My family wasn't at all like yours. I'm an only child, for starters."

His grin was quick and immediate, and Evangeline felt it blow through her with all the force of a hurricane. "That's not a problem in the Colton family." That smile soon faded. "But your questions aren't just because you're an only child. Are they?"

"I've never seen anything like it. A bond like that. I know anger and rage and then silence. But not easy laughter at the table and welcoming visitors into your home with open arms."

Later, she'd likely tell herself she shared all those things because she was tired and her guard was down and the sketch work with Desiree had forced her to draw on her last reserves of emotional strength.

But right now, she said the words because she needed to say them.

Troy nodded, that furrowed brow as serious as before.

Only before he said anything, an electrifying series of pops lit the air. Quick, heavy bursts of sound suddenly bombarding them from all sides.

And then the lights above the car went out, plunging them into darkness.

Chapter Ten

Troy immediately reached for Evangeline, pressing his hand to the crown of her head and forcing her down in the seat to take cover. The noises continued but as his initial burst of adrenaline wore off to the point he could think over simply reacting, he realized the sound remained outside. There were no shot-out windows. No broken glass, even. Just that continued loud popping and bursting.

And then it stopped.

"Troy?" Evangeline unfurled from where she'd slunk down in her seat.

"Stay there," he ordered, his phone already in hand to call for backup.

He needed to wait to get out of the car but people from her condo complex were already opening their doors, lights appearing at the same time on some of the floors above.

In clipped tones, he relayed to dispatch what had happened and what little he knew of the scene before giving the warning that never failed to make his skin crawl. "Possible active shooter."

He got quick reassurance that several patrol cars nearby were already on their way.

"An active shooter?" Evangeline asked. "At us?"

"We can't know."

"Those were gunshots?" Evangeline glanced around frantically, twisting in the small space of the front seat. "What are all these people doing outside?"

"I'm going to go ask everyone to go back inside their homes. Stay here."

"You can't—"

He cut her off. "Stay here. Patrol is en route and we can assess once they're here. I'm a trained officer and I can handle this."

The quick nod was all he got but it had to be enough, especially as more lights went on behind darkened windows and a few more neighbors stepped out their front doors.

Troy got out and pushed as much authority into his tone as he could.

"Grave Gulch Police! I need everyone to go back in their homes until we know what's going on."

Various shouts rang out from the people who'd come outside or who'd lifted their windows to take in the scene.

What right do you have?

This is my house.

What's going on?

"I repeat! Grave Gulch PD." He ran through the particulars again and by the time he'd finished, the sound of sirens was already audible, flashing blue lights visible shortly after.

The sensation of being an open target refused to leave him. His gaze kept darting through the now-darkened parking lot as he sought to narrow in on anything suspicious or out of place. He kept his back to Evangeline's building and his body angled toward the ground, hoping to minimize himself in a shooter's vision.

Although that wait dragged on, he knew by the sound of sirens that he and Evangeline had only been waiting a few minutes at most. In another thirty seconds he had police cars filling the parking lot, cops milling around the area.

A strange sense of relief filled him when Brett jumped out of one of the cars, Ember on his heels. Brett assessed the situation, his gaze as careful as Troy's had been as he dissected the parking lot in quadrants. Satisfied he saw no one out in the open, Brett gave the all clear to the surrounding officers and then they swarmed through the parking lot and on into the grass.

Troy eyed Evangeline through the windshield and gestured for her to stay down, despite the clearance. He still wasn't comfortable, nor did he feel it was safe for her yet out in the open. When he saw her subtle nod in return, he shifted his attention to Brett.

"Fancy meeting you here," Brett said, his grim smile and active gaze that continued to scan the area around them proof that this wasn't a social call.

"I hear you. This is getting to be a bit of a habit."

"Evangeline?" Brett was discreet and never even tilted his gaze toward the car, but Troy knew the detective was aware of Evangeline's presence.

"Yeah. I took her over to my sister's so Desiree could do a police sketch tonight. We just got back and then this happened."

"Want to walk me through it?"

Troy gave Brett the details, explaining how they had parked and were finishing up a discussion covering the evening's events. He avoided all mention she'd made of her family, recognizing that was personal and not relevant to the discussion anyway. He then detailed the punching noise that had broken through the evening stillness before the lights went out.

"But you don't think it's gunshots?" Brett asked.

"No. I don't see anything. There aren't any casings on the ground, and we weren't hit with any bullet holes in the car windows. Not even a scrape on the paint."

Brett tilted his head back and stared up at the structures that kept the condo's parking lot well lit for residents and visitors. He tilted his head once more, obviously trying to get a clear gaze at the light directly over Troy's car. "Do you have a flashlight in your glove box?"

Before Troy could go get it, one of the patrol officers handed over a flashlight from his belt. "Here you are, Detective."

Brett shined the narrow beam upward onto the oval shape of the light. "Isn't this interesting?"

Troy stepped closer and stared up, following the line of Brett's gaze.

"Light's been shot out, Buddy. Right over Evangeline's passenger side door."

"But there aren't any shell casings on the ground." A quick glance showed the other lights all continued to glow, a fact he was already cursing himself for not noticing.

The assembled officers all had their flashlights in hand, and began inspecting the ground, but nothing else glittered.

What the hell was going on?

The light had obviously been blown out, and those pops had echoed like gunshots, loud and persistent and much too close to the car.

"Detectives! Over here."

Troy and Brett walked over to where a young rookie

pointed at the ground. Troy recognized her, one of their fresh-faced new recruits who had joined the GGPD in the last couple of months. "What did you find, officer?"

"It looks like a string of firecrackers. Look here." She pointed where small, seemingly innocuous poppers had exploded off of their pasteboard holders. "Is it possible this is what you heard?"

It was entirely possible. And as Troy reconsidered that quick burst of noise, he realized that small firecrackers made sense.

"You think someone's playing a prank?" Brett dropped to his knee and lifted one of the discarded paper casings.

"A prank? This close to Evangeline's house?" Troy pushed back. "No way."

"Troy, come on. It's June already. And it's summertime. Everybody starts getting excited for fireworks this time of year."

"Detective, sir?" Grace Colton, Troy's sister and one of the newest rookies on the force, stepped forward. She was diligent about treating him with the respect of his rank, and while he appreciated it, it always made him feel a bit awkward when she went into formal mode. "Is it possible some kids were here playing? And when they realized it upset you, they ran."

Although Troy had been focused on Evangeline when they pulled into the parking lot, and even more so once he cut the ignition and turned to face her, he didn't recall seeing anyone milling around the lawn. He might be into her, but he certainly would have recognized a group of kids. Even if they hadn't been making mischief, he would've seen them and carefully navigated so that he didn't come too close to one or potentially run over a bike. Children were careless in summer when they had their freedom from school and he always paid extra attention when he saw one anywhere in close proximity.

Plus, it was after 11 p.m. Would they still be out playing, summer vacation or not?

And why so close to her home and nowhere else?

"I suppose anything is possible, Grace. But it feels like a long shot."

Brett didn't respond and Troy heard a world of information in that lack of answer.

"Long shot? What makes you think that?"

Once again, Brett proved himself the consummate partner, and pulled Troy to the side, out of the way of anyone who might hear them. "Come on, man, you really think this is anything?"

"Do you think it isn't? She's been under attack for almost thirty-six hours."

"Under attack? If it's even that, it's an attack by things no one can see but her."

"Because the threat is hiding out of view."

Brett stared up at the darkened light again before returning his gaze fully to Troy's. "I'm not saying it's not strange, but I don't think it's a problem that necessitates half the GGPD out here. And for the second time today."

Troy knew that resources were stretched to the bone. The Davison case as well as all the other things Randall Bowe had deliberately blown up needed every bit of the precinct's focus. But he simply couldn't stand down on this one. "Something is happening to her, Brett. I know it. I feel it. This can't be a coincidence."

"Look, I get it. Instincts are a huge part of this job. But are you sure your instincts are right on this one?"

It was because of both the respect he heard in Brett's

voice and the seriousness that he saw on the man's face the Troy was willing to end the conversation right there.

But it was the first clue that he might be up against more than a few doubts. First Melissa's that afternoon, and now Brett's.

If his closest allies had questions, it was only natural to assume that the GGPD did not believe that Evangeline Whitaker was in danger.

Yet however he spun it, Troy couldn't conceive of any way that she wasn't.

WATCHING THE BODY language of the cops from her safe perch in the car, Evangeline wanted to scream with the frustration of it all.

They didn't believe her.

It hadn't taken much in the way of intuition to read the skepticism painted across the various officers' faces. Nor did she need clairvoyance to understand what Detective Shea was saying to Troy.

It was one more problem laid at her feet.

And she hadn't even called this one in to the GGPD.

But there are still a dozen police officers swarming your home.

As that thought filled her mind, the urge to sink lower in the car expanded in her lungs until she nearly burst with it. Which was the exact reason she sat up straight and opened the door. She'd worked too damn long and hard to overcome the frustrations of her childhood to sit and cower. Digging her keys out of her purse as she crossed toward her door, she had them in the lock before Troy caught up to her.

"Hey. I want you to stay in there."

"And I want to be in my home."

"But it's not safe."

Evangeline blew out a hard breath and turned to face him before flinging out a hand toward the flashlight-illuminated officers. "I've got a dozen cops on my lawn. I think I'm fine."

"Let me at least do a sweep of the house first."

"I'm *fine*, Troy."

The words spewed out, harsh and bitter, but try as she might, she couldn't pull them back. They were the culmination of more than a day's worth of fear and exhaustion, layered on top of months' worth of the same. Twisting hard on the key, she shoved on the door and pushed into the house. She had no interest in being the center of gossip in her condo complex, nor did she have any interest in seeing the mix of what was sure to be pity and censure in Brett Shea's eyes. Hell, his dog would probably wear the same expression at this point.

"Let me." Troy followed her into the house, flipping on lights as he went. "I'll do a sweep of the house."

"I've got this."

He stilled at that, laying a hand on her forearm. She expected him to say something but when he remained silent, she finally looked up.

"Please let me do this."

The emotional fire that had carried her inside suddenly sputtered out and all she could do was nod. "Okay."

Although she refused to huddle on a chair underneath a blanket this time, she did remain in the living room as he did the same sweep as the night before. Onward toward the back door, flipping on lights and opening closet doors. Then back down the hall and on into her two bedrooms. He finished the search in a matter of minutes. "All clear."

"Good."

"Thank you for letting me check."

"No, thank you. I'm sorry I was so petulant and ill-behaved."

Something flashed across his features. It was quick— if she'd looked away from him for even a moment, she'd have missed it.

But in that flash, Evangeline thought it looked a lot like anger.

PETULANT AND ILL-BEHAVED?

Troy was still rolling those treasures around on his tongue a half hour later as he went back outside to wave Brett and Ember off and out of the condo parking lot. They were the last to leave, the other officers on scene all having dispersed already, after getting all clears from Troy or Brett.

Troy had requested they take in the firecracker casings, and the officer who'd discovered them had quickly complied, securing them in evidence bags. Brett might have his doubts but Troy wanted those casings in to CSI and he knew his cousin Jillian would make them a priority. She might only be in her first year on CSI but she was good and she was motivated to succeed. A fact that had only grown exponentially when Randall Bowe tried to pin his criminal evidence techniques on her.

It had been a bad time, Troy thought, as he headed back toward his partner. Jillian had struggled for quite a while as Bowe's transgressions came to light. Each and every time, their CSI head tried to pin the faults on his junior investigator, even though Jillian's work was impeccable.

Her work ethic even more so.

Yet Bowe had still managed to make her doubt herself.

Which brought him back to his own problem. He'd only worked with Brett for a few months, but he trusted the man implicitly. Melissa had partnered them up on the Davison case and they'd shown great promise as a working pair. Yet here he was, arguing with Brett's instincts and forcing his own.

"I'm sorry about before."

Brett glanced briefly away toward Evangeline's front door. "Look, I get it. She's in some sort of trouble. Too much is going on to think this incident is totally innocent. I'm just not so sure it's as sinister as you believe it is, either."

"I can see that."

"Sleep on it and we'll put fresh eyes to it in the morning?"

Troy took the proffered hand that came with the offer and shook it, satisfied he and his working partner were absolutely finding common ground. "I'll be in before eight. Coffee's on me."

Brett called for Ember and the two loped off to his car. The urgency with which they'd arrived had faded and Troy didn't miss the weight that rode Brett's shoulders as he watched him cross the parking lot beneath the working lights.

Wasn't he feeling the same?

That endless weight that had settled over the entire GGPD when Len Davison and Randall Bowe's crimes were discovered?

One that seemed to have Evangeline in its grips, as well.

I'm sorry I was so petulant and ill-behaved.

There it was again. That odd apology that suggested

Evangeline believed she'd acted like a child. She was a woman in danger and that was all she could come up with? Some apology for it all?

I know anger and rage and then silence. But not easy laughter at the table and welcoming visitors into your home with open arms.

Things had happened so fast in the car that Troy hadn't had a lot of time to process her last comment. But now that he did, he considered what she'd said. And all that lay beneath those words that spoke of fear and tension and a volatility that shaped the way she thought of families.

How she believed they acted.

He'd been a cop for a long time and he wasn't a stranger to the more terrible things people did to one another. That was as true of how family members treated one another as it was in the crimes he saw committed month in and month out, year after year.

What he hadn't expected was that Evangeline might have lived with that in her own life.

The strong, competent attorney he'd observed for years was a grown woman apparently still processing the sins of her upbringing.

He took a deep breath on that knowledge, not quite ready to head back into her house yet. He was determined to stay another night, not comfortable with leaving her alone. A feeling that had only grown stronger with the reality that the large light closest her home was out. She had a front door light but its radius offered limited protection, and as far as he was concerned, it wasn't enough.

So he'd stay. He'd argue the point if he needed to or sleep out front in his car, but he'd stay. But before he did either, he needed the soothing quality of the evening air and a few minutes with his racing, roiling thoughts.

With nothing more than observation in mind, Troy walked the perimeter of the parking lot. He took stock of the way cars were stationed in front of the building—which he assumed was meant for the residents. And then there were additional spots that spread out as a paved parking lot, providing additional spaces for guests.

He counted the number of overhead lights, similar to the one in front of Evangeline's door. And as he looked up at each one, the bulbs were bright and shining.

Coincidence?

"What are you looking at?"

Troy turned to see a woman, likely no more than twenty-two or twenty-three, staring up in the same direction.

"Nothing. Just curious that the light's out."

"I heard all that noise earlier." She shrugged. "My boyfriend told me to ignore it. 'Ella,' he said, 'why are you always so nosy about what the neighbors are doing?'"

Troy wasn't so certain it was nosy, but he took full advantage of the young woman's curiosity. "It's good to keep an eye on your surroundings."

"That's what I said!" she said and brightened at Troy's ready agreement. "I want to know what's happening where I live."

"And what did you find?" Troy asked.

"Nothing." Ella kicked the grass at her feet. "Probably just a bunch of kids playing around with fireworks."

Her boyfriend hollered down from a window above and she glanced up before backing away. "I've been out here a while. I'll see you later."

Troy took a solid look at the boyfriend. Although Ella seemed awfully quick to do his bidding, Troy didn't see much in the man's gaze other than annoyance his girl-friend was traipsing around the parking lot at midnight.

The interlude hadn't taken long, but as Troy reconsidered the lamps, he went back to his original frustration.

There was no way the lights going out over Evangeline's door was a coincidence.

Everything in him fought back at that idea. If she hadn't had the panic over the bloody shirt earlier, he might have said it was possible. But now? Two incidents within a few feet of her home?

No way.

As he continued working his way around, he ended up at the end of her particular building. It was one of four that made up the overall condominium complex. The front door of the first unit was painted just like hers, a color scheme that was repeated all the way down the building. There were two other overhead lights, spaced at equal intervals from the one that was now dark.

If he hadn't been looking, he'd likely have missed it. But now, as he stared up at the second light, the one closer to Evangeline's, he saw it. A thin thread that connected that lamp to the one in front of her building. Curious, he turned to gauge the same distance between the middle lamp and the one at the opposite end of the building, but nothing was visible.

That strange thread was much too high to reach, the oval of the lamp at least as high as the second story of condos, but it was visible all the same. Hastening back, he ran to his car to get his flashlight.

Cursing the oversight, he snagged the flashlight out of his glove box. There had been a dozen cops here, and every one of them had missed it. It irritated him, even as he acknowledged they were all on edge and stretched far too thin. Especially when it had become evident the cause of the lamp going out had been a firecracker.

Crossing back to the lamps, he positioned the beam directly on the thread. As he'd originally suspected, a thin wire was strung between the two lights, ending at the now-empty socket. He pulled out his phone and snapped off a few photos. Was it a fuse of some sort?

It was more plausible than whatever else they'd come up with. But it also meant that whoever set it off had still been relatively close to the car as he and Evangeline talked. Had Troy been that oblivious to his surroundings when he was with her?

Troy moved back to the light still lit and snapped a few more photos for good measure before shoving his phone in his pocket.

He'd send Jillian a text tonight and have her meet him here first thing in the morning. They'd need a ladder anyway, so he'd have her bring the big investigation truck the CSI team brought out to sites.

That lamp going out practically over his and Evangeline's heads wasn't a coincidence. And they were going to get the evidence to prove it.

HE WAITED UNTIL the cop was gone, irritated that some dumbass punk kid had steered him wrong about the fireworks. He'd asked, hadn't he? How to set a fuse that would light the poppers from a distance?

And he'd been given minute details on how to make the thin braided fuse do the work.

Only it hadn't incinerated like he'd believed it would. And now there was a link from where he lit it and where it detonated.

That damned, persistent cop had seen it.

All his plans would go to hell if he left any evidence behind. The goal was to make the lawyer look like she was making things up so no one believed her. But if the cops started finding evidence, his entire plan would fall apart.

There was no way he was letting that happen.

He'd lain low down by the end of the condo building, waiting for the melee to die down. He couldn't risk going to his car with all the cops around, especially for the second time that day. And he wasn't walking back to downtown, either.

He'd intended to get in his car and leave once the cops were gone. It had only been the last-minute urge to count to a thousand and let the scene lie a bit longer that gave him what he needed. If he'd left a few minutes before or after he'd have missed the cop's late-night investigation altogether.

But now that he'd seen it, he had to do something.

The setup earlier that day had been easy. He'd played local handyman and had even changed the light bulbs for good measure. No one had even noticed him up there on a ladder *or* before he'd left that doctored shirt on her doorstep.

Did anyone ever notice anything?

Wasn't that why he was in this damn mess? Tampered evidence no one bothered to notice. A problem the damn DA's office couldn't even see? How was that justice?

It wasn't.

The rising anger that always burned in his stomach like battery acid welled up again and he savored it. Used it.

That damn lawyer was why he was in this position. His business was nearly bankrupt and he owed more people than a bookie after a game upset. And to hell with it all, he wasn't going down without a fight.

The cop took a few more pictures with his camera before heading back inside the lawyer's fancy digs. He'd give it another minute or two and then he was pulling down what was left of the fuse. The damn cop might have pictures but he wasn't going to have any evidence.

And like the lawyer's shoddy prosecution had shown him, evidence was the only thing that mattered.

Chapter Eleven

Evangeline listened to Troy's recounting of what he'd observed outside and shuddered at the idea of more deliberate action against her. "You think someone did that on purpose?"

"Yes."

"Against me?"

"As one more way to make you frightened, at minimum. It's also the personal nature of doing it at your home. I don't like it and that's why I'm staying again tonight."

"You don't have to do that."

"Consider yourself in possession of a roommate for the foreseeable future. I won't make a mess and you'll barely know I'm here."

She wanted to argue with him. Realistically, she knew how to take care of herself. She had been active in strength training and various forms of self-defense her entire life.

But she'd be lying if she didn't admit that having a cop with a gun in her home went a long way toward making her feel safer.

Which was the exact opposite reaction of her hormones. Because there was nothing safe about Troy

Colton's effect on her. She realized that now, after spending a few days with him, as well as seeing him with his sister and her family.

But even if she found him attractive, Evangeline knew she had to manage her expectations. He was here to help her. Yes, they'd kissed and exchanged some lingering glances, but it wasn't enough. And it certainly wasn't something she needed to explore here in the midst of whatever was going on against her.

Or, more to the point, to her.

"Tell me more about this string between the lights."

"I don't know exactly, but it's strange. To be fair, it could be nothing more than a string that's been there for quite a while. Did your complex ever have any decorations up there? Or any sort of sign that the sales office might've put up?"

"No, not that I remember. But I was one of the last residents to buy a unit here. I suppose it could have been placed up there, welcoming people to the condominium complex and encouraging them to look at the model units."

And to be fair, it could have been. She had been in her condo for a few years now, but the complex overall was relatively new. Although, would string like that have lasted that long?

"It's suspicious—that's all I need to know. If I had a ladder, I'd get up there myself right now to take it down and log it in as evidence. But I already got a text back from my cousin Jillian. She'll be here first thing tomorrow morning, with a ladder."

"Jillian's the one in CSI?"

"Yes. And as Randall Bowe tried to make her his scapegoat, she's got an ax to grind and a willingness to review any and all evidence, no matter how remote it might seem."

"His crimes were endless, weren't they? I mean, Davison is scary all on his own and his crimes are horrifying. But the way Bowe did it? Operating behind the scenes. It's diabolical, really."

"A lot of his motives came to light as we were investigating Everleigh Emerson."

"The woman who was accused of murdering her ex-husband?" When Troy nodded, Evangeline added, "I wasn't involved with that case, one of my coworkers was. But it was a strange case from the beginning."

"What makes you say that?"

"Well, Ms. Emerson got a divorce from the ex. By all accounts, that suggested she'd moved on. Yet somehow she's suddenly a suspect in her ex-husband's murder? Obviously, we were following the evidence prosecuting the case, but I remember when we discussed it in a team meeting thinking how odd it was."

"You don't think a marriage gone bad can be a reason for murder?"

"I've done this long enough to realize anything can be a motive, regardless of how irrational it seems to anyone else. But in this particular case, there was just something about it all that never quite fit. Here is a young woman who found a way to move on from a bad time in her life, yet suddenly she comes back?" Evangeline shrugged. "It just always rang false to me."

"It did for my cousin Clarke, too. He took on her case. Now they're a couple and planning their future."

She shook her head, smiling as Desiree's words from earlier sank in. "Your sister made a comment, and in this instance it's very clearly true. Sometimes the things in our life that are unpleasant or difficult lead us to something wonderful on the other side."

"Dez said that?"

"She did. Or my paraphrased version of it."

He quieted, the light smile fading from his lips. "Your opinion on Everleigh's case, and some of the things that you said earlier…in the car… Does that all have anything to do with your perspective on your own family?"

That sudden feeling of exposure hit fast and hard. Why had she said those things in the car? Yes, her guard was down a bit from the pleasant evening they'd shared with Desiree, Stavros and Danny. And in the darkened interior of the car, it had felt safe somehow. A quiet place where she could share her thoughts.

"I was just a bit surprised, I guess. Your family is special."

"Is that all?"

She should have expected he wouldn't take a simple answer or platitude in place of the truth. Although that *was* the truth. His family was special. Despite the trauma of losing his mother in the way that he had, he and his sister clearly had a deep and special bond. And the way he described his stepmother, Leanne, the day before was further proof of that.

So how did you explain those feelings of envy and confusion when confronted with someone whose experience had been so different from your own? More, how did you reconcile that with your own experiences growing up?

Maybe you didn't.

And in the quiet acceptance in Troy's golden gaze, Evangeline tried to explain. "My parents had a volatile marriage. I spent my childhood living with that. But there are times, when I observe other people's lives or hear other people's experiences, that I realize we aren't all the same. That not everyone grew up the way I did."

"Was there violence?"

"Physical, you mean? No." She shook her head, the idea of her father exacting his rage with that sort of violence as off-kilter as thinking he could ever remain silent on any subject.

He'd prided himself, in fact, that he was above "those men who use their fists to make a point." Hadn't she heard that over and over?

Yet hadn't that "self-control" he prized vanished with the swift lash of his tongue, over and over?

"My father had issues managing his emotions. Presumably he still has that problem but neither my mother nor I live under his roof any longer. Anything and everything could set him off, but once unleashed, he'd rage and rage."

"Lashing out emotionally is a form of violence, as well, Evangeline."

"Yes, it is." While she wouldn't have believed that as a child, she'd worked through the slow journey toward understanding it now. Both through her own therapy and through her casework, she'd come to understand that emotional abuse was real and could do damage, just like a fist.

"He refused to accept any of his own faults or any responsibility for his choices. If my mother ever dared to complain, he'd verbally strike out, claiming she was anything from a harpy to a madwoman for her thoughts."

"Are they still together?"

"Thankfully, no. They divorced when I was in college."

Her mother had stayed in her loveless, emotionally

troubled marriage for far longer than she should have. Evangeline had always known it was because she'd feared leaving her only child to battle those forces alone. And still, it bothered Evangeline that her mother had felt the need to do that. That she'd given up her own happiness for so long.

"I'm glad you and your mother are out of that."

"I am, too. But it still can't change the fact that I'd rather have a real, functioning relationship with my father. Instead, we have cool and distant conversations once a month."

It was a situation that had come to suit them well and she had long ago stopped crying about it. Yes, it chafed every so often, a wound that never fully healed. But she'd moved on.

And had determined to live a better life for herself.

"Is it at all possible the altercation you saw in the alley yesterday was triggered by your experiences?"

It was a fair question. She knew that and understood it. As a prosecutor, it would be a question she'd ask herself if she'd evaluated this case through a legal lens. Most of all, based on the time she had spent in Troy's company, she recognized he meant it in a collaborative way.

Despite all those things, she couldn't help but feel the sharp point of his doubt.

"You think I made it up? That because my father couldn't control himself, suddenly I'm seeing women murdered in alleyways because of it?"

"I didn't say that."

"Are you sure? Because that's exactly what I heard."

"That's not what I said."

"Right. Because I tell you about a piece of my past that I don't discuss with anyone and suddenly it's the reason

I'm seeing women murdered in Grave Gulch. I sat in that car out there, Troy." She pointed in the direction of the door. "I saw the doubt in everyone's eyes."

"I'm not doubting you, Evangeline."

"That's exactly what you're doing. I've seen enough of it for the past two days to know that I'm right."

"ARE YOU INCLUDING me in that number?" Troy struggled against the rising ire, the bile nearly overriding his quiet tone. But even in his frustration, he recognized yelling wasn't the answer.

By her own admission, she'd lived with enough of that growing up.

When she said nothing, he pressed on. "This isn't about doubt. This is about understanding what is happening to you."

"What's happening to me is that I saw a woman murdered in an alley. I saw the blood spread across her white shirt. I didn't make that up. Especially since said shirt showed up on my front doorstep."

Only it hadn't stayed there.

He'd raced over here at top speed, several officers in pursuit behind him, and they'd arrived to find nothing. No shirt, no blood and no remnant of either existed, let alone proof that it had been placed in front of her home.

"I know what's being said about me," she finally said.

"Not by me."

"But you've thought it. Come on, Troy. How couldn't you?"

"It's not about what I think. It's about understanding what's happening to you."

"PTSD over my father isn't what's happening here." She shook her head and stood. "I need some water."

As he watched her walk out of the living room, Troy had to admit that he wasn't being entirely honest with her. He believed her…to an extent. Almost like that belief was just out of reach, in view but not quite in his grasp.

He knew how he wanted to feel, but what was in his heart kept warring with the facts as he knew them.

And much as he struggled to admit it, between Melissa, Brett and then, this evening, Stavros, he did have doubts. Legitimate ones. The sort of doubts a detective was supposed to have when working on a case.

It was the man who was attracted to her who didn't have them.

And wasn't that the whole problem?

He followed Evangeline into the kitchen, and found her with her back against the counter, a cold bottle of water in her hand.

"I'm sorry I can't be the person you need me to be," he said. "I'm sorry that my job keeps getting in the way. But I need to keep my focus on the Davison case."

"I get it."

"Do you?" He moved in closer, his hands planting against the counter on either side of her waist. "Do you really?"

"You're in a difficult position. We both are."

He was enamored by the way her pulse tapped there, in the hollow of her throat. He saw the slight flutter and had the overwhelming urge to press his lips to her flesh.

Because she wasn't unaffected.

He lifted his gaze from temptation, his voice dropping to a lower register. "What are you going to do about it?"

"For starters, I think you need some distance from this case. I appreciate the help you've given me, more than you can ever know. But I think you should get back to work and quit worrying about me."

"I don't think I can do that."

Her pulse continued to pound, a fact that must have finally caught up to her when her voice trembled, breathless. "Why not?"

"Because all I can think about is doing this."

Temptation roared back in and he recognized fully that he was past the ability to resist. Bending his head, he pressed his lips against her throat, trailing his tongue over that throbbing pulse. Her light moan filled his ears and provided all the encouragement he needed to keep going.

His lips traveled the tender skin of her throat, nipping beneath her chin, before he took her mouth with his. Those light moans became deeper, more urgent, as she opened her lips beneath his. And as his tongue swept in and met with hers, Troy finally acknowledged to himself the problem all along.

As a detective, he needed objectivity.

But as a man, he had none.

EVANGELINE FELT THE water bottle slip from her grip and was abstractly happy she had remembered to put the cap back on. Not that a backsplash of cold water would hurt her right now.

He was so hot.

Like a furnace. He was pressed against her now, with the most delicious sort of heat. With her hands now free, she gripped the shirt at his waistband, the fistfuls of material soft to the touch. As his lips moved over hers, more of that delicious heat branded her, as their glorious kiss spun on and on and on.

Bolder, her hand shifted from his waist to drift over

his back. He was so solid, the strength beneath her fingertips an impressive testament to the way that he kept his body in top shape.

His hands shifted over her body, as well, stroking and coaxing the most delicious responses. When one large hand closed over her breast, his thumb rubbing against her nipple, Evangeline's knees went weak. Pleasure, an impossible thought over the past few months, was suddenly present, ripe with possibility.

She wanted him.

And while she knew it made no sense, nor was it something they could indulge in at this point in time, the opportunity to steal a few moments in his arms was priceless.

With that thought foremost in her mind, she took. She took all that pleasure and sweet need and drank in as much as she could. Tomorrow would come soon enough. The events swirling around her that made no sense, the ones that were as real and tangible as the man holding her in his arms, would still be there.

So for now, she took.

And when he lifted his head to stare down at her, his hazel eyes drugged with desire and his lips still wet from their kiss, she smiled.

No, he wasn't unaffected at all.

"What do you do to me?" she whispered.

His question, voiced in that husky whisper, was a surprise, and her smile faded at the confused look that painted his face in harsh lines. "Inconvenient attraction?"

"Really?" That was how he saw this? What was between them.

"How is it anything else?"

Or more to the point, how *could* it be anything else?

She wanted to be angry. And some small part of her was hurt. Bruised feelings, really. But if she were honest, she also recognized what he was saying. Because it was nearly impossible to think that this could be real. That this fire between them could be a product of something deeper, instead of the tense, fraught situation she found herself in.

"I don't know. I honestly don't know." He sighed. "But I've never been tempted like this before. I know my job and I know my responsibilities. That is as clear to me as my own name. As the love I have for my family. As the next breath I'm going to take. Yet with you, I question my responsibilities."

"You're a good cop, Troy. You're well respected, and you know how to do the job. Whatever has happened to me over the past few days, you can't doubt your work. The value you bring to the badge, that's important."

"I know it is. That's the problem, isn't it? The badge *is* important. For a long time, it was everything. But see, these past few days, I've realized something."

"What?" It almost hurt to ask the question, but she had to know.

"You, Evangeline. You're important, too. And it scares the hell out of me."

RANDALL BOWE PICKED up the burner phone, one of several in his possession, and dialed the number he knew by heart. The line rang, and rang some more, each peal a resounding endorsement of his wife's betrayal.

Probably out with someone, he thought. Screwing around again, just like she had before their separation. His heart slammed in his chest with the anger and injustice of it all, just like the day he'd discovered her infidelity.

"Hello?"

Her answer was a surprise, but now that he had her on the line he couldn't keep quiet. "You mean you aren't out right now cheating and defiling yourself with someone else?"

"Randall." That was all she said, his name coming out on a strangled breath.

"Yeah, it's me. Who'd you think it would be?"

"You shouldn't be calling me. You know I'm going to have to call this in to the police."

"Like I care." And like it mattered. They'd never trace the call anyway.

"Randall, what are you doing? Where are you?"

That familiar anger churned, low in his gut. It was so dark, so deep.

So overwhelming.

Until he'd finally figured out how to use it. How to mold it and shape it, really, so that it became something more than grief and anger. So that it became useful. Like a tool he could wield to derive justice.

She'd done him wrong, and someone had to pay. And since she hadn't seemed particularly contrite, or particularly interested in being the one to pay, he'd channeled all that anger toward others.

He ignored her question about where he was. He missed her to a degree that bordered on stupidity, but even he wasn't that dumb. "It's not what I've done. It's about what *you've* done."

"I've done nothing."

"You call cheating on me nothing?"

She sighed, but it was nothing like the way her sighs had sounded when they were first together. The sweet, delicate ones she'd make when he pulled her close, into his arms.

"I'm sorry that I didn't wait until I found a way to talk to you about my unhappiness, but you have to know we both needed to move on."

"No!" The shout tore from his lips. "*You* needed to move on. I thought we were perfectly happy."

"Happy? I've thought about it a lot these past months. We were miserable, Randall. All the time. You have to remember it, too."

Lies.

Lies she told herself, no doubt to make herself feel better about the cheating. Because if she could make herself out to be a victim, claiming their marriage was a dead end, then she could walk away from it all without any guilt.

Damn it, it didn't work that way. She *was* guilty. And now, anyone else who behaved like her was guilty, too.

And he could make it public.

He had that power. Or he did, until the damn Everleigh Emerson case blew it all to hell.

"We made a vow. A commitment."

"No, Randall, we made a mistake."

"How convenient of you to think that now. But it's because of you I'm in this situation."

"The one where you lied at your job, falsified information and helped a serial killer go free?" Her voice rose on each point, a slamming indictment of him and how she thought of him. "That situation?"

"Davison was an upstanding citizen for years. He was *faithful* to his wife." He deliberately emphasized the word "faithful," well aware his own wife was unable to grasp that concept. "And after nursing her through cancer, then losing her, he couldn't deal with it."

"So it drove him to become a killer? Grief doesn't work that way."

"He deserves his revenge, too."

"Stop this. You're talking nonsense."

He might have believed her. Once, he really might have. But now, after seeing what it was to have your marriage dissolve—not because of a virulent disease, but from your spouse's innate desire to walk away from you—he knew better.

"No, sweetheart, it's not nonsense at all. It's justice."

Chapter Twelve

Evangeline lay in bed and stared at the bright sunlight that streamed in through the curtains. She'd had a restless night and the sun seemed like a particularly sharp insult as it hit her bleary eyes.

Was it a sleepless night because Troy lay in the bed down the hall? Or was it because she couldn't get her thoughts to still, no matter how hard she tried. Their kiss had played out every time she tried to close her eyes, like a movie running on the backs of her eyelids.

A sensual movie. One that had been full of action and very little conversation.

After their honest admittances to one another in the kitchen, they'd both made quick excuses to head to bed. He still needed to check email, he'd claimed, to make sure his cousin Jillian would be over in the morning.

And she'd needed to escape.

It was still hard to believe she had told him about her father. The stories of her childhood were things that she kept to herself and it was odd now to think that someone else knew. Someone outside of her own family. Yet at the same time, she trusted Troy implicitly. The situation she currently found herself in was far from normal, but she did trust that he would keep her confidence.

Sitting up, she rubbed the grit out of her eyes and reached for a hair tie on the end table. Pulling up her hair into a loose knot, she swung out of bed and hunted for clothes. Attraction or not, Troy had stayed to watch out for her last night and she at least owed him some hot coffee. Maybe even a frozen waffle. She thought she had those in the freezer.

Padding down to the kitchen a few minutes later, she got the coffeepot set up and went hunting for the waffles.

And let out a small yelp when she turned to find Troy sitting at the kitchen table, his phone in hand.

"I'm sorry, I didn't mean to scare you."

Realizing she must look like a Gothic heroine, with her hand pressed against her chest, Evangeline dropped it. "I'm not sure how I missed you sitting there."

"You seem sort of focused on your task." He smiled, the look a sweet cross between sheepish and amused. "And for the record, I would've put the coffee on. I only beat you here by about two minutes. I just wanted to check my email first."

"It's fine. You are a guest. You shouldn't be expected to start your own coffee."

"Jillian should be here soon. She was swinging by the precinct to trade her car for the CSI vehicle, so she'd have the materials she needed. Namely a ladder."

"Okay."

His cousin's impending arrival was a swift reminder of what they'd dealt with last night.

And of the danger that still lurked outside her door.

"Are you hungry?"

"I can get something on my way to work."

"I have frozen waffles." She busied herself with opening the freezer, tossing back suggestions that she peered inside. "I also have some raisin bread I can defrost. Or some chicken tenders, if you prefer protein."

"I'm okay. But fix yourself something if you're hungry."

She closed the freezer door without pulling anything out. What was wrong with her? Chicken tenders? For breakfast?

Willing the awkward thoughts away, she focused on action. "Is there anything I need to do? For Jillian?"

"No, she'll take care of everything. I'll stick around to help her quickly with the ladder and gathering the sample and then we'll get back to the precinct so she can take everything to the lab."

"That's great."

And it was great. That wire was the first real evidence they had toward finding out what was going on around her. And while it could be nothing more than a string that held up a sign or some sort of lingering condominium project, it felt like something.

Something tangible.

Which had been woefully lacking to this point.

"Look, I was thinking about it. And while I appreciate all of your help, you don't need to come back later."

Troy looked up at her from his seat. Setting his phone facedown on the table, he stood up at her words. "What's this about?"

"You have a life. You have an active caseload. And there's a killer on the loose. Your attention is needed there."

"My attention is needed where there's a problem. You've been having a problem, Evangeline."

Again, that ready willingness to help her meant more than she could describe. But his cousin would be here soon and would be collecting the wire as evidence. That should get her case moving in the right direction, and they could get things figured out. He didn't need to be wasting his time with her.

"It'll just be easier that way. You don't need to keep checking up on me like I'm your responsibility."

"Where is this coming from? You need help right now. Not only that, but we have an active and open case dealing with what happened in that alley the other night. I'm here to help you."

"By moving in?"

"I hardly think sleeping in your spare room for two nights qualifies as moving in."

Why was he being so calm and collected about this? She was trying to make a point, damn it. But either he didn't hear her, or he refused to listen.

"Look, I just don't think you need to put all this time in on my behalf. You got me connected with Desiree and now there's a police sketch. I'm sure that'll be enough."

Before he could respond, a heavy knock came at her front door. He walked toward the exit of the kitchen but stopped to fully face her. "I'm sure that's Jillian. I'm going to get set up with her outside. But we're not done talking about this."

And then he was gone.

As the coffee maker made its last gurgle, Evangeline fixed herself a cup. What was she going to do with him? While she might have exaggerated a bit, Troy had sort of moved in over the past couple of days. His scent lingered in the air, and even though he made the bed neat as a pin, she still knew he had been there. In her home.

Add on the fact that the GGPD was clearly questioning his judgment about helping her and she knew they needed to put some distance in place.

And then there was the kissing. And the sleepless night she'd experienced because of the kissing.

She couldn't do too many more of those. That acute sense of nonfulfillment because she knew how good it could be between them.

It wasn't possible to keep on the way they were. And it was even worse to think about having him so close but not be able to progress things between them.

She considered one of those frozen waffles once again and crossed to the fridge to pull one out of the freezer. She barely had the door open when a shout came from the front of her condo.

"Evangeline! Get out here."

"I'M SORRY, TROY, I don't see anything." Jillian Colton stared down from her perch high up on her ladder, near the dome of the streetlamp that stood sentinel in front of Evangeline's door.

"There's nothing there?" Evangeline had joined them outside and stood on the other side of the ladder, helping him hold it in place.

Troy looked up toward his cousin, squinting into the early morning sunlight. "You're honestly telling me it's disappeared?"

"I'm telling you, there's no wire. There's nothing hanging between the two lamps."

"Jill, I saw it last night. I took pictures of it."

Jillian stared down at him, her gaze direct. "You want to come up here, then?"

"Damn it." He shook his head. He'd had trouble seeing the thin wire connecting the two lamps this morning but had assumed it was a function of the bright, early morning sunlight. But if there was nothing strung between the two lamps that meant someone had removed it. He'd stood here less than eight hours ago and laid eyes on it himself. "Come on down."

"What's going on?" Evangeline asked.

"I can only assume whoever put what looked like a wire up there was actually stringing the fuse to the firecrackers."

"And?"

"And they're the same person who pulled it back down."

"Right outside my door?"

"Yeah." Right outside her door. All while he was inside, kissing her, completely distracted from his surroundings. He let out a quiet curse, before reaching for Jillian's hand to help her down the last few ladder steps.

Jillian squeezed his hand gently. "I'm sorry, Troy. I just don't see anything."

"Because it's gone." Troy had already shown her the photos on his phone, but he flipped to them again, handing the device over to Jillian. He was disgusted, but also knew they were on to something.

Finally.

"Based on what you described, that had to be the fuse," Jillian scrolled through the digital photos. "Because at this point, if it was just some innocuous leftover from another event, it would still be hanging there."

He couldn't deny how good it felt to have Jillian's support on this as she handed him back his phone. "That's what I'm afraid of."

"Help me move this ladder over to the other light. I do want to take some scrapings from up there and see if we can get a handle on the firecrackers that were used. It's a long shot, especially now that it's summer and they're being sold in about a million places, but it's a place to start."

Grateful for something to do, he folded the ladder and moved it to the lamp closest to Evangeline's door. He didn't miss the way she'd gone quiet, giving them space to do the work. Nor did he did miss the rising fear, evidenced by her thinned lips and clasped hands. Even with her fear, she did step forward as Jillian began the climb back up, holding her side of the ladder and ensuring Jillian had a solid space to work.

His cousin was thorough, and it didn't take her long to get what she needed. She wore a utility apron tied around her waist, and pulled out any number of tweezers, plastic bags and evidence labels as she worked.

"She's good and very prepared," Evangeline said.

"She is. She's one of the best CSI team members we have. Just one more reason to be monumentally pissed off at Randall Bowe."

"Because he didn't appreciate her?"

"Because he tried to pin his misdeeds on her."

The fear he had observed so recently shifted and changed as Evangeline's black eyes lit with fury. "That bastard. Is there anyone's career in Grave Gulch he didn't try to mess with or ruin outright?"

"At this point, I'm afraid not many."

Evangeline quieted, and he could see that fury shift and take on a new dimension, almost as if she channeled it. "Is it possible he did this?"

"Set the fuse?"

"The firecrackers, placing and removing the fuse. If

he knows how to tamper with evidence, presumably he knows how to set it, too."

"That's an interesting take. The latest intel we have suggests he left Grave Gulch, but it's entirely possible he hasn't."

"If this is his home base, why would he?"

It was a good point and something he would add to his ongoing list of all things Randall Bowe. He had been working on Bowe's background, looking for any information he could find, including a brother the man was reported to have. Part of the hunt for the brother was to get information on Randall, but to also see if he had provided a hidey-hole.

It had seemed like the most likely choice, but Troy was grateful for the fresh perspective. A chance to bounce his working theories off someone was priceless. "True, but why would he stay? He can't go out. We're hunting for him to take him in and prosecute him for his crimes. If he's stayed close, he's got to have some sort of system set up to keep himself fed and off the radar."

All the more reason Bowe's brother, Baldwin, made sense as a probable hide out. Melissa had already been in consistent contact with Randall's estranged wife, Muriel, and the woman swore up and down she'd had no contact with him. She swore even more vehemently she wouldn't harbor him if he did show up and ask for help, and her protests hadn't been all that hard to believe. While anything was possible when dealing with people and emotions, he'd gotten the solid sense the man's estranged wife would likely be the last person to step up and help him.

"It's all about the revenge quotient," Jillian added as she climbed back down the ladder.

"How do you mean?" Evangeline asked.

"He's mad at the world. His wife, most of all."

That was interesting. Everything they'd understood so far was that infidelity had been the reason Bowe made the decisions he did. He manipulated evidence to incriminate anyone he believed to have cheated on their spouses or partners. "You think his marriage was in trouble?"

"Oh, yeah. He was in love but he didn't act like someone in love. Instead, he was jealous of her and always sabotaging them in some way." Jillian stopped and glanced at Evangeline. "I'm sorry. I don't normally talk about other people this way but he did a number on me. And, well, you know. I've got eyes."

Evangeline nodded, her expression free of judgment or censure. "You don't owe me an explanation. Besides, what you observed is important. Understanding someone's situation is essential to figuring out their motive."

Jillian smiled at that, her grin wide. "So I'm not coming off like a vindictive bitch?"

Evangeline smiled back, her first easy smile since they were at Desiree's house the evening before. "Nope. Not at all. I think you sound eminently reasonable."

"I LIKE HER."

Because they left Evangeline's condo at the same time, he and Jillian had arrived back at the precinct within moments of each other. Troy had already walked around to the back of the CSI van to help his cousin with the bags she needed to take back inside to the lab.

"Evangeline, I mean," Jillian added, as if the statement required clarification.

"I know. And I agree. She's great."

"Something's going on for her, too. Even if I'm desperate to catch Randall Jerk Face Bowe and it's my fondest wish we nab him as quickly as possible, I do recognize this particular situation might not be his work. But that doesn't change the fact that she's still dealing with a problem."

"You believe it?"

"I know it. She's scared and you don't make that up or fake it."

"Why are you mentioning faking it?"

Jillian stared him down, her gaze far more worldly than her twenty-seven years might suggest. "Come on, Troy. I get it, and I've even been there recently. You're getting blowback from everyone saying that she's making it up for sympathy. That she was responsible for the mess-up in the DA's office."

"Not exactly."

Jillian lifted one perfectly arched brow. "In any way?"

"Okay. Yeah, a bit. It's like this phantom argument sitting under the caution to be careful and to watch my back."

"Right. And all the while you are the one who can see exactly what's happening and know there's a problem."

He knew his cousin had experienced a rough go at the start of the year. Randall has used Jillian's status as one of the newest members of CSI to make her a scapegoat. She'd ultimately proven herself and pointed toward the work that was actually at his hands, but she'd been in a bad place.

"I'm sorry if I wasn't as understanding as I should have been when you were going through that."

"You stood by me. The whole family did."

"Yeah, but you still needed support. I hope you know we're always there for you."

"I know that." She stepped up and pulled him close for a hug. "We're Coltons. It's what we do."

"We are." Troy tightened his hold once more before letting her go. "And yes, it's what we do."

"We're also involved with one another and up in each other's business. You all know me which is why you stood up for me when Bowe was gaslighting me over the evidence. Now someone else needs help."

There it was again.

Gaslighting a person to make them feel off-kilter. Or worse, to scare them into thinking they are the problem.

It was the same thought he'd had the prior night and it was odd how neatly it meshed with Jillian's experience.

Before he could press her, Jillian kept on with her train of thought. "From one Colton to another, I am going to use my familial privilege to poke a bit more."

Despite the gleam in her eyes, Troy was still blind-sided at what came next.

"You have feelings for Evangeline and I think she has them for you in return. Don't let this strange situation circling around you both keep you from recognizing that."

"It's not like that."

"Oh no?" Her lone, lifted eyebrow suggested just how much she believed him, but her next words proved it. "You're crazy about her, that much is obvious."

"She's part of an active investigation. That's all."

"Keep telling yourself that, cousin." Jillian reached down and hefted one of her bags of evidence. "Just keep telling yourself that."

When she took off in the direction of the precinct, all Troy could do was follow, her words trailing him the entire way.

LESS THAN AN hour later, Troy cursed Jillian for her perceptiveness. And for the endorsement she'd given for him to pursue Evangeline.

You have feelings for Evangeline and I think she has them for you in return. Don't let this strange situation circling around you both keep you from recognizing that.

Entirely inappropriate feelings, he amended.

He was a cop and a good one. He knew how to keep his head and he knew how to assess danger. Yet despite his attention and oversight, this case had moved from bizarre to sinister in the span of a heartbeat. A shift that had happened while he was kissing her in her kitchen, brainless from the *feelings* coursing through him.

That length of fuse, strung between lampposts, was the proof he needed that something was going on outside of Evangeline's imagination. But just like everything else she'd experienced so far, the evidence of wrongdoing had disappeared. And he'd been too distracted to keep an eye on the evidence before it disappeared.

Settling in at his desk, he pulled up his files. He'd promised Brett coffee and then he'd had to text him early that morning that he was waiting for Jillian instead. His partner had taken it in stride, wishing him luck.

And now here Troy was, with nothing to show for it anyway.

Which had done nothing for his mood. There had to be something he'd overlooked. Tapping in his password, he waited as his files booted up. As he did, he considered Jillian's theory on Randall Bowe.

Troy had been working on running down the brother, Baldwin Bowe, but hadn't found the man yet. He knew the two were estranged—or at least had been, based on last intel on either of them. But estranged or not, familial bonds could get someone to act on behalf of a sibling or parent.

If Randall was hanging around Grave Gulch, it gave a bit less credence to the idea he'd holed up with his brother. Troy wasn't quite ready to close the line of inquiry, but it was something to think about.

"One unsugared coffee, piping hot." Brett strolled in and set the to-go cup on Troy's desk. "Or more aptly named, why bother?"

"I call it high-test and I could say the same about your chocolate and sugar-laden coffee that doesn't deserve to carry the name."

"It's called energy, my friend." Brett pointed toward the computer. "And you look like you need it. What happened with Jillian this morning?"

Troy caught Brett up over coffee, the two of them bouncing theories back and forth.

"You've got photos of the fuse?"

"Yep." Troy called up the photos on his phone, handing them over. "It's thin but you can see it. And I got it from a few angles."

"And then it was gone this morning?" As Troy nodded, Brett pressed on. "I owe you an apology, then."

Troy considered Brett across the desk. They'd paired up well and worked well together and he knew Melissa was leaning that way. He wanted a partner who would be honest with him and who could call him on his bs.

That sense had always been true for him. It was even more true now, as the GGPD faced one of its biggest challenges in the history of the department.

"No, you don't. Not for doing your job and asking the right questions."

"Yeah, but you also trusted your gut. And now you've got proof."

"It all depends on what Jillian finds in the lab. She took some evidence from the blown-out streetlamp. We'll see what she turns up from that."

Brett took a sip of his coffee, considering. "Your angle on Bowe is still a good one. We've been pursuing the idea he's outside of Grave Gulch. I know we haven't ignored the idea he's stayed local, but maybe we need to put a bit more focus there."

"He can't access his files. It's seemed more likely he'd cut and run."

"But he's got enough spite and anger to stick around. You know what I mean?" Brett added.

Troy did know what he meant and that assessment fit Bowe to a T. He was about to say as much when Melissa filled his doorway.

"Good. The two people I wanted to talk to." She came in and stood before them.

"What's going on?" Brett stood to greet Melissa.

"Randall Bowe."

"Yeah?" Troy asked. "Funny enough, we were just talking about him."

"I just got off the phone with his very frightened, still-estranged wife. He called her last night. Acted like an ass and accused her of a lot of things with respect to their marriage."

"You think we can get a trace?" Brett asked, sitting forward on his chair.

"Ellie's already on it."

Their tech guru, Ellie, had already been invaluable in this case. She'd been the one to recover Bowe's stolen files while the whole case broke open and had been working on tracking him since.

"Did Bowe give her any sense of where he was?"

"No," Melissa replied, before adding, "and she admitted it was a mistake on her part not to try and get more information. He caught her off guard and she's pretty shaken up. We've already started the paperwork to put her into protective custody."

"Good." Troy nodded. "That's good. What time did he call?"

"A little after eleven."

Troy did the quick math. Although it wasn't impossible, if Bowe was calling and picking a fight with his wife at that time, it was increasingly unlikely he was also at Evangeline's property, setting off fireworks and later drawing down evidence.

Which put them right back at square one.

No theories and some faceless threat lurking around Evangeline's home.

Troy quickly caught Melissa up on that detail as well as the news that Desiree had already sent through a police sketch for the file.

As he'd known she would, Melissa assessed the situation quickly and succinctly, cutting straight to the chase. "A fuse? So the job was done remotely? Or out of sight from where you were parked?"

Troy nodded. "It was quick and clean and I saw no one out of place by the time I got out of the car and did a visual inspection of the grounds."

"Is Evangeline all right?" his cousin asked.

"She is. Shaken, but okay."

Melissa took the seat beside Brett, dropping hard into the chair. "Maybe we've been looking at this all wrong."

It briefly crossed his mind to suggest Brett and Melissa *had* been looking at the situation all wrong, but Troy held his tongue. They were all under pressure, and reminding his colleagues—who were also friends and, in Mel's case, family *and* his boss—of that felt petty. Instead, he opted for "How so?"

"Based on the time of Evangeline's nine-one-one call and the report from the couple whose home he invaded, the would-be killer she observed wasn't Len Davison." Troy tapped his chin. "But what if Len is inspiring others?"

Brett took a sip of his coffee, thoughtful. "A sort of copycat?"

"She described a gunshot. That's Len's MO, too."

"But he's killing men," Troy argued. "A copycat would likely do the same, right?"

"Would he? Or might he use the killings as inspiration?"

There was hardly anything inspiring about Len Davison's actions. But Melissa's point still held.

Was it that hard to believe that all this recent confusion had turned husband against wife? Neighbor against neighbor? Friend against friend?

Or worse, had inspired the sort of mad fantasies better left alone?

Chapter Thirteen

Evangeline peeked through the curtains once more, consoling herself that she was playing neighborhood watchdog and not indulging in mindless, paranoid behavior.

Yeah, right. If the shoe fits, Whittaker.

What she was doing was talking to herself and going slowly bonkers here in her living room all alone. Even her precious lists hadn't done a good enough job of quelling the mix of fear and anxiety that had been her constant companions since Troy had left that morning, and the legal pad she'd stared at determinedly for the past half hour was still blank.

And yes, while she might have encouraged him to go back to the precinct to handle his work and not worry about her, now left to her own quiet home, she had to admit that the push was rather shortsighted.

Had someone really lit a fuse on a bunch of firecrackers to blow out the light in front of her door? It seemed like an odd way to scare someone, yet it made a strange sort of sense, too. It was summer and firecrackers were a ready part of people's recreation in the evenings. No one would notice them going off. Nor would it look immediately suspicious as a scare tactic.

Heck, if she hadn't already witnessed the violence in

the alley and experienced the scare of someone being in her home, she'd have ignored them completely, thinking them a prank gone slightly destructive.

The heavy ring of her phone pulled her out of her musings. When she saw it was her mother calling, she dived for it like a drowning woman going after a tossed lifeline. "Mom. Hi. How are you?"

"Sweetheart, I didn't expect you to answer. I expected you'd be working and I was just going to leave you a quick message to call me later."

Although she hated the fact that she'd kept her enforced leave quiet, she hadn't had the heart to tell her mother, either. While her mother knew about the outcome of the Davison case—who didn't?—Evangeline hadn't wanted to share more information. It felt too much like a failure.

"I've got a few days off."

"Oh, good. I hope you're making the most of them."

Right. Huddled in my house.

The urge to say just that—to have the words spill out so she could tell her mother everything—was nearly overwhelming. Instead, she forced a bright smile on her face and hoped it translated to her voice. "Well, it's lucky I can talk now, then. What's up?"

"I had some news I wanted to share with you." She heard her mother's quick inhale of breath before she pressed on. "Well, I've been seeing someone. Dating him, actually. He's a lovely man. His name's Bill."

"Oh." Realizing how that must have sounded, Evangeline quickly added, "Oh, Mom, that's wonderful!"

"I can't wait for you to meet him. And, well, it's a strange time right now, with all that's going on in Grave Gulch. But we met and it seems right. We're being careful and I won't let him walk in the park, even if he's with me."

Although she suspected Bill was a bit older than the men who'd been targeted by Len Davison, Evangeline was glad for her mother's caution. For the mysterious Bill and for her mom's own safety. "That's wise. We have to all hope this situation will clear up soon but until then I'm glad you're being so careful."

"You have to be. Even the protests downtown have me concerned. I respect the right of peaceful assembly, but it seems like a crowd like that could hide a person attempting to do harm, too."

Although their discussion was about a scary and dangerous topic, she could still hear the joy that floated beneath her mother's words. It was something she'd missed for a long time and it was only now, as she heard her mother's voice, that she understood what that sound was.

Hope.

"You sound really happy, Mom. I know you weren't for many years and, well, I'm glad you are now."

"Thank you for saying it. And it wasn't that bad."

Evangeline started to protest but her mother pressed on.

"What I mean is that it was bad, but I'd do it all over again to keep you safe."

"That wasn't a reason to stay in such a bad situation."

"Oh, sweetie. That's every reason and it's the only reason, all rolled into one."

Once more, that desperate urge to tell her mother all that was going on swelled deep in her chest but Evangeline held back. She'd never heard her mother this happy and there was no way she wanted to ruin that or dim it in any way with worrisome news.

News that was still too amorphous for comfort.

She could picture the conversation now. *So, Mom. I saw someone shot in an alley but there's no body, no blood and no sign that it ever happened. There was a mysterious book showing up in my house and someone's lurking outside my front door.*

Nope. No way. Not when her mother had finally found so much joy of her own.

Instead, she opted for a different tact. "When can I meet this Bill? Check him out myself."

"He's visiting his children this weekend down in Kalamazoo, but maybe next weekend?"

"I'd like that."

They spoke for a few more minutes and Evangeline promised to call later in the week to set some time for the following weekend. It was only when she hung up that the tears tightened her throat and the oppression of what she'd been living with for the past few weeks finally came crashing down.

An oppression she faced all alone, unable to even tell her mother.

She kept her gaze on the blank legal pad in front of her, the thin blue lines quickly going blurry with her tears.

MELISSA COLTON HAD no problem doing her job. Whatever was needed in her role as chief of the Grave Gulch Police Department, she was willing to do. That included seeing difficult cases all the way through to conclusion, investigating disturbing crime scenes and testifying against worthless weasels when they finally got their day in court.

But as a woman, she avoided poking into other women's business like the very plague.

Which made her visit to Evangeline Whittaker's condo as out of place in her day's agenda as if she'd decided to take half a day off and go skinny-dipping in a nearby watering hole with her attractive fiancé.

Actually…she thought as she shut off car, that last one wasn't a bad idea. And with Antonio in the forefront of her thoughts, she quickly dialed his number.

"I was just thinking about you." His greeting brought a smile to her face and she marveled at how easy that had become since Antonio Ruiz had come into her life.

"Fancy that, since I was thinking about you." She gave herself thirty seconds to indulge in what she'd mentally dubbed the kissy-kissy aspects of their relationship before shifting gears. "I have an idea brewing and I wanted to see if you could reserve a private table in a private corner of the hotel's restaurant."

"For us?"

"Not us this evening but my cousin. Troy's been putting in quite a lot of overtime and I'm ordering some R and R. My treat."

"Our treat, darling. And a private table suggests that the R and R is with someone."

"That's my plan."

Antonio's laughter came rolling through the phone. "I'm not going to bet against you on that one."

Melissa indulged in fifteen more seconds of the kissy-kissy stuff before ending the call. With her smile still humming as she walked up to Evangeline's front door, she stared up at the parking lot lamps that had caused such a stir this morning. She'd looked at Troy's photos from the night before and there was clearly something strung between the two lights. But now, as she looked at them, it was obvious it had been removed.

Which meant she not only owed Evangeline an apology, but she also owed Troy a bit more of her attention on this case. The situation downtown was still puzzling, with a K-9 as well as the CSI team finding nothing that suggested a murder or any sort of gunshot wound.

But harassment at home was another layer that wouldn't be ignored.

Melissa knocked on the door, brisk and efficient, even as a small voice inside began to waver. The cop part was easy to handle. The woman part, not so much. What was she doing here? And would her overture be received in the way she'd meant?

Or maybe a better question, what did she possibly hope to accomplish?

The question vanished as she came face-to-face with Evangeline. And as she took in that tear-stained face, it was easy to see she'd shown up at just the right time. "May I come in?"

"Of…of course."

Evangeline waved her in, keeping her face turned slightly away. "Would you mind giving me a minute?"

She nodded, moving more fully into the condo while Evangeline disappeared into what looked like the master bedroom. Melissa looked around, unwilling to hide her curiosity or her perusal of the home. The ground floor unit made it more readily accessible off the bat, with two entrances in the front and back of the home. The first-floor windows also offered someone intent on doing harm an easy view into the layout of the house.

A unique choice for an ADA. While Melissa firmly believed a woman should do what she wanted—and that included her choice of home—her cop's mind recognized the increased risk in selecting this unit.

"I'm sorry." Evangeline came back into the room. Although her eyes were still red, she must have splashed cold water on her face because the lingering vestiges of tears had vanished. "Thanks for giving me a few minutes."

Melissa took a seat on one of the pretty red chairs that flanked the couch, the color complementing its abstract print. "Nothing to worry about. And it's me who should be saying sorry."

Evangeline took a seat on the couch, her shoulders heavy. "You don't need to. I've used far too many resources from your department over the past few days and I can't tell you how sorry I am for it."

"You've used the resources afforded to you as a resident of Grave Gulch. There's nothing to apologize for and if I gave you that impression it's equally on me to correct it."

Those shoulders drooped a bit farther and Melissa considered what she knew about Evangeline Whittaker. They'd worked in the same community for over a decade and since they managed opposite ends of a case, from open to closed, their separate jobs ensured they spent minimal time together. Melissa came to court when needed and Evangeline had deposed her on a few occasions, but that was where it ended. A general awareness of one another instead of any real friendship or professional acquaintance.

Despite all that, she knew Evangeline to be a strong prosecutor. She'd worked for Grave Gulch County for years and until the Len Davison case, her reputation had been impeccable.

As a woman who prided herself on her reputation, and who knew the pressure the GGPD was dealing with that hit her directly, Melissa had a deep sense of how it would feel to see that vanish in a matter of days.

"But more important, I owe you an apology for not believing you."

Those red-rimmed eyes widened, but Evangeline's tone was measured when she finally spoke. "I know what's happened the past few days has been unusual. The lack of evidence is hard to understand, no matter how I twist it around or think through what I *know* I saw. But it's also on top of the past few weeks that have had me professionally upside down. My leave of absence has been kept quiet, but it's not exactly a secret. I can see where that would add suspicion in anyone's eyes that I'm making this up."

It wasn't a secret but Melissa believed that the lack of gossip surrounding Evangeline's leave was a sign of respect for the ADA. She had a strong reputation. Yes, that reputation had taken a hit with the Davison case, but it didn't change all that had come before.

Nor should it.

"The Davison mess has us all upside down. A serial killer is unusual, despite what modern entertainment wants us to believe. But that, coupled with Randall Bowe's betrayal of the GGPD, has put the entire law and legal communities on edge. That doesn't mean you aren't being subjected to some sort of problem right now."

"Thank you for that."

The apology seemed to go a long way toward relaxing Evangeline, the stiff lines of her body softening. "Your cousin Jillian was here this morning. Whatever else you can say about Randall Bowe, his behavior has lit a fire under her. Troy mentioned how determined she is to prove herself and to catch him in the process."

"I know I might sound biased because she's family, but Jillian has an amazing future in CSI. She's only been in the role for about a year, but she's proven herself incredibly dedicated to the work."

"That's great to hear. We need more professionals like her. And especially after going through the experience she did with Bowe's behavior, I'm glad it hasn't turned her off the profession."

Melissa considered the genuine praise from Evangeline and added one more check in the "yes" column for all the reasons why she'd come here today. "I am here to apologize. You deserve that and it's important that you know that. But there is something else I'd like to discuss."

"Oh. Of course."

"What you've been dealing with over the last few days has put you in close proximity with Troy. He's a good man and he's dedicated to his work."

"That's so easy to see. The way he's handled my case, but even before that, I've recognized that quality about him. Anytime I've seen him in court, he's always incredibly well prepared and quite passionate about his job."

That was one way to describe it, Melissa thought. Workaholic tendencies without taking any time for himself could be another. "He is. Sometimes to the distraction of everything else."

"It's a big job. And it's been an extraordinarily difficult year."

"It has been, for everyone at the GGPD. And if I'm being honest, for the Colton family, as well. But I also know that Troy has borne the brunt of it. The search for Randall Bowe and all the work to expose the depth of his cover-ups. The ongoing hunt for Len Davison. And the continued frustration that both remain at large. It can be overwhelming sometimes."

Although Evangeline's red-rimmed eyes had calmed from their obvious crying jag, an unmistakable sheen filled them once more. "That it can be. I keep telling myself I should try to relax a little bit and enjoy this leave of absence. I haven't had personal time like this in quite a while." She held up her hands, gave a rueful smile. "But it's hard to relax when the time off isn't by choice."

"When it's time off it feels like an indulgence. When it's forced, it feels like punishment."

"Yes!" Her eyes lit up at that, the thin sheen of tears fading. "That's exactly how it feels."

"I was put on desk duty earlier this year. I earned it fair and square and it's a policy I require for my team, so I expect to follow it, too. But it was still hard."

"This was the Orr case?"

Melissa nodded, surprised at how fresh it all still felt. She'd believed herself past it yet couldn't deny that there were times when it reached up and grabbed her hard around the throat. Drew Orr had faced a jail sentence, but that hadn't been good enough and he'd tried to kill her, thinking somehow he'd get away with it. She didn't regret firing her weapon, but she also believed that if she didn't feel the impact of taking a life, no matter how depraved, she didn't deserve to wear the badge.

She thanked the heavens every day she had found Antonio. Finding him and falling in love had upended her world, in the best way possible. And in the months since she'd shot Orr, Antonio's deep, endless support had meant more to her than she could have ever imagined.

It meant everything.

Which was why she wanted the same for her cousin

Troy. It was slightly presumptuous of her to be here and to press the issue, but if Troy didn't pick his head up once in a while and try living, there was going to come a day when he no longer could.

She'd nearly been there herself, before Antonio, and had no interest in seeing a beloved family member make the same mistake.

Especially when his interest in Evangeline Whittaker was so clear.

"I'm fortunate that the case is behind me and while I regret the loss of life, I would do the same again if my feet were held to the same fire."

"Orr faced a life in prison and instead of paying for his crime he tried to kill you." Evangeline stared down at her hands before looking back up. "And even with that truth I have to imagine it's still an impossible decision."

"It feels like that some days. Which is why Antonio is such a miracle. I don't have to face those days alone any longer." Melissa waited a beat before laying down her cards. "It's why I worry about Troy and his future."

"He's committed to his job. And his family, too," Evangeline added.

"A lovely thing, to be sure, but he needs more. Which is why there's a table with your name and his on it this evening at the restaurant in the Grave Gulch Hotel."

"Oh no, I couldn't. I mean, *we* couldn't. I mean, it's not like that."

"I know." *But it could be.*

Melissa kept that last piece to herself and kept on pressing. "It's a dinner, nothing more. A quiet evening for two people to relax and put the world around them in the rearview mirror for a bit."

"It's a lovely gesture, but—"

"It's already done. Antonio has it all set up."

"And Troy said yes?"

Spoken like a lawyer, Melissa thought.

But since she'd come this far, there was no way she wasn't going to see this through. "He will."

"What if he has plans?"

"He's spent nearly every day working late at the precinct for the past two months. He's entitled to a night off."

"But—"

Melissa leaned forward. "Please, Evangeline. Let me do this. As both an apology to you and as a much-needed evening off for my cousin."

"I don't know what to say."

"Say yes. It's an all-expenses-paid evening and I can personally vouch that the shrimp scampi is the best I've ever had."

Melissa saw Evangeline wavering and gave it her final push. She wasn't above playing dirty and if it meant she could try out her Cupid skills all at the same time, then she'd take it. "He needs a change of scenery and a break from the Davison case. The two of you get along well and I know you've been under a lot of stress from the same. It's a dinner. Enjoy the evening and forget about life for a few hours."

It's just dinner.

That thought had gone through her mind, over and over, since Melissa Colton had walked out of her home an hour ago. She'd gone from restless and upset to restless, upset and—oddly—in possession of a date.

Even though it wasn't an official date.

But it was a dinner at one of the nicest restaurants in Grave Gulch with Troy Colton.

Evangeline had already gotten a text from him that he was looking forward to dinner and would be by to pick her up at six. Which meant his cousin had managed to talk him into it. Or ordered him into it, as the case might be.

Which only added to her panic level. A forced date was even worse than calling it a date when it really wasn't.

She stared at the silk sheath she'd pulled from the closet. It felt too formal—and *way* too date-like—but she also knew the restaurant in the hotel lobby. The darkened interior was full of soft lighting and elegant tables, with small votive candles in the center. And the pretty aubergine shade of the dress always made her feel her best.

"To hell with it." Evangeline shrugged herself into the dress, determined to quit stomping around like an idiot. She had a nice evening planned. On some level, wasn't that enough?

So what was the problem?

But as she turned to stare at her reflection, she knew full well what the problem was.

She wanted the evening to be more.

To mean more.

And she wanted *more* of all of it with Troy.

With quick movements, she ran a brush through her hair and finished her primping with a soft coral lipstick that had been her favorite brand since college and gave herself one last glance in the mirror.

"You haven't been on a date in too long to count. Whether tonight is or isn't a date, go and enjoy yourself."

That admonition carried her out of her bedroom and on into the living room. She'd just reached the couch when her front doorbell rang. The drapes that hung in pretty brocade waves on the window were already drawn, a caution from Melissa before she'd left. That subtle change nearly had her crawling back into the bedroom and diving for the covers, with nothing more than a text to Troy to tell him she couldn't make it, but Evangeline forced herself forward.

She would not hide. Nor would she cower.

Even if she wanted to.

With a quick check through the peephole, she confirmed it was Troy and pulled the door open.

And just like that, Evangeline no longer wanted to hide.

The man that stood on her small front porch was everything she'd imagined as she'd gotten ready—and so much more. He stood there, looking strong and capable and incredibly handsome in the dark slacks and gray button-down shirt.

"Hi."

"Wow. Evangeline." He exhaled her name on a heavy breath before he seemed to catch himself. "You look great."

"Thank you. So do you."

"You ready to get going?"

"Sure. Let me just get my things." She gestured him into her home before turning to get the small purse and wrap she'd left on the chair. It was only as she turned back to face him that she realized his intention.

His heavy footfalls had already echoed away as he marched down the hall toward the kitchen and her back door. From where she stood, she could see him check the locks and confirm all was in place.

The happy bubble of anticipation that had formed as she'd gotten her first look at him fell away. Just like the drawn drapes, she was forced to see the evening for what it was.

Her time with Troy Colton for what it was.

A duty.

Nothing more.

Chapter Fourteen

Troy sensed the change in Evangeline almost immediately, yet had no idea why. She'd greeted him warmly when she'd answered the door, her shy smile shooting sparks through him with all the finesse of a lightning strike.

It was because of those lingering aftershocks that he'd needed a few moments to compose himself before walking her out to the car.

The woman was gorgeous. Her long, straight hair fell, glossy and smooth, down her back. Her arms, sculpted by her active kickboxing workouts, were shown to perfection in the silky confection that covered her. And the slim legs that were already amazing had gone off the charts with the addition of thin heels that put the two of them at eye level.

Had he ever seen a more beautiful woman?

Or one he'd wanted more?

The answer was a resounding no as he opened the passenger-side door for her. He waited for her to slide in, hoping for another one of those smiles, but it never came. Instead, she gracefully slipped in, swinging her feet into the car and keeping her gaze straight ahead.

Determined to have a nice evening, he ignored the

deep freeze. He'd figure out what was going on soon enough. And, if he were guessing correctly, he suspected Melissa hadn't given her a particularly big choice in going out that evening.

His fearless chief had come back into the precinct like a whirling dervish, ordering him to get up from his desk and go home to get ready. She'd informed him there was a reservation in his name and that he *would* be taking Evangeline Whittaker out that evening.

Brett had laughed at the set of orders but Troy didn't miss the slight note of panic in the other man's eyes when Melissa turned her serious gaze on him. Troy would have laughed at the unnerved bachelor routine if he weren't being steamrolled into leaving work early and taking Evangeline to dinner.

Which wasn't exactly a hardship.

Troy climbed into the driver's seat and backed out of his spot in front of her home. Part habit, part heightened vigilance, he scanned the parking lot as he drove slowly toward the main road, seeking anything out of place. Satisfied nothing lurked around Evangeline's home, he took his first deep breath as he headed for downtown and the Grave Gulch Hotel.

"I'm glad you could come out tonight." He kept his tone light, conversational, and was completely surprised by the continued cool response.

"Melissa seemed insistent we do this."

"You don't want to?"

He took his eyes off the road just long enough to see her subtle shrug. "It's nice to get out of the house."

Wow, he thought. Chalk that one up to a ringing endorsement. She might have mentioned taking a trip to the grocery store or scraping mud off her shoe.

"I know I'm looking forward to the evening."

When Evangeline remained silent, Troy kept his gaze on the road and focused on the short drive to the Grave Gulch Hotel. At least he'd see a friendly face when Antonio met them at the front desk.

The silence between them was heavy as he drove and it was only as it grew more and more oppressive that Troy realized why. In all that had happened over the past several days, there hadn't been silence. Despite her fear and anxiety, Evangeline had *talked* to him. She'd discussed how she felt and she spoke with him on any number of topics from her work to her family to the external situation they were dealing with in the faceless threat that stalked her.

And now?

Silence.

It was jarring in the extreme, and as Troy thought over the past twenty minutes since his arrival at her home, he racked his brain to come up with what had set her off.

He drove into the hotel parking lot, pulling up to the valet station. Melissa had given strict orders there, too, ensuring his car would be well cared for while he and Evangeline ate. As he handed over the keys, he hoped whatever malaise had settled over Evangeline would fade once they were seated in the restaurant.

Or they were going to have a long night ahead of them.

EVANGELINE KNEW HER behavior was terrible. She'd spent enough time growing up to know the damage emotional tantrums—and their counterpart, dead silence—could do.

Yet try as she might, she couldn't muster up any enthusiasm or excitement for the evening. Especially when

Troy had made it abundantly clear he saw this whole dinner as a commitment, nothing more.

He did a damn sweep of her home, for heaven's sake. A thorough check of the locks and doors, ensuring no one could get inside while they were gone for the evening.

It wasn't a rational reaction, especially after spending the afternoon convincing herself this evening wasn't a date. Yet at the same time, there was something about watching him inspect her condo that had landed like a cold bucket of water on her hopes for the evening.

Hopes she didn't need to be having.

Yet ones she'd had all the same.

"Troy!" A man she knew to be Antonio Ruiz met them at the maître d's stand at the front of the restaurant. The tall, elegant figure turned toward her, his smile broad. "And you must be Evangeline. I'm Antonio Ruiz. It's a delight to have you dining with us."

"Hello, Antonio. Thank you for having us this evening."

"It's my pleasure. And please consider yourself guests of Melissa and mine."

He led them to their table and Evangeline didn't miss the way several discreet gazes followed them on the walk through the room. She suspected it was due to the fact that she and Troy were guests of Antonio's, but she couldn't deny the feeling of being on display. After spending several weeks in a mix of isolation and hiding, it was an odd sensation to find herself in view of so many people.

It was only when they were seated at a small table in the back, in a private corner, that she finally began to relax.

Antonio waited until they'd sat, and with a final request that they enjoy the evening, he departed.

"I'm still getting used to the fact that he's about to be Melissa's husband." Troy smiled as he opened the heavy leather menu from its perch on the charger plate in front of him. "We've spent years looking out for this place at the GGPD, ensuring its high-end clientele were always safe while here. It's funny to now think of him as family." Troy glanced over the top of his menu. "And I say that in the best way."

"Melissa seems really happy."

Troy set his menu back down, his smile easy and genuine. "I've never seen her happier. A lot of responsibility rests on her shoulders as chief of the GGPD. Responsibility she's earned and wants. But it doesn't mean that it's not hard. And facing that alone, without a personal support system at home?" He shook his head. "It's a tough life."

Melissa's words from her earlier visit ran through Evangeline's mind.

Troy has borne the brunt of it.

The search for Randall Bowe and all the work to expose the depth of his cover-ups. The ongoing hunt for Len Davison. And the continued frustration that both remain at large.

It can be overwhelming sometimes.

He was deep in the morass that the GGPD was dealing with. Hadn't she seen that herself these past few days? Yet even with the pressure and stress, she'd not seen him crack under it.

No, instead, he did just as Melissa suggested: he bore up under the weight of it all.

She was entitled to her anger from earlier, but did she

really want to be petty and ruin a thoughtful evening provided by someone with seemingly the best intentions? Sure, this evening might not be what she'd secretly hoped. But it was still an evening out with an attractive man. A *good* man. One who deserved the simple enjoyment as much as she did.

Wasn't that some of what the past few weeks had taught her? She believed in her work and the long, long hours that she'd put in throughout her career. But the Davison case had also taught her that she wasn't infallible. More than that, her instincts were valuable and worthy, but every situation she found herself in wasn't going to be black-and-white. It was in the shades of gray that the real work happened.

Resolved to look at the evening with fresh eyes, Evangeline picked up her menu. Troy was owed a nice evening, too, and she wanted to be a fun, charming dinner companion.

The word *date* didn't have to factor into it.

And he did look really good this evening. The attraction she was determined to fight was having a hard time remembering the "not a date" part, even as she reveled in being out with such a handsome man.

And in the end, wasn't that something?

Whatever inconvenient feelings she might have for Troy Colton, she couldn't deny how much she enjoyed sharing his company. He was easy to talk to and they had a common bond with their work. She admired his commitment to the job and the focus and dedication that he brought to everything he did.

Her life might be wildly challenging right now, but she wouldn't regret the fact that its temporary strangeness had given her an opportunity to know Troy better.

The cop she'd admired from afar, in their limited inter-actions during court cases, had become a real person.

Tangible.

Human.

And incredibly interesting.

"What are you having?" Troy asked.

"The steak looks wonderful but Melissa already gave me the heads-up that the shrimp scampi was amazing."

"I'm trying to decide myself. And while I love shrimp, I'm not sure I can turn down a steak. Especially when the scents coming from the kitchen are so amazing."

"This really is a beautiful place." She looked around, the dark paneling throughout setting off a bar on the far side of the room that ran to white lighting and yards of glass shelving. Those glass bar shelves glistened like diamonds in the light and she considered what a pretty, intimate setting they'd managed to create here. Grand without being imposing. "I've been here for drinks after work on occasion, but that's been it."

An ADA's salary wasn't designed for steak dinners and lavish appetizers but being here now made her real-ize that it was okay to indulge every now and again. She worked hard and while she had never regretted going into the district attorney's office, perhaps she'd been a bit too focused on her job and on saving for her home.

"Those look like more serious thoughts than choos-ing between the filet or the shrimp."

With one last glance at those glistening glass shelves, she turned back to Troy. "I was just thinking about my life. Before going on leave."

"Oh?"

"I've been so focused on being frugal that I think I might have missed a few opportunities to live a bit."

A trait from her father? He'd spent years launching into a tirade at her mother for the barest infractions, from a splurge on cookies at the market to a new pair of shoes. Had she minimized her needs to avoid a confrontation?

Or worse, looked at any sort of indulgence as so frivolous that it was to be avoided?

"There's nothing wrong with saving what you earn."

"No." She twisted her hands in her napkin, searching for the right words. "There isn't. And I'm proud of the home I worked for as part of that savings."

"So why the sudden sadness?"

"More of my father, I suppose. The strange way he used whatever was at his disposal to control my mother. It was like he always needed to keep her on her back foot. I wonder how much of that I picked up, even subconsciously?"

As the conversation with her mother earlier replayed back through her mind, Evangeline couldn't help but smile. "But on a happier note, I spoke with my mother today and she's seeing someone. A man named Bill who makes her happy and who is from Kalamazoo."

Evangeline shook her head, surprised at how easy that admission came. And how truly excited she was for her mother as she embarked on this new relationship.

"You don't have to brush it off, Evangeline. Those were difficult years. Just because you got out of them and moved beyond them doesn't mean they didn't do damage."

Before she could answer, their waiter came over, balancing a bottle of wine on a tray. "Compliments of Mr. Ruiz."

Although she didn't know the full ins and outs of wine, Evangeline had enough of a working knowledge to know the bottle Antonio had sent them was special. "How lovely."

"May I pour?" Their waiter set two glasses down on the table and made a big show of the wine.

Evangeline gave the man his moment, grateful that the dramatic flourishes gave her a chance to regather her thoughts. Why had she gone there about her parents? As the complimentary wine suggested, it was meant to be a lovely evening out, away from their cares and concerns. Yet here she was, the meal not even served, rambling on about her father and his emotional abuses.

Scintillating conversation, Whittaker.

They waited until their waiter had departed, their orders in hand, then Troy lifted his glass. "To a lovely evening with a beautiful companion."

She felt a flush spread over her skin at his words. "Thank you." She tapped her glass against his, the delicate crystal making that satisfying clink.

The evening flowed from there and Evangeline felt her cares float away on the engaging drift of conversation and food and wine. She'd dated off and on through the years, but in all that time, she couldn't remember a man she'd shared so much with, or whose company she'd enjoyed more.

It made that push-pull of emotion—was it a date? wasn't it a date?—that much more challenging. It was only as their waiter wheeled over the dessert tray that she finally found an answer to both questions.

Did it really matter all that much?

She was out for the evening. Whatever moniker she wanted to put on it, the fact remained she'd had a lovely time. A truly enjoyable evening.

As their waiter wheeled the cart away, with their orders of crème brûlée for her and chocolate mousse for him, Troy's gaze turned serious. "Can I ask you something?"

"Sure."

"Earlier. In the car. I upset you." He stared down at his hands before those hazel eyes met hers, the gaze bold. "Did I offend you in some way? Complimenting you at the door or making you feel as if Melissa forced you to come out this evening?"

Something cracked wide open inside at his honest question. At the fact that he was willing to ask it at all.

"It was the sweep."

He frowned at that, confused. "What sweep?"

"Of my house. Before we left. I thought we were about to go out and you marched in and looked for signs of intrusion."

"And that upset you?"

"No." The answer was out before she could stop it, an unfortunate habit of denying what really mattered to her. With her earlier thoughts about choosing what she wanted in life and making some decisions that could be entirely frivolous in nature, Evangeline forced herself to reconsider. "I mean, yes. Yes, it bothered me."

"Why?"

"I was ready to go out, and you treated the evening like a job."

"But I—" He stopped, genuine surprise still painting his face. "I'd chalk it up to an occupational hazard but that's not fair."

"It's fine now. I'm over it."

"I appreciate you saying that. But regardless of how you feel now, I'm sorry I made you feel that way before."

That was it. A simple *I'm sorry.* Not all the accusations she'd heard through the years, each one lobbed at her mother and, at times, herself, like grenades.

You're overreacting.

That's not what I meant.

You never listen to me.

But never, in any iteration, had there been an *I'm sorry.*

"Thank you." She couldn't quite hide the strangled whisper and reached for the cup of tea she'd requested with dessert. "That means a lot."

As their waiter set down their desserts, Evangeline realized his apology had meant more than a lot.

It had meant everything.

TROY WAS STILL reeling from Evangeline's revelation over dessert. He'd been mostly honest with her. It was customary for him to check locks and doors, especially in a location he knew had been breached.

But his walk down her hallway had been about so much more.

Desire.

Desperation.

And an overwhelming sense of despair that his feelings for her were rapidly spiraling out of control. Feelings he had no business having for a woman under his protection and part of an open investigation.

He was a professional, damn it. He knew how to keep his own emotions in check and do the job. And he was good at it. He'd learned the skill early, a coping mechanism to ensure no one would ever have reason to ask him off the force or find a way to push him out of the GGPD.

He was a cop.

It was all he'd ever wanted to be and all he'd ever seen himself becoming.

He'd spent his life accepting that his mother's killer would never be found. Oh, it had never stopped him from following up on leads or reviewing her cold case file with what he hoped were fresh eyes. But it was because of the fact that her case was cold that he'd never wanted to give anyone a reason to think he took the job so personally that he couldn't be objective.

So why now?

And why her?

Evangeline Whittaker needed his help and all he could do was think about getting his hands on her.

So yeah. It was an "occupational hazard" as he'd claimed, marching through her apartment like a man on a mission. But it was more a disguise—a moment to find some much-needed composure—in order to control his raging need for her.

It was why he had put up an argument when Melissa had told him he was having dinner this evening. The protest was token at best, but he had to try.

Only, when faced with his cousin's insistence—and the opportunity to spend an evening with Evangeline— he'd caved pretty quickly.

Some cop you are, Colton.

But wasn't that the problem? He was good at his job. He didn't doubt that. He worked hard and knew the importance of what he did. The emptiness his family still lived with over his mother's murder was something he fought hard every day to ensure other families didn't have to. He couldn't always provide positive news, but he could provide closure.

And for someone in the process of trying to heal, that mattered.

For all those reasons, he knew his badge deserved better. Evangeline deserved better. He couldn't stay focused on her case if he was too focused on her. Hadn't that been proven more than once this week?

Even as he told himself to remain strictly professional, he was also abundantly aware that the genie was out of the bottle.

They had kissed. And spent time together. And even had this evening together.

And she mattered.

In the end, wasn't that really at the heart of it all?

"I hate to leave that wine behind." Evangeline glanced at the almost half-full bottle still perched at the edge of the table. "But two glasses are my limit."

"And one for me since I'm driving." He eyed the bottle, as well, before smiling. "Though to be honest, I'm not sure Antonio will mind. I've seen the wine cellar in this place and our leftover half a bottle isn't making a dent."

"I suppose that's true."

They stood, gathering up their things. In his own inimitable fashion, Antonio had already dispensed with the bill, ensuring Melissa's desire for an evening out was honored. Nor did Troy miss the satisfied smile from across the room where Antonio caught his eye, but he did nothing more than wave goodbye as an acknowledgment. Troy appreciated the dinner, but if Melissa had any inkling how close she'd come to playing matchmaker this evening, he'd never hear the end of it. A sure step in avoiding that was ensuring he didn't tip off her fiancé.

They walked back out and Troy kept his gaze trained on their surroundings. Although he didn't want to let his guard down, he knew the sort of security Antonio ran at the hotel and could at least breathe easy as their car was pulled around to the valet stand with prompt efficiency.

Troy opened the door for Evangeline, helping her slip into the car. His gaze caught hers as he took her hand and something deep and sharp and painful sliced through his midsection.

Did he honestly think he could stay immune to this woman?

She settled into the seat, their gazes lingering, and Troy had to pull away and force himself to walk back around to his side of the car.

Drive her home, Colton. Then get back into the car and drive your lovesick ass home. Look at crime scene photos if you have to, but get her out of your mind and certainly out of your blood.

All very solid direction, Troy thought, as he opened his own door and swung in.

Ridiculously solid, he lamented, as he put the car into Drive and headed for the exit of the hotel.

He'd barely turned out of the parking lot when he heard the sharp intake of breath followed by a piercing scream.

Slamming on the brakes, he turned to stare at Evangeline. Light from the overhead streetlamps at the edge of the hotel property flooded the car and in the glow he could see she'd gone a ghostly shade of white.

Terror glossed her eyes, rapidly transmitting toward him as his gaze tore over her face and upper body.

Was she hurt?

In pain?

"Evangeline!" Her name tore from his lips as he tried to get through the agonizing shrieks.

It was only when that terrified scream fell into a throaty whimper that he saw her gaze actually had a destination.

As his own gaze shifted course, he saw it. The balled-up white shirt on the floor of the passenger seat, streaks of blood soaked into the material.

Chapter Fifteen

"What in the ever-loving hell is going on here?" Antonio Ruiz paced his office from one end to the other. "My valets are trained and they know the penalty for allowing anyone access to a car in our garage."

"We're getting to the bottom of it." Melissa tried to reassure her fiancé but it was obvious she wasn't getting through. The pacing had ratcheted up to stalking a hole into the carpet as he moved back and forth in front of his desk. It had taken Melissa's quiet yet firm order to keep him near his desk and stop him from rushing down to the crime scene in the garage.

Troy could hardly blame Antonio, since he wanted to be down there, as well. But knowing Brett and Ember were there gave him some peace of mind as he kept close to Evangeline and they all waited for news in the office.

She still looked deathly pale, a state that hadn't changed, even with both hands wrapped around a warm mug of tea one of Antonio's assistants had brought in for her.

Her grisly discovery in the car had momentarily stunned him but he'd finally gotten his wits when another patron departing the hotel behind him laid on their horn. Whipping back around into the parking lot, he'd already speed-dialed Melissa to tell her what happened. He'd pulled up in front of the hotel and barked out orders to the valet station to find him a spot to set up in the garage.

The team had complied, the fact they already knew him going a long way toward their cooperation, even before he had his badge out.

Melissa had arrived shortly after, Brett and Ember on her heels.

"What happened?" Brett's question was out before he'd even cleared his car.

"The shirt," Troy had told him. "We got back into the car after dinner and Evangeline found it at her feet on the floor on the passenger side."

"Son of a bitch."

"I know. This is too close." Troy stared at the shirt, still visible on the floor of his car. *Too damn close.*

"Which is concerning all on its own. But worse knowing that shirt's been in play for a few days now." Brett shook his head. "So where's the body?"

The crime scene techs had arrived and were getting set up. Troy was grateful to see Jillian in the mix. She'd do right by the evidence, which meant she'd do right by Evangeline.

Brett had gone to work then, too. He set Ember up with the scent from the shirt and then began the repeated motions, working their way from the car outward, looking for a scent.

Troy had wanted to stay but Melissa's orders, barked at Antonio through her phone to stay put in his office with Evangeline, had sent him running back into the hotel.

Yet even as he ran toward her, determined to shield

her as best as he could, Brett's last question rang over and over in his mind.

Where was the body?

When it was just an investigation into a disappearing crime, Troy had been able to keep that thought at bay. They'd reviewed open files for any missing women in the area, but when no one turned up that fit Evangeline's description, they'd moved on.

But now? With the evidence some crime *had* been committed? It was challenging not to follow it all the way through to its natural conclusion.

There was a dead woman undiscovered and unaccounted for somewhere in Grave Gulch.

Pushing that grisly image aside until they had the details from the CSI team and whatever Ember could suss out in the garage, Troy turned his attention back to Evangeline. Her gaze followed Antonio as he criss-crossed his office, but other than her polite thank-you to the man's assistant for the tea, she'd said nothing else.

Which made her next words that much more of a surprise. Her voice was steady and strong as she leveled a question at Antonio.

"Who has access to your garage?"

Antonio stopped and turned at the question. "The valet staff. Hotel staff. Laundry deliveries, too. Big deliveries go through the loading dock but laundry is in the garage as the entrance goes straight to housekeeping."

"Is a badge required?"

"Yes."

"Cameras?"

"Of course."

Antonio nodded before Melissa jumped in. "Ellie's on it and already working with the IT office. If there's something to find she'll find it quickly. There was a limited window of time when someone could get to Troy's car."

Just like the comfort he took knowing Brett and Ember had the garage and Jillian had the forensics on the shirt, he was pleased Ellie was running point on the tech.

And he still hated sitting in the office, away from it all. He knew Melissa felt the same and figured she'd finally give in and let Antonio come with her for no other reason than she wanted to be down in the garage. He'd nearly said as much when Jillian came racing into the office.

"Mel!" Jillian came to a halt when she saw the assembled group. "Even better. You're all here."

"You found something?" Melissa asked.

"The blood. On the shirt."

Troy felt Evangeline stiffen beside him. Before he could ask for more details, Jillian was already excitedly revealing her discovery. "It's not human."

"What?"

The question went up as a collective, all of them talking at once.

"It's a fake." Jillian waved the phone in her hand, tapping the face to pull up a photo. "Look at it."

She set the phone down on Antonio's desk and they all gathered around.

"It's not a person's blood?" Evangeline said, her excitement palpable as she stared at the phone.

Troy heard the distinct notes of hope in her voice and hoped like hell Jillian was right. He didn't doubt his cousin, but after all Evangeline had been through, they couldn't afford to make any missteps here.

"I secured the evidence from the car and was going to take it directly to the lab. I still will, but there was something about the spatter pattern that bothered me."

Troy gave his cousin her due, listening patiently to her overview of blood spatter and the seemingly random nature of what was on the shirt. "But the kicker was when I realized what was missing."

Evangeline's harsh intake of breath had Jillian smiling and nodding, all at once.

"No bullet holes." Evangeline's breath flew out on a hard whoosh. She eyed the phone again before turning her attention fully back to Jillian. "You can see it even in the photo."

"So whose blood is it?" Melissa demanded, snatching the phone off the desk to expand the image of the shirt.

"It's synthetic. Someone wanted this to look pretty damn scary, but the blood isn't human. I'll run full tests on it and log it in evidence, but I'm pretty sure that is not human blood. And based on the integrity of the fabric, no one was shot wearing it, either. The blood spattered like it came out of an exploding capsule. The sort they use in TV shows to fake an accident."

"I don't understand." Evangeline ran her hand through her hair, her gaze steady on Jillian. "I mean, I'm happy no one was shot. Relieved, really. But what is this all about?"

"It's a joke." Melissa's gaze was dark as she set the phone back on the desk. "A nasty one. On you and on all the good cops trying to get to the bottom of this."

Throughout his life, he'd had plenty of experience with seeing Melissa mad. From family squabbles to workplace blowups, her threshold for anger was something Troy wasn't ignorant of. She was levelheaded and calm and didn't cross that line often, but she was human, too. Add on the high-stress job and she'd been known to lash out a time or two.

But never, in all his life, had he seen the sheer fury

that now painted her face. Her crystal-blue eyes had gone dark with it, her slim frame fixed in hard, tense lines. She gripped one of the guest chairs in front of Antonio's desk, her knuckles going white.

It was only after she'd stared at each one of them, Evangeline the longest, that Troy saw that fury channel itself into action. "We're going to find whoever did this and take him down. And if I find out this has anything to do with Len Davison or Randall Bowe, there is no rock either one of them can hide under that I won't pull them out from."

Troy moved close, laying a hand over hers and squeezing tight. "That makes two of us."

EVANGELINE YAWNED AS Troy turned into the parking lot of her condo. She'd believed getting back into his car would be difficult but she'd been so exhausted by the time they finally reached the parking garage that her fear never took root.

It doesn't hurt, knowing the blood wasn't human.

Which was entirely true, even if she couldn't deny the sheer menace of the situation. Yes, it was creepy to know someone had done such a malicious prank. But it was still a wild relief to know a human being hadn't been harmed in the process.

The various GGPD teams had finally wrapped up in the parking garage about two hours after Jillian's revelation in Antonio's office. And while it had buoyed Evangeline's spirits to know a person was unharmed, those same spirits had taken a second hit when Ellie had come in about an hour later and confirmed she hadn't been successful in finding anything on video.

Antonio's outburst had sent him marching off toward

the hotel's IT office, leaving her and Troy behind. She'd encouraged him to go down with the rest of the GGPD but he'd insisted on staying with her.

A kindness she appreciated, even as she warned herself not to get too comfortable with the attention.

While it wasn't definitive proof, whatever she witnessed in the alley seemingly wasn't a murder. A crime of some sort, yes, but not something that had resulted in murder. Melissa had vowed the GGPD would get to the bottom of things, but Evangeline knew the decreased likelihood of a murder meant the already-stretched staff would double down on its efforts to find Len Davison and Randall Bowe.

A move Evangeline not only agreed with but insisted upon. Police resources had to be prioritized where they were most needed and a serial killer at large needed to be everyone's focus.

Even though it meant she'd see far less of Troy.

"I'd like to stay one more night." Troy turned off the car and turned to her. The parking lot lamp was still out but the light she'd left on over her front door gave some illumination to the car.

"You don't have to. I know a lot happened tonight. And I know the shirt thing is creepy and we have to get to the bottom of it all, but I can't tell you how relieved I am that no one was murdered."

"We don't know that."

"No, we don't. But we're a lot closer to thinking someone's playing a nasty, disgusting prank than anything else."

He still didn't look convinced and Evangeline reached out to lay a hand on his forearm. "You've been so good to me this week. But the GGPD needs you. Totally focused on finding and securing Len Davison." She paused, well aware she'd had a part in that. "I know that better than anyone."

"You don't still blame yourself for that?"

"I do."

"Randall Bowe is responsible for it."

They could go round and round but it wouldn't change anything.

Troy's support of her was sweet and oh-so-caring, but she owned her role in all that had happened. In all the challenges the town of Grave Gulch currently faced. And in the questions the community now rightly asked of its public servants.

He looked ready to argue with her but only nodded. "Let me at least come in and check everything out."

What had seemed insensitive and rote earlier left a new sensation in her chest now. It felt good to be cared for.

Wonderful, actually.

With no small measure of shock—and an amazing shot of clarity—Evangeline realized that she hadn't had that in a long time.

Maybe ever?

Her mother was warm and caring, but so much of Evangeline's childhood was overshadowed by the behavior of her father that those quiet moments with her mother weren't as fixed in her memory.

She'd dated off and on since college, a few of the relationships moving to something steadier and more serious, but she'd always held those men at arm's length. Almost as if the distance could protect her should they turn, their personalities morphing with the same sort of anger and rage as her father had.

It was only now, faced with the innate kindness, warmth and true decency that was Troy Colton that Evangeline recognized all she'd missed.

Or never had to begin with.

And with that realization came one she hadn't expected. Yet now that she recognized it, she couldn't deny it.

She wanted him.

It would be so easy to chalk it up to the stress of the past few days, piled onto the distress of the past few months. A need that could assuage the strain and anxiety and provide a pleasurable reprieve from all she was living with.

But even as she rolled that thought through her mind, Evangeline knew it was an excuse.

The current situation had given her proximity to Troy in a way she'd never had before. And with it, she'd had the opportunity to see all the qualities she'd believed he possessed but hadn't known for sure.

The first time they'd crossed paths in the Grave Gulch County courthouse, she'd seen an attractive man with a strong jaw and sexy smile. As she'd deposed him for cases, she'd seen a man who cared about justice and wanted the best for each and every one of their citizens.

It was only now that she could acknowledge how surface attraction had turned to deep-seated interest. How the knowledge of his professional commitment could make him even more appealing on a deeply personal level. And how attraction, always left on simmer up to now, could leap up and grab you by the throat with sharp, needy claws.

"I'd appreciate that." She took a deep breath and wondered if she could press for more. "Thank you for making sure I'm safe."

He carried the protection even further, asking her to remain in the car until he could come around and get the door for her. It was sweet and chivalrous and the insistent need that had begun thrumming in her bloodstream at the thought of intimacy with Troy began to beat.

His grip was firm as he held her hand, helping her out of the elevated seat of the SUV. She felt her heels hit the concrete and, even with her balance steady, she held tight to Troy at the sudden trembling in her knees.

Did she dare pursue this?

And could she live with herself if she didn't try?

In the span of a few short minutes, they were inside her condo, no external threat detected during the short walk from the car or the time it took to unlock her front door.

Unwilling to stand there twiddling her thumbs, she went to the kitchen while Troy did his check of the house. Surprised to see her hand trembling, she dug out a bottle of water from the fridge. She'd just unscrewed the cap and lifted the bottle to her lips when Troy walked back into the kitchen.

"The house is fine."

She fumbled the water at his unexpected arrival, spilling it over the front of her dress. The thin material was already quite sheer and the water only added to that, the wetness spreading over the top of her chest.

"I'm sorry." Troy's gaze drifted over her breasts before he turned away to grab a towel from where it lay draped over the edge of the sink. "I didn't mean to startle you."

"You didn't."

His eyes remained level with hers as he handed over

the towel, his smile sweet and boyish. "You always spill water all over yourself?"

He'd given her the perfect opening and Evangeline recognized this was her shot.

Now or never, Whittaker.

"I'm clumsy when I'm nervous."

His demeanor changed immediately, any lingering humor from her spill vanishing. "You're worried about staying in the house? I checked everything and the doors and windows are secure."

She dabbed at the water stain with the towel, her tone easy. "I know."

"Then what are you nervous about?"

Evangeline set the towel on the counter and turned her full attention to Troy. "That you'll say no when I ask you to stay."

His eyes, that warm, rich hazel, turned a deep gold with desire. He understood what she was asking, but she wanted to make absolutely certain.

More, she needed to. Needed to know he wanted, just as she did.

"With me, Troy. I'd like you to stay with me."

TROY HEARD HER. He even understood her.

But he couldn't believe it was happening.

The woman he wanted more than anything—more than he could ever remember wanting a woman before—wanted him to stay. And there was no way he could act on it.

His job was to protect her. Hell, he'd just done a sweep of her home, ensuring she wasn't in danger or under possible threat of attack from the nameless, faceless stalker who had set their sights on her. There was no way he could cross the line and sleep with her.

"Evangeline. You know I can't do that." He saw the pulse beating wildly at her throat, even as her gaze stayed level on his. "Even if you are the only thing I can think about right now." He hesitated, before adding, "And the only one I want."

"Why can't we have this? In the midst of all that we've both dealt with, why can't we have this?" She moved a step closer. "Why can't we take it?"

"I have to protect you."

"That's an excuse, Troy, not a reason."

"It's a damn good reason. You said yourself, the GG-PD's efforts need to be focused right now. On capturing Davison. On securing Bowe and making him account for his lies. And they need to be focused on what's been happening to you. That shirt tonight isn't the end of things."

He hated to scare her, but if that was what it took to make her see reason, he wouldn't sugarcoat the situation, either.

Oh, who was he kidding? If it was what it took to convince *himself* to keep his head and not give in to passion, then the words were even more important.

"That shirt is an escalation. Sneaking around to place it in my car, knowing you'd be the one to see it? Even more so."

"You think I don't know that? Just because I'm glad there's now a high likelihood a woman isn't dead from a gunshot at close range doesn't mean I'm ignorant of what's going on."

He let out a hard sigh, the frustration of so many unanswered questions more than evident in that hard exhale. "You tell me then, Evangeline. What's going on?"

"Someone has it out for me. Maybe it's someone I prosecuted or someone who's got a problem with the Davison case. Who knows?"

Who did know?

She was the one who hadn't gotten a conviction for Davison, for Pete's sake. And she could be as upset about that as she wanted, but Troy had to believe it hardly made her the first person Davison would change pattern for and come harm.

And Bowe?

In a lot of ways, her use of his data to get Davison off on all charges had reinforced the man's motive. So once again, seeing her as his enemy and stalking her just didn't fit.

Which put him back to more questions with no answers. And a series of incidents that felt off-kilter and *way* off pattern.

"I care about the answer, Troy." She pressed on, her conviction clear, even as she remained close enough to touch. "I care about finding out who's been after me and why these things are happening. But right now? I care about you more. About exploring this need between us. And about letting the rest of the world fall away for a while."

It would be so easy. To simply take what he craved so desperately. To be with her and find a way to get past all the endless questions that roiled in his mind, seemingly without answers.

Because while the mystery of what surrounded her had no answer, in so many ways, it didn't matter.

She was the answer.

To him. For him. And with this wild attraction he'd never expected or anticipated.

From the first night here in her kitchen, he'd had this unrelenting need for her. It kept whispering through him, suggesting she was meant to be in his life.

And meant for him.

Troy knew he stood on a precipice. But as he stood there and saw the need in her eyes—need that matched his own—he recognized something else.

There was nothing on earth he wouldn't do to protect this woman. Nothing he wouldn't do to keep her safe.

Making love wouldn't change that. More to the point, it *couldn't* change that. His commitment to her as a cop was unwavering.

Just like his need.

"I'm still not sure this is a good idea."

He saw victory flash in her eyes, matched by the smile that filled with the knowledge of all that was to come. "I know."

And then there was no more talking. What was the point?

There was only feeling.

Need had already wrapped around them both, but as he pulled her close, his lips sinking into hers, he found that it had shifted somehow. The greedy claws and snapping jaws that had driven him faded, replaced with the gentle need to explore. To touch. To fill them both with pleasure.

It was no less urgent, but it was different. As if the mere act of finally deciding to be with Evangeline had calmed the beast.

Moment flowed into moment as they drifted, never losing touch of one another, even as their clothing was lost somewhere between the kitchen and the bedroom.

A shoe here. His shirt there. Her dress somewhere in the hallway.

And when he finally laid her down on the bed, covering her naked body with his own, he knew joy. The feel of her, so soft to his every touch, was like some sort of happy magic. Troy cupped the rounded curve of her breast, his thumb brushing her nipple, and lost himself in her. Especially when the act pulled sounds of pleasure from her throat and he felt an answering need curling low in the belly.

Want and need were no longer enough. No longer sufficient to describe what she did to him and what he wanted from her.

He wanted all of her.

Every bit she could give him and then he wanted more.

Her hands flowed over his skin, a matching exploration of her own. Over his shoulders, down his triceps, before curling around to his chest. Her touch moved over him, over the hard lines of his stomach, before drifting lower, then lower still to wrap those long, glorious fingers around the pulsing length of him. As she took him in her palm, Troy knew he was lost.

Utterly, completely lost.

"Troy. Now." The words whispered against him, powerful in their simplicity and featherlight against his ear. He reached for the condom he'd set beside the bed and, quickly sheathing himself, moved back into her arms.

They found a rhythm, increasingly urgent as the pleasure built and built between them. He felt her tighten around him, her deep cry of pleasure a match for his own as her release crested.

And as he sank into her, burying himself in the glory

that was Evangeline, Troy knew with absolute certainty why he'd resisted for so long.

He'd believed it was because she deserved better than a guy making the moves on her while she needed help. Then he'd convinced himself that he needed to keep work and personal separate, that his job required his full and complete focus. He'd even told himself that his inability to find a partner in life was a result of the fear for a loved one that had been instilled in him at the earliest age.

All were true.

It was only now—now that he'd made love to her— that he knew what his conscience had only whispered. Because all those things were only excuses. They'd covered up the truth.

He'd been in love with Evangeline Whittaker far longer than he'd realized.

And for all those reasons, there was no way he could have her.

Chapter Sixteen

In the morning, he was gone.

Evangeline knew he would be. She'd mentally prepared for it, even as she'd gone willingly into his arms. But even with that knowledge, she'd given all she felt—all she *knew* down to the depths of her soul—to Troy.

She'd wanted him. And the feeling had been gloriously mutual. They'd spent the night wrapped up in each other. For all the time they'd spent talking since he'd come to her aid on a street downtown, their night together had held little conversation. It was almost as if the words had taken a back seat to action.

She didn't regret it. She'd never regret it. But she'd dearly hoped she'd be wrong about the morning after.

Sitting up, she pulled on a robe and made quick work of her morning routine. In moments her face was freshly scrubbed and her hair was pulled up into a loose bun on top of her head. She ambled down to the kitchen for coffee, touched to see he'd started a pot for her. He'd even had a cup, his mug now rinsed and sitting in the drainboard next to her sink.

All without waking her.

Her gaze caught on the note on the table and she picked it up. It might be cliché, the "morning after" note, but knowing him now as she did, she also recognized it as purely Troy.

Evangeline—
   It's an early day and I need to meet Brett to go over the latest on Bowe. We've been trying to run down Bowe's brother and Brett has a contact who might be able to help.
Troy

As goodbye notes went, it was nicer than most, she imagined. She wouldn't know, exactly, as she'd never received one. But it was clear that he had a job to do and she'd do well to remember that.

A killer was still on the loose, as was the department criminal who'd enabled him. Her night with Troy was a gift for them both. One that had allowed them to escape that for a while. But now, in the fresh light of a summer morning, they had to return to reality.

And she needed to return to some sense of normalcy.

A shower and then a call to Arielle was first on her list. She wanted to set a timeline to return to her job. Because despite the unrest in Grave Gulch and in her own personal life, she needed to be doing something. And sitting home day in and day out wasn't the answer.

An hour later, she returned to the kitchen, hair and makeup done and clad in her favorite work-casual blouse and pressed slacks. She wanted every ounce of confidence she could muster for her call with Arielle and wasn't immune to the benefits of a good session with the eyelash curler.

Evangeline had her phone in hand and was about to ring her boss when the glass face lit up with a call. The number came up, one she didn't recognize. She would have let it go to voicemail, but considering how many people were working on her behalf at the GGPD, she decided to answer. If it was a robocall, she could always hang up.

"Hello?"

"Evangeline." Her name came out in a frightened whisper.

"Who is this?"

"Shh. Shh. He'll hear me."

Hear her? Who?

The voice trembled before the woman continued on. "It's Ella, Evangeline. I live upstairs from you."

Instantly, an image filled Evangeline's mind's eye. The young woman who lived upstairs was small and waiflike and, if she remembered correctly, worked at one of the restaurants downtown.

"Ella. What's wrong?"

"It's him. He's out of control. I'm hiding in the bathroom."

"Who?"

"He's mad. He's in a rage because I broke up with him."

They didn't keep the same hours, and other than their casual conversation earlier in the week, Evangeline hadn't seen much of Ella, but she did remember the day she moved in. She had a large, muscled boyfriend who looked about the same age. Although he hadn't been super-friendly, he hadn't struck Evangeline as a problem, either.

You can't always tell on the surface.

That idea whispered through her mind as an image

of her father's face, red and mottled as he screamed, rounded out the thought.

"I'll come up. I can help you."

"No!" The urgency was there, but Ella managed to keep her voice low. "He hit me and split my lip. He'll hurt you, too."

"No, he won't." While she had no way of knowing if that was true, Evangeline hoped she could help defuse the situation and get Ella out of there. "I'm going to call the police."

"No! You can't. He'll kill me if the cops show up."

"All the more reason for me to do it," Evangeline pressed urgently.

"Oh no! He's coming. He's trying to break through the door. He's going to strangle me if he finds me!"

"I'll be right there."

Evangeline disconnected, immediately dialing Troy. She was already rushing out of her door, the baseball bat she kept in her hall closet in hand, swinging around to the landing that held the stairwell to the second floor.

"Evangeline." He answered on the first ring.

Although it seemed incongruous after what they'd shared, she didn't have time for anything sweet or pleasant. "My neighbor. Upstairs. She's in danger. Her boyfriend is trying to strangle her."

"Stay downstairs. I'm on my way."

"I can't do that. He could hurt her."

"Stay downstairs!"

She wasn't going to argue, and while she recognized the reason for the direction, she was sick and tired of waiting while things went on around her. Whatever happened in the end of that alley had vanished because she didn't go down there and engage.

She wasn't letting her neighbor suffer the same fate.

Fully aware of how rude it was, she kept climbing the stairs anyway.

And hit the disconnect button.

Someone needed help. And she wasn't sitting around waiting for someone else to handle it.

TROY SLAMMED HIS phone on the desk and let out a string of curses as he dragged on his sports coat.

"What is it?"

"Evangeline's neighbor is in the middle of a domestic dispute."

Brett was already up and following him out the door, Ember in their wake.

"I told her to stay put."

"And she's rushing in to help."

The two of them ran for their vehicle outside, Brett hollering instructions to dispatch as they moved through the precinct.

Troy flew through the streets of Grave Gulch, his lights flashing. Brett got on with dispatch the moment they were in the car, Mary's voice echoing through the car speaker.

"I've got two officers nearby en route."

Troy barked out the layout for the condo complex, the access points to the second floor and the likely condo number for Evangeline's upstairs neighbor.

The other officers were already there, their car parked and flashing in front of Evangeline's building as he pulled into the parking lot. Troy swung into the closest spot he could find and leaped out of the car as soon as he cut the ignition.

Panic swam in his veins. For her, for the situation. And

for the rising sense of unease that Evangeline would be in the middle of some new mess.

He took the metal stairs to the second floor two at a time, and heard the calm, steady voices as soon as he cleared the landing.

"Ma'am. Nothing is wrong here."

"But he's inside. She's frightened and afraid."

"I'm not afraid. Of anything."

Troy puzzled through the different voices, from Evangeline's rising one to the steady voices of everyone else. It was the same voice someone used when trying to calm an animal or a small child.

And as he came down the landing he could see by the look in Evangeline's dark eyes that it wasn't working.

Her gaze kept darting between the half-open door, filled with a sleepy-looking woman in a T-shirt and short-shorts and two uniformed officers outside the door.

Her hand was white-knuckled around a bat, but the piece remained firmly at her side. "But Ella, you just called me. You said he was coming after you to strangle you. You said you were locked in the bathroom with a split lip."

"There's no one here. I already told you that, like, five times." The young woman still lounged against the doorframe and Troy took in the odd look on her face.

Whatever was going on—and it increasingly looked like Evangeline was wrong again—still didn't match that reaction. Even if Evangeline had imagined whatever had gone on, the woman's casual pose struck him as off.

It also hit him that he'd met her before. Staring up at the building, trying to figure out the situation with the firecracker fuse.

Ella, he remembered on a rush.

"Officers." Troy moved up to the door, his badge out. He eyed Evangeline, willing her to understand his silent instruction, before turning to the woman in the doorway. "Ma'am. I'm Detective Colton. What's going on here?"

"My neighbor is all freaked out for no reason." The young woman stood taller at his approach, her gaze darting toward Evangeline. "She's been pounding on my door and screaming about letting her in. She woke me up."

"But you called me," Evangeline said from behind and Troy turned once more, his gaze dark.

"I didn't call you," Ella said, her voice rising. "How many times do I have to tell you that?"

Brett and Ember joined them on the second-floor landing and the woman's eyes went wide at the appearance of yet another cop and a dog. "Whoa. Look. I'm not sure what you're all doing here but I didn't make any calls. I was sound asleep up until a few minutes ago and her knocking."

Evangeline must have gotten the message because she said nothing else and Troy ratcheted up the charm. "I'm sorry that you were disturbed, Ms.—" He left it hang there and she picked it up.

"Fields. Ella Fields."

"Ms. Fields. I'm sorry for the inconvenience." He lowered his voice, well aware her casual pose and insistence that nothing was wrong could easily be a ploy to protect the boyfriend. "If there's anything you need, we're happy to help. And if it would set your mind at ease, we can do a sweep of your home."

The woman swung the door wide and extended her hand toward the interior. The layout was similar to Evangeline's and while he couldn't see the full condo from the doorway, it didn't appear as if anyone had gone on a rampage through the apartment. "I have nothing to hide. No one's here."

"We have permission to enter your apartment, ma'am?" Brett stepped up.

"Sure." Ella shrugged. "But just you guys. I don't know what her problem is but I don't want her in here."

Brett moved forward and Troy gestured the officers to follow.

"I'll just take Ms. Whittaker back to her home. Thank you for your time, Ms. Fields."

"Troy!" Evangeline started in the moment he moved up beside her.

"Shh." He let the word out in one quick order and took her hand, giving it a gentle squeeze. "Not now."

He didn't miss the puzzled look on her face but she said nothing further. He retraced his steps back down to the first floor and escorted her to her home. The moment they were through the door, he closed it behind them. "Stay here."

Gun drawn, her swept her apartment, the sudden realization he'd had upstairs looming large in his mind. What if the girl upstairs was a diversion? A way of getting Evangeline out of her apartment so an intruder could get in?

The sweep turned up nothing and Brett's text a few minutes later that Ember hadn't found anyone else reinforced the idea taking root.

As he walked back into the living room, he purposely kept his mind blank, desperate to avoid the images that wanted to take hold. He would not think about the way he'd retrieved his clothing off the hallway floor this morning. Nor would he remember the way they'd used every inch of her big bed, making love several times throughout the night.

"You hung up on me."

"I had to help her."

He wanted to be stern. More than that, he needed to be. She put herself in danger, responding to a call that required the police. But the raw fear that had iced him cold on the drive over needed an outlet, too. Without considering all the declarations he'd made to himself—those uncompromising ones about leaving her alone—that very morning as he rinsed his coffee mug, he pulled her close, his mouth crushing hers.

Evangeline responded immediately, her arms wrapping around him as she answered the deep pull within him.

He did need to walk away. But first, he needed to satisfy himself that she was all right. Needed to feel the life that beat within her and confirm that all his dark fears, the ones that had loomed so large on the drive to her home, hadn't come true.

So he pushed all he felt into the kiss. As if he could convince her how much he cared and brand her at the same time. Because after this, he had to walk away.

She was in his blood now and it was something he never expected. Or needed. Or wanted.

With one final press of his lips to hers, Troy pulled back.

He didn't miss the empty look in Evangeline's eyes. He figured it was a match for how she likely looked this morning when she'd woken and he was gone.

He wanted things to be different. But they couldn't be. And because of that simple fact, he leaned into the job and used it as a shield to protect his heart.

"Now. Let's walk through this one from the beginning and figure out what's going on."

THE MORNING INCIDENT at Evangeline's had put him behind but Troy wasn't quite ready to let it go. Her upstairs neighbor had protested, but Troy had seen Evangeline's call log. He'd taken down the number and the time of the call and hoped it would be enough for Ellie to work her tech magic. If not, Evangeline had agreed to come into the precinct to let Ellie look at her phone.

Which had circled Troy right back to where he'd begun his morning: Randall Bowe.

"Still no luck finding the brother?" Brett asked around a mouthful of sandwich. One of the two he'd picked up on his way back to the precinct from Evangeline's.

"No. I can't find any record of a Baldwin Bowe and I've done some serious searching." Troy took a bite of his meatball sub and considered all the effort he'd put into this case. As he chewed he remembered Brett's offer a few days before.

"How did I forget?" Even as he asked the question, Troy knew exactly how he'd forgotten. Evangeline. She'd been at the forefront of his thoughts, crowding out the work. His cases.

Everything.

Pushing it aside, he refocused on Brett. "You offered to ask your friend. The US marshal who has an inside line to the witness protection program?"

Brett shook his head and grinned. "You haven't gotten to your email yet. Oren got back to us and nothing popped on WitSec."

Troy wiped his hands and turned to his computer, scrolling until he saw the name Oren Margulies. "You spoke well of him." Troy scanned the man's email, the reason for Brett's solid endorsement evident in the crisp, clear words and the genuine offer of help. "I can see why. He's thorough. And doesn't have any detail on a Baldwin Bowe or any hints the man was even considered for protection."

"Another dead end." Brett balled up the wrapper from his sandwich. "There is another angle, though. Would you want to be close to Randall Bowe? The guy's a worm, from everyone's recounting. It's entirely possible Baldwin just doesn't want anything to do with his family."

"True."

Much as he hated thinking of any angle as a dead end, Troy knew Brett was right. The Coltons might be tightly woven and all up in one another's business, but that didn't mean every family was the same.

What also didn't translate was why Baldwin Bowe was so damn hard to find. Everyone had a digital footprint. It was so standard at this point that Bowe's lack of one was a red flag in and of itself. It had become so odd that it might be worth putting Ellie on it to see if she could come up with something.

Which made the woman's arrival at his office door less than thirty seconds later both odd and reassuring. "Troy. Brett. The people I want to see."

She barreled into the office, her trusty laptop in hand as she took the guest chair next to Brett. "Wait'll you see what I found." She angled her laptop so they could both see the screen and tabbed through a few of the apps she had open.

"The number you gave me this morning. It was shockingly easy to track." She eyed Troy directly. "Like, stupid easy."

"What do you mean?"

"The number that called Evangeline's mobile line? It's the number registered to her upstairs neighbor, Ella Fields. The woman didn't even call from a different phone or try to hide what she was doing."

"Someone could have spoofed the number," Brett interjected, but Troy could see his attention was caught on Ellie's screen.

"They could but based on the logs I pulled from the phone company—" Ellie toggled to a new screen "— there was a call made from that number through those stodgy old phone lines that crisscross Grave Gulch. The girl didn't even use an untraceable cell phone."

"And it was made to Evangeline's cell."

Ellie nodded. "At nine thirty-two this morning."

Which made sense, because Evangeline's call to him had come in four minutes later.

Ellie shook her head as she closed her laptop. "Someone's gaslighting her. That's all there is to it."

Which was the final tumbler in the lock, Troy realized.

He'd questioned the idea and, while not impossible, it had seemed like an awfully complicated way to hurt someone.

But in Ellie's words, Troy knew the truth.

The incredibly simple, *obvious*, truth.

Someone was purposely taunting Evangeline, attacking and undermining her credibility.

As the cloud of confusion lifted, a layer of guilt took its place.

He hadn't believed her. Not fully, anyway. A big part of him might have tried, but there had always been something holding him back, so he'd never fully given Evangeline his trust.

"You mean making her think there's danger when there really isn't?" Brett clarified.

"Yep. Like that old movie. The one with Ingrid Bergman. The creepy husband keeps trying to make her think she's seeing things." Ellie added, "They actually made us watch it in the academy along with one of our domestic abuse workshops."

"It all makes sense. Every bit of it." Troy tried to remain calm, but he couldn't deny the slamming of his heart against his ribs and the rising anger. All at himself.

He'd doubted her. Even when it was clear she was desperate to have someone believe her, he'd held back.

"First the incident in the alley. The weird stuff in her house and the sense of being watched. The bloody shirt. Now the neighbor."

"But who's doing it?" Brett pressed the question. "A woman, and one this soon after his last kill, is a serious break in pattern for Len Davison. And Randall Bowe has no reason to come after her."

Troy was already on his feet. Now that he knew what he was looking for, he had an entirely new approach to keeping Evangeline safe. And it started with the lying upstairs neighbor.

"I don't know. But we're going to find out."

EVANGELINE TRIED TO focus on the positive call she'd had with Arielle Parks and her boss's agreement that it was time for her to come back to the DA's office and not on the weird incident with the upstairs neighbor.

What was going on with Ella?

The call had been real but so had the sleepy eyes and disdain for being woken up. But it was also strange the woman had called her. It wasn't like they'd exchanged phone numbers, yet somehow Ella had hers? They'd met the day Ella moved into the condo complex and were cordial to one another when they passed in the parking lot and that was it.

Yet Evangeline was the first one she called?

The ping of a text pulled her away from the puzzle and she couldn't stop the smile as Troy's name lit up the face of her phone. It was a wholly unnecessary reaction, especially given her current situation and the reason he was texting her, but it made her smile all the same.

Got a lead on your neighbor. Can you meet me? The diner just past the edge of town?

She texted back that she could and quickly cleaned up her breakfast dishes. In a matter of minutes, she'd left the house, locking the door behind her. The sense of action felt good. Better than good, she admitted to herself as she navigated her way toward the diner Troy had noted.

She felt more like herself than she had in months. Like she had purpose again.

"That was fast," Troy said as she climbed out of the car. "Things are coming together. Including the fact that your silly young neighbor did call you this morning from her home, just above you."

"That was her number?" Evangeline stared at Troy across the expanse of the hood of her car. Of all the things she expected him to say, that wasn't it. A hello would have been nice, too, but she ignored that spurt of disappointment. "Why would she do that and then pretend she didn't?"

"That's what we're going to find out. Ellie did some

quick work on her social media pages and found she works here. She's going to meet us."

Evangeline glanced around the parking lot. "There—" She pointed to a small red compact car. "That's her car."

"I'd normally do this alone but I want her to look at you when I ask her questions."

It was a tactic Evangeline recognized and it made a lot of sense. As of yet, the woman had behaved suspiciously, but they needed to know more. Her presence might be the key they needed to get Ella talking.

"Thanks for bringing me into this. I'd really like to understand what's going on."

"What's going on is that we think you're being gaslighted."

"What?" Evangeline stilled as images of her father's tactics on her mother rushed through her mind. "Why do you think that?"

"Ellie had the idea and it's the only one that fits. You are a strong, competent woman. And all these things that keep happening to you and then vanishing? They're setups."

The wash of relief was palpable, even as the memories of her father's behavior left an oily residue in her midsection. "I'm not imagining things."

He came around the car then to stand in front of her. The hard lines of his face, set in place ever since that last, lingering kiss in her home, finally faded. In its place, his mouth creased into a small smile. "No, you're not. You never were. But someone wants you to think you are." She'd heard of that behavior. She'd even seen it a time or two over her career. Sadistic, psychotic behavior, perpetrated on innocent people to make them feel less-than.

And while she was happy to finally have answers, she was angry, too.

How dare they?

Whoever "they" was.

Just like that morning, when she woke with the express desire to call Arielle and get on with her life, that same feeling filled her now. On a nod, Evangeline pointed toward the glass front door, determination straightening her spine with steel. "Let's go get this done."

She walked beside Troy into the diner, her gaze sweeping the room for Ella. Although the diner was large, the post-lunch crowd had thinned out and it wasn't hard to find Ella as she moved around, cleaning off tables and pocketing tips.

"Miss Fields?" Troy approached her, casual and easy. Evangeline had spent enough time with him now to recognize the act and how the smile didn't quite meet those hard cop's eyes.

But anyone sitting around listening wouldn't have known that.

"May we have a few minutes of your time?"

"Um. Well. I'm not due for a break for another half hour."

Troy kept that smile firmly in place, even as his tone remained unbending. "I'm sure your manager won't mind but I can clear it if I need to."

"No, no. The lunch crowd has died down. I'm sure it'll be fine."

Evangeline didn't miss how the young woman's eyes kept darting her way but kept her own smile firmly in place.

Troy led them to a quiet corner of the diner, in a seat Ellie had already grabbed when she came in.

"Who's this?" Ella asked, that cornered look growing more pronounced in her eyes.

"This is Ellie Bloomberg. She's our queen of all technology at the GGPD and she found something interesting this morning with Ms. Whittaker's phone."

"I'm not sure what this has to do with—"

"It seems as if you made a call to Ms. Whittaker this morning," Troy cut her off, pressing his advantage. "A call Ms. Bloomberg was able to confirm quite easily."

Whatever reaction Evangeline was expecting—especially after the sleepy bravado routine this morning at Ella's condo—wasn't in evidence. Instead, her neighbor's shoulders fell as she blurted out, "Damn. I forgot to use that cell phone he gave me."

"Would you like to make a statement, Ms. Fields?"

The young woman's head snapped up. "Am I under arrest?"

"You made a fake phone call with the express intent of harassing someone."

Evangeline stepped in before Troy could add anything further. "I work for the district attorney's office, Ella. I'm quite sure we can talk to Detective Colton's chief as well as my boss and gain their leniency if you can help us with this."

Ella nodded, her eyes filling with tears. "It was a quick hundred bucks, ya know? And it didn't seem that bad at the time."

"What didn't seem so bad?" Troy's voice had gentled and in his compassion Evangeline saw more of what she loved so much about him.

He recognized that the people he was sworn to protect didn't always make the best decisions. But even when they erred, it didn't mean he lost his compassion for them.

"All I had to do was call and rile her up a bit. It was just pretend. Acting, the guy told me." Ella turned her tear-filled eyes to Evangeline. "I really didn't mean to hurt you or upset you. I can see now how I did."

"Do you have any other information?" Troy asked.

"Yes." The waitress nodded, swiping at her eyes. "I have a note in my bag. Let me just go get it."

Ella slid out of the booth to head toward the back of the restaurant. Evangeline figured there was no need to follow her since they knew where she lived. But it seemed odd, anticlimactic, even, to be sitting here waiting for a note.

"She got in over her head," Evangeline started in, curious if Troy would agree. "I meant what I said. I see no reason why we can't figure out a deal. I don't want to press charges."

"Don't be too hasty."

Troy barely had the words out when Ella came rushing back up to the table, a crumpled piece of paper in her hand. "Here. I knew I had the number. He said to call him if there were any problems."

Troy glanced at the small slip of paper before passing it to Ellie, who began tapping on her oversize cell phone. In moments, she had what she was looking for. "It's a local number." With a glance for the young woman who'd helped them, she tapped the piece of paper. "I need to take this with me."

"Go ahead." Ella lifted her hands up, palms out. "I don't want anything to do with it."

They wrapped up quickly, getting the details of how Ella was approached and a description of the guy who'd paid her. Other than making the young woman even more scared than she already was, there was little to be gained after getting the details.

The waitress was obviously remorseful and while Troy might not be quite ready to let her off the hook, Evangeline had worked long enough in the DA's office to recognize young and naive over criminal any day.

What still remained was what was going on with the person who put her neighbor up to this.

Ellie turned to them when they got into the parking lot. "I didn't want to give her any more details, but that number appears to be tied to some of the back-end operations of a local restaurant. I got the type of business off of their tax filings."

"What restaurant?" Troy demanded.

"I can't see it on my mobile device. I need to dig into the computer back at the office. Shouldn't take me long to get it for you."

Ellie was already climbing into her car to head back to the precinct.

"I'll let you go, then." Evangeline dug her keys out of her purse. "Thank you for including me in this. And for your kindness to Ella."

"She's not out of the woods yet."

"She should be. She did a stupid thing. She's young and she saw the money and thought it was a phone call."

"She committed a crime."

Evangeline let out a hard sigh. That stony, stoic look had returned to his face and suddenly, she wasn't able to face it any longer. They'd made love the night before and while she wasn't expecting declarations of everlasting devotion, his lack of acknowledgment stung. Terribly.

"Please let me know what you find out about the phone number."

He only nodded and it took everything inside of her to get in her car and keep the tears at bay.

The drive back to her condo passed in a blur of tears and sobs and the deep desire to climb into her bed and pull the covers over her head.

How had she been so stupid? Because as she drove the winding miles through Grave Gulch back home, she knew the truth. She'd fallen in love with Troy. Beyond her better sense or any modicum of reason, she had and there was nothing to be done for it.

Swiping at her eyes, she dashed away what was left of the tears. She was stronger than this. Hadn't the past week shown her that? Hell, the past few months. She'd get past this and move on and someday she'd find a way to stop thinking about Troy Colton with every fiber of her being.

But that day wasn't today, Evangeline admitted as she got out of the car and walked to her front door. She slipped the key in the lock and only barely registered the ease with which the door swung open, even before she turned the key.

If she weren't distracted, maybe, she'd have reacted differently when a big, beefy hand clamped around her wrist and dragged her inside the house.

But she couldn't even summon a scream as a second hand clamped over her mouth.

Chapter Seventeen

Troy could still picture Evangeline's face a half hour later as he tried to work his way through a response to Oren Margulies. The US marshal had been kind enough to offer to answer any additional questions Troy might have and Troy wanted to see if the guy had any insight or experience that might help them find Baldwin Bowe.

Even as he typed, then deleted, then typed some more, Troy couldn't find his focus.

All he could see was Evangeline's face when she turned away from him in the parking lot and got into her car.

He'd hurt her. That much was evident. More than evident, he admitted to himself, because he knew it was purposeful. And much as it pained him to do it, he needed to begin making the break with her.

The discovery of the gaslighting had broken the case open and now that they had a phone number they were running down, he and Brett would go deal with the restaurant owner and get the entire situation resolved. This nightmare she'd been living in would all be over.

Just like him and Evangeline.

It was the right thing to do. More than right, he considered as he typed another paragraph to Margulies. The Davison and Bowe cases needed his full attention.

His full focus.

So why did he feel so miserable?

"Ellie got us a name and an address." Brett's voice flowed into the office a few beats before he walked in. "Sal Petrillo. Guy owns That's Amore, an Italian restaurant downtown."

Troy knew the place. He'd been there on a few dates and had done takeout a time or two. "I know it. It's been there a few years. Guy opened it after moving down from Detroit, best I remember."

"Your intel matches Ellie's. She also said she's heard rumors the reason Petrillo moved down from Detroit was that he had some debts up there he never really paid off."

Troy hit Send on his email. "Oh, he does?"

"Since I've learned in the very short time I've been here that Ellie is always right, who am I to argue?"

"You learn fast, Shea."

"I like to think so."

Troy texted Evangeline to see if she knew anything about the restaurant or had any run-ins with its owner. As he hit Send, a small shot of remorse filled him at the simplicity of the text and the way he'd shot out an order to text back, but he had to ignore it. He needed an answer and he wasn't composing damn love notes.

In a matter of minutes they'd arrived at the restaurant and Troy looked around as he got out of the car, pushing the text to the back of his mind.

"It's not that far from Evangeline's alley."

"No, it's not." Brett pointed in the direction of the row of buildings that spread before them. "I'd say one major block over, give or take a few storefronts."

"Right you are."

Troy considered it as they walked up to That's Amore. A neon Open sign was lit over the door and they walked into the scents of tomato sauce and baking pizza. Although this place didn't back up to the alleyway where Evangeline saw the purported shooting, it would be easy enough to squeeze through a few buildings to come out to this one.

Again, he filed it away as a hostess greeted them. "Can I help you? The dining room's closed until dinner but we can still do take-out orders."

"I'm actually looking for someone." Troy shared the number that had been included on Ella's note. "I have a number and I understand it's associated with this restaurant."

For the first time the woman looked uneasy and Troy pulled out his badge, as did Brett. "We need to know if you recognize it."

It had been a deliberate gamble, but they'd not called the number in advance, instead hoping to catch the owner here. The hostess's response confirmed it was the right one.

"Yeah, that's Sal's number. He's the owner. He's in the back. I'll just go get him."

"Clumsy move to use his phone and to get dumb kids to make calls for him," Brett observed as he moved around the small waiting area. There were a few framed newspaper articles on the walls, the sort local restaurants put up to affirm they were part of the community. Troy scanned them for any insight into the mysterious Sal and it was only as his gaze alighted on the last one that he recognized the image.

From the sketch his sister had done.

He was about to call Brett over when the hostess walked back out from the kitchen.

"I'm sorry, Detectives, but Sal left, apparently. Right after the lunch rush wrapped. Or what passes for it these days."

"Do you know where he went?" Troy asked, that same uncomfortable feeling that had ridden him in his office flaring high like a bonfire.

The woman shook her head. "I don't know."

Troy grabbed his phone from his belt to check. No answering text from Evangeline filled up the screen. He turned to Brett, his gut screaming that they already knew the location of the elusive Sal. "Let's go."

EVANGELINE STRUGGLED AGAINST the bonds at her wrist but didn't dare move too fast. The big, beefy man who'd been at the heart of all that had happened to her was surprisingly quick and had done an even quicker job jamming her into a kitchen chair.

One that he'd already rigged with a bomb underneath.

One he'd told her about as he slammed her into place, tying her hands behind her.

Thoughts raced around in her mind as she desperately tried to come up with a plan. She had no experience with bombs but based on the gingerly way he'd maneuvered around her once he had it set, she had to assume the situation was sensitive.

And highly deadly.

"Why are you doing this?"

"You've ruined my life."

"Me? I don't even know you."

It was the wrong thing to say and it had his ire flaring, his face turning a mottled shade of red. "You've ruined my business. It's your fault that piece of scum is out on the streets. No one's willing to go out anymore. I was getting by on a shoestring as it is. And now they've found me."

"Who found you?"

He turned bloodshot eyes, buried deep in his face, on her. "Some guys I owe money to back in Detroit. I guess I didn't run far enough away. Figured this dump of a town would be plenty of protection. Why would anyone look for me here? I'd get back on my feet, run a good business and make my money back, and then I could pay what I owe."

While she took serious offense at hearing her home characterized that way, antagonizing him wasn't going to help the situation. "I can assure you, I'm as upset as you about the murders. I was put on leave because of the Len Davison case and I'm heartsick to know he's killed more people."

"Keep your sob story to yourself. My business is down fifty percent. No one can pay off a loan when they can barely pay the rent. And that's damn hard when no one wants romantic dinners when a killer is on the loose. All the publicity your case drummed up for the loser put me smack in the crosshairs of my loan sharks. One of 'em saw me on TV, standing in front of my restaurant waving away those damned protestors."

Evangeline had no idea how the man had twisted the story around to suit himself, but it was obvious he had.

Even more obvious: Whatever story he'd told himself had become his truth.

Her legal case with Len Davison, terrible as it was, had no bearing on unpaid loans to unsavory people. And if she'd hoped that sharing her sob story would build a kinship between them, she was sorely mistaken. His eyes only turned meaner. "Figured the cops would ignore you and think you were crazy. Make it all so easy for me. Only they've gotten closer than ever."

"You were the one behind it all?"

"Figured I'd have some fun with you for a while. You've given me enough sleepless nights. Thought I'd toss some your way."

Although she had little hope she'd be successful, Evangeline tried once more. "Look. I'm sorry your business is failing but I'm sure we can figure something out. Make a deal or something. I'm part of the county DA's office and I'm sure we can work with the city to help with some of your mounting financial problems."

He laughed hard at that, the mirthless sound seeming to rattle around the kitchen. "Just like every other lawyer I've ever known. You think you can talk your way out of everything. Only, you can't."

As she stared at him, Evangeline knew the truth.

She couldn't talk her way out of this one. Just like she couldn't run far enough away from the bomb, even if she did manage to get her hands free.

And no one knew she was here with a madman and a bomb.

No one at all.

"THE SHADES ARE DRAWN." Brett sized up the front of the condo from where he and Troy sat in the cruiser. Brett was in the driver's seat and Ember rode in the back. And Troy felt like a caged animal in the passenger seat.

"I need to get in there."

"We need to assess the situation and get backup."

Backup Troy had already been assured was on its way.

"We're going to start with a perimeter search with Ember. See if she picks up a scent."

"You can't ask me to wait that long."

"I'm asking and I'm telling." Brett turned to face him fully. "It's what partners do. You have to trust me. I know what I'm doing. And I trust my K-9 to tell me what's going on."

Brett had already picked up the stained white shirt from the evidence room before heading out to Evangeline's. He reasoned that the lingering scents on the clothing would be enough for Ember to suss out if Evangeline's stalker was here.

Troy knew it was the right approach. He had nothing to go on except the lack of response to a text. If they went in guns blazing and she was in danger, they could do more harm. If they sat it out and ignored every clamoring nerve ending that said she was in danger, she could be hurt then, too.

And then he'd never get to tell her he loved her.

That thought lodged in his chest like an immovable boulder, heavy and suffocating.

He loved her.

And he had to get the chance to tell her.

"Ember will be quick and then we'll know what we're dealing with."

Troy nodded and got out of the passenger seat. Brett had parked several spots down from Evangeline's front door, hiding them from immediate view of anyone peeking through the blinds in her front window.

With careful precision, he folded the shirt so that the stains were on the interior and the areas of the shirt untouched by blood could be sniffed by Ember. Troy feared that even with those precautions the synthetic blood would act as a block to Ember catching a scent, but Brett didn't seem to harbor the same concerns.

After sensitizing Ember with the shirt, Brett gave his orders and she was off.

She moved around the front, sniffing along the perimeter of the building. It was only as she got to the edge of Evangeline's condo that she stopped and sat.

Brett heaped praise on her before pulling her away from the front door. "Let's head around back."

As his partner suggested it, Troy recognized the benefit. Sal might have lurked around the front of the house but if they could get behind the building they'd likely have a better shot at catching him unawares.

Troy visualized Evangeline's home and the layout from the back door to kitchen, then on down the hallway to the living room and bedrooms. If they could catch him unaware…

They moved as a team down the front of the condo building, around its side and then to the common area on the opposite side of the condo complex. The summer day ensured there were a few people out but all seemed to be focused on sunning themselves. As Ember continued smelling the perimeter, Troy heard the quiet step behind him.

His sister Grace moved up beside him.

"You shouldn't be back here."

"I got the call. I'm here." Her words along with the mulish expression shut him down before he could get a head of steam going. He still struggled knowing his baby sister was a rookie but he had to trust in her training.

Had to trust in her.

He quickly directed her and her partner to get the sunbathers off the property and away from the back of the complex. Grace nodded, clearly intent on answering his request immediately, before she turned back. "We're pulling for you and her. All of us. Oh, and there are three more pairs of officers out front waiting for instruction."

"Thanks."

With his sister's words still ringing in his ears, he caught up with Brett. And stilled when he saw the wide-eyed look his partner gave the K-9 as she sat abruptly, her face turned toward Evangeline's back door.

"Did she find something?"

"Yeah."

"Evangeline?"

Brett's expression was perfectly neutral. "Ember found a bomb, Troy. Based on where she's perched, it's through that door."

"The bastard has a bomb? What if she's wrong?"

"She's not wrong." Brett shook his head. "She's trained for this. That nose is never wrong."

Troy wanted to rant and rail and say that no system was infallible, but he knew it was useless. Brett trusted Ember and he trusted Brett.

And Ember knew her world through smell. His sister Annalise was a K-9 trainer. Hadn't she bragged about her dogs through the years? Their ability to scent off the most minute detail?

Brett pulled Ember away from the door, setting them up a few yards down to avoid being heard. "We need to call in the bomb squad. Now."

"We don't have time for the bomb squad. He's got her in there and he's got no reason to keep her alive."

Brett considered for a minute before nodding. "I know how to dismantle it and I've got gear in the car. I know it's precious minutes but it's the best I can give you."

Troy nodded and was already on the move. He waved Grace over since she was closest, her partner still rounding up sunbathers, and gave her the details as they walked.

"You can't go in there," Grace argued.

"I don't have a choice."

"Mom will kill me if anything happens to you," she finally muttered before pulling him in a tight hug. "I'll radio the rest of the team out front."

Brett stepped in, handing Ember's leash to Grace. "Keep her as far away as possible."

Grace did as requested and moved off to join her partner, Ember obediently following. Troy and Brett jogged to the car and Brett gave a set of orders as they dragged on the gear.

Troy didn't doubt for a minute what he was doing, but as they headed around the back of the building to make their entry, a big part of him kept expecting to hear an explosion. Kept waiting for the reality that they weren't fast enough.

"Remember," Brett said as they got to the back door. "He's not pulling any trigger until he's out of there. Nothing about his behavior has suggested suicide mission up to now."

It was an oddly comforting thought and Troy hoped like hell Brett was right.

The life of the woman he loved depended on it.

As he reached for the doorknob, intent on picking the lock, he felt the door turn in his palm.

One hurdle down.

It looked like the bastard was aiming to make a quick escape.

EVANGELINE HATED THE helpless feeling that had washed over her. The raw fear and the endlessly cycling thoughts of Troy, her mother and how much she wanted to be alive to talk to both of them again.

Yet even with the panicked thoughts, another flew through her mind on the same loop. She'd believed herself helpless these past few months, too.

And she couldn't have been more wrong.

It was only now, strapped to a bomb, that she understood how strong she had really been. How much power she actually had to make a difference, the case against Len Davison be damned.

And how much she had to live for.

The man—did she even know his name?—had stalked around her a bit more, checking a few things on the chair and grunting as he bent his bulk over to look at the wiring before standing back up and looking at a small device in his hand.

A detonator?

The raw terror that had kept her on high alert spiked once more and Evangeline was shocked that she didn't leap up off the chair from the sheer rush of it.

But it was when he took a few steps back and stared her dead in the eye that Evangeline realized there was nowhere to go.

And nowhere to hide.

So she might as well get her answers.

"How'd you do it?"

"Do what?" His voice was gruff but she saw the slightest flicker of respect in his eyes. Like he admired that she'd finally started asking questions.

"The woman. The alley. That looked awfully real."

He guffawed at that—actually laughed—and Evangeline fought the need to scream.

"You mean my little acting job. It was easy to pull off. Been acting since I was a kid. I know all the tricks and I even do a decent make up job. It's how I got out of Detroit in the first place.

"I'm real good, too."

"Good enough to hide DNA?"

"That's easy," he said and waved a hand. "Pour a few cans of soda on the ground and you wash away any DNA left behind. Or you leave it so sticky, no one's finding anything."

Evangeline struggled to take it all in, but figured it was better to let him talk. As long as he was talking she was alive and that counted for something.

It had to.

"You really should take more care in your surroundings. You were easy to follow and it was even easier to break into this place. Ground floor." He shook his head and Evangeline knew in that moment that if her hands were free she'd have smacked him.

"I had my friend all set up and she wore a blood packet. All we needed to do was get your attention and then the rest was easy. We ginned up that fake fight and you fell right for it."

"That was fake blood?"

"Fake blood. Fake fight. Most of my waitresses want

to be actresses anyway. A few hundred bucks and a day off." He shrugged. "Easy."

For a moment, she thought he was going to tell her more about the fake play he'd put on in downtown Grave Gulch.

Which made his next comment that much more surprising.

"This was never my intention, you know. Hurting you. At least, not at first."

"Oh no?" She heard the quaver in her voice and hated it, but couldn't help it around the adrenaline jangling her system.

"It's just all gotten to be too much. I was so close to paying off my debts. Living without that hanging over my head, until you let that guy go free. And I finally realized, someone else has to suffer, too. You know?"

He turned on his heel then and left. As if that was somehow an explanation for what he'd done. Or a reason she should blithely accept his justifications while she sat strapped to a bomb.

She nearly let loose the scream that was building in her chest when she saw the flash of movement through the doorway to the kitchen. A loud grunt echoed from the direction of the living room as Brett Shea raced into the room.

"Evangeline! Don't move!"

He was by her side immediately, his attention fully focused on the chair.

"He's got a detonator. You have to leave! Now, Brett! You and Troy. You have to leave!"

"We're not leaving without you."

"But he's going to blow us up."

"Troy's got it."

"You—" Her voice trembled, raw in the throat from the urgency of it all. "You need to go help him."

Brett nodded, understanding the import of her words. But it was the ones that came back to her that gave her the first kernel of hope. "He's got a lot of incentive to ensure we're all walking back out of here."

TROY SLAMMED A fist in Sal's gut, the impact ringing through his wrist and up his arm. Damn, but the bastard was a grizzly bear. He was paunchy but big and he had a lot more power behind him than Troy expected.

He also had a detonator.

Brett had already shouted it from behind him as he sought a way to get at the detonator.

Troy wanted to scream at his partner to go to Evangeline, but for the moment, that detonator required their full focus. The presence of the police ensured the guy knew he was caught.

Which meant he had precious little motivation to keep them all alive.

Troy dodged a jab at his kidney but took a beefy fist to the ribs that nearly had him doubling over. It was only the reality of the stakes that kept his hand still locked hard on the man's wrist, unwilling to give him any opportunity to press the button.

Brett moved in closer and Troy grunted as he tried to keep Sal pinned. But it was Brett's quick stomp on the man's exposed arm that ultimately did it. The combination of Troy's hold on the wrist and Brett's boot to the elbow had Sal screaming in pain, his fingers opening.

Brett snagged the detonator and raced to the kitchen. Troy moved equally fast, taking the temporary advantage and using it to turn the man over and dragging his hands behind his back. Sal's Miranda rights were already falling from Troy's lips as he tugged the handcuffs tight over those two meaty wrists.

Satisfied Sal was subdued, he opened the front door, his hands up. It was only when he got an "all clear" shout from Melissa, holding the line across the parking lot, that Troy screamed further orders.

"Stay where you are. Suspect is subdued but the bomb is still live."

Melissa's pale visage was the last thing he saw before he turned and ran toward the kitchen.

"Just a few minutes more, darlin'." Brett's voice was steady and calm and Evangeline figured it was costing him a lot to stay that way. And she wanted to believe him. She wanted to sink into that calm, reassuring voice and lose herself there.

Only she couldn't because he was stuck under her kitchen chair, in close range of a bomb and Troy was sitting beside her at the table, his hand cradling hers.

"You need to leave. Please leave," she'd asked, over and over, but the stubborn man refused to move.

Both men had put on bomb vests, after freeing her wrists and settling one over her, but it wasn't enough. They needed to leave. It pressed on her, preying on her mind in an endless loop until a well of sobs finally took over, the adrenaline coursing through her body obscuring anything but the desperate prayer that they'd leave her and save themselves.

The sobs continued as she was lifted from the chair, wrapped in Troy's arms as he walked her out of the house to the ambulance waiting in the parking lot. And they kept on when he climbed in behind the paramedics, riding with her to the hospital.

Later, she'd learn that Brett had executed the bomb's defusion perfectly. She'd also learn that the bomb squad had come in for a formal sweep of her condo and all the other homes in her complex, declaring the entire facility safe. She'd even learn the name of the attacker, Sal Petrillo.

But all of it seemed so distant and foreign as she lay in the big hospital bed, machines beeping around her long into the night.

TROY STRETCHED FROM his position on the chair beside Evangeline's bed. He'd wanted to call her mother but had ultimately waited until morning. He knew she'd kept the news of her ordeal quiet and since it had been so late by the time she was fully checked out and brought to her room, he made the decision to err on the side of fresh morning light.

The doctor couldn't give him much beyond the reassurance that she'd experienced a major trauma but would be all right with some time. So he'd stayed and waited and wondered how he could help her until her mother had shown up.

And after giving the kind woman with the even kinder eyes—Evangeline's eyes—the details, he left. And went back to the precinct to write everything up. A steady stream of people came in to greet him throughout the day, all doing a mix of checking in and getting the latest on what had gone down. It was only when he finally confirmed that he'd tell everyone everything but he needed some quiet that the line outside his door finally died down.

Which was when Melissa showed up.

"You didn't follow protocol yesterday."

"No, I didn't."

"And because of that, you saved her."

It was high praise from his chief. But it was the understanding in her eyes that was all family. Melissa closed his door before crossing to the chairs in front of his desk. "You doing okay?"

"Sure. It's the job. We're just fortunate those days are few and far between."

Not that he'd ever been part of a bomb defusion six inches away from his body. And certainly not one for the woman he was in love with.

Which only added to all the reasons he needed to walk away. He'd been a detective on cases that Evangeline prosecuted. One of those cases involved the town serial killer. Davison had to be Troy's full focus right now.

"I know you, Troy Colton. Why are you torturing yourself about this? And why aren't you with Evangeline?"

"We need to stop spending time with each other. It's as simple as that. We both have jobs to do, even if the past few days have made us lose sight of that."

"Jobs? You both almost died yesterday."

"But we didn't."

"Troy—" His name hung there and much as he wanted to just send her away, he finally gave in. Throwing down his pen, he gave his cousin his full attention.

"You didn't see her in that chair, Mel. The fear in her eyes. And the adrenaline crash when the dam finally burst. She was in danger and has been all along and I spent half the time doubting her. Our jobs are too much at odds with one another. I knew it from the start and this has only proven it."

"That's bs and you know it."

"Is it?" He might be sick of his own thoughts but he didn't need his family's interference, too. "How is it bull? Tell me how our professional lives haven't complicated the situation."

"It doesn't matter if things got complicated. The point is that you care about each other." He saw her grow still before she pressed on. "That you love each other. That doesn't come along every day and to hell with some job standing in your way."

"What good did that do my mother?" The words tore out of him, landing between him and Melissa with sharp, spiky edges. "She needed attention. She needed justice. But someone, somewhere dropped the ball. That's why her murder is unsolved to this day."

"You know as well as I do, we don't close every one of them. It's not a statement on the work, Troy. It's a reality of the job."

That might be the case but he'd spent a lifetime living with that reality. And he couldn't stand the fact that his closed-mindedness and his inability to see the bigger picture of what was happening had nearly gotten Evangeline killed.

"The job takes everything. It's just the way it is," he said.

"I'm sorry you feel that way." Melissa stood then and walked out of his office, leaving him to the empty thoughts that swirled in his mind, refusing to calm.

A WEEK. EVANGELINE had been home a week. Her mother had fussed over her, making her favorite foods and sitting up talking with her late into the night. It had taken a few days but her mom had finally approached the question of why Evangeline had kept her in the dark about the leave of absence from her job.

After a lot of tears and "I'm sorrys," Evangeline had finally shared the truth. That she was afraid of upsetting the new life her mother had built.

After getting a stern talking-to, full of Dora Whittaker's abundant love and frustration, Evangeline could only laugh. How had she thought her mother couldn't handle the truth? It was only after that storm passed that her mom had moved on to the subject of Troy.

Since that subject did nothing more than get Evangeline's own ire up, her mother had ultimately changed the subject.

And now here she was.

The entire GGPD had checked in on her, Melissa at the front of the line. Brett and Ember had showed up with lunch one day earlier in the week. Grace and Ellie and Jillian had all come to see her, as well.

But Troy had stayed away.

Everyone diligently avoided mentioning his absence, but it loomed large all the same.

Which was why Evangeline ultimately moved on. The thoughts that had swirled so strong and sure during the experience with Sal Petrillo had morphed into purpose and, finally, action.

She loved the time she'd spent at the DA's office, but it was time for something new. Through the years as a prosecutor she'd seen any number of women who'd been through similar situations as her mother. Families that had been torn apart by violence, physical and emotional, and who needed help and support to get back on their feet. It was something she'd thought about for years, but it finally felt like the time to make a change.

She'd given Arielle plenty of time in her resignation letter, but effective two weeks from now, Evangeline was beginning the courses needed to become a licensed social worker. It would be hard work to juggle the courses and her ADA job, but it was time to make a change.

Time to make a difference in the community in a new way.

It was a decision that felt right and good and she was ready to get started.

But first, she needed to close the current chapter of her life.

On the drive into downtown, she took in the familiar street signs and buildings she'd seen her entire life. Despite Sal Petrillo's crimes against her, Grave Gulch was a good place to live. A good place to work and to build a life.

Evangeline was determined to find both.

She pulled into the parking lot at the GGPD and headed into the precinct. The steady hum of activity she always associated with the place was in full swing and she saw an active bullpen.

"Can I help—" Mary Suzuki broke off with a broad smile. "Ms. Whittaker. It's good to see you. I'm so glad to see you're doing okay."

"Thank you. I wanted to see if Detective Troy Colton is in?"

"He is. Let me call him." Mary was about to dial when Melissa materialized at the front desk.

"That won't be necessary, Mary. I'll walk Evangeline back."

"Oh." Mary's eyes widened as she keyed in to why their chief was stepping in. "Thanks, Chief."

Melissa gestured Evangeline through the door beside Mary's desk, walking her through the bullpen. "I hope you brought your boxing gloves."

"They don't match my outfit," Evangeline deadpanned, even as she caught onto Melissa's meaning a lot quicker than Mary had.

"A solid choice, by the way. And those heels are awesome." Melissa patted her back, giving her an encouraging smile as they reached Troy's door. "No mercy."

The obvious support buoyed her, giving her the final push she needed to get into Troy's office. She had dressed carefully and the other woman's notice added an extra shot in the arm.

Now or never, Whittaker.

"Troy. I'd like a few minutes."

He looked up from his desk, the circles under his hazel eyes an obvious and outward sign of his exhaustion. "Evangeline."

"You've been quiet this past week."

"I've been trying to catch a killer."

"I understand. Which is why I don't need much of your time." She turned and closed the door behind her. Whatever the outcome of this discussion, it was between her and Troy and no one else.

"I came to tell you a few things."

She saw his mouth open in question but he quickly snapped it shut, saying nothing.

"I finally stopped crying. It took a few days, but I got it out of my system."

"I'm sorry you had to go through that."

"I'm not. Those tears gave me a lot of clarity. Some things I hadn't been willing to admit or address in my life."

His eyebrows narrowed in question, adding additional creases to those dark circles. "Clarity on what?"

"I'm no longer interested in working for the DA's office. I've had a good run but I think my talents can be put to better use somewhere else."

"That's a loss for Arielle and for Grave Gulch."

"I don't think so and neither does she. I'll see out all my current cases for the foreseeable future, but I'm starting classes in a few weeks. My new focus will be social work. Hopefully I can help people before they find themselves in need."

"Congratulations."

"Thank you. But to be honest, that's not why I'm here."

"Why are you here, Evangeline?"

"I thought it was important to tell you that I love you."

"I don't—"

She held up a hand. "I don't expect you to say it back. I also don't expect you to do anything about it. But I do expect that you won't lie to me."

She saw the flash of heat in his eyes. Good. The jab hit its mark and she didn't even need boxing gloves to do it.

"I haven't lied to you," he said.

"Then you've lied to yourself."

As more anger flashed, Evangeline knew she'd landed another direct hit.

"You've somehow convinced yourself that the calling you have for your job means you can't have a life. And that's a steaming pile of crap."

"It's true."

"No, actually, it's not. Do you want to know how I know?"

She saw it then. The moment when everything shifted.

When the walls he'd put up to protect himself began to crack. "How do you know?"

"Because I was there, too. I believed more of my father's lies and abuses than I realized. I convinced myself that I didn't have what it takes. Or that I had a hand tied behind my back because I always had to prove myself. That I was emotional. Or hysterically reacting to a situation. I wasn't, but I forced myself to remain calm and dispassionate to make my choices."

She let out a hard sigh. "Because of it, I let Len Davison slip through my fingers. I read the data but I didn't truly read the evidence."

"I've told you from the start that's not all your fault."

Oh, this sweet, sweet man, Evangeline marveled. Still singing that tune.

"But you see, Troy. It is my fault. That's what I've had to come to accept. That data and details are just that. Items that sometimes add up and sometimes don't. It's what's inside—" she moved closer, laying a hand on her chest "—what's in here that matters."

"Why are you telling me this?"

"Because you've convinced yourself the only way you can honor your mother is to keep the cop separate from the man. But it's the man you are that makes you an amazing cop. One your mother would be proud of." Evangeline doubled down, full well knowing it was the truth. "One she *is* proud of."

He came around his desk then and stood before her. "I can't be someone I'm not."

"I'm not asking you to."

"Then what are you asking?"

"That if you love me you'll take the chance on us. That

you'll fight for us. And that you'll still be Detective Troy Colton every day, too."

Whatever lingering ire filled his eyes vanished, replaced by a haunting vulnerability that skewered her clean through. "What if I don't know how?"

"We'll figure it out together."

He closed the remaining distance between them, pulling her against his chest and bending his forehead to hers. "I do love you."

"I love you, too."

He lifted his head, his gaze never leaving hers. "Do you think it's enough?"

"I think it will always be enough."

And as Evangeline's lips met Troy's, she knew, with absolute certainty, that she was right.

Epilogue

Troy stared at his bride-to-be across the expanse of the restaurant at the Grave Gulch Hotel and considered how far they'd come in only a few weeks. The night he and Evangeline had shared here, having dinner, had been something special. Until it wasn't, as Sal Petrillo had lurked in the shadows.

But no matter how scary that evening was, it had been the catalyst to crack Evangeline's case wide open and ultimately bring them to this moment.

He would have preferred they'd gotten here without the risk to her life, but now that Petrillo was in their rearview mirror—and awaiting trial in Grave Gulch County—Troy had begun to breathe easier.

Evangeline mingled around the room, Desiree excitedly chattering beside her as she introduced Evangeline to their assembled guests.

"Has she met the family yet?"

Troy turned toward his brother, Palmer, and they clinked the tops of their beer bottles to one another in greeting. "She's getting there. Every time I think she's met everyone, someone new pops up and I realize I'm wrong."

Palmer laughed at that, lines creasing the skin around

his vivid green eyes, tanned from all the time he'd spent outside on his ranch. "There's always another Colton to meet."

Troy eyed his brother and realized that he'd seen Palmer staring in the direction of Soledad de la Vega more than once this evening. The fraternal twin of Dominique de la Vega, their cousin Stanton's fiancée, had been invited to join them all for the evening.

With a nod to the beautiful baker, Troy pressed Palmer, "You see something you like?"

"Come on. You know me. I'm a perpetual bachelor."

Troy heard his brother's words but didn't miss the distinct notes of longing before Palmer shut it down. Nor did he miss Palmer's rush of excuses to head to the bar for a refill when Dez and Evangeline walked up to join them.

"Did someone say bar run?" Desiree smiled, linking her arm with Palmer's. "Count me in."

Troy put his arm around Evangeline, taking joy in how simple it was to pull her close as Palmer and Desiree headed for the bar.

Why had he fought this for so long?

It was a question he'd likely ask himself for many years to come, only there was another part of him that knew the answer. Until the past few weeks, he'd admired Evangeline from afar, but had never really gotten to know her. His interest, up until then, had been superficial at best.

But now...

Now he knew so much more. And even better than the knowing, he recognized that they'd have a lifetime of learning all there was to know about one another. It was a heady thought, one that caught him unawares at the oddest moments.

Yet as he stood there, looking out over the room full of the people he loved, he had to admit that his sister had been right all along.

Love did find you at the most unexpected times.

As he bent to press a kiss to Evangeline's forehead, Troy knew another truth. One he'd had to learn for himself.

When you found it, you needed to hang on with both hands, and never, *ever* let go.

* * * * *

COMING SOON!

We really hope you enjoyed reading this book.
If you're looking for more romance, be sure to
head to the shops when new books are
available on

Thursday 10th June

To see which titles are coming soon, please visit

millsandboon.co.uk/nextmonth

LET'S TALK
Romance

For exclusive extracts, competitions and special offers, find us online:

f facebook.com/millsandboon

𝕏 @MillsandBoon

⃝ @MillsandBoonUK

Get in touch on 01413 063232

For all the latest titles coming soon, visit
millsandboon.co.uk/nextmonth

MILLS & BOON

THE HEART OF ROMANCE

A ROMANCE FOR EVERY READER

MODERN

Prepare to be swept off your feet by sophisticated, sexy and seductive heroes, in some of the world's most glamourous and roman locations, where power and passion collide.

HISTORICAL

Escape with historical heroes from time gone by. Whether your passio for wicked Regency Rakes, muscled Vikings or rugged Highlanders, av the romance of the past.

MEDICAL

Set your pulse racing with dedicated, delectable doctors in the high-pr sure world of medicine, where emotions run high and passion, comfo love are the best medicine.

True Love

Celebrate true love with tender stories of heartfelt romance, from the rush of falling in love to the joy a new baby can bring, and a focus on emotional heart of a relationship.

Desire

Indulge in secrets and scandal, intense drama and plenty of sizzling he action with powerful and passionate heroes who have it all: wealth, sta good looks…everything but the right woman.

HEROES

Experience all the excitement of a gripping thriller, with an intense ro mance at its heart. Resourceful, true-to-life women and strong, fearles face danger and desire - a killer combination!

To see which titles are coming soon, please visit

millsandboon.co.uk/nextmonth

JOIN US ON SOCIAL MEDIA!

Stay up to date with our latest releases, author
news and gossip, special offers and discounts, and
all the behind-the-scenes action
from Mills & Boon...

 millsandboon

 millsandboonuk

 millsandboon

might just be true love...

MILLS & BOON
True Love
Romance from the Heart

Celebrate true love with tender stories of
heartfelt romance, from the rush of falling
in love to the joy a new baby can bring,
and a focus on the emotional
heart of a relationship.

MILLS & BOON
MEDICAL
Pulse-Racing Passion

Set your pulse racing with dedicated,
delectable doctors in the high-pressure
world of medicine, where emotions run
high and passion, comfort and love are the
best medicine.